THE PAIN
KILLERS

By
John Avanzato

KCM PUBLISHING
A DIVISION OF KCM DIGITAL MEDIA, LLC

CREDITS

The Pain Killers by John Avanzato

ISBN-13: 978-1-955620-09-3

First Edition

Publisher: Michael Fabiano
KCM Publishing
www.kcmpublishing.com

This book is dedicated to the anesthesiologists of Auburn Community Hospital in Auburn, New York. Some of the finest physicians I have ever had the privilege to work with.

Cheryl

Always and Forever

Other Novels in the John Cesari Series

Hostile Hospital

Prescription for Disaster

Temperature Rising

Claim Denied

The Gas Man Cometh

Jailhouse Doc

Sea Sick

Pace Yourself

The Legend of the Night Nurse

Hilton Dead

Bleeding Heart

Under the Weather

Contents

THE PAIN
KILLERS

Chapter 1

"What's wrong with him, Hugo?" asked the Sommelier.
The naked man strapped to the chair in front of them, bloodied and battered, drenched in his own sweat, had suddenly arched his head back, rolled his eyes upward, and was frothing at the mouth as he twitched uncontrollably.

Hugo, the Sommelier's chief of security, wore a black plastic apron over his dress clothes. The tools of his particular trade rested on a metal table nearby save for the pair of pliers in his right hand. He studied the man and poked him with the tip of the pliers without eliciting any obvious change in his condition.

He turned toward the Sommelier and shrugged. "I think he's having a seizure, Michel."

"I can see that, but is he faking? Do something. It's unnerving."

Hugo walked over to the table with the tools and returned with a ball-peen hammer. He smashed it into the man's right kneecap and stepped back to see the result, but the man continued to spasm and lurch as if nothing at all had happened.

The Sommelier sighed loudly, stepped close, and suddenly slapped the man hard across the face. He said, "Dave, snap out of it... Snap out of it now."

Dave suddenly pissed himself.

The Sommelier stepped out of harm's way, drolly commenting, "I guess he's not acting."

"What shall I do?"

"That, Hugo, is a very good question," the Sommelier responded slowly, rubbing his strong chin with a massive hand as he thought it over.

They were in a specially designed, sound proofed room in the sub-basement of his office building on Randolph Avenue in Mine Hill, New Jersey. The Sommelier ran a financial investment company and the man in the chair had recently been caught embezzling from the business. His name was Dave Werner, and up until that day had been the Sommelier's senior investment manager and most trusted lieutenant. Presently, he was a mostly macerated, pulpy piece of meat clinging to life by painful, gasping breaths taken through purple swollen lips. What the Sommelier and Hugo were trying to determine just moments before all the convulsing began was if he had acted alone in his duplicity or was in collusion with others in the firm. So far, it seemed to have been a unilateral action, but the man's current status precluded further questioning.

The Sommelier hated to give up and said, "Certainly, he can't go on like this forever?"

Hugo replied, "I have no idea."

"Fine, stay with him until dark. If he has not recovered by then dispose of him in the usual manner but remember to save the head. Pack it in ice and bring it out to my chateau in Bernardsville. I…"

His phone buzzed before he could finish that thought and he retrieved the device from his pocket, glanced at the screen, and answered it. It was one of his receptionists upstairs.

"Yes, Marsha?"

"I was just about to close up for the evening and go home when two men entered. They wish to speak to you. I told them the office was closed but they were adamant."

The Sommelier glanced at his watch, a two hundred thousand-dollar Patek Phillipe. "Do they have badges?"

"No, they're doctors from Manhattan. One said his name is Arnold Goldstein and that you would know what it's all about."

The Sommelier let out a deep breath into the receiver. "In fact I do. Show them into my office and I'll take care of it."

"Should I stay?"

"No, Marsha. You can leave, and thank you."

He put his phone away and said, "We have unexpected visitors, Hugo. I must tend to them."

"Will you be needing assistance?"

"No, but thank you. It shouldn't take too long. It's a couple of doctors who are confused about their role in the world."

"I trust you will set them straight."

"I always do, Hugo. I always do. I will see you later then, and don't forget the head."

The Sommelier straightened his tie, checked to make sure he could see his reflection in his shoes, swept his dirty blonde hair back, popped a breath mint, and left the room. There was a small elevator in the hallway, but he was in great shape and bounded up the stairwell to the main floor. Not quite thirty-five, he was six feet five inches tall, two hundred and eighty pounds of solid muscle, and nearly as hard and lean as during his college wrestling days. Fair-skinned with clear blue-eyes, he was distinctly Nordic in appearance and could trace his lineage back to the Alsace-Lorraine region of France. He took great comfort and pride in his genetics and one of his greatest personal heroes was the gallic King Vercingetorix, who had led a great rebellion against Roman rule around 52 B.C. Coming within a hair's breadth of victory, he was eventually defeated by Julius Caesar, brought to Rome, imprisoned, tortured, placed on public display, and ultimately executed for the entertainment of the mob. The Sommelier had an instinctive disdain for Italians and sometimes wondered if it was coded into his DNA stemming from that period of history.

He entered his office with an air of confidence. The two men sat facing away from the door and turned at the sound. As they started to rise, he waved them back, both as a friendly gesture and a dismissive one. He scooted around his desk to his plush leather chair and sat down. His office was large, fifty feet by fifty feet, and contained all the amenities of a small apartment, including a wet bar, private bathroom, a ten-foot sofa and a coffee table on one side. On the other end of the room was a massage table and a variety of exercise equipment including a steel squat cage. The metal bar was racked in place and loaded with over three hundred pounds which the Sommelier used as a warm-up. On his desk were four large monitors, two laptops, and a variety of tablets all wired into the markets, and through the use of spyware, into all the other computers in the office as well.

He sized up his guests. One was an older man in his sixties, pudgy and balding, gray at the temples wearing bifocals. His name was Dr. Arnold Goldstein, and he was the acting CEO of St. Matt's hospital in lower Manhattan. They had met on multiple occasions over the past year when Dr. Goldstein had elected to invest the hospital's capital in what was then a red-hot market. Now that things had cooled and become somewhat bearish, Dr. Goldstein was developing angst and had started calling every day for updates and explanations.

The other physician was new to him, significantly younger, just south of forty he guessed. He was sitting but the Sommelier guessed he was at least six feet tall. Decent shape by the look of him, broad shouldered and solidly built, maybe two hundred and ten pounds, maybe a little more. He sensed that he knew his way around a gym and probably spent a lot of time there when he was younger. He was clean shaven, with a full head of dark hair, inquisitive brown eyes, and olive complexion. Both were dressed in neat but plebeian fashion. Everything about them screamed ordinary, vanilla, unremarkable. Yet there was something about the younger man the Sommelier couldn't quite put his finger on. Something he didn't necessarily like. As if he were to scratch past the first layer of paint and find something wholly unexpected.

He turned to the older man and smiled. "Dr. Goldstein, it's a pleasure to see you. To what do I owe this unexpected honor?"

"Thank you, Michel, and please call me Arnie. Before I begin, I'd like to introduce you to Dr. John Cesari. He's the chief of gastroenterology at St. Matt's and a personal friend of mine. He's also my driver. I rarely leave Manhattan other than by plane and would get lost in a traffic circle. Cesari, this is Michel Beaujolais, the CEO and president of Fidelity Financial Services Inc."

Cesari felt obligated to rise and so he did, extending his hand across the desktop. Likewise, the Sommelier stood, and they shook hands. He said, "Dr. Cesari, the pleasure is all mine, and I go by Mike or Mike B. Michel makes me feel like I'm a child at my aunt's house in Lyon."

Cesari replied, "Nice to meet you, Mike or Mike B., and you can call me Cesari. I've never been comfortable with titles."

They sat back down, and the Sommelier studied Cesari for a moment before saying, "Cesari, is that Italian?"

"Even better, it's Sicilian."

A slight grin spread across the Sommelier's face. "Why is that better?"

"We're smarter than the rest of the Italians and they know it."

The Sommelier chuckled softly. "I'll bet you are."

Arnie interjected good naturedly, "Stand down, Cesari. We have business to discuss. We don't want to waste his time with your chest thumping."

The Sommelier said, "No problem, Arnie. I appreciate a man with a sense of humor. It certainly is a good way to break the ice. On that note, may I offer your intellectually superior companion and yourself a drink? It's after five, and I have wine, scotch…."

Cesari glanced at Arnie and then back at the Sommelier. "It's been a long ride and I wouldn't mind a glass of wine if you have one that's good."

"I think I'll be able to find you something worthy of your palate. And you, Arnie?"

"Sure, why not?"

The Sommelier walked over to the far wall, opened a door, and stepped out of sight. When he returned five minutes later, he held a corkscrew, three wine glasses, and a very old looking bottle of wine. Placing the glasses and wine down on his desk, he retrieved a clear glass flask from a nearby cabinet. He then gently uncorked the bottle and decanted the liquid through a filter into the flask.

He said, "It really should rest, so we'll wait a bit while we chat."

After he put the bottle down with the label facing Cesari, he sat in his chair and powered up a laptop. Cesari read the label and looked confused.

The Sommelier noted his puzzled expression and asked, "Is everything all right, Doctor?"

Cesari looked at him. "Am I reading the label right? The vintage looks like 1885 or is that a misprint?"

The Sommelier smiled politely. "You read it right, Doctor. Château Pape Clément is a Bordeaux from the Pessac-Léognan appellation. I was able to get one of the last known cases of that vintage at Sotheby's. It cost me an arm and a leg; although, I really must apologize in advance. It's not nearly as good as the 1890 vintage but those are rarer than hen's teeth."

Cesari snorted, "I'll bet. I was looking for one in a liquor store last week and they were all out."

"You like wine, Dr. Cesari?"

"I should say so. We Italians invented wine you know."

The Sommelier tried not to react to that, but it was yet another reminder of why he held Italians in such contempt. He never met one who wasn't extraordinarily garish. He said jokingly, "Was it the Sicilians or the Italians, Doctor? My memory fails me on that one."

"Mine too. Maybe it was a collaboration."

"Perhaps one day you will indulge me and allow me to show you my wine cellar."

"Perhaps one day I will."

"That would be splendid," the Sommelier said enthusiastically. He then hesitated before adding, "May I ask a medical question before we get started?"

Cesari said, "Go right ahead."

"Do either of you know anything about seizures?"

Chapter 2

Two hours later, they left the Sommelier's office. Arnie was red-faced and fuming as he got in Cesari's car. He wasn't just ordinary angry. He was irate. If he was anymore apoplectic, his head might explode.

He said, "What the hell was that all about, Cesari?"

But Cesari was unconcerned and hummed merrily as he started the engine. It was a ten-year-old, black, four-door Honda Accord. The body had a few random dings in it and the interior upholstery had seen better days. No doubt it wasn't the sexiest of cars, but it got the job done. It had a hundred and five thousand miles on it and all he ever did was change the oil. He had owned a Porsche outright once, leased a Mercedes twice, and rented a BMW on vacation. It all came down to getting from point A to point B reliably, and nothing did that better than his Honda.

Cesari responded to Arnie's comment, "I'm not sure what you mean. I really like that guy. Would you mind buckling up? This car's got a nasty temper when you don't."

Arnie fastened his safety belt and said, "You're not sure what I mean? Well I'm not sure I'm comfortable with you driving, Cesari. I think you're drunk. Did you have to ask him to open a second bottle of wine? We were supposed to be there on business."

Cesari smiled. "We were there on business and you're lucky he didn't have time for a third bottle. Was that good wine or what? I really like that guy."

"So I've come to understand, but that guy you like so much just lost one hundred million dollars of the hospital's endowment fund so stop saying you like him so much. He's the enemy and I brought you with me for moral support. You were supposed to be on my side, not his."

The engine coughed and then started and Cesari pulled out of the parking lot much too fast causing Arnie to rock back into his seat aghast. Cesari laughed as he settled into cruising speed. "Relax, Arnie, he didn't lose anything. Your money is just temporarily not accessible to you. Furthermore, he's not your enemy, I'm not drunk, and I am on your side."

"You could have fooled me on all counts, and why don't you get a real car?"

"You don't like my car?"

"It's okay, I guess, if you were a freshman in college or just got your first job."

Cesari scoffed, "This car is great, Arnie. I don't touch it for months at a time and it starts like a top whenever I need it."

"Okay, fine. Forget about the stupid car. Focus, Cesari, focus. Mike B., remember him?"

"Well I thought he explained himself very well back there. Did you see all those graphs? High cap, low cap, annuities, stocks, bonds, short term, long term, blue chip. Asset allocation, mutual funds, index funds, hedge funds, market capitalization, price to earnings ratio... I mean, he really knows his stuff."

Arnie was wide-eyed in disbelief. "I didn't understand a thing in there. He was clicking through those graphs at the speed of light and talking even faster. Besides, I don't care how smart he is. The bottom line is, I signed off on a two hundred-million-dollar investment with him six months ago and now it's only worth half that. I have a board meeting tomorrow. They're going to skin me alive."

"Look, I'm sorry about the board, but it's not a real loss unless you pull the plug on whatever's left of the investment.

You heard him. Markets rise, markets fall. It's not his fault if an oil tanker capsizes here or they suddenly decide to raise the corporate tax rate there or an earthquake rocks Tokyo. The market will come back, Arnie. Be patient. The graphs showed that this downturn is just a blip on the radar, and when the market does come back... Man, oh man. Drill, baby, drill."

"Will you stop that already? This isn't funny at all."

"Hey, I'm starving. Maybe we should stop to grab a bite and hydrate a little."

"Fine, as long as you stop being Mike B.'s cheerleader."

They spotted a place called the *New Jersey Bar and Grill* coming up fast and Cesari said, "That place looks like it will have decent burgers."

From the outside it looked like a stereotypical roadhouse with flashing neon lights advertising inexpensive beer and good times. Arnie said, "It looks like a dive to me, and you've had enough alcohol... I don't think this is a good idea at all, Cesari. What's with all the motorcycles parked in the lot? It looks like a Harley convention."

Ignoring his protests, Cesari drove into the parking lot and cut the engine. As they walked toward the side entrance, Cesari said, "I want you to lighten up, Arnie, and look at the situation from the glass half full point of view. Mike B. is a great guy. I'm perceptive about people and he's a keeper. I'm convinced that in six months' time we'll be laughing about this while we roll around in freshly minted one hundred dollar bills."

"I hope so, and stop saying he's a great guy, all right? Just because he poured you a glass of wine doesn't mean he's your friend."

As they entered the tavern, pounding blues-rock music assaulted their ears. Arnie rolled his eyes as he glanced around at the packed bar and restaurant area. Beefy guys in leather jackets drinking bottled beer regaled each other with stories and back slapping jokes. A waitress wearing tight jeans, sneakers, and a black tee shirt with the word *STAFF* in bold white letters emblazoned across her large chest indicated they should seat themselves. Sensing they were a little out of their element, she pointed to a small table as far from the bar area as possible where they sat opposite one another.

Not quite finished tormenting his overwrought friend, Cesari continued their conversation, "Wine? Arnie, don't be gauche. That wasn't just wine. That was a heavenly elixir. Each bottle cost him twenty-five thousand dollars and except for the one glass wasted on you, I got to share the rest of the divine liquid with him."

Arnie was shocked. "Twenty-five thousand dollars a bottle? When did he say that?"

"He mentioned it when you were in the bathroom."

A different waitress with an equally large chest approached and handed them menus and took drink orders. Arnie ordered a light beer and Cesari stuck with water. Arnie shook his head in frustration. "That's not what I wanted to hear, Cesari. The hospital is down a hundred million bucks and the guy managing the money is drinking twenty-five-thousand-dollar bottles of wine as a pre-dinner cocktail."

Cesari looked over the menu and said, "This is pretty interesting bar food."

"I have to agree. I think I'll get the fresh tuna tacos."

"They have eggrolls. That's interesting. I knew a guy who made eggrolls like these back in Manhattan."

"Well maybe he branched out."

"I find that hard to believe. Last I heard, he was on the run from the law."

Arnie shook his head in exasperation. "Do you have any friends who aren't on the lam?"

"There's you of course."

"Can we order please?"

Their waitress came over with their drinks and they ordered dinner. After she walked away, Arnie said, "You're not really going to take him up on his offer, are you?"

Cesari was still thinking about the eggrolls. He looked up and asked, "What offer?"

"Your new pal, Mike B. invited you to his home in Bernardsville to see his wine cellar, remember?"

"Oh yeah... Of course I'm going to take him up on it. Why wouldn't I?"

"What a pair that guy has. He bankrupts a hospital and then announces he lives in the wealthiest town in the United States."

"Arnie, drink your beer, please. Class warfare is unattractive on you. He's probably very good at what he does and is compensated commensurately. That doesn't bother me."

"You're very good at what you do, and you don't live in Bernardsville."

"I can't make graphs the way he does, but if you're offering me a raise, I accept."

"Will you shut up about those graphs. I just lost the hospital's shirt to that guy. He probably bought a new yacht with the money. The board is going to tear me a new one and instead of being appropriately concerned, you want to have Mike B.'s baby? What gives, Cesari? I never pegged you for a turncoat."

Their food came and they got down to business. Cesari munched happily on the house specialty, Philly cheese steak eggrolls with a habanero ranch dipping sauce.

In between mouthfuls, he protested, "I am concerned, Arnie, and I don't want to have his baby. Although if he invited me to Monaco for the weekend, I'd strongly consider it. By the way, if your plan was to trip him into a confession by showing up unexpectedly like that, you failed miserably. I feel I should point out that he had all his facts at his fingertips and was able to account for every penny. You have to admit, that was a pretty impressive impromptu presentation."

"There you go again, Cesari. Stop telling me how great he is."

Cesari got serious. "Look, Arnie, I don't mean to be flippant. I'm just trying to keep you from jumping off the ledge, all right? Of course, you're right to be concerned, but the fact of the matter is that you still have a hundred million dollars, and that's a far cry from bankrupt."

"That's easy for you to say. For a hospital the size of St. Matt's, a hundred million is chicken feed. Operationally, we were twenty million in the red last year alone and we're in the process of building a new cardiac cath lab with a price tag of thirty-five million bucks. The radiology department needs an upgrade. I don't even know yet what that's going to cost, and if the nurses' union gets their way, I'll be shelling out an extra seven hundred grand a month in payroll and benefits. Not to mention, the state doesn't like to bail out hospitals that piss their own money down the drain with bad investments. That hundred million you speak of will possibly keep us afloat for another year and a half assuming nothing unforeseen happens. When I invested the money, the idea was to turn two hundred million into four hundred million not one hundred. I could've done that myself in Vegas. Are you getting the picture or am I not explaining myself well enough?"

Cesari grinned. "You're doing great. Well, it's out of your hands now, and Mike B. seems to be perfectly capable. I assume you checked him out before you signed over all the hospital's money?"

"Of course I checked him out. Brennan, the CFO, recommended him highly. They went to Columbia together where Beaujolais was a prodigy, graduating with high honors in just three years. Beaujolais's relatively young but he's hot. He's got a degree in accounting and an MBA from the Wharton School of business, and he's been a licensed stockbroker for fifteen years. There are no complaints against him with the SEC. He worked for Goldman Sachs for a couple of years before setting out on his own five years ago. He's got rock solid reviews from everyone he's ever worked with or for."

Cesari said, "Okay… That sounds good. Brennan's kind of new. I don't know him too well. How's he feel about this sudden reversal of fortune?"

"He's from the don't worry be happy school of financial investment, but then again, what else would he say now that the shit's hit the fan. He really can't afford to be negative. It was his idea to go with this guy just because they played racquetball together back in the day."

"Out of curiosity, why did you have me tag along instead of Brennan? He would have been a more logical companion. He is a money guy after all."

"I know that, but Brennan's biased because he and Beaujolais are old pals, and I thought it would be helpful or perhaps sobering to have someone of your demeanor with me."

"What that's supposed to mean?"

"It means that you look like a tough guy, and Brennan looks like an accountant. I wanted Beaujolais to know that I meant business."

Cesari laughed. "Well, I don't think that angle worked out too well. From the amount of weight he had racked up in his office, I'd say he could handle himself against two or three guys my size."

Arnie cracked a smile. "Yeah, I'd forgotten how big he is."

Cesari cleared his throat. "Well, I don't know a whole lot about these things, Arnie, but my gestalt is that if Mike B. isn't worried and Brennan isn't worried, then you probably shouldn't be either."

"Yeah, I keep telling myself that, but then I remember that's exactly what they told the passengers on the Titanic when they hit the iceberg."

"Hey Arnie, I have an idea. How about we change the subject. This food is amazing. Isn't it?"

Arnie reluctantly agreed. "Yes, it is… As long as we're changing the subject, how is Valentina?"

Cesari chuckled. He stepped into that one. Valentina was an OR nurse he had been dating on and off for close to a year. They had even temporarily moved in together, but it didn't work out too well, so he moved back out a month later. Lately, they had been more off than on, and recently had agreed to see other people, not that Arnie would know that. Valentina's biological clock was ticking loudly in both their ears, and he just couldn't bring himself to go in that direction. It didn't help that the entire OR was privy to the most intimate aspects of their relationship and didn't hesitate to offer their opinions on a daily basis, which chafed at him immensely.

He said, "We're sort of taking a break right now."

"Really? Was it mutual or a Cesari executive decision?"

"She didn't put up much of a fight if that's what you're getting at, so I'd have put it in the mutual column."

"Is that wise? She's a beautiful woman, Cesari. She won't be lonely for long if you get my drift."

"Yeah, I get your drift. In fact, I think she's on a date with Joe Fusco tonight."

"Fusco? The hand surgeon? He's loaded. I heard he drives a Lamborghini."

"Good for him. I drive an Accord."

"No offense, Cesari, but you can't compare a Honda to a Lamborghini. That's like comparing a Big Mac to a twenty-ounce, dry-aged New York Strip steak at Peter Lugers. Besides, as your friend, I feel I should point out to you that a ten-year-old four-door sedan is kind of girlie. You know what I'm saying?"

"Suddenly, you're Enzo Ferrari?"

Arnie said, "Just joking, Cesari. How did you hear about her date tonight?"

"Six or seven OR nurses texted me this morning, but that number's down from the ten or twelve who texted me last week about her rendezvous with the cardiothoracic surgeon."

"I'm sorry to hear that... But you're okay with Valentina dating other doctors at the hospital?"

"It's fine. Valentina and I will always be good friends and like I said, we're taking a break, so what choice do I have?"

"Good point... So how are the mystery novels coming along? You've published two, right?"

"Three, but who's counting? They're doing okay. No best-sellers yet, but money's coming in."

"How much money? Are you a millionaire yet?"

"If I was, do you think I'd still be taking orders from you?"

"Maybe..."

Cesari snorted, "Good one, Arnie. You could have a career in comedy."

Arnie grinned. He liked that. "If I'm a comedian what's that make you?"

Cesari thought it over and replied, "I'm an artist, Arnie. I use the printed word rather than a paint brush and paper instead of canvas."

Arnie scoffed, "Art? More like soft porn, Cesari. I over-heard several nurses talking about your books."

"I like to keep it real, Arnie," Cesari bristled. "But maybe you should read one and find out for yourself."

"Okay, Michelangelo, take it easy. Just promise me one thing..."

"And that is?"

"That you won't forget me when you make it big. I want you to promise to be there for me when I need you, okay?"

"You know I will, Arnie."

"Then say it out loud."

"I promise to be there for you, Arnie."

"That's better. So the next time I trash my financial guy, I expect you to agree with me whole-heartedly, all right?"

"Fine."

"I heard it's a beautiful fuchsia."

"What is?"

"Joe Fusco's Lamborghini."

Chapter 3

They paid the bill and left the bar at close to nine. It was dark and the night air was cool. It felt like it was going to rain. Cesari stretched and said, "C'mon, Arnie. Let's get you home. It's past your bedtime."

"Yeah, I'm going to need a good night's rest before tomorrow's board meeting."

They walked to the back of the lot past a long row of Harley-Davidsons and found the Accord. As Cesari fetched the key from his pocket, he heard a thumping sound and a muffled voice. He scanned around until he found the source of the noise. It came from a car parked in the far corner of the lot under the shade of a huge maple tree and obscured from the lights of the bar. The car was parked crudely and one tire had hopped a short curb before coming to a rest on grass. It wasn't in a designated spot and appeared that someone just wanted it out of the way.

As they went toward the vehicle to investigate further, the sound grew stronger. Up close, they could see it was obviously not an ordinary car. It was a vintage silver Rolls Royce in mint condition. The thing was enormous and Cesari guessed it had to be at least forty years old. They didn't make cars that boxy anymore with trunks like this one had. Even closed you could tell it was large enough to fit a whole family. The thumping sound came from within the trunk.

Arnie said, "I don't like the feel of this, Cesari."

"Neither do I, but we have to do something."

"We can call the police."

"How about we help whoever it is first?"

Cesari leaned near to the lid and spoke to the person inside, "Hey, pal, I can hear you."

"Then let me out, you stupid fuck," came the belligerent reply in a high pitched, slightly nasal voice.

Cesari glanced at Arnie, who raised his eyebrows at the less than friendly exchange. Cesari then reached under the lip of the trunk and felt around for a button or a switch but found nothing.

He asked the guy, "How do I open it?"

"Are you some kind of retard? See if the driver's door is open. If it is, there's a latch on the inside."

Cesari went around to the driver's side door and grabbed the handle. The door swung open, and he spotted the car keys sitting on the front seat. The trunk release was right there and he pulled on it with a satisfying clicking sound. When he returned to the rear of the vehicle Arnie was helping a little guy out onto the asphalt.

The guy brushed himself off, spat on the ground, and turned to them. He was about forty years old, five feet four inches tall, and not an ounce over a hundred and fifty pounds. He had curly brown hair and a nose that looked like it had been broken and reset multiple times like a boxer or a scrappy streetfighter. He was dressed neatly in khakis and a blue shirt. The guy's dark eyes said it all. He was pissed and not in the mood to take prisoners. Otherwise, he was none the worse for his experience.

Cesari handed him the car keys and asked, "You okay?"

"I was locked inside a trunk for over an hour. What do you think?" He turned to Arnie and said, "Please tell me he's not the smart one."

Arnie didn't say anything, so Cesari said, "You got a name?"

"Gerry... Gerry Acquilano and you?"

"John Cesari and the quiet one over there is Arnie Goldstein."

"That's great. Now where are they?"

"Where are who, Gerry?"

"The asshole bikers who put me in my own trunk."

"They're in the bar but I wouldn't go looking for an apology if I were you."

"Oh, you wouldn't?"

"No, I wouldn't. There's about a dozen of them in there and they've been drinking. It might not go over too well. What happened out here?"

Gerry had steam coming out of his ears. "One of them said I cut him off entering the parking lot and that I took his space. He told me to apologize and move my car. I told him to shove it up his ass. That's when then they took my keys and cellphone and threw me into the trunk."

Gerry closed the trunk and went to the rear door of the Rolls, opened it, reached down into the foot well and came out with a black pump action twelve-gauge shotgun. It was a Mossberg 500. A fine weapon.

Arnie whispered urgently, "Cesari, do something before this gets any worse than it already is."

Cesari put one hand on Gerry's shoulder and with his other hand grabbed the barrel of the weapon. He was much larger and stronger than Gerry and wrenched it free without difficulty.

"Don't make me regret letting you out of the trunk, Gerry. If you're not happy, call the police. You can use my phone. We'll stick around as witnesses."

"Call the police? What for? It's my word against theirs and they'll never admit to anything."

"You're probably right, but you're about to make a mistake so cool off. It sucks what they did but you're okay, right?"

Gerry thought it over and seemed to calm down. He said, "I'm fine, I guess. It just pisses me off and...."

Gerry's jaw dropped and he let out a primal scream. Cesari and Arnie looked in all directions. Nothing. Gerry pointed at the car's doors. There was a long scratch mark in the paint job from the front end of the car to the back.

Gerry shrieked, "Those bastards keyed my car. What kind of animals are they?"

Cesari took a deep breath and replaced the shotgun back into the footwell. "Let's be glad they keyed the car and not you, Gerry. Why don't you go home and have a scotch or two? Try to forget tonight. It can be fixed. It's just a car."

"Just a car? You putz… This is my livelihood. I was delivering this to my buyer in Manhattan. It's a 1989 Rolls Royce Silver Spur. It sold new for $145,000 and has the original Rolls Royce engine. The color is Silver Sand. No one has made that color in thirty years. The interior is beige leather, piped in dark brown, with real walnut accents and picnic tables in the rear compartment. There are lighted vanities so the women can powder their noses, and lamb's wool floor mats… They don't make cars like this anymore. It only has six thousand miles on it and has been kept covered and in a climate-controlled garage. I went all the way to Chicago to pick it up for the guy and you say it's just a car."

They stood there for a minute as Gerry got emotional over the damage to his prize. Eventually, Cesari said, "I stand corrected, Gerry. Obviously, you know a lot more about how special this particular vehicle is but it's still not worth going to jail over so please go home or continue on your journey. You can always have the car repaired and then deliver it to your customer."

"You don't get it. I promised this guy a mint condition car and now all I have is garbage. And you don't know the kind of people that pay cash for these kinds of automobiles. You promise them a mint car, you'd better provide a mint car."

Cesari said nothing and Gerry just shook his head and looked like he was going to cry. He let out a deep breath and silently got into the driver's seat of the Rolls and closed the door. He sat there for a long minute leaning his head against the steering wheel. Reassured that the crisis had passed, Cesari and Arnie walked back to the Honda and got in. They sat there watching the Rolls Royce.

Arnie said, "Jesus, that was unbelievable."

Cesari nodded. Arnie was a tenderfoot. His idea of an exciting night was having an extra scoop of ice cream for dessert or playing bingo. Cesari said, "It certainly was."

"He didn't even say thank you."

"For letting him out of the trunk?"

"Yeah."

"He was upset. I can forgive that."

"You haven't started the engine. What are you waiting for?"

"I'm waiting for him to drive away, and it appears that he's waiting for us to do the same."

"You don't think?"

The Rolls Royce engine turned over and fumes shot out of the rear exhaust. Cesari breathed a sigh of relief as Gerry's headlights came on. Gerry put the car in drive and pulled the car gently off the grass onto the smooth pavement of the lot and drove to the exit. The brake lights suddenly came on and he slowly backed up into a reverse U-turn.

Cesari said, "Oh shit!"

There were twelve Harley Davidson's lined up in a row next to the side of the bar. Twelve very large and very expensive Harley Davidsons, and Cesari sensed what was about to happen as the front of the Rolls was now fifty feet away and perfectly lined up with first of the bikes. Gerry revved his engine and it snorted like a bull.

Arnie gasped, "Oh my God. He's crazy."

Cesari got out of his car in an attempt to stop the insanity, but he was too late and too far away. Gerry gunned the Rolls. The engine roared, rubber peeled, and the Rolls rammed into the side of the first Harley. It crashed into the second which crashed into the third and like a row of dominoes they all went down in a noisy tangled heap. The first two were probably damaged beyond repair. The next two or three were most likely unrideable tonight. As for the rest it was hard to say. Leaking gas perfumed the air. Gerry got out of the Rolls to inspect the carnage just as Cesari and Arnie arrived at the scene. Gerry had a big smile on his face.

Things happened quickly after that. People came out of the bar to see what the racket was, and word percolated back to the bikers. Soon Arnie, Cesari, and Gerry were facing twelve very large and very angry men. The leader was a bearded, tattooed guy with a black do-rag and a jean jacket. An inch taller than Cesari, he had about a fifty-pound advantage. Cesari immediately started to think through his options as the guy stepped forward. The first thing he did was take a pace toward the guy to position Arnie and Gerry behind him. Arnie didn't need any further hints and retreated several feet backward. Cesari couldn't see what Gerry was up to.

"What the fuck happened here?" the biker growled menacingly.

Cesari said, "It was an accident. My friend lost control of his car."

"Your friend? What friend?"

Cesari turned and saw Gerry walking nonchalantly toward the Rolls. The biker caught his gaze and said, "The dwarf with the mouth is your friend?"

"More like an acquaintance."

"How'd he get out of the trunk?"

"I let him out."

"You let him out? Now I see where the problem is. I didn't give anybody permission to let him out. So you let him out and he did this. That makes you responsible. Does it not?"

The guy and his men stepped closer at the ominous implication. Cesari said, "I had no idea he was going to do this. I advised him to go home and not make trouble."

"I guess he didn't listen. But still, you let him out. You shouldn't have done that. Guys…"

With that signal, two gorilla-sized bikers grabbed Cesari by the arms and the boss wound up and punched him in the abdomen. Cesari coughed and gasped. Nausea gripped him but he fought back the urge to vomit. He might have fallen over except for the guys holding him up. The boss man grabbed Cesari by the hair and was about to slam him with a right hook when an explosion filled the air, freezing them all in place. Gerry had retrieved the twelve gauge from the rear of the Rolls and fired a round over their heads. He walked toward them as he ratcheted another shell into the chamber.

"Let him go, assholes," he shouted. "I got five more rounds of buck shot. There's more of you than I have ammo but the question you need to ask yourself is this…" He pointed the gun right at the leader. "Do I feel like lucky tonight?"

The boss man nodded at the two apes who let Cesari go. Cesari was still sucking wind and stood there waiting to see what was next. Gerry said, "That's better. Now it's a fair fight. My guy wins, we go in peace. You win, you get the Rolls."

Cesari's eyes went wide. The biker smiled and turned back to Cesari. Cesari held his hand up and said, "Hold it… What about ground rules?"

The guy said, "Ground rules?"

While his mouth was still open, Cesar launched a massive uppercut plowing the bigger man's lower jaw into the top half. The guy staggered back and spit out a tooth and blood. He was dazed but recovered quickly and wound up for a lethal roundhouse at Cesari's head which might have decapitated him had it landed. Cesari stepped into the arc of the swing just as it was coming forward and punched the guy as hard as he could on the inside of his bicep. The guy's blow landed weakly on Cesari's left shoulder. The bicep shot hurt him a lot and he grimaced. Cesari moved quickly and slammed his right foot down hard onto the top of the guy's left foot. Before he could howl in pain Cesari swung around and hammered him in the temple with his elbow. It was a clean shot delivered with all the force and momentum he could muster. And it was effective. The guy crumpled to the ground, disoriented, clawing at the air. He was barely conscious and clearly out of the fight. Cesari didn't wait to see if he would be declared the winner. He signaled Arnie and they walked hurriedly to the Honda as Gerry backed away to his Rolls. The bikers stood there in stunned disbelief as their captain threw up beer and chicken wings onto one of the disabled Harleys.

As they drove away, Arnie who was staring blankly ahead suddenly blurted out, "You're a fucking animal, Cesari. That guy was twice your size. How did you do that?"

"It's all about speed and surprise, Arnie. Hit them in places they don't expect and hope for the best."

"Damn... Why couldn't you do that to Mike B.?"

Chapter 4

They followed the taillights of Gerry's Rolls down Rt. 46 towards the entrance to I-80 East toward New York. They were both heading in the same direction, but a couple of miles into the journey, the Rolls began spewing black plumes into the night air. The emergency lights started blinking and Gerry pulled the big car into the parking lot of a local ice cream stand called Cliff's. They followed him to see if they could help. Cesari wanted to yell at him anyway for all the trouble he caused.

Gerry parked the Rolls as far away from the other vehicles as he possibly could. The place was packed with cars and people eating ice cream at tables and standing in long lines waiting to order their favorite flavors. They pulled into the spot next to him as Gerry got out and lifted the Rolls' hood to allow the heat and smoke out. Cesari and Arnie got out of the Honda and watched as clouds of rancid burning oil billowed upward.

Gerry looked at them and said, "Shit. I'm leaking oil. Look at what those guys did."

Cesari rolled his eyes and replied, "What they did? I told you to go home and have a scotch... Your front fender is about to fall off, and I'm pissed at you. You almost got me killed back there."

Gerry grinned. "I knew you could take care of yourself. You remind me of Carmine."

"Who's Carmine?"

"He's my cousin. We're in the Rolls Royce business together. We're small time but high quality. We procure and deliver high end and rare Rolls Royces to discriminating customers. We travel all over the world searching for the best products available."

"Where's Carmine now?"

"Finishing up a prison sentence in Ossining. He might even be out as soon as next week. Good behavior and all that. He got caught procuring a sweet deal from a garage in Nyack."

Cesari and Arnie glanced at each other. Cesari asked, "Gerry, is this car hot?"

"Who wants to know?" Gerry retorted pugnaciously.

Cesari was getting annoyed. "I do."

Gerry shrugged. "My buyer doesn't want to know, and neither should you. You'll live longer that way. All the buyer's going to care about is the ten grand he gave me in advance for expenses to get the car. I mean look at this hunk of shit, and it's not even my fault."

Cesari's jaw dropped. "It's not your fault? Gerry, it's all your fault. You have to learn to control your temper."

"Kiss my ass, Johnny boy."

Cesari let out a deep breath. Despite everything there was something about the guy that Cesari liked. "Look, can I drop you off somewhere? It's late. No one's going to look at this until tomorrow, and if the car is stolen, you may not want to make too much noise about it anyway."

"I know, but I hate to just abandon it. My big problem is the customer. He's not going to be happy, and he's not the kind of guy that takes disappointment well." He sighed and added, "Help me transfer my stuff to your car and then we'll wipe down the car for prints."

Besides the shotgun, Gerry had a duffle bag with his personal effects and a change of clothes. They used a couple of rags he had to wipe down the car as best they could and then they all piled into Cesari's Honda with Gerry in the back.

"Where to, Gerry?" asked Cesari.

"I don't know. I was supposed to drop off the Rolls in Little Italy on Mulberry Street and meet my client in a little café to finish the deal. Twenty-five big ones. Cash. Now I'm in the hole for ten. I'll be lucky if I come out of this without any broken bones."

Arnie was becoming increasingly shocked at the conversation. First, a biker brawl outside a bar, then a stolen Rolls Royce, and now broken limbs over a failed transaction. He was turning pale.

He whispered, "Jesus…"

When Gerry mentioned Little Italy and Mulberry Street, the hair on Cesari's neck stood at attention. He asked, "What's your buyer's name?"

"I'd better not say it out loud. Trust me. The less you know about him the better."

Cesari said, "Is it Vito Gianelli?"

"You know the guy?" was Gerry's surprised response.

"I've heard of him."

Vito Gianelli was a lifelong career criminal in a certain organization that J. Edgar Hoover once testified before congress never existed. He and Cesari had been friends since childhood when Vito had saved Cesari from a gang of bullies intent on feeding him knuckle sandwiches for lunch one day. In return for that one act of kindness, Cesari spent the next twelve years doing Vito's homework and helping him cheat his way through all his final exams. Thanks to Cesari, Vito was ranked as one of the smartest kids to ever graduate Holy Rosary grammar school in the Bronx, at least it appeared that way on paper. The nuns thought he might go to Harvard one day or possibly become president. It was the most perfect example ever of why you should never accept favors from mob guys. Your debt never ended.

"Then you must have heard that he's got a nasty disposition."

Cesari nodded. "That he does."

Arnie said, "You know this guy, Cesari?"

"We grew up together in the Bronx. You know, grammar school, high school. That sort of thing. He went his way, and I went mine. Gerry, do you have a place to stay tonight?"

He shook his head. "Gianelli was going to put me up for the night after the deal went down, and then I was going to take off again on my next job. There's a '69 Rolls convertible coming into the Port of Newark from London in a couple of days. I got a hot tip from a guy I know down there. It's not in as good condition as the one tonight and needs a little work, but it'll put food on the table."

"Where do you live?"

"Here and there. I'm on the move a lot. If I survive the night, I'll get a room in a motel somewhere."

"So your intention is to meet with Gianelli tonight even without the car? Is that wise?"

He nodded glumly. "I still have a couple of grand of his money I can return. If I try to run, he'll come after me. I'd rather not have that happen. Better to take my lumps. I'll have a chance that way."

"Gerry, maybe you should stay with me tonight. I'll give Vito a call and see if I can smooth things over for you."

"Just like that? Are you nuts? You don't just call a guy like that and tell him to take a chill pill."

Arnie added incredulously, "You can't be serious, Cesari? You're already involved too much."

"Have some faith, guys."

They dropped Arnie off at his apartment and drove back to Cesari's place on Sixth Avenue just north of Washington Square Park. He rented the third-story loft of an old building. The first and second floors were owned by the street level Polish delicatessen. After Gerry settled in on the sofa with a scotch and was watching TV, Cesari retreated to his bedroom to call Vito in private.

"Cesari, it's almost midnight. What's up?" asked Vito gruffly in a deep baritone voice made gravelly from years of smoking unfiltered Camels and Pall Malls.

"I ran into a friend of yours tonight. A guy by the name of Gerry Acquilano."

"Gerry? I was supposed to meet him two hours ago and he's not answering his phone. He stood me up. How do you know him?"

Cesari reviewed the events of the night but changed the story around a little. In his version, the bikers trashed Vito's Rolls Royce with crowbars and ripped up the interior with knives without the slightest provocation.

"Holy shit. These guys are savages."

"You're telling me? I wouldn't have believed it if I didn't see it with my own eyes. They even pissed on the seats. You wouldn't want this car now for any amount of money and Gerry was lucky to get out of there with his life. If I had shown up five minutes later, they would have been pissing on him too."

"But why?"

"Why? Two dozen bikers all liquored up doesn't have a why, Vito."

"I guess you're right about that. Where's Gerry now?"

"He was pretty shaken up, so I let him spend the night here. He was terrified that you were going to hand him his ass in a sling when he didn't show with the Rolls. The situation was totally out of his control."

"I understand that, but he took ten grand of my money and now I have nothing to show for it, and that doesn't explain why he didn't call me."

"He didn't call you because the bikers took his cellphone, but he'll get a new one tomorrow. I promise. Look, I talked to Gerry about the situation. He's got another Rolls coming into the Port of Newark in a few days. It was supposed to be for another customer, but he'll give it to you. It's a '69 convertible. It's not quite as nice as the one he was bringing you tonight. It's got a few scuff marks, but nothing a little touch-up paint won't fix. He thinks you'll like it. He said he'll pick it up for you at half the usual fee."

"Half?"

"You heard me."

Cesari waited for a minute while Vito thought it over. Eventually, Vito said, "How big is the trunk? I wanted the Silver Spur because of the trunk. You could fit three guys in there."

"Isn't that sort of cliché?" Cesari asked. "You know, putting dead guys in trunks?"

"It's not for dead guys. It's for me. The FBI have set up surveillance on my apartment. It's a great way for me to get around without being tailed."

"How exactly would that work?"

"They know about my Cadillac, but they don't know about the Rolls. When I leave my apartment, they'll follow me to the parking garage. The Caddie has tinted windows. When it pulls out, they'll assume I'm in it. Fifteen minutes later, I'll come out the other side of the garage in the trunk of the Rolls just in case they're watching both exits. In that particular garage you have the option of exiting on Mulberry Street or around the block on Mott Street."

Cesari tried to picture this in his mind's eye. Vito was six feet three inches tall and two hundred and sixty pounds of solid muscle. The trunk of the Silver Spur was certainly big enough, but Vito never went anywhere without being impeccably dressed in hand tailored suits, imported shoes, and enough bling to finance a small war. Then there was the issue of his personal grooming. He had a thick mess of curly salt and pepper hair that he had trimmed professionally every week along with a proper shave. Popping out of the trunk of a car could severely mar the image he was trying to project.

"Out of curiosity, why a Rolls and not some other car or an SUV?"

"Because they'll never suspect I would use a Rolls Royce. They'll think it's way too classy for me, and an added benefit is the trunks are lined with lamb's wool. It'll take all my strength not to fall asleep in there."

Cesari turned to Gerry, cupped the receiver, and said, "They line the trunks of Rolls Royces with lamb's wool?"

Gerry nodded. "Some doctor you are. You didn't even notice back in Jersey when I got out of the Silver Spur?"

Cesari returned to Vito and said, "It sounds like a great idea. Look, I'll check with Gerry about the trunk, but pending that should I tell him you have a new deal or that he should flee the country?"

Vito hesitated and then said, "Tell him we have a deal as long as I can fit in the trunk easily. If not, the convertible's mine and he eats his finder's fee, and make sure he gets a phone tomorrow and calls me."

Cesari turned to Gerry and gave him a thumb's up.

"All right then. I'll let him know we're a full go."

"One more thing, Cesari. No offense, but I don't appreciate you interfering with my business dealings. Gerry should have reported his sad story directly to me. This secondhand bullshit is disrespectful."

"Give the guy a break. He was profoundly traumatized tonight. I almost had to take him to the emergency room for sedation."

"That doesn't sound like the Gerry I know."

"Well, trust me. These bikers were badass."

"That's another thing. Do you have any names or colors for these guys? They were disrespectful too and I'd like to discuss it with them."

"I don't have any names, but they were at the New Jersey Bar and Grill on Randolph Avenue in Mine Hill. They seemed pretty comfortable there like they were regulars."

"Good enough."

Chapter 5

Just about the time Cesari was taking a punch from the biker, the Sommelier's chauffeur-driven Rolls Royce limousine pulled up to the wrought iron gate guarding his mansion. The Chateau was a hundred thousand square foot, four story, twelve-bedroom, fifteen fireplace, stone and brick Tudor-style modern-day castle, nestled on two hundred and fifty acres of deeply wooded land in Bernardsville, New Jersey. The combined income of the town's seven thousand uber-wealthy residents was more than the GDP of half the nations of South America and Africa. The Chateau was complemented by riding stables, outdoor and indoor swimming pools, outdoor and indoor tennis courts, a seven-lane bowling alley, a shooting range, an underground parking garage, and a smaller residence attached to the main domicile for the multitude of house staff.

The driver rolled down his window to identify himself to the approaching guard. Security was tight throughout the property, and everyone was armed, trained in the use of deadly force, and conditioned to not trust anyone. The chauffeur himself was an ex-navy SEAL and combat veteran who carried two Glock 17's and a ten-inch knife on his person. The limo had two Remington 12-gauge semi-auto shotguns loaded, chambered, and strategically placed for easy access of both driver and passenger. Security cameras watched every access point and were monitored continuously by his men in the basement of the mansion. Every two hours, a team of security guards with Dobermans walked the perimeter of the property where visibility of the cameras was limited by the natural terrain. Personally worth more than Switzerland, he couldn't afford to take any chances and even as the guard spoke to his driver, the Sommelier had one of the car's shotguns trained on the man's face.

The Sommelier had business dealings far and wide and had witnessed first-hand what corruption and greed did to men. Loyalty was as ephemeral as life itself and he personally had bribed many of his enemies' most faithful employees into betrayal and ultimately the downfall of their masters. But all was well, and they were waved on uneventfully through the gate. One hundred yards ahead, the driver stopped the car to let him off at the main entrance. Two other men were waiting and opened the door for him. As he exited the Rolls, he instructed the driver to sweep the car for electronic listening and tracking devices, an action which was performed twice daily.

Entering his home, he walked briskly through the massive great room passing by a twenty-foot-wide marble fireplace, grand piano, crystal chandeliers, and original oil paintings illegally obtained on the black market. Rembrandts, Monets, Van Goghs and Picassos. Wherever and whatever he could get his hands on, decorated the hall. The center of the room was dominated by a sixteenth century bronze reproduction of Donatello's fifteenth century masterpiece, David. The original was housed in a secure museum in Italy, but as far as reproductions went, this one was considered a work of genius in its own right. No price was too high and no methods too low in order to obtain his objectives. At the far end of the room, he was greeted by a woman in her early thirties wearing a modest skirt and top. Attractive and business-like, she was tall and lithe with long dark hair and seductive, almond-shaped brown eyes. She was his right-hand woman.

He greeted her warmly with a slight peck on either cheek. "Good evening, Simone. I know I'm running late. I trust you've been keeping my guests entertained?"

She nodded. "Of course, Michel. They are right this very minute enjoying a glass of wine in the library."

"Whatever would I do without you?"

"Thank you."

"Has Hugo arrived?"

"He is waiting for you in the trophy room downstairs."

"Good. I will go there first. Tell our friends I won't be long."

"Certainly… The governor's office called earlier. He wanted to thank you for hosting the fundraiser for his re-election here at the chateau next Saturday."

"Again? He thanks me every two days. What did he really want, Simone?"

She smiled revealing perfect, white teeth. "He was wondering if you would mind if he gave one of his staffers a private tour of the upstairs part of the house either during cocktail hour or perhaps in between one of the courses."

"He wants to bang one of his chippies in one of my bedrooms during his own fundraiser with his wife in the same building? The man has gall. That's for sure."

The Sommelier handed her his briefcase. He was exasperated. "Tell him I said fine, but I won't be held responsible if his wife catches him with his drawers down. Simone, I swear that one of these days he's going to push me too far… Although I suppose he's been a useful enough tool that I should accept his flaws and occasional transgressions. It's a lot easier than training a new governor. They always come in riding their white horses and wearing their self-righteousness like an overcoat. Did he say what kind of a contribution he expects this time around?"

"He said a million is a nice round number."

The Sommelier snorted disapproval. "He is the worst kind of robber baron. You can tell him I said a hundred thousand is also a nice round number. Send his campaign a check for that amount. If he complains tell him the cost of making sure there are no cameras in the bedroom with him is exactly nine hundred thousand dollars."

"Yes, Michel. Will there be anything else?"

"Not at the moment."

There was a massive staircase up, twenty feet wide at the bottom tapering to ten feet at the top. The bannisters were made of ornately carved mahogany and the steps were lined with plush carpeting. On the back side of the steps leading upward was an equally magnificent down staircase. Off to the side was a private elevator accessed by a four-digit electronic code. Simone walked away and the Sommelier felt the need to stretch his legs, so he walked down the staircase two levels. The upper lower level contained an Olympic-sized swimming pool, the steam room, the sauna, and the squash and tennis courts. The lowest level of the mansion was home to the wine cellar which was the largest single room in the mansion and housed more than three hundred thousand bottles of wine, the largest private collection in the world. The cellar's temperature and humidity were strictly controlled, and the wines were arranged by country, grape, vineyard and vintage with reds on the right and whites on the left. There was an enormous oak table in the center of the room where the Sommelier held lavish dinner parties.

At the far end of the wine cellar was a four-inch-thick steel door, nondescript and ordinary, reinforced on all sides. Only he and Hugo had keys to the giant deadbolt which guarded it. There was no other way in and more importantly, no other way out. The Sommelier estimated that no ordinary means could break it down. In fact, from the way he had it constructed, he was sure that nothing less than an Abrams M1A1 tank could force its way in. He inserted his key and turned it. The sound of the mechanism clicking open always reassured him.

The room was circular, twenty-five feet in diameter with a four-foot square metal table in its center. There was a hose and sink along one wall and a drain in the center of the room. The ceiling was fourteen feet tall with fluorescent lighting. Hugo stood by the table with an ordinary red and white cooler next to him on the floor.

"Were there any problems, Hugo?" he asked.

"None whatsoever, Michel."

"Then show it to me, please. I have been able to think of nothing else."

Hugo placed the cooler on the table and opened it. Reaching in, he grabbed the head by the hair and pulled it out, holding it high in the air, proud of his handiwork. The Sommelier studied the ghastly remains of what used to be a valued employee and smiled.

Loosely quoting Shakespeare he said, "Alas, poor Dave. I knew him well."

Hugo allowed himself a quiet chuckle. "Didn't we both? He should have known better... He had a girlfriend. She'll be asking questions."

"We sent him to Singapore on urgent business, Hugo. Falsify a plane ticket and travel log."

"Would he have left without calling or saying goodbye?"

"Tell her three other beautiful young women have already asked us the same question. Each one swears that he was in love with them and only them."

"That should slow her down."

The Sommelier had leaned in to examine the head more closely. After a while, he remarked, "Well done, Hugo. Well done. How did you get the cut line so smooth?"

"As with anything, practice makes perfect. I first removed the head with a band saw in my workshop. Then using a surgical scalpel, I trimmed off any ragged edges and polished the bones with fine sandpaper."

"You are definitely an artist. Have you embalmed it yet?"

"No, I didn't have time. I will do that now and mount it once you have chosen a suitable spot."

The Sommelier looked around the room. Mounted on the wall were the heads of various big game from around the world. A lion's head from the Congo. A giraffe from East Africa. A snow leopard from the Himalayas. Multiple species of antelope, deer, elk, moose, water buffalo, and at least three dozen human heads mounted in similar fashion, representing hated enemies and rivals, or as in this case, a traitor.

The Sommelier walked over to the wall nearest him and glanced upward at his prized possessions. He said, "I want him mounted here next to the hyena. What do you think about that, Hugo?"

Hugo nodded his approval. "It's fitting, and probably better than he deserves."

"I agree… Well, get on with it. I have guests to attend to."

"Yes, right away…How did it go with the doctors?"

"It was no problem. One of them was that pest, Dr. Goldstein. I've told you about him. He invested the hospital's endowment fund with me and seems to think he has a right to ask for the money back now that he's taken a loss."

"Did he take a loss?"

"Of course not. I siphoned off a hundred million to use in a pump and dump. It hasn't had enough time to mature and with regulatory agencies crawling up everyone's butt these days, I've had to move slowly. The poor doctor was beside himself."

Hugo looked concerned. "Will he be a problem?"

"If you mean your kind of problem, then no. At least not yet. Fortunately, I had an unlikely ally in the room. Goldstein came with another doctor for moral support, a Dr. Cesari. After a couple of bottles of wine, this Cesari character was literally telling Goldstein to stop asking silly questions about where the hospital's money went."

Hugo grinned. "It was that easy?"

"No, I had to pull up some heavily doctored graphs and accounts from a different client. I adjusted the numbers and the dates as we sat there drinking Bordeaux. Dr. Cesari was quite impressed."

"Not so much the other one?"

"No, Dr. Goldstein was nearly as upset at the loss of his money as he was by his friend's shifting loyalties. It was quite amusing really. Try to picture someone of ordinary breeding, from the Bronx of all places, guzzling whole glasses of fine Bordeaux in one long swallow and then wiping his lips and belching."

Hugo cringed. "Seriously?"

"I kid you not. Part of me wanted to write Goldstein a check and be rid of them both, but I have rules. And you know what my number one rule is, Hugo?"

"Tell me, Michel."

"There are no give-backs in my line of work."

"Nor should there be."

"Exactly…one more thing. Please do a background check on this Dr. Cesari for security purposes. I extended a perfunctory invitation to him to visit the wine cellar, and apparently, he thought I was serious. Rather than rescind the offer, I thought it may prove useful to cultivate him further. He seems to exert a fair amount of influence over Dr. Goldstein. Not that I'm worried, but he seemed skittish, like the type to make a phone call to the SEC, and I'd rather avoid that if possible."

"Should I keep an eye on Dr. Goldstein? It wouldn't be that difficult."

"How close an eye?"

"A simple listening device in his office."

The Sommelier thought it over and then said, "Sure, why not? It couldn't hurt. His office is on the tenth floor of St. Matt's hospital on Third Avenue in Manhattan. Will you do it yourself or use our asset?"

"I'll discuss it with our man there. It may be simpler to let him handle it. Most hospital security systems are painfully lacking even in this day and age of terrorism and random gun violence. He'll probably be able to just walk in any time he wants… I'll get on it right away as well as the background check on Cesari… He sounds Italian."

The Sommelier laughed. "Even better, Hugo. He's Sicilian. They're the smart ones. He told me so himself."

Hugo looked concerned. "I feel as if I should counsel you against bringing him here, Michel. I am not as comfortable with the lower classes as you are."

"Fear not, Hugo. From the moment Dr. Cesari opened his mouth, I knew there would be a special place in my home for him."

He finished that thought by looking upward at the wall of mounted heads.

Chapter 6

Several days later, Cesari meandered through the hallways of St. Matt's Medical Center in lower Manhattan looking for trouble or coffee or something sweet to eat like an apple fritter or a donut. It was eight in the morning, and he was hungry and caffeine deprived. The combination frequently led to him saying things to people he shouldn't say. He had decided to let Gerry stay with him a few days and the experience was making him edgy. The guy wouldn't shut up and wanted to fight about everything, but thankfully, when Cesari woke up this morning, he was gone. He assumed that sometime after they had gone to bed Gerry must have received a call from his friend at the Port of Newark about the arrival of the Rolls Royce.

Cesari's first scheduled colonoscopy was a no-show so he had nothing to do for the next thirty minutes and toyed with the idea of going to the cafeteria to deal with his alimentary needs. They had breakfast sandwiches there. Overcooked egg with melted plasticky cheese and a dried out, burnt sausage patty served on a raw untoasted, unbuttered, soggy, cold English muffin.

Cesari had calculated that an average gastroenterologist in New York State generated on average between five to seven million dollars in revenue per year for an average hospital. How could it possibly be then that an average gastroenterologist could drive to an average McDonalds and pay on average twenty percent less for a similar breakfast sandwich which on average would taste a thousand times better? Wouldn't it be a good idea to fire the chef in the hospital's cafeteria and use the money to pay a courier to go to Mickey D's every morning and pick up a suitcase full of assorted breakfast sandwiches? The hospital would save money and the morale of the staff would increase ten-fold, minimum. Win-win.

He pondered these life-altering questions as he walked into the cafeteria and picked up a soggy sandwich and inspected it. He shook his head in frustration. Why was it considered taboo to toast the muffin? He would bring it up with Arnie, he thought, as he poured black coffee into a styrofoam cup. As a matter of fact, he had time to kill so he would bring it up with him now. He paid for his meal and headed to Arnie's office on the tenth floor.

As he exited the elevator, he shoved the last of the sand-wich into his mouth and followed it up with a long pull on his coffee. Arnie's door was closed but unlocked so he let himself in and found the room fully occupied. Arnie was sitting behind his desk and four anesthesiologists were standing in front of him. These were the pain management branch of the anesthesia department. Arnie only had two consultation chairs so Cesari assumed that the guys thought it would be rude for two to sit while their comrades stood. Hence, they all stood. Like Cesari, they wore blue surgical scrubs and white lab coats with stetho-scopes hanging out of their pockets.

Arnie looked up and the others turned to him. They were an interesting assortment of people and Cesari liked them. Two were Indian; one from Mumbai and the other from Queens, New York. The one from Queens was Sikh and wore a blue tur-ban and sported a full beard. The kind of thick, fluffy beard that made you want to pull on it to see if it was real. His name was Jaskaran but went by Jay. The one from Mumbai was nearly seven feet tall, lanky, and wore old-fashioned dark-rimmed eye-glasses. His name was Parikh and he called everybody, sir. Xi was second generation Chinese American and was hard core conservative. He liked to say that if you cut him, he would bleed red, white, and blue. Last but not least was Jeremy, who also went by Jay. He was African American with a thin mustache and hip European glasses. They all liked scotch, which was good in Cesari's book, but Jeremy liked cigars too which was better. And when not in scrubs, he was a sharp dresser. Whenever and wherever he showed up after hours, he raised the bar for everyone else. All of them were in their mid to late thirties, intelligent, and excellent physicians.

They were reliable and easy to work with, and since their arrival as a group a year ago, much of the hospital's anesthesia woes had gradually disappeared. Parikh was in charge and towered over everyone else in the room. In the hospital, they were known as the Pain Killers. Cesari was pleasantly surprised to see them all here and greeted them warmly with a smile.

"Hey guys. I'm sorry for interrupting. I can come back later, Arnie. I just wanted to file a complaint about the food in the cafeteria."

The four pain guys chuckled, and Arnie said, "No, come on in. I need you here. You're acting Chief Medical Officer and should be in the loop."

Cesari raised his eyebrows, glanced at the others and said, "Chief Medical Officer? Since when?"

Arnie glanced at his watch. "Since five minutes ago. I can't be CEO and CMO at the same time."

"Do I get a raise?"

"Will you close the door and stop fooling around?"

Cesari closed the door behind him. "Fine, now what's with all the serious faces?"

"In exactly thirty minutes a New York City police detective is going to walk through that same door and inform me of a criminal complaint that has been filed against these doctors and the hospital. Is that serious enough for you?"

"Okay....," Cesari said slowly, trying to decipher the meaning of that. "I'm all ears. What happened?"

"I got called an hour ago by a Detective Tierney..."

Cesari interjected, "I know him."

"You do?"

"Yeah, I do. Our paths have crossed socially on several occasions."

"Well, isn't that a coincidence? He sounds like a real prick. Anyway, he informed me that a woman died in her bed three nights ago several blocks from this hospital and that one of these fine young men is a potential suspect."

"Are they real suspects or just potential suspects?"

"What's that supposed to mean?"

"Is Detective Tierney coming here to arrest anyone or simply ask a few questions?"

"He didn't say."

Cesari looked at the four anesthesiologists who were standing there meekly and asked, "Did any of you guys kill anyone in their bed three nights ago?"

They all shook their heads in unison. Parikh said, "No, sir. I would remember if I had."

Cesari grinned. "I didn't think so." He turned back to Arnie, "Do you know the substance of what happened?"

"Not yet. He was going to fill in the gaps when he arrived. I called these guys in as soon as I hung up with him to see if they knew anything."

"And they don't?"

They all shook their heads again.

"How does Tierney even know it involves one of them?"

"I don't know. All he said was that our pain management doctors were on the short list of suspects."

"Okay..." Cesari said again just as slowly as before. "Well look Arnie, I have ten patients waiting for me in the OR for their colonoscopies. As much as I'd like to stay and help you with Tierney..."

Ignoring him, Arnie picked up the phone and dialed the OR. A few seconds later, he was talking to Emily, the nurse manager. "Hi Emily. This is Arnie Goldstein. Dr. Cesari is helping me stamp out a fire that's just come up. Unfortunately, I need him more than you do. He tells me that he has quite a few colonoscopies scheduled. Please start calling his patients and if they don't wish to be rescheduled then tack one or two on to each of the other GI guys' schedules and let them know how much I appreciate their cooperation. Thanks."

Arnie hung up and looked at Cesari. "You were saying?"

"I'm not sure how professional or ethical that was, Arnie."

"Look, Cesari, I don't really care. St. Matt's can't afford to have one of its doctors be accused of murder. This is an all-hands-on deck situation. You know this detective who's coming here, and you may be able to sway him to our way of thinking."

"Which is?"

"We don't accuse a doctor of murder unless we are one hundred and ten percent certain. It would smear the hospital, destroy his or her career and undermine our ability to deliver care to the community. The damage would be incalculable. Besides, look at these guys. Do any of them look like they're capable of murder?"

Cesari studied them, and after a minute said, "Well, Parikh's kind of big. It makes me uncomfortable the way he's always staring down at me. Plus, the way he blocks out the sun, a guy could die from vitamin D deficiency or get rickets or something. Not a pleasant way to go I'm told."

Indian Jay laughed at that, and Parikh unconsciously slouched to diminish his size saying, "I am sorry about that, sir."

Cesari added, "What are you laughing about, Jay? You could be hiding a .44 magnum in that beard of yours or a grenade under the turban and no one would notice."

Now they were all laughing. Cesari turned to Xi. "Xi, you own an AR15 and lots of ammo. You're practically a one-man militia. That says something, doesn't it?"

Xi replied defiantly, "Yeah, it says that I'm ready to fight all of my country's enemies both foreign and domestic so don't tread on me, Cesari."

"You sound like a Soviet sleeper agent who's memorized right wing propaganda. And last but not least, Jeremy Macallan. How am I supposed to trust a guy who's named after my favorite scotch? You smoke Cuban cigars, don't you Jay? While not the crime of the century, they are illegal and hints at an underlying subversive personality disorder, and possibly commie sympathies. I'm sorry Arnie, but if I was on a jury, I'd convict them all just because."

Arnie was getting annoyed. "Cesari, shut up and sit down. This is serious and you're playing games. The rest of you can go back to work, but you've been forewarned. I suggest you figure out where and whom you were with three nights ago in case this thing takes on steam, and for the record, I think this is total bullshit."

They thanked Arnie for his support, waved at Cesari, who they found thoroughly entertaining, and turned to leave. Cesari called out as they reached the door. "Happy hour tonight anyone? Cigars and scotch at the Light House Saloon in the Village? Say 6:00 p.m.? And Jeremy, if you bring me a Cuban, I'll consider not turning you in."

They thought it over and one by one nodded. Jeremy said, "You got it."

After they left, Arnie shook his head in frustration. The angst was etched deeply into the lines of his face. "As if I didn't have enough on my plate. I lose a hundred million dollars of the hospital's money, the board wants my head, and now this. I'm telling you, Cesari, they can't pay me enough."

"Heavy is the head that wears the crown, Arnie."

"Isn't that the truth? What's with the happy hour? You the new cruise director?

"C'mon, Arnie, you just told four young doctors that a New York City detective was coming here to accuse one or more of them of murder. They're going to need to unwind a little after that assuming one of them isn't walked out of here in handcuffs."

He nodded. "You're right. If it was me, I'd be a basket case."

"You are a basket case, but I think your assessment is one hundred percent correct. This is total bullshit. None of those guys would hurt a fly. Changing the subject, anything new with the financial guy?"

"Mike B.? Not really, although I put a call in with the SEC and the Attorney General's office yesterday."

Cesari raised his eyebrows. "You're kidding?"

"I couldn't help myself. This is eating at me. Something about that guy doesn't seem right to me. He's too slick."

"What did they say?"

"Nothing yet. I made appointments with agents from both offices. The SEC is tomorrow, and the attorney general's appointment is the day after. They wouldn't take complaints on the phone."

A knock on the door interrupted them.

Chapter 7

Detective Robert Tierney was a stiff-assed, brushed-cut, clean-cut, an inch over six feet, twice-divorced, fifty-year-old former marine, who suffered from bouts of PTSD from one too many combat tours in Iraq and Afghanistan. He wore a brown tweed three-piece suit, crisp white dress shirt with cufflinks, striped bowtie, and a bowler derby hat. This was his uniform which he wore three hundred and sixty-five days a year. The chain from a gold pocket watch looped down from his vest and he munched on the stub of an unlit fat cigar while holding a Starbucks latte in one hand. It was rumored that he lived with an overweight calico cat named Stonewall, who was his only friend. It was also rumored that he made two gin martinis every night, dirty, with three olives. One for him and one for Stonewall. He and Cesari had crossed swords in the past with neither party able to claim victory. They weren't enemies nor were they exactly friends. But they did have a certain degree of respect for each other.

Tierney stood in the doorway and said, "Good morning, doctors."

Arnie and Cesari stood to greet him. They all shook hands and sat down. Tierney rested his hat on the corner of Arnie's desk and took the cigar out of his mouth. "I didn't know you were going to be here, Cesari."

Arnie said, "He's the newly appointed Chief Medical Officer of St. Matt's."

Tierney cracked a sarcastic grin. "So crime really does pay. Well, congratulations to you, Cesari."

Cesari retorted, "It's a pleasure to see you too, Detective."

Arnie wasn't sure what to make of the back and forth between the two but was eager to find out what was going on. "Detective, I hope you don't mind but I'd like to get right to the point. You made a very serious allegation on the phone so tell us what happened."

"Sure thing, Dr. Goldstein."

He placed his coffee cup on Arnie's desk next to his hat and then retrieved a small notepad from his jacket pocket. He made a big deal about flipping through a few pages until he came to the pertinent one.

"Three days ago, an eighty-year-old woman, named Carol Loomis, was found dead in her apartment. The coroner's preliminary report placed the time of death somewhere around midnight the night before which would have been Saturday night. The cause of death appears to have been a drug overdose. Everybody with me so far?"

Arnie nodded and said, "You said there was a murder. People overdose all the time, even the elderly."

"I'm getting to that part, but the lady's name doesn't ring a bell?"

Cesari and Arnie shook their heads and Tierney continued, "Mrs. Loomis lived alone in a one-bedroom apartment on East 9th Street just a short distance from this hospital. Her husband died several years ago. She has a daughter across the river in Hoboken. Mrs. Loomis had a variety of medical conditions, mostly routine stuff like high blood pressure and osteoarthritis. Nothing too dramatic until three months ago when she began experiencing abdominal pain and weight loss. A CT scan and blood work revealed metastatic pancreatic cancer. She was considered too far gone for chemotherapy or surgery and was referred to your pain clinic for palliative care. Apparently, she was in a lot of distress."

He paused to take a breath and a sip of coffee. Cesari took the opportunity to make a point. "I think I know where you're heading with this Detective. One of our pain guys prescribed a narcotic in order to alleviate her pain and she overdosed, either accidentally or purposefully. A sad situation for sure but I'd hardly call that murder."

Tierney's eyes burned a hole right through Cesari. "Relax, Perry Mason, I'm not finished. So Mrs. Loomis was referred to your pain management clinic roughly three months ago. She was terminal and with few options available. She saw..." He turned the page of his notepad and read down before continuing, "She saw two of the four guys listed on your website in that department. A Dr. Jeremy Macallan and a Dr. Jaskaran Singh. Over the course of several weeks, they provided her with several prescriptions for fentanyl patches and oral narcotics in the form of hydrocodone in escalating doses but well within the range one would expect for a cancer patient."

Arnie fidgeted in his chair. "How do you know all this? I don't remember receiving a request from the NYPD to review her medical records."

"Deep breath, Doctor. We're getting there. First of all, as I mentioned Mrs. Loomis has a daughter in Jersey. When her mother didn't answer the phone Sunday morning, she called the police and has been very forthcoming about her mother's medical care. Secondly, yesterday I made a quick visit to her primary care physician's office, and he didn't mind showing me her records once the daughter gave him permission."

"Fine," Arnie said. "But what's this got to do with murder?"

"This is where it becomes interesting. Mrs. Loomis knew she was dying. No big mystery there. She was wasting away. Her daughter knew she was dying too. She had accepted that from the moment the diagnosis was made. Her primary care physician had told her that it could be weeks or months. No one could predict, but that it wouldn't be years. Mrs. Loomis was okay with it. She had made her peace with the world. She was also determined to live her life as well as she could as long as she remained functional and independent, which she had been doing a pretty decent job of. A visiting nurse checked on her three times weekly. Her daughter called her every day and took her to all her clinic appointments. She had offered for Mrs. Loomis to move in with her and her family in Hoboken, but the invitation was declined. Mrs. Loomis did not wish to be a burden on anyone."

Cesari glanced at Arnie as Tierney took another deep breath before the big reveal, which was obviously just around the corner. No one said anything as the anticipation mounted.

Finally, Tierney said, "On the night she died, Mrs. Loomis called her daughter at around 10:00 p.m. to say goodbye and to tell her one last time how much she loved her. She said that she was waiting for an angel to come and take her to heaven."

Arnie's eyes went wide, and he said, "What happened then?"

"The daughter was upset and thought her mother was hallucinating from all the narcotics."

Cesari offered, "That's not a bad guess."

"I agree," added Tierney. "The daughter toyed with the idea of driving in to check on her, but her mother didn't appear to be in any distress otherwise. In fact, she said her mother was lying in bed watching TV when she called and sounded very rational except for the angel part. The daughter had a very long and tiring day herself, and she decided to wait until morning to reevaluate the situation. In the morning, she phoned her mother repeatedly and eventually called the police."

Cesari said, "Is it safe to assume, there's more to this story, Detective?"

Tierney nodded. "When the police arrived, they found Mrs. Loomis dead in her bed. Cold and stiff as you would expect. She had two fresh fentanyl patches on her, a half-empty bottle of hydrocodone on the nightstand, and no signs of foul play or forced entry. Superficially, nothing was out of place. But there were a couple of anomalies that made my boys in uniform reach out for more direction. One, the door to her apartment was un-locked when they arrived. That's kind of unusual in Manhattan, isn't it?"

Cesari nodded. "Sure, but she was on narcotics and could have been confused. She might have forgotten to lock it. What else?"

"That's what I thought when I got there, but then there was the glass in the kitchen sink. Mrs. Loomis had a mostly empty water glass on her night table which made sense but there was second glass in the kitchen sink and guess what?"

Arnie sighed, "What?"

Tierney relished the cat and mouse stuff. Like most cops he lived for the melodrama. "The glass on the night table was loaded with the old lady's fingerprints, but the glass in the kitchen sink had absolutely no prints on it at all."

"Meaning what?" asked Cesari.

"Meaning somebody had either wiped it clean or was wear-ing gloves. Either way, it suggests there was a second person in the apartment and that in itself raises the possibility that Mrs. Loomis's death was no accident."

Cesari and Arnie took that in and waited. Tierney went on, "The most important finding, however, was this."

He took a four by six photograph out from his coat pocket and handed it to Cesari who examined it and handed it to Arnie who did the same. It was the plastic cap of a syringe.

Tierney said, "That fell out of the bedsheets when they removed the body. Mrs. Loomis wasn't taking any injectable medications and there were no syringes in the apartment. Upon examination, a small puncture wound was found in her left groin by the femoral vein. The syringe cap had no fingerprints on it but did have a miniscule amount of a substance in it that has been identified as propofol, a commonly used sedative. I believe you are both familiar with it."

Cesari gulped and nodded. He could now see clearly where this was going and his mind immediately shifted to other possible explanations. "Yes, of course we know what it is. Not only is it commonly used in this hospital, it's commonly used in every hospital and outpatient surgical center in the entire country."

"I knew you would say that, Cesari. It's the Michael Jackson drug. Isn't it?"

"Yes, it is. But in that instance, it was improperly obtained and improperly used as a home sleep aid."

Tierney agreed with a nod. "Is it safe to say that a syringe full of propofol in the setting of an old, malnourished woman on narcotics could easily prove fatal?"

"Yes, that would be safe to say, but who gave it to her would be the real question."

Tierney smiled. "Now we're on the same page. Who would have access to this kind of medicine? Certainly not some schmuck on the street. What about you, Cesari? Could you just write a prescription for it and pick it up at your local CVS?"

"No, of course not. It's only for use by licensed anesthesia providers in the hospital setting and even there it's strictly regulated and accounted for. Every drop, I assure you. The Michael Jackson tragedy made sure of that. Every hospital and pharmacy in the country tightened its grip on access and distribution."

"And yet here we are. We found traces of a controlled anesthetic in a dead woman's apartment, a puncture wound in her femoral vein, and circumstantial evidence that there was another person there with her. You just admitted that the only people who have access to that particular drug are anesthesiologists. And two of your anesthesiologists were intimately involved in her care. A really nice guy might think that one of your pain management people took mercy on the woman and decided to end her suffering. She might even have begged him to do it. I can empathize with that, but it's still a crime, mind you, and I don't give a rat's ass what his motivation was. That's not my job. I'm a cop. The judge and jury will have to decide the rest."

You could have heard a pin drop as Cesari and Arnie held their breath. The wind in their sails had been completely knocked out. Their bubble had burst. Cesari asked, "What would a not-so-nice guy think?"

Tierney replied, "That one of your anesthesiologists is a deranged savage who takes advantage of dying people to get his rocks off by delivering the coup-de-grace."

"There could be other explanations for this, Detective. I'm sure you are aware of that."

"I sure am, Cesari, but none that make any sense or fit the narrative. For instance, maybe the old lady somehow purchased it on the street from her local dealer, shot herself up, and threw the syringe out the window before she died. Why she would do that is anyone's guess. Pretty unlikely though... Maybe she copped a syringe left carelessly lying around the waiting room in the clinic when she arrived for her appointment?" Tierney scrunched his nose. "I don't like that one either. How about this one? Some anesthesiologist from Mount Sinai heard about her case, swooped in from mid-town and killed her to frame your guys. You know...one of those make the competition look bad kind of things."

Cesari said nothing.

"No, I'm sorry, Cesari, but one your guys did it and you know it. Before you go full-court press on me, I should let you know one more thing about Mrs. Loomis."

Arnie was totally defeated. "What?"

"The daughter remembered something about the conversation she had with her mother the night she died. Mrs. Loomis had said she was waiting for an angel to take her to heaven. Well, the daughter remembered that when she would take her mother home from pain clinic, she would refer to the doctors there as angels."

Cesari said, "Shit."

Chapter 8

There was a long silence before anyone spoke again. The mood in the room was somber. Eventually Cesari said, "So what happens next, Detective?"

"What happens next is that I speak to your anesthesiologists and take statements from them off the record for now."

Arnie asked, "You're not going to arrest anyone?"

"Not today, Doctor. The evidence is compelling but too circumstantial and would never hold up in court unless someone confesses or we find matching fingerprints or their DNA in the apartment placing them at the scene. I wouldn't want to act prematurely. The optics for the hospital wouldn't be good and would be even worse for the department if we couldn't prove our case. I came here to give you a head's up that you may have a bad seed. Also, I would like your full cooperation in allowing me access to Mrs. Loomis's medical records and all four doctors' personnel records. I'll need to know if anybody has filed any complaints against them. I'd hate to have to get a warrant, Dr. Goldstein. God knows what kind of rumors that would start and could potentially slip to the press. In the meanwhile, you tell your guys to play nice with me and maybe we'll get through this without too much rancor. You may want your pharmacy to count up the propofol to see if any is missing."

Cesari said, "I don't understand. All four doctors are under suspicion? But the old lady only had a relationship with two?"

Tierney turned to him. "The others would have had access to her chart and would have known she was terminally ill as well as where she lived. Unfortunately, if one is a suspect, they're all suspects. I will be as discreet as I can, doctors, but I have no intention of cutting anyone any slack because they have a college education. Are we clear on that?"

They both nodded and Arnie said, "Are you going to interview them here?"

"No, they'll have to be fingerprinted and submit DNA samples, and I'll need photographs to show to people in the building to see if anybody recognizes them and possibly saw them that night. I'll try not to interfere with patient care as best I can, and we can do most of it after work in the early evening."

"We'll do whatever we can to facilitate the process, Detective," Arnie affirmed. "Do you want to meet them now?"

Tierney shook his head, stood, finished his coffee, and threw the cup in Arnie's trash can. "No, I want to give you time to talk with them to soften the blow. I'd like to see Mrs. Loomis's medical records and their personnel files first. Let them know that I'll be calling them to set up times to come down to the precinct for interviews. Needless to say, no one should leave town. It would look bad. Here's a bunch of my cards to give to them. I'll grab their cellphone numbers off their files. Now maybe someone could direct me to the record room."

Cesari stood. "Arnie, you start calling the guys and let them know what's on the horizon. I'll walk the detective to medical records. Almost everything's computerized but we have a private room with a secure terminal you can use, and I'll get you access. I'll need to stay with you of course, partly to help you navigate the system and partly to keep the staff away. At this point, there's no need for anyone to even know who you are or what you're doing."

"Good thinking, Cesari," Arnie said. "If anyone asks, just say he's from the state reviewing policies and procedures in the OR. All very routine."

Tierney grinned, "Hey, you guys are pretty good at cover-ups. I'll try not to be suspicious about that."

They left Arnie who was already on the phone before the door even closed. In the elevator on the way down to the basement of the hospital where the medical records department was located, Tierney asked, "How's your friend, Gianelli?"

"Vito's good. Staying out of trouble as far as I can tell. I'll tell him you asked."

"You do that, and Gianelli wouldn't know how to stay out of trouble if his life depended on it, Cesari. A word of advice, if I may. I know you and Gianelli are tight, but having a best friend who's a known organized crime underboss may negatively impact your ability to defend your anesthesia guys if the shit ever really hits the fan. Think of how that would look if it ever came to light."

"Bad optics?"

"Exactly... If I were you, I would consider hiring a PR person for the hospital. Do yourself and everyone else a favor and stay out of sight if the media comes sniffing around. You should be the last person who gets in front of a camera, and your pal, Goldstein, doesn't have the temperament. He'd fold like a cheap suit. Let the professionals handle the press."

"You're protecting us?"

"I live in this community, Cesari. I might wind up in St. Matt's emergency room one day with a gunshot wound or a heart attack. I don't want this place to get a blackeye unnecessarily. It would be sad if your friends are innocent but St. Matt's takes a hit because their new Chief Medical Officer is all mobbed up."

"I'll bring it up with Arnie, but it sounds like a reasonable idea. Thanks."

They exited the elevator and found the records room deep in the bowels of St. Matt's. Cesari let them in with a swipe of his ID badge against the electronic control panel. The door opened with a click and the first thing that struck Tierney were the massive rolling racks of paper charts that seemed to stretch for miles in every direction. Six feet tall, two feet wide, and eight feet long, there dozens upon dozens of them on a series of long metal floor tracks vaguely resembling a busy railyard.

He commented, "What gives with all the paper, Cesari?"

"One of the great mysteries of modern technology, Detective. Everybody thought that when computers came along all this paper was going to disappear, but they made several miscalculations along the way, not least of which is that as a class of people most healthcare workers are hopeless luddites. Then there are the cumbersome, not-so-user-friendly medical records systems that are designed to maximize billing potential and the ability of the state to track us, not optimize efficiency and patient care. Finally, there are the endless problems inherent with computers and the internet in general. We're always one power surge away from total incapacitation in our ability to deliver care. Without being online, we can't even give a patient an aspirin or start an IV. And the ever-present threat of viruses and hackers makes paper charting an absolute necessity for redundancy, but fear not, Detective, the government is here to help."

Tierney glanced in all directions before saying, "Interesting...I had no idea."

As they walked past the file cabinets, Cesari said hello to several workers. They eventually came to a room with multiple laptops set up on individual small desks separated from each other for privacy. They sat down in front of one and Cesari typed in his username and password. He pulled up Mrs. Loomis's records and let Tierney review them to his heart's content. They were fairly extensive, since her primary care and consulting oncologists were on staff and ordered all of her x-rays and lab work at St. Matt's.

Tierney clucked from time to time, asked Cesari to explain a few medical things, and jotted down a few notes. After close to an hour, he looked up and said, "Anything in here look suspicious or unusual to you, Cesari?"

Cesari replied, "Nothing at all."

"All right. What about those doctors' personnel files?"

"We'll have to go to Human Resources on the second floor. Anything important will be on paper under lock and key."

"Will there be anything important?"

"I doubt it. I was part of the committee that hired them. I saw all their resumes, spoke with their references, and interviewed them. In addition, I've worked with all of them closely over the last year. I would have heard if something was off. Sorry to disappoint you, Detective, but they're squeaky-clean, garden-variety nerds just trying to make a living before the politicians destroy what's left of healthcare in the name of progress."

"Got a pretty dim view of our representative government, do you?"

"I have a pretty dim view of anybody who thinks that just because they won a popular vote by promising people free lunch, they can suddenly micromanage physicians like me who had to train ten years after college to do what I do. In my career, I've seen more people die than most combat veterans. Do you really think I'm going to take suggestions well on how to prac-tice medicine from some fresh-faced newly-elected congress person spewing out soundbites for the press corps?"

Tierney smiled. "I hear you, Cesari. Loud and clear. Now picture yourself sitting on a mountain top in Afghanistan trying to figure out if the same bureaucrat is going to support you or sell you down the river depending on which way the political winds are blowing."

Cesari nodded. "I guess that wasn't right for me to compare my own situation to the sacrifices you made."

"Maybe not, but I see your point and it's a valid one. A lot of people are crying about how bad things are in our healthcare system and what you're saying is that they haven't seen any-thing yet. Just wait until the drunks on Capitol Hill are running things."

"Exactly... Here we are."

Cesari opened the door to the HR department and spoke with the secretary there who had been alerted to their arrival by Arnie. She directed them to a small conference room where the personnel files were already pulled and waiting for them on a table. They sat down on metal folding chairs opposite each other. Tierney picked up one of the manila folders and weighed it. They were all quite thin.

He leafed through each one, taking notes. At one point, he raised his eyebrows. Cesari asked, "What is it?"

"These guys are pretty smart. Harvard, Columbia, Yale, Princeton..."

"Yes, and they're very good at what they do too. They're not just book smart, although they have plenty of that."

"You seem to be a big fan of theirs."

"Doctors are easy targets these days, Detective. They deserve the benefit of the doubt."

"You mean like cops?"

"That's exactly what I mean."

"I'll keep that in mind... It says here that one of them is seven feet tall. Is that right?"

Cesari grinned. "Yeah, that's Parikh, and he's very self-conscious about it so..."

Tierney nodded. "I won't bring it up. It also says that he's a permanent resident with a green card for ten years. Is there a reason he hasn't applied for his citizenship?"

"I never asked him about it. More than likely, he's just been very busy living his life, studying and training. Things like that. He's married, owns a house and has two kids. I'm sure you understand."

"Yeah, but if he wants to vote he needs to be a citizen."

"Says who? I'm not even sure you need to be alive to vote in this country."

Tierney laughed. "You're in an awfully misanthropic mood this morning, aren't you, Cesari?"

Chapter 9

The Light House saloon was an upscale pub on Thompson Street in the Village. Cesari and the pain guys had met there on multiple occasions for drinks after work. There was an outdoor patio with tables and ashtrays where they were permitted to smoke. This time apparently wasn't going to be a cigar and scotch night. He found them inside squished into a small wooden booth looking morose as they stared at their hardly touched beers sitting in front of them. Arnie had brought them up to speed on Tierney's visit and they had already received a phone call from the detective inviting them to come down to the precinct for a chat. Cesari pulled up a chair at the end of the booth and signaled a waitress for a drink.

He glanced around, and said, "Look guys, I realize this isn't the best thing that has ever happened, but you're innocent so there's no need for the glum faces. There's just been a misunderstanding that will soon be cleared up."

Parikh shook his head. He was worried. "I am not so sure about that, Dr. Cesari. I am not a citizen. They may deport me."

"First of all, Parikh, it's just Cesari. No need for doctor. We're all equals here. Second of all, no one's getting deported. You didn't do anything."

Not in the least reassured by this, Parikh countered, "I don't agree, sir. As a foreigner, I will not be treated well."

Before Cesari could reply to that, Jeremy commented cynically, "You think being a foreigner is bad, Parikh? It's always the black guy that takes it up the ass when there's an unexplained crime. As long as I'm around, the rest of you guys are safe."

Cesari looked at him. "Jesus, Jay, was that supposed to be helpful? Everybody, please stop. No one's taking anything up the ass. It's not even clear that a crime has been committed."

Xi said, "From what you and Arnie told us, it's only a matter of time."

"Not necessarily," explained Cesari. "But we might as well get our ducks in a row. You guys all have alibis, right?"

Parikh said, "I was at home with my wife and children."

Cesari said, "There you go."

Xi said, "I was on call doing C-sections. Lots of witnesses including nurses, the obstetrics guy, Hamilton, and the pediatrician, Lewis. We were there all night."

Jeremy nodded. "I'm covered too. I was at my girlfriend's. We had dinner with friends and then went to her apartment to watch a movie."

Cesari added, "So far so good."

Jaskaran was quiet and Cesari asked, "What about you, Jay?"

He shook his head. "I was alone."

Cesari said, "Seriously? A good-looking guy like you? All alone on a Saturday night? That's sad. I thought you were seeing that nurse in the ICU?"

"I was, and she was seeing about five other guys, so you don't need to rub salt in the wound, Cesari."

"Sorry about that... So you don't have an alibi?"

"No, I don't."

"Then you could be guilty."

"Shut up, Cesari."

The dam broke and a soft chuckle percolated around the table as tensions eased slightly. Cesari grinned. "Just kidding. We'll figure something out. Worse comes to worse, you were with me watching Formula One racing."

Jaskaran laughed. "At midnight?"

"Sure, they have races in Asia, don't they? We stayed up late to watch the Grand Prix in India."

"I suppose it's possible, but this is ridiculous. I'm not going to lie to the police. Then I'll really be in trouble."

"Okay, tell the truth but if this goes anywhere and you wind up on trial, we resort to plan B about you being with me watching TV, okay?"

His dark complexion turned pale at the thought of a criminal trial. "How about I just stick to the truth and take my chances with the criminal justice system?"

"You could do that," advised Cesari, "but then we'll all know who's going to take it up the ass... Talk some sense into him, Jeremy."

"I'd listen to Cesari, Jay."

Xi added. "I'm not sure I like the idea of lying to the authorities either."

Cesari said, "It's only if it looks like things are getting out of hand, Xi. But it probably won't happen that way. The bottom line is I know this detective. He's tough but he's fair and open-minded. He's not looking to destroy anyone if he doesn't have to."

Xi said, "And if he has to?"

"Then it's going to suck being you."

"Great....How do you know this guy anyway?"

Cesari hesitated and then said, "I hate to report this to you, but I've been caught in his investigatory crosshairs on one or two occasions myself in the past and he's always given me a fair shake."

Now they were all curious. One of them asked, "What did you do?"

"I didn't do anything. That's the point. He came, he asked questions, and then he left me alone. Okay, now would someone care to explain to me how a syringe cap with traces of propofol found its way into the old lady's apartment?"

Their faces went blank as they thought it over. Indian Jay said, "It couldn't have come from the outpatient pain clinic. No one uses propofol there. Was she in the OR for some reason or the surgical center?"

Cesari said, "No, I reviewed her chart this morning with Detective Tierney. There was no mention of any recent surgical procedures or visits to the OR."

"She could have gone to a surgical center not affiliated with St. Matt's," offered Xi.

"And did what?" asked Cesari. "Steal a syringe full of propofol while no one was watching? And then go home and shoot herself up with it in the femoral vein?"

"No, sir, but maybe she had some type of procedure there and they got careless and accidentally dropped the cap on her stretcher," hypothesized Parikh. "And then possibly, it got caught in her clothing or fell into her bag. Perhaps the puncture wound is nothing more than a bug bite."

Cesari mulled that over. "Possibly, but as implausible as that sounds, it's good to have some alternative explanation... I'll ask her primary care physician if he knew of any trips she might have made to another medical facility. But let's be real, the woman was dying from metastatic pancreatic cancer. Does it seem logical that she would go to another medical center and different doctors at this late stage?"

Jeremy shook his head. "No, it doesn't make sense at all. She and her primary physician would have wanted to consolidate her care in one place."

"That's what I think, but hey, you never know. I'll look into it. Now here's a big question I want you all to start thinking about the answer to because it's bound to come up." Cesari paused and scanned their faces before saying, "Think long and hard about your personal feelings concerning physician-assisted suicide and end of life care. I have no doubt that it will come up."

Xi asked, "Why?"

"It will come up because everyone's going to want to understand you as a person and your mindset as a physician, and now's not the time to promote personal philosophy or politics. Whether or not any of this goes any further than a simple inquiry to criminal charges may have a lot to do with how Tierney feels about you personally. If you walk into the interview telling him you don't think we should be wasting valuable resources on eighty-year-olds with cancer, he may think you're capable of acting out on those sentiments. The other thing to keep in mind is that news of this is undoubtedly going to leak and then you'll have to contend with the court of public opinion, which is a much harsher court. So prepare your canned responses and keep them neutral, articulate, and consistent with the ethics and guidelines of your profession and modern medicine. Don't stray from the script even if you're provoked. Flippant comments or speculation on what you believe a perfect world ought to look like will make you seem like you could possibly have an agenda."

Parikh asked, "Excuse me, sir, but don't they need evidence to convict a man?"

Cesari snorted, "Yeah, sometimes. It certainly helps, but if the prosecution paints you as a Dr. Kevorkian wannabe, then maybe not. The goal is to keep this thing from ever reaching that point. Everybody understand?"

They nodded slowly and sipped their beers. Jeremy asked, "Should we lawyer up?"

"I can't answer that for you Jay. Tierney told me that everything's off the record right now, but a friend of mine in law enforcement once told me that nothing is ever off the record with cops. My gut feeling is that you can trust Tierney, but if you feel more comfortable with a lawyer then by all means. It's your money and your life."

Xi said, "Won't it seem suspicious if we get lawyers too soon in the process?"

Cesari thought about that for a while before saying, "I can't answer that one either, but probably not. Tierney's been around a long time. I'm sure he knows today's events would undoubtedly make you guys a little jumpy."

"Maybe that's what he's counting on," Jaskaran speculated. "You know, stir the pond and see what jumps out."

Cesari cracked a smile, "Interesting analogy and possibly right."

Jaskaran picked up his phone and started a google search. Cesari asked, "What are you looking up?"

"I'm searching for any Formula One races that might have taken place in India the night the woman was killed in case I need to take you up on your offer of an alibi."

Cesari said, "That's the spirit. I want you all to start thinking like Jay here... Okay, I have to wrap things up. Everybody stay calm and carry on. Freaking out isn't going to help anything. Keep working hard and take great care of your patients the way you always have. Nothing's changed, but try to lay low and stay under the radar for a while. Most of all, don't discuss this with anyone else in the hospital."

Chapter 10

Walking through Washington Square Park on his way home, the dilemma of the pain killers weighed heavily on Cesari's mind. He looked up at the sky. Clouds had gathered and the wind was picking up. A flash of light overhead, followed by rumbling thunder, and suddenly he was drenched to the bone as mother nature dumped on him. People ran in every direction for cover, and he quickened his pace. An appropriate finish to an extraordinary day, he mused.

He trudged up the three long flights of old stairs to his apartment, dripping rainwater and absorbed in the day's events. Somewhere in the back of his mind, he wondered how Gerry had made out at the Port of Newark. On the other hand, he would be perfectly happy if he didn't know and never saw or heard from the guy again.

At the top of the steps he hesitated when he heard sounds emanating from inside the apartment. The door was unlocked, and he pushed it inward. It swung open revealing a full view of the loft; kitchen to the left and living room to the right. Two large men sat on the sofa watching T.V. while a third peeked out a window furtively from behind its curtain. Vito and Gerry were in the kitchen arguing over red wine and pizza.

They were both a little hot under the collar. Vito spotted Cesari first and waved him in. None of his guys moved. As Cesari sat down at the table, Vito handed him a kitchen towel to wipe his wet face, and then poured him a glass of chianti. The open pizza box had one slice left with pepperoni, sausage and banana pepper toppings.

Vito said, "Damn, you're soaked, Cesari. It wasn't raining an hour ago." He turned to his men in the living room. "Hey, one of you mopes go get a real towel from the bathroom for him to dry off with."

Cesari took a sip of wine and said, "Did I miss something?"

"Yeah, you missed a lot," Vito explained. "This mental case just brought the whole world down on us."

"I meant you all being here in my apartment without permission."

"Give me a break, Cesari. We had to go somewhere. My place is being watched and probably tapped too."

Gerry was in an usually ill-tempered mood himself. "I'm not a mental case. I did you a favor."

Vito towered over the little man and glowered at him. He was literally twice Gerry's size and his voice boomed, "Did me a favor? You call pinching a twenty-five-million-dollar custom made car and bringing it to my apartment in Little Italy where the FBI are watching a favor?"

Cesari grabbed the last slice of pizza and took a bite as he studied the odd couple. Despite his size disadvantage Gerry more than made up for it in attitude. "You didn't say not to bring it there. Besides, I only stopped for five minutes before driving away. No one saw nothing."

Vito shook his large head. His cold gray eyes and large beaked nose made him look like a bird of prey. "This is the hottest car in the country right now. If it's not on the news already, it will be by tomorrow. Cesari, have you watched the news today?"

"No, I haven't. I've been tied up at work. What happened?"

Gerry said, "I'll tell you what happened…"

Vito cut him off. "Shut up. I'll tell him… This schmuck went to pick up a 1969 Rolls Royce Silver Shadow destined for some collector in New Jersey. Street value about fifty to sixty grand, tops. No big deal, right? I mean a Corvette costs more than that. I did some research. The Silver Shadow wasn't the greatest car ever built and this one had seen better days anyway. It cost a lot but it's not the end of the world if it disappears. Most insurances will cover sixty grand without blinking."

"I assume there's more to the story," Cesari said.

"Yeah, there is. Gerry goes down to the port at 2:00 a.m. and his friend lets him in to where the car is being kept. They open the container and instead of seeing a '69 Silver Shadow, they find a spanking new Rolls Royce Boat Tail convertible, retail value of twenty-five-million-dollars, minimum. There have only been five of them made and he brings it down to Mulberry Street so the FBI can snatch pictures of it in front of my apartment. He had barely stopped when a crowd of people surrounded it with their cellphones."

Cesari's jaw dropped, and he glanced at Gerry who was still defiant. "I thought you'd be happy. It's an upgrade."

"So what happened?" Cesari asked Gerry as one of Vito's guys handed him a bath towel to better dry off.

"I don't know exactly," replied Gerry. "The paperwork said it was a 1969 Silver Shadow in more or less good condition. Not mint but not bad. Needed some minor body and engine work here and there, but drivable. It was purchased by a private collector in Morristown. Some Dutch guy bought it way back when. The guy died and left it to his son who had no interest in it and put it up for sale."

Cesari scratched his head. "Does that make sense? Could they have mislabeled the container accidentally?"

Vito shook his head. "I've been thinking about it and I don't think that's what happened. They mislabeled it all right, but it wasn't an accident. I think the guy who bought the car didn't want anyone to know the real value of what was inside the container and worked out a deal with the seller to misdirect people."

Cesari thought about that and nodded. "I guess it worked."

Vito said, "Yeah, it worked and now I have a shitstorm to deal with because, like it or not, I'm involved with the heist of the century."

"How'd you get here? Did you get in the trunk?"

"No, when Gerry pulled up in the Rolls my guys knew right away it wasn't a smart idea, so they called me and I called Gerry. I directed him to drive to one of my warehouses on the West Side where the car is now covered and out of sight. It's possible the agents who are watching my apartment were unaware of the significance of the car when Gerry pulled up, at least that's what I'm hoping. And another thing, Gerry, no one can fit in the trunk of that car. It has one of those funny two door trunks that fold up in the middle. Supposed to be classic or something."

"Yeah, but you could lie on the back seat and cover yourself up in a blanket," Gerry shot back.

Vito rolled his eyes. "That would look great at a red light. It's not like anyone's going to stare at a car like that. Gerry, you fucked up. Admit it."

"Bullshit. You could get ten million for that car tomorrow."

"What don't you understand, shortstack? Selling that car would be like selling the *Mona Lisa*. Sure, a lot of people would want it but it's too risky."

"Who you calling shortstack?"

Cesari intervened, "Okay, okay. Everybody calm down. Vito, you never answered me. How'd you get here then or is there a van full of FBI agents across the street with binoculars pointed in this direction?"

"We're fine. My guys have been watching. So I went very visibly to the garage where I keep my Caddie. I had my driver pull out a few minutes later and take the feds on a joy ride to Queens. We were deciding the best way to leave the garage when we heard an ice cream truck passing by. You know, the one that plays pop-goes-the-weasel over a loudspeaker and specializes in soft serve. So I sent a guy out to commandeer it."

"You hijacked an ice cream truck?" Cesari asked trying to get a mental picture.

"I didn't hijack it. I gave the guy two bills for his effort. He brought the truck into the garage and picked us up. Carmelo sat up front with the driver. He's the one guarding the window over there. Me and the two Gunthers hung out in the compartment where he serves the ice cream through that little window. Man, the aroma back there... totally to die for."

Cesari glanced over at the two fat guys on the couch. "They're both named Gunther?"

"That's what I said, didn't I?"

"Are they related?"

"I don't know. I don't speak German."

"Since when do you hire guys named Gunther?"

"Why is that important?"

Cesari said, "Fine... I guess I don't understand all the sub-terfuge. Why can't you just call an Uber or a yellow cab and have them come into the garage to pick you up?"

"Cesari, you're not thinking straight. If I get into the trunk of a yellow cab or an Uber that would make the driver suspicious, and if I don't, there's a chance I might be spotted. Just for the record, I can't have one of my guys rent or borrow a car either. I have to assume if I'm being watched, then they're all being watched, including their credit cards. Right now, they think they've got me covered and I want to keep it that way."

"Why all the surveillance anyway?"

"Why not? They got bloated budgets from 9/11 and since there aren't enough terrorists running around, they need to do something to justify their existence."

"So they harass innocent civilians like yourself?"

"Exactly."

"All right, so what happens now?"

Gerry jumped in. "What happens now is he pays me my finder's fee and I disappear."

"You ain't getting nothing, Tiny Tim. You just stirred up a hornet's nest and now I have to deal with it. The car's mine and you don't go nowhere until I decide what to do with you."

Cesari offered, "Maybe you can return the car to its rightful owner and shut down the fireworks before things get out of hand."

Vito sipped his wine and mulled that one over. "You know, Cesari, that's not a bad idea. Whoever can afford twenty-five million for a car probably can afford a few extra million to have it returned."

"You're going to ransom the car?"

"Sure, why not? It'll be the safest way of cashing in on it. I certainly can't drive around in it, and nobody I know is going to chance buying it. I like it... Okay, Gerry, this is what we're going to do. You start working on finding out who the real owner is. Tomorrow you go out to visit that collector in Morristown whose name is on the invoice. Maybe we'll get lucky."

"Me? Why do I get to do that?"

"Because if it really is his car, I don't want him to see me, meet me, or hear my name or the names of any one of my men. You'll be acting as the go between so we can hammer out a deal."

"Oh that's just great. So he gets to meet me? What if there's an army of cops out there?"

"That's the price you have to pay for your mistake. Now man up."

"What do I get out of this?" Gerry asked.

"You get to keep your kneecaps for starters, but if it works out, then you'll deliver the car for me and collect the finder's fee. I'll give you the full amount I was going to give you for the Rolls you let the bikers vandalize the other night."

"Twenty-five grand? That's all?" he whined. "You're going to make millions. You cheap mother..."

"Don't piss me off, Gerry. I'll throw you out the window right now onto Sixth Avenue."

Cesari said, "Boys, simmer down."

"Fine," said Gerry.

Cesari asked Vito, "Do you really think the collector listed on the invoice is the real buyer?"

"He might be, or he could be fronting for someone else. I doubt a collector would go through all this trouble to disguise his purchase. And would a collector really buy a brand new, one of a kind, custom-made model, literally the most expensive car on the planet? Usually collectors are looking for vintage makes, classics, vehicles that have some history behind them, things of that nature. I mean, it's possible but it just doesn't feel right. The car on the invoice, the '69 Silver Shadow makes sense. Not this thing. So why hide it? I don't know. Maybe it was just a ruse to keep thieves away, but then why not hire massive security? Once again, I don't know. Maybe he's the kind of guy that shies away from that kind of publicity and didn't want the whole world to know he just bought a twenty-five-million-dollar car."

Cesari grinned. "Well, the whole world's going to know now."

"Maybe not. Now that I've had a couple of minutes to reflect, a really rich guy may not stir this pot too vigorously. Like I said, he may be smart enough to know that most people aren't going to be sympathetic to a guy that could afford to spend dough like that on an imported toy."

"Yeah, but he's going to want his toy back."

"Sure, he'll make private inquiries, hire private detectives, things like that," Vito explained and then smiled. "But the more I think about it, this may not make the news at all."

Cesari could tell that Vito was back in the driver's seat. Cesari said, "Guys that wealthy generally don't take defeat well. This will burn a hole in his gasket for sure."

"That's not my problem, Cesari."

By 10:00 p.m., they had all left but Gerry. It seemed prudent to Vito to let Gerry cool his jets another night in Cesari's apartment. He was in the living room lying on the sofa. Cesari lay on his own bed when his phone buzzed.

It was Mike B.

Chapter 11

The Sommelier walked down the long, dark, carpeted corridor past the many doors on either side until he arrived at his destination. He stood in front of the entrance to one of the numerous bedrooms on the fourth floor of the mansion. This room had no TV, radio, telephone jacks or internet access points. The windows had steel bars and faced the rear of the property with nothing but thick woods in view. The solid oak door was massive, nearly eight feet tall and four feet wide. The old triangular shaped wrought iron hinges and lock mechanism gave it a distinctly medieval feel.

He placed the key in its slot and turned it. With a loud creak the door swung open and he stepped inside, spotting her on the canopied, four poster, king-sized bed where she lay motionless, awaiting his approach. Her eyes were puffy from crying, which she did almost continually. Barely out of her teens when they wed, she was thoroughly unprepared for the nightmare that was to be her life for the next ten years. Now at thirty, she was still amazingly beautiful with long dark hair and big brown, sad eyes. Not obvious at the moment but she was tall and had the high cheek bones and full lips of a model although no makeup presently adorned her. The rest of her voluptuous figure was hidden under a sheet. There was a tray next to the bed with her afternoon tea and a half-eaten croissant.

Although not the largest bedroom in the mansion, it was gigantic compared to those in ordinary homes. One hundred feet wide and long, with a ten-foot embossed copper ceiling, a gas fireplace, a six-foot sofa, sitting chairs, and a bathroom larger than most garages. There was a refrigerator and microwave installed for her convenience, and several Monet's adorned the walls. As far as prisons went, this one was far from the worst. She sat up, wrapped the sheet defensively around her torso, and let out a deep breath as he lowered himself to sit beside her.

He asked, "Are you well, Martine?"

Her voice trembled and a tear rolled down from the corner of one eye as she pleaded, "Please, Michel. Let me go. I will not tell anyone. I just want to be with my baby."

Several weeks ago, she had made the unfortunate mistake of letting her curiosity get the better of her and had entered the trophy room while he was away on business. Cleverly pilfering the room's key while he slept, she had made a duplicate on a shopping trip. Unfortunately, she was unaware of the surveillance cameras in that room when she had made her gruesome discovery. Fully appreciating that there was no turning back, she had tried to make a hasty getaway with their toddler, Jean-Claude. Using the ruse of visiting a sick family member in Boston, she took off that same day. She had moved quickly, but not quickly enough. Just hours after her departure, the tape had been reviewed and an immediate course of action decided upon. Tracking her by the GPS unit he had planted in her Mercedes, the Sommelier and Hugo caught up with her in a small town in Connecticut where she had stopped for gas and a bathroom break, and now here they were. Ten years of a loving relationship down the drain.

He looked at her and was clearly conflicted. His voice was stern but not unsympathetic. He had kept her locked up in the room in total incommunicado. Jean-Claude was three years old and although he missed his mother, he was used to being with nannies and had many distractions. Jean-Claude had been kept from her the entire time as her punishment. She was not close with her family and despite the attempted escape had not called anyone to alert them. At the time of her flight, she was in a state of great emotional unrest and hadn't decided what her best course of action should be. She was even concerned that perhaps she would be considered an accomplice.

"Certainly, you can understand my dilemma, Martine?" he asked calmly. "I don't know which hurt more, betraying my trust or attempting to take my child from me. You knew you were never to enter that room. We've been over it many times."

She nodded and began sobbing. "I know, Michel. I am sorry...so sorry."

"But is sorry enough?"

Her body shuddered as she choked back her emotions. "It is all I have."

"Do you still think that I am a monster?"

"I am sorry for that too. I was in a state of shock at the time. Surely, you can appreciate that."

He nodded. "I was as well." He let out a deep breath and relented, "I will have Simone bring Jean-Claude to you, but the visit will be supervised. She will remain with you the entire time. Before that, however, you must give me something in return."

She looked up suddenly filled with hope. "Anything, Michel. Anything."

"I want you to call your sister in Maine and tell her that you and Jean-Claude will be leaving the country for a grand tour of Asia and Africa that could take several months and that much of the time you will be unable to communicate except for the occasional email."

Her eyes went wide as he took her cellphone out of his pocket and handed it to her. She said, "I don't understand. Why?"

"Until we sort this situation out, it would be best if your family didn't try to call or visit. Now, do you want to see Jean-Claude or not?"

She took the phone and dialed her sister. It took several minutes but she played her part well. Her sister was used to the lavish and excessive lifestyle Martine and the Sommelier led and so the planned holiday abroad did not seem quite as outlandish as it might have. They were always private jet-setting to distant parts of the globe for business and pleasure.

When she was finished, she clicked off and handed the phone back to the Sommelier who said, "I will send Simone in with Jean-Claude. You will have exactly one hour. If you are good and do not make a scene with him, I will consider allowing you to see him again tomorrow."

She breathed a sigh of relief and said, "Thank you."

He stood to leave. "I will give you fifteen minutes to prepare yourself for the visit. Pull yourself together and dry your eyes."

Outside in the hallway, he locked the door and walked back down the long corridor. His phone buzzed in his pocket. It was Hugo.

"Michel, something's come up and we need to talk privately."

"Where are you?"

"In the lobby."

"Meet me in the bar and open a bottle of the Opus One 1992 Cabernet. I will be there at once."

As the elevator descended to the main floor of the mansion, the Sommelier called Simone and gave her instructions and strict parameters for the visit with Jean-Claude. There were to be no exceptions to the rules. There would be no crying on Martine's part and no badmouthing of the Sommelier. Any violations and she was to terminate the visit immediately. When the time was up, she was to leave with the child without delay.

He caught up with Hugo in the mansion's bar, which for all intents and purposes looked like any other bar you might find in a Ritz-Carlton or its equivalent. The counter was highly polished teak wood with eight leather swivel stools and several round wood tables scattered about the room with plush armchairs. Hugo stood behind the counter and had just opened the wine. He poured a small amount into one of the large glasses in front of him and then proceeded to do the sniff and swirl thing. Satisfied, he filled two glasses with copious amounts and handed one to the Sommelier who gathered himself into one of the swivel stools.

"So what's the problem, Hugo?" asked the Sommelier as he sipped the fine wine.

"As you recall, I had a bug placed in Dr. Goldstein's office in St. Matt's to keep an eye on him. I just found out that he has made overtures to the SEC and plans on filing a complaint against you. He has an appointment with them tomorrow afternoon. I have already contacted our man inside the SEC who will run interference for us as best he can..."

"And?"

"Our man can buy us some time, but he won't be able to completely bury the complaint, and it gets worse. Goldstein has also made an appointment with the attorney general's office. Apparently, he either believes in duplication of processes or doesn't fully believe in the ability of the SEC to police itself."

At that, the Sommelier let out a deep sigh. "When is that appointment?"

"The day after tomorrow."

"Our asset in the hospital couldn't dissuade him?"

"No, he was the first person I called when I found out. Dr. Goldstein is on a mission... I don't suppose there is time to replace the money?"

The Sommelier shook his head. "To replace the money? No, I could transfer personal funds into the account though. That would make him happy but would not withstand scrutiny by the authorities if it came to it. And if I were to precipitously withdraw my investment in its entirety from where it is sitting, it would invite its own disastrous consequences. The idea with these things is always to make as little noise as possible so as to not attract attention. If I sell off a hundred million dollars overnight, from a company whose stock values I just recently inflated one thousand-fold what it is actually worth, it would trigger a massive sell-off. Somebody somewhere down the line will lose his shirt and file a complaint and I would be standing there with the smoking gun as they say. Not a good look at all. Not good at all. Pump and dumps need to be a teeny bit more subtle these days, I'm afraid. It appears we are caught between the rock and the hard place."

The Sommelier shook his head in frustration and Hugo asked, "What should we do?"

Strumming his fingers on the bar counter, the Sommelier replied, "Clearly, it would be in everyone's best interest if Dr. Goldstein were to fail to make it to his meeting with the SEC tomorrow. It would have the added advantage of minimizing the exposure to our guy there."

"What about his appointment at the attorney general's office?"

"If he doesn't show there, what is the likelihood that anyone will follow up?"

"Slim to none, I would guess. They're overworked, underpaid civil servants. They won't give it a moment's thought."

"Exactly, so the only risk is from some low-level office worker possibly wondering why some citizen never showed up for his appointment. Then he or she gets to have an early or extended lunch because of it. Sounds like there will be nothing to worry about on that score. I'll take those odds any day."

"I agree," Hugo concurred.

"Then, it's settled. Collect the good doctor before he gets to his appointment. You won't have much time to plan things out."

"I'm not worried about that. I've been listening to him for hours every day. He's very predictable and likes to walk. He will most likely travel by foot to the SEC, which is not that far from St. Matt's. It's no more than a thirty-minute stroll, which is nothing for a Manhattaner. The real question is what shall I do with him?"

"The real question, Hugo, is what if he brings his lapdog, Cesari, with him?"

"Then it's two for the price of one."

"I'm not sure I like that. I met Cesari. You didn't. I don't like the vibes he gives off. Despite his lack of breeding, he could spell trouble, like a cornered rat if you know what I mean. Did you find out anything about him, by the way?"

"Not much so far. Single, no children. Very little footprint online. No social media accounts. Appears to have a clean bill of health at St. Matt's where he's been working for ten years. In good standing too. Dr. Goldstein just promoted him to Chief Medical Officer, but I'm still digging."

"A promotion? Fascinating... Well, I'll take care of him. I'll provide a distraction he won't be able to resist. A five-course wine-paired lunch in the wine cellar. I'll have my limousine pick him up tomorrow and drop him off afterward."

"Will he be able to accept your hospitality on such short notice?"

"I'll tell him that I have an office on the west coast and business concerns may force me to fly out there soon. If he takes a pass, I will understand, but the opportunity to entertain him may not come up again for weeks, possibly months. I'll even tell him to bring a friend... He won't refuse. If you saw him guzzling my wine the other day, you'd understand."

"I think it will work. From the tone of the conversation between the two he doesn't approve of Dr. Goldstein's activities anyway, so he may relish the offer."

"But then we're back to the question of what to do with Goldstein, which is truly an excellent question. I'm not sure he's worthy of a place in the trophy room. We could keep him on ice somewhere until I divest his money from the pump and dump, but that needs to be done slowly and could take weeks. On the other hand, weeks of house arrest like that could lead to all sorts of unintended consequences."

"I did learn something else that may or may not help with this decision..."

"Go on, Hugo."

"There was an unexplained death of a cancer patient who was being treated at St. Matt's. She was terminal and in great pain. A police detective visited with Dr. Goldstein and Cesari to discuss the matter. Apparently, there is at least some mild suspicion that one of their anesthesiologists may have gone rogue and put the poor woman out of her misery."

The Sommelier raised his eyebrows at that. "You don't say?"

"I do say. A syringe cap was found in the old woman's apartment containing propofol, a controlled substance that only the anesthesiologists had access to. So far, it's not clear what happened."

"Now that is interesting." The Sommelier glanced at his watch and added. "I better call Dr. Cesari and make that invitation before it gets too late."

Chapter 12

A rnie sat there dumbfounded and slack-jawed glaring at
Cesari who sat across from him. He said, "I can't believe
my ears. You're going to have lunch with Beaujolais at his mansion in Bernardsville today while I'm going to the SEC to file
a complaint against him for gross incompetence and possibly
worse? Did I hear that right? I thought you were on my side,
Cesari?"

"Take it easy, Arnie. I am on your side but an opportunity
like this may never come up again. When's the last time you
heard of someone getting an invitation to see a three hundred
thousand bottle wine cellar let alone get a five-course meal prepared by a private chef in that same wine cellar?"

"You sold me out for the price of a lunch? I wanted you to
come with me for support."

"You'll be fine, Arnie. Nothing's going to happen anyway.
They must get thousands of complaints like yours every year.
No one's happy when they lose money. It's always got to be
somebody else's fault. I really don't think I need to be there, and
I definitely know I don't want to be there. It's going to be embarrassing for you. You remind me of those patients that no matter how many times you warn them of the risks of a procedure,
the minute something goes wrong they're on the phone with
their lawyers crying about how they had no idea there could be
complications. You can even show them the consent form they
signed, and they will still swear they were never told anything."

"That's one hell of a comparison you just made there, Cesari."

"But an accurate one, unless you're going to tell me that at close to seventy years of age, you had no idea that there were risks involved with the stock market."

Getting testy, Arnie said, "Fine, but I'm still filing the complaint. Something is fishy out there in New Jersey and I don't like it. Go have your lunch. See if I care."

"If you were nice, I'd offer to take you. Mike B. said I could bring a guest."

"I have an appointment with the SEC, remember? And the last thing I want to do is to hang out with that snake oil salesman in my spare time."

"I knew you would say that and that's why I already invited African Jay."

"Who's African Jay?"

"Macallan."

Arnie looked as if head was going to explode. "You call him African Jay?"

"Only when he's not in the room."

"Are you insane, Cesari? That's so racist. This is the twenty-first century."

"How else am I supposed to differentiate him from Indian Jay?"

Arnie slapped his hands over his face and groaned. "No, no, no. You need to stop this immediately. I cannot condone this in my hospital."

Cesari grinned. "It's okay, Arnie. I'm the Chief Medical Officer. I'll report me to myself."

"Get out. Please, just get out…And stop doing that."

"I'll call you after lunch to see how it went."

"Fine."

Cesari left Arnie's office and called Jeremy. "Dude, you ready to roll? The limo will be here in fifteen minutes."

"Oh yeah, I'm all pumped. I was just about to sign out to Indian Jay."

"See you in five in the front lobby."

"Roger that, Cesari."

Cesari clicked off and stepped into the elevator. He got off on the second floor and went to the surgical locker room to swap his white lab coat for his sport jacket. He was dressed more or less in doctor casual. Khaki pants and loafers, white shirt, and striped tie with a blue blazer. Just about every doctor in the country had this ensemble in his closet. As he came out of the locker room he froze and held his breath. Coming straight at him was Valentina, his ex-girlfriend, and Joe Fusco, the hand surgeon with the Lamborghini.

Damn, she was beautiful. Long blonde hair, blue eyes and a perfect figure. Too bad she was crazy. She only had one thing on her mind 24/7 and it wasn't sex. It was making any relationship she was in permanent like cement. She and Fusco wore surgical scrubs and appeared to have just come out of a case. He had no escape route available except to turn around and duck back into to the locker room. But that would have been lame. And to no avail. They both saw him a split second after he spotted them.

She wrapped her arm through Fusco's as they neared in a deliberate attempt to provoke him and said, "Hey, Cesari. How've you been?"

"I've been very well. Thank you for asking. Hey there, Joe."

Fusco smiled and wrapped a huge arm around Valentina. He was several inches taller than Cesari, extraordinarily good looking with chiseled features, and very buffed. Hand surgeons raked it in hand over fist and had plenty of spare time to hang out in gyms and hire personal trainers.

He nodded at Cesari and greeted him with a simple, "Cesari."

"Soooo," Cesari said uncomfortably. "I was just heading out. It was nice running into you both."

As he turned to walk past them, Valentina placed her palm on his chest and pushed him back into position. Smiling she said, "Where's the fire, Cesari?"

Fusco added, "Yeah, what's the rush? You got a hot date?"

Both Valentina and Fusco laughed at that and Cesari's cheeks turned red. He replied, "Actually I do. There's a girl in administration I'm meeting for lunch at the diner across from the hospital."

Valentina said, "Really? That's sweet. I usually have my ear to the ground about these things, but I guess I missed this one. What's her name?"

Cesari racked his brain, but all he could come up with was, "George... Georgina, and she's pretty hot."

"Is she?" said Valentina, clearly amused. "I'd like to meet her sometime. Maybe we could double date for dinner. We'd have to meet at the restaurant though. Joe's Lamborghini only seats two."

"You should see it, Cesari. What a dream. Seven hundred horsepower. Cost me two hundred and fifty big ones, but that's just pocket change."

"That's a lot of muscle, Fusco. Are you sure you can handle her?"

In response, he squeezed Valentina tight and she started to giggle. "Tell him about my muscles, Valentina. Go ahead and tell him."

"Trust me, Cesari, he can handle anything," she laughed. "He really knows how to take care of a girl."

Cesari felt his breakfast coming back up. He said, "I'll bet. Well, I really have to go. I'm sure you understand."

They stepped aside and Fusco said, "I sure do. If my ex was hanging around with a guy like me, I wouldn't linger too long either. It would be too painful...The head-to-head comparison, I mean. No hard feelings, all right? I'd like us to be friends."

Cesari let that sink in, didn't overreact and replied, "No hard feelings at all, Fusco. I want us to be friends too. Now, if you'll excuse me..."

As he walked past them, Valentina called out, "It's fuchsia."

He turned back and looked at her quizzically. She added, "Joe's Lamborghini. It's fuchsia."

"Thanks," he said, and then resumed his trip to the lobby where he found Jay waiting for him at the front entrance to the hospital. He was holding a leather briefcase.

They high fived and Cesari said, "Are you ready to party, my friend?"

"Oh I am. I really am," Jay replied enthusiastically.

"Looking sharp, Jay."

"You're looking pretty snazzy yourself, Cesari."

"Thanks but as usual you outclassed me."

Jay was wearing essentially the same outfit but had a spiffy red carnation in his lapel, a gold tie pin bracing the knot of his tie and matching cufflinks. "Purely unintentional, Cesari."

"I bet. You bring any cigars? This guy Mike B. said we can smoke if we want."

"Are you kidding me? Do I ever go anywhere without cigars? I brought six of my best Cubans. I've got them in the briefcase in a travel humidor along with lighters and cutters."

He lifted the case as if Cesari had x-ray vision and could see inside. Cesari grinned. "Good man, Jay. Good man."

"I'm pretty pumped up about this. Thanks for the invite. When did you hear about it?"

"Late last night. He called me out of the blue, and I called you right after that."

"What did I do to deserve this?"

"Well, I wanted to bring my favorite anesthesiologist with me to share the experience. But since the other guys were un-available, I settled on you."

Jay laughed good-naturedly, and said, "Thanks, anyway. I'm still honored. How long do you think we'll be in Jersey?"

"Let's see, a five-course meal, cigars, a tour of a wine cellar the size of a super Walmart. I'd think we'll be coming back well after five or six tonight. Maybe later. Why? What are you thinking?"

"I'm thinking I should have brought more cigars."

"Hey, Jay, you know I'm Chief Medical Officer now, right?"

"Yeah, I was there when Arnie promoted you."

"Well, I have to bring up something sensitive and I don't want you to take it the wrong way."

Jay was puzzled. "Just say it."

"Well, you know how Arnie gets dramatic about everything, right?"

"Cesari, what is it?"

"You know how you call Jaskaran, Indian Jay, from time to time?"

"So? He is Indian."

"Arnie says you're a racist and you have to stop saying that."

Jeremy's eyes went wide. "Arnie says I'm a racist? How did he even know?"

"I apologize but when I called you before I had you on speakerphone and he overheard," he lied. "Look, it's not that big a deal, but... You know what I mean?"

"This is such bullshit. You and Xi say it all the time too. Even Parikh says it and he's Indian."

"I tried to tell him, but you know how Arnie gets with this politically correct stuff. I told him I'd talk to you on the QT and that he shouldn't make a mountain out of a molehill about it."

Jay was annoyed. "What did I tell you, Cesari? The black guy always gets screwed around here."

"No one's getting screwed. I had your six. Arnie knows you're a nice guy. Now, let's put it behind us and have some fun."

"Should I say something to Arnie when I see him?"

"I wouldn't. I've known Arnie a long time. By morning he will have forgotten all about it. You bring it up and the next thing you know he'll form a committee to look into it."

"You're a good friend, Cesari."

"Thanks."

Chapter 13

The limo dropped them off at the Chateau in Bernardsville at twelve o'clock sharp and Mike B. was right there at the entrance waiting for them, impeccably dressed in a dark suit and tie. Cesari introduced Jeremy and they were given a grand overview of the property before touring the house itself. They spent nearly forty minutes in the great room alone studying the artwork. Jay didn't want to leave the bar and asked if he could live there. Mike B. liked that and decided to start the party there by uncorking a 1972 Domaine de la Romanee-Conti Romanee Conti Grand Cru, a lively pinot noir from the cote de nuits region, just south of Dijon in France. At just over forty thousand dollars a bottle, Cesari calculated that each sip cost about sixteen hundred dollars.

An hour later, they were feeling really good and made their way down to the wine cellar. It was close to 2:00 p.m. and it was obvious by then that this was going to be the longest lunch either one had ever experienced. They walked around the room like kids in a candy factory, their mouths agape, staring at the myriad of wine bottles racked nearly floor to ceiling in all directions. The impossibly long wood table in the center of the room was decorated on one end with a delicate white linen tablecloth, lit candles in brass holders, fine China plates, Irish crystal glassware, and sterling silver cutlery. Three waitstaff in black tails and white gloves held out their chairs for them. Mike B. sat at the head of the table with Cesari and Jay to either side. The rest of the fifty-foot-long table looked empty and lonely, but another bottle of expensive wine soon preoccupied them as the first course of perfectly seared foie gras was plated.

Most wine-paired multiple course meals usually consisted of two or three ounces of wine per course. Not this one. The server filled each glass to the top, emptying each bottle into three large glasses. To compensate for the inordinate amount of alcohol being served, large glasses of ice water were kept filled and each course was separated by thirty-minute intervals with enough time to stretch one's legs, use a nearby bathroom, and examine the cellar in greater detail. Cesari noted oversized glass ash trays on the table and Mike B. caught his gaze.

He said, "Feel free to light up, Dr. Cesari."

"Right now? While we're eating?"

"Certainly, if Dr. Macallan doesn't mind. I'll have one with you."

Jeremy smiled. "I'm pretty sure I don't mind."

Cesari said, "Won't it hurt the wine?"

"Not a chance. I have one of the most advanced ventilation and climate control management systems in the world installed down here. Less than one percent of any puff of smoke leaving your lungs will ever reach further than three feet from your lips before it is sucked through an activated charcoal and water filtration system and then channeled to the roof top chimney and into the atmosphere above. Did you bring any good ones?"

Cesari glanced at Jeremy. "Jay is my cigar dealer. Jay, you're on."

Jay reached down, lifted his briefcase to his lap, opened it, and said, "They're Cubans."

Mike B. countered with, "Excellent mid-meal cigars."

Jay took out three, six-ring, full-bodied Montecristo's and handed them out with cutters and lighters, which were unnecessary as the waitstaff snapped to attention at the sight of the smokes and whipped out their own lighters and cutters.

Cesari contentedly puffed away as Mike B. studied his cigar, took a draw, and said, "Nice choice, Jeremy. Where did you obtain them?"

"In Montreal, no one really cares anymore about the embargo."

"Nice. After dinner with some cognac, you'll have to try one of mine. I have business dealings in Havana. When I was there last year, I picked up a box of their Cohiba Behike, their fortieth anniversary edition. They only produced one hundred boxes. I'm sure you'll enjoy it."

"I'm sure I will. I bet they cost a pretty penny."

"Eighteen thousand a box but who's counting."

Cesari studied the magnificent room and said, "Mike, this is a pretty big table. It looks like you could have quite a dinner party down here."

"Indeed. This table sits fifty to sixty guests comfortably, but as you can see there is plenty of room so when I have a big social gathering like the fundraiser for the governor's re-election this Saturday, I'll have extra tables set up all around to accommodate the larger crowd. Of course, I have to leave enough room for the band and a modest dance floor."

"A fund-raiser for the governor? That's impressive."

"He's a complete boor. Believe me, but it's a necessary evil. In order to survive in business, you try to stay as neutral as possible in politics, but there comes a time when you have to at least appear to choose sides."

"What's a guy have to do to get an invitation to something like that?"

Mike B. blew a smoke ring at the ceiling and said, "Not much, Dr. Cesari, just have more money than God and be willing to sell your soul."

"I guess I'm out," Cesari said, and then looked across the table. "But I think Jeremy qualifies."

They all laughed at that.

The third and main course came, and they settled into a delectable chateaubriand, medium rare, with brown sugar glazed baby carrots and roasted fingerling potatoes smothered in garlic and fresh rosemary. By the end of that course, they had polished off four full bottles of wine and were stuffed and glad they weren't driving themselves home. Thankfully, the last two courses eased up a bit. There was a cheese course accompanied by a light salad and a brisk chardonnay, and then they finished up with small ramekins of raspberry crème brulee paired with a 1988 Sauternes.

French press coffee arrived at 7:00 p.m. and Cesari thought he might explode if anyone offered him anything else to eat. Glancing at Jay, he noticed his eyes were glassy and he had a permanent grin plastered on his face. Cesari hoped he didn't pass out, at least not until after they returned to Manhattan. If Mike B. was inebriated, he hid it well. After coffee, Mike B. wanted to finish the tour of the wine cellar and then head back upstairs to the bar on the main floor where they could relax in leather chairs with cognac and Mike's Cohibas.

Cesari was a little tipsy as they walked down the long aisles of wines listening to Mike reveal the various histories of each vintage and decided to wander away a little on his own to study some of the older, dust covered bottles. He was having a little trouble paying attention and thought it was extraordinary that Mike B. didn't seem in the slightest bit impaired by all the alcohol they had just consumed. Six full bottles of wine split three ways. That was a lot by any standard. Granted it was over the course of several hours and with food but still... He was well within hearing range of Mike B. chatting with Jeremy, but had drifted behind, turned a corner and was now out of sight.

It was hard to fathom a collection such as this as he scanned row upon row of ancient bottles. He didn't even know there were that many vineyards in the entire planet and some of the dates on the bottles were incomprehensible in his limited experience with such things. He reached a section that had a placard saying Vintage Circa 1750, Italian, Umbria.

Unbelievable.

At the end of this long aisle was a plain metal door. Cesari wondered if it might be an emergency exit or door to a supply room. It caught his attention mostly because it seemed out of place, but he didn't have time to dwell on it very long.

"Dr. Cesari, I was wondering if we might have a sip or two of cognac now. Young Jeremy seems to be wavering on the subject and I was hoping you might persuade him to not be faint of heart."

They had come up behind him and he turned around and said, "I think we should take a rain check on the cognac, Mike." He glanced at Jeremy and then his watch and added. "My oh my, it's after eight. Young Jeremy and I have to work tomorrow and need to get a good night's sleep. Thank you so much for your hospitality, though. I really can't remember when I've had a better time."

"Me too," concurred Jeremy and then hiccupped. "This was an outstanding day all around."

Mike B. grinned. "Are you sure? It's Louis XIII."

Cesari hesitated and after a long pause, smiled, "Louis XIII? Why didn't you say that in the first place?"

They all laughed at that and as they turned to leave the wine cellar, Cesari's gaze drifted back toward the strange looking, out of place, steel door. He asked, "Say Mike, what's this?"

"Oh that. That's the door to the maintenance room where the air conditioning, heating elements and plumbing machinery are housed along with all the other items and tools necessary to manage and repair a large home. As you can imagine, it takes quite a large effort behind the scenes in order to maintain a place like this. There's a fully furnished and operational woodworking and refinishing wing in there as well. I keep a full-time groundskeeper, plumber, carpenter and electrician on my payroll, and they are never idle. I never go in there myself. The smell and the noise are brutal to one's senses."

Cesari said, "I'll bet." He was drunk but not stupid. "You let your staff walk in and out of the wine cellar whenever they need to do some maintenance work or grab a rake?"

The Sommelier scoffed, "Heaven's no. This is my personal entrance if for some reason I need to access the room to find one of my staff. There is a much larger entrance on the other side of the room, a couple of hundred feet away, that leads to the underground garage. That door is large enough to accommodate a tractor or a forklift. This door here is deadbolted to prevent accidental entry into the wine cellar by the workers. Interestingly, it's been so long since I've entered the room, I'm not even sure where the key is. Come now, doctors. Louis XIII waits for no man."

They spent another hour in the library, drinking cognac in snifters and smoking Cohibas. All in all it was a grand experience.

At 10:00 p.m., Cesari said, "Well all parties must necessarily come to an end and so it is now. Mike, once again, thank you for being such a wonderful host, but we really have to go."

Jeremy was sleepy and officially sloshed, slurring his words, "Yes, Mike. Thank you. You're the best."

Mike B. smiled. "You two are welcome in my humble abode anytime."

They thanked him again and said goodbye. Cesari helped Jeremy walk to the limo. He had been doing okay with the wine, but the three glasses of cognac pushed him over the edge, and he was borderline comatose. In the back of the limo, there was a lot yawning and contented sighing.

Cesari asked, "Did you have a good time, Jeremy?"

He replied, "Oh yeah."

"I'm proud of you, Macallan. You didn't make one racist comment all night. That must have been difficult."

Jay was too tired to respond, but with his eyes closed, he raised the middle finger of his right hand and aimed it at Cesari.

Chapter 14

A rnie's eyes fluttered open. He was groggy, disoriented, and his mouth was dry. The room was dark save for the glow of a gas fireplace twenty feet away. The bed he lay on was soft and comfortable. He glanced around in all directions and slowly his eyes accommodated to the gloom. He propped himself up and tried to get his bearings but wasn't even close to understanding where he was or what had happened. He touched himself all over to make sure that he was intact, and he was. He wasn't restrained, he wasn't in pain except for a mild headache, and nothing appeared to be broken. Someone had gone through the trouble of removing his shoes and he wiggled his toes.

The room was quiet. Too quiet.

Where on earth was he? The last thing he remembered was walking to the SEC in the early afternoon, but he never made it there. It was around 2:00 p.m. and it was a straight run from St. Matt's down Broadway past City Hall, make a right on Vesey Street and there you were, give or take. He remembered crossing Canal Street and then…something happened. There were crowds of people, heavy traffic, and lots of noise. He had been distracted, rehearsing in his mind what he would say. Thinking about the potential fallout. Someone called out his name. He looked up and saw a guy he didn't know waving at him. The tires of a vehicle screeched behind him. Strong arms grabbed him roughly. He didn't remember much else after that.

He swung his legs around and stood on a plush Persian rug. Without too much effort, he found a wall switch and flipped on an overhead light. His eyes traveled back and forth across the room in amazement. He had either died and gone to heaven or someone had mistaken him for royalty. It was the most extravagant and largest bedroom he had ever been in. At least a hundred feet wide and long, he estimated. The ceiling was fourteen feet high with a crystal chandelier glimmering in the light. The king bed was a magnificent four poster thing with a canopy. There was a sofa, chairs, a refrigerator, coffee maker, and even several bottles of wine on a desk with a glass and a corkscrew. His wallet, house keys and hospital ID lay on the desk next to the wine, but his cellphone was nowhere in sight.

Picking up his personal items, he placed them in his pockets. It was the kind of routine action one performed unconsciously as if he were going to leave whenever he felt like it and might as well be ready, but deep down he suspected he wasn't going anywhere fast. He needed to pee urgently and went to the bathroom and was stunned by its size and grandeur. It was easily larger than his living room, dining room and kitchen combined. It had its own chandelier.

When he returned, he opened the refrigerator and saw a six-pack of bottled water, orange juice, beer, and several sandwiches wrapped in plastic. In the small freezer were six containers of Häagen-Dazs ice cream. He grabbed a bottle of water, unscrewed the cap, and drank half of it in one long draught. Feeling refreshed, his energy returning, his mind clearing, he walked to the door and cranked on the knob. It was locked.

Naturally.

He banged on it forcefully and called out. There was no answer as he continued to jiggle the knob in frustration. Tiring, he turned around and that's when he noticed there were no television, radio, or telephone. The windows on either side of the bed had been boarded up with thick planks of three-quarter inch plywood, hammered into place with multiple nails. He had no hope of removing them without proper tools. Clearly, he was a prisoner but in a very nice prison.

But why?

He spent the next hour kicking the door, turning the knob, and calling out at the top of his lungs to no avail. Finally, overcome by fatigue, stress, and confusion, he lay down on the bed and wept. The only thing on his mind at that moment was the thought of his wife, Sylvia, worrying about him. He called her every day at close to five, just as he was getting ready to leave work. He looked at his watch. She would certainly have tried to reach him by now. Several times, in fact. They had 7:00 p.m. dinner reservations that night at their favorite restaurant. She would be disappointed.

****

After Cesari and Jeremy left the mansion, the Sommelier retired to his private office on the main floor where he found Hugo waiting to update him, sipping brandy from an expensive glass.

"How'd it go, Hugo?" the Sommelier asked.

"As well as possible, Michel. We had him in the van in less than five seconds. Less than a minute later, the van was lost in traffic. I left a man on the scene to sow confusion, but he said no one even noticed and if they did, didn't seem to care. As far as he could tell not even one person reached for their cellphone. Goldstein slept the whole way here and didn't wake up until long after we placed him in the bed. I hadn't the time to place a camera in his room but according to the guard in the hallway, he paced for hours, banged on the door, cried out for help, but now apparently seems resigned to his fate."

"Well done, and the van?"

"We switched vehicles in the long-term parking area at the Newark airport and brought him here in one of our cars. The van was stolen of course, wiped clean of fingerprints, and left there in the lot. It will be weeks before anyone even notices it."

"Sounds as if it couldn't have gone any more smoothly."

"Not really. He didn't put up any fight at all, and we maintained complete anonymity. He hasn't a clue as to what has happened or who is behind it. I was concerned from the way he was breathing on the way here that maybe we had been too rough or given him too much chloroform, but he eventually recovered."

"And the propofol?"

"A more difficult although not insurmountable problem which should be resolved by tomorrow afternoon. The drug is not available over the counter nor is it routinely stored in commercial pharmacies. My men have identified several hospital-based pharmacists who may be susceptible to our advances, and we are currently reaching out to them with the urgency of our need. I am offering a king's ransom for a small supply. I am certain we will find one who will cooperate. Propofol, apparently, is a little bit easier to make disappear from pharmacy shelves than narcotics."

Curious, the Sommelier asked, "Why is that?"

"I am not entirely sure. In my brief research on the subject, it appears that although the drug is a wonderful sleep-inducing agent with rapid onset and rapid metabolism it is not necessarily a fun drug in that it doesn't produce the high addicts and recreational users are looking for. You simply go to sleep and wake up."

"No fun in that."

"None at all. Unless you desperately need a good night's rest. The good news for him is that since he has no idea who kidnapped him or why, he can be returned whenever you wish."

"You mean if I wish. The verdict is still out on that."

"Yes, of course... So how was your afternoon with the doctors, Michel?"

"Not nearly as tedious as I thought it was going to be. Cesari of course is an unmitigated oaf, but he brought a friend with him. A black doctor named Macallan. He was well bred and interesting. The contrast between the two couldn't have been more striking. Although both of them were lightweights in the alcohol department and could barely walk out of here afterward." The Sommelier snickered at the memory. "The most adorable thing. This Macallan person brought knock-off Cuban cigars he obtained in Canada. He didn't realize they were knock-offs which is the biggest scam going up there. Americans spend millions of dollars in Canada on Honduran and Nicaraguan cigars labeled as Cuban which they could get for a third the price anywhere in the U.S. They weren't awful mind you, just not Cuban."

"Macallan, you said?"

"Yes, Jeremy Macallan. Why?"

"He's one of the four anesthesiologists under suspicion for the death of the old woman I mentioned to you. I heard his name mentioned multiple times along with the others when the detective came to speak with Goldstein in his office."

"Seriously, Hugo? Are you sure?"

"Very sure."

The Sommelier rubbed his chin. "What an interesting twist of fate, and it raises some interesting possibilities."

"How so?"

"I am not one hundred percent certain yet, but it strikes me as having a certain amount of karma that he walked into my lap the way he did. Find out what you can about Dr. Macallan. It may prove valuable."

"As you wish. What about Dr. Goldstein's wife? She will undoubtedly notify the police."

The Sommelier shrugged. "I am counting on that. In the meanwhile, she knows nothing, and no one saw anything. He will be another missing person in a city of millions. An old man wanders off and doesn't return home with no signs of foul play. It happens every day. Maybe his dementia kicked in or perhaps he took a jet to some island with a woman half his age, but that will be the least of her problems by the time I'm finished with them. Cesari's the one I'm most concerned with."

"Why? Do you think he will personally search for Dr. Goldstein?"

"I have no doubt he will, Hugo. He and Goldstein are obviously good friends, but that is not the real issue. The real issue is that he knew where Dr. Goldstein was going today and what his purpose was."

"Aside from our asset at St. Matt's, he may be the only one though."

"You mean the only one we know of for sure. There could be others."

"Yes, of course."

"Realistically speaking how many people would Goldstein want to know about his disastrous financial decision that will cripple the hospital for years to come. Not many, I would guess. Therefore, his decision to go scorched earth with me at the SEC would not have been widely broadcasted. Much too humiliating. Seriously, Cesari is the only one who even vaguely worries me."

Hugo was puzzled. "Why is that exactly, Michel? I don't fully understand your fear."

"I can't put my finger on it exactly. There's something primitive about him. I've met him twice now and twice I've had a peculiar sensation like…" The Sommelier thought about it for a minute trying to find the right words. He then said, "Remember going to the zoo as a child, Hugo?"

"Yes, of course."

"Remember the indoor exhibits with the tigers? The thick plexiglass plates were all that separated you from their fangs, their teeth, their ferocity. No tiger, lion, or bear could possibly break through the glass barrier. Deep inside you knew you were safe. Yet when they came close to study you, you still felt your heart race and bowels loosen. There was always that element of dread that the beast might come crashing through his prison at any moment and devour you. That's the feeling I get around Cesari."

Hugo nodded. "Too bad. We had him here all day. It would have been so easy to fix that."

"Easy Hugo. Finesse, my friend. Remember, I invited him here and picked him up in one of my limos. Who knows how many people he or Macallan may have told of their trip here? Besides, he's the perfect alibi if anyone ever tries to link me to Dr. Goldstein's disappearance."

Hugo nodded. "I don't like him."

The Sommelier laughed. "Just wait until you actually meet him. You will absolutely hate him. Did I tell you he wandered off and accidentally discovered the door to the trophy room this afternoon?"

Hugo paled. "How is that possible? It's nearly a hundred yards from the dinner table through a circuitous maze of wine racks in the most poorly lit section of the cellar. I get lost myself half the time trying to find it."

"Not to worry. He was snockered at that point, and I sold it to him as the entrance to the maintenance room."

Hugo shook his head in alarm. "Not good at all, Michel."

"Relax, Hugo. The evening went remarkably well. I assure you, they were putty in my hands. Now tell me about my new Rolls Royce. Have they located it yet?"

Hugo cleared his throat. "There seems to be a problem in that regard. It appears that it may have been stolen."

"Stolen?" the Sommelier asked incredulously. "From the Port of Newark?"

"That part is not clear. When our men reached the port, the container was sealed, but there was nothing in it."

"Meaning?"

"There's the rub. We can't be sure if the vehicle was ever on the ship. It's possible that it was either never packaged or was taken before the ship left Southampton."

"Have you spoken to London yet?"

"I was tied up with Dr. Goldstein earlier and now with the time delay it is the middle of the night over there."

"Wake them up, Hugo. Wake them up now."

Chapter 15

Cesari's alarm squawked loudly awaking him from a deep slumber. By the time the limo had dropped Jeremy off at his apartment and then brought him home it was past midnight and he had been exhausted. This morning he wasn't hungover, but he wasn't too shiny either. He had that groggy, cobwebby feel that came with excessive alcohol, rich food, and tobacco. He looked at the time and realized he was late for work. Adrenalin surged through his body, and he ran to the bathroom to shower and shave.

Twenty minutes later, he flew out of his apartment stopping only to grab a cup of coffee from the Polish deli that occupied the ground floor of his three-story building. He was tempted to get a bagel for later, but the line was eight persons deep and he didn't have time. Coffee was a much simpler, faster matter. He could help himself and throw a few bucks down as he waved to the cashier. He knew the owner, Piotr, personally and professionally and had performed colonoscopies on him and his babushka-wearing sisters who were in the back rolling out pierogies. Everyone in the deli knew him and waved him on.

As he speed-walked the half-mile to the hospital, he wondered how Vito had made out with the Rolls. Part of him was dying to know but another part of him said it would be infinitely better not to. His loyalty to Vito was too strong to worry about the legality of his friend's activities just as long as they didn't land him personally in the slammer. Vito was one of those old-fashioned mobsters. He didn't believe in drugs, he didn't hurt women, and tried never to involve civilians in his nefarious affairs. He had a code of sorts and stuck by it, but for those in his profession who were dumb enough to cross him, he was a holy terror. Basically, if you were another mobster, you were fair game for anything his imagination came up with. And it came up with a lot. Holding a rich guy's Rolls Royce hostage struck Cesari as a more or less victimless crime though, and Cesari's curiosity got the better of him, so he made the call.

"Hey Vito. How'd you and Gerry make out with the Rolls' collector in Morristown?"

"I'm glad you called because I need your help. The Rolls' guy was no collector, but he does run a Mercedes dealership in Morristown and picks up exotic cars from time to time. The people out there got money coming out of their ears. Gerry said there was high end everything in the guy's lot including a couple of Rolls Royces. Anyway, his name is Alan Chamberlain and according to Gerry he didn't know anything about a Rolls Royce at the Port of Newark."

"Where does that leave you?"

"Well, his name and business address were on the invoice, so I have to believe that's not random. He probably knows who the real buyer is and fronted for him. Why, I don't know, but Gerry was in no position to find out the truth so he left it at that." He sighed into the phone and continued, "Gerry found out this guy Alan's home address and I was thinking of going out there tonight. I didn't want to get involved on that level, but I don't think I have a choice. Feel like taking a ride?"

"To Morristown? Why would I want to do that?"

"Because I need a ride and you already know my circumstances."

"Yeah, but I don't want to be part of this particular situation, if you know what I mean. Grand theft auto of a Rolls Royce sounds like a potentially long prison sentence."

"What are you talking about? You don't even have to get out of the car. You park in the driveway, and I'll go talk to the guy. Maybe I'll agree to buy a Mercedes from him in exchange for his cooperation."

"Afraid I'm going to have to take a pass, bud."

"Yeah, I thought you'd say that. Spoken like a true friend. You know, Cesari, there are times when I think I should have let those guys pummel you like they wanted to."

"Back in the first grade?"

"Yeah, I think ever since then you've taken our relationship for granted."

Cesari rolled his eyes, waited a moment, and said, "No guns, knives or baseball bats? We're just going to talk, right?"

Vito hesitated before saying, "Sure… Pick me up at seven."

"I have to pick you up?"

"The feds, Cesari. Remember them? The Mott Street entrance to the parking garage, the third floor. I'll send the Caddie uptown. That should keep them busy."

"Look, I have to go. I'm about to enter the hospital. See you at seven and when we're done, we're going to have a long conversation about when my debt to you from the first-grade ends."

He hung up as he walked into the lobby of St. Matt's and raced to the OR. Putting Vito out of his mind, he returned to his real life. He couldn't wait to run into Jeremy today and relive the night before at the Sommelier's mansion. The poor guy probably had the mother of all headaches today. Last night he had to practically carry him into his apartment in Chelsea where his girlfriend was waiting for them. She was a cute cardiac rehab nurse with short, dirty blonde hair. She had rolled her eyes and clucked disapprovingly when she saw Jay's condition. Cesari was sure she would never let them go out together again.

He quickly changed into scrubs and found the OR in its typical state of controlled chaos. The schedules were heavy and the nurses were short staffed. He finished his coffee and went directly to the endoscopy room. Opening the door a crack to see inside, he saw a patient lying in position on a stretcher, Cindy, his nurse, sitting at her desk charting, and Beth, the nurse anesthetist, playing on her phone. The lights were down low. He glanced at the wall clock and saw that he was only fifteen minutes late. Not bad, all things considered, but they were one nurse short, the one who was supposed to assist him during the procedure. She was the important one. No offense to anyone else in the room, but they were superfluous.

He entered and greeted them all, starting with the patient. "Good morning, Mr. Colantonio. I see you're a little early for your procedure. I'll be happy to get started."

The old guy looked up. "Early? I thought you were late."

"Not according to my schedule, but it's no problem. I'm just glad I showed up when I did."

"Are you sure?"

"Very sure."

"Well then, thank you. Now, can we get this over with?"

Beth laughed quietly to herself, and Cindy frowned disapprovingly. He said, "Is there a problem, Cindy?"

"None whatsoever, Doctor. And don't listen to him, Mr. Colantonio. He's the one who's late. He's just being a wise guy."

Cesari made a face at her, and the patient grinned, "A wise guy, huh? Well, as long as he's as good as everyone says he is, I can take it."

"We're going to take good care of you Mr. Colantonio and I apologize for being late. I stopped to rescue a puppy from a burning building, but I'll be fine. Just a few scratches."

Cindy almost fell off her chair and the patient started laughing. Cesari signaled Beth to start the sedation and for Cindy to perform the timeout. The timeout was the preop ritual to identify the patient and nature of the procedure to all the participants in the room to make sure everyone was in agreement as to what they were about to do. The idea was to prevent someone from accidentally cutting off the wrong leg or operating on the wrong part of the brain. What it had to with colonoscopy had never been made clear to Cesari. Anybody who spent the night taking laxatives and then undressed and stuck their butt up in the air knew exactly what was about to happen. There was no wrong colon to operate on, and if you had inadvertently come to the wrong place for your cataract surgery why would you undress from the waist down?

Cindy said, "We have to wait for the scrub nurse before doing the timeout. She went to the bathroom."

"The bathroom?"

"Natured called, Cesari, and you weren't here."

"Fine, who is it? Melissa?"

"No, she called in sick this morning."

"Karen?"

"No, she's in another endo room with Veronica."

"Are you going to tell me who it is or should I just go through the entire roster."

On cue, the door opened, and Valentina entered the room. Cesari became very quiet and probably a little pale, but the room was quite dark, so no one noticed.

"*Jesus,*" he thought. "*I can't catch a break.*"

"Hi, Cesari," Valentina said with an upbeat tone.

"Hi, Valentina."

She closed the door, gowned and gloved up, and then stood side by side with him as Cindy performed the timeout. When she was done, Beth sedated the patient and Cesari started the colonoscopy. Negotiating the tip of the scope around the usual twists and turns was no big challenge for Cesari, an experienced endoscopist who had performed thousands of colonoscopies. He could probably do the procedure blindfolded while drinking coffee.

No, the big challenge today was standing inches away from Valentina, arguably one of the most beautiful women he had ever dated and pretending not to notice. Her hair was in a ponytail, her scrubs and gown clung to every curve and she smelled nice. He wasn't sure what the scent was. It could have been her body soap or her shampoo or her perfume or possibly some sort of feminine pheromone she released whenever she was around him. He had no doubt that women could do things like that. It fit right in with all the other magical powers they held over him.

"What are you doing in endoscopy, Valentina? Are you being punished?" he asked.

She grinned. "No, I volunteered when I heard Melissa called in sick. It's not as glamorous as orthopedics or plastic surgery or even vascular or general surgery for that matter, but I feel it's important to stay well rounded."

Cesari thought about the last time he saw her naked and how well-rounded she really was. The thought made his mouth a little dry. But she was also nuts. It was always that way it seemed. The more beautiful the rose, the sharper the thorns, he mused silently.

He cleared his throat and said, "Well, that's really nice of you. Most of the other OR nurses pretty much hate coming to work in endoscopy."

"I know. That's such a shame. I think it's kind of fun... So how was lunch with your girlfriend yesterday?"

Cindy and Beth looked up simultaneously. Cindy said, "You didn't tell us you had a girlfriend, Cesari."

"Who is she?" asked Beth.

"Georgina, in administration. That was her name, wasn't it, Cesari?" offered Valentina helpfully.

He nodded, not liking the sudden turn the conversation had taken. "Yes, that was her name."

"How long have you been dating?" asked Cindy.

"Not long and I think calling her my girlfriend is a bit of a stretch. We've only been out a couple of times. She's more of a friend than anything else."

"It's kind of peculiar though," Valentina said. "I had to go to administration yesterday afternoon to fill out some paperwork for my health benefits. I asked around but no one knew anybody named Georgina."

Cesari blushed in the dark. He was quiet for a long while as he tried to come up with an explanation. Finally he said, "Well, she is kind of new. Maybe she just hasn't made the rounds yet. She's really cute. You can't miss her. Wavy, shoulder length brown hair, five foot four, perfect figure."

Valentina nodded but Cindy was perplexed, and said, "That's odd that no one knew her. It's not that big a place."

Valentina added, "That's what I thought."

Cesari said, "Well, I wish I could help you guys sort it out but at the moment I'd like to focus on the patient in front of me."

"Georgina's a different kind of name too," Beth reflected. "Not very common. You think people would have remembered it."

Cesari took a deep breath and let it out. They weren't going to let go of it any time soon. "You think we can talk about something else, guys?"

Valentina said, "Why? Don't you like talking about your imaginary girlfriend?"

Beth and Cindy started laughing.

Chapter 16

It was the longest morning of his life as the nurses yanked his chain mercilessly about Georgina but thankfully it came to an end at a quarter to noon. When it was over, he pulled Valentina aside and out of earshot of the others.

He was irritated and said, "What was that all about?"

Smiling devilishly she said, "I'm not sure what you mean."

"You know exactly what I mean. You went to administration to look for the girl I told you about. That was over the line, Valentina."

"You mean, Georgina?" she asked innocently and giggled. "There is no Georgina, and you know it. Although I'm flattered you felt the need to make up a fictitious girlfriend to prove to me you're all right. It didn't work though. I see the way you look at me. You can't live without me, and we both know it."

Damn, she was a pain in the neck, but he wasn't ready to surrender, and said, "I didn't invent a girlfriend. I don't have to. She's as real as you are. I just didn't want to tell you where she really works because I knew you would do something like that."

Valentina laughed hard at that. "You're hopeless, Cesari. Did you know that? Well, if she's real then pick a date. Forget it. I'll pick a date. Saturday night. Bring her to The Palms Steakhouse in mid-town. Say eight o'clock. Fusco and I would love to meet her. There, you have two nights to find a girl with wavy, brown, shoulder length hair and a perfect figure."

"She can't make it to dinner Saturday night. Georgina is visiting her mother on Long Island this weekend."

"How convenient," she scoffed. "Well, I'm going to need proof of life and so are the other nurses or you'll be in danger of becoming a laughingstock around here. Georgina... please... What kind of name is that? I don't think a girl has been named Georgina in a hundred years."

"It's a very nice name. I like it."

"Later, player..."

She spun around and bounced away before he could finish. That pissed him off even more. She did that a lot. He watched her and despite his irritation, couldn't help marveling at her perfect ass. He took in a deep breath and let it out. She was trying to bring him to heel, and he knew it. He must resist at all costs. The crazy ones never ran out of energy.

Preoccupied with the fake girlfriend debacle, he hadn't given much thought to Arnie and his appointment at the SEC. He had meant to call him yesterday but got waylaid by the booze, the food, the cigars, and the grandeur of Mike B.'s not-so-humble home. He went to Arnie's office on the tenth floor and let himself in, but no one was home. Probably wandering around the hospital pressing the flesh the way politicians do or possibly in a meeting somewhere in the bowels of the hospital, he thought. Either way, he was a little surprised that Arnie hadn't called him. He couldn't have been that annoyed.

Although Arnie was acting CEO since the sudden and ignominious departure of his predecessor, he hadn't relocated his office to the inner sanctum of the hospital on the main floor where the offices were more spacious, the coffee machines were of better quality and the secretaries wore shorter skirts. If and when he was ever confirmed as permanent CEO, he would move there but it hadn't happened yet, so he continued to share secretarial staff with several other physicians on his floor. Cesari went to the central reception area twenty feet from Arnie's office and found three middle-aged, very bored, very indifferent women busy at work answering phones, receiving and sending faxes, filing important and not-so-important documents. They all looked like they were dying for a cigarette break or a donut.

He asked them, "Anybody know where Dr. Goldstein is?"

One looked up and replied nonchalantly, "Haven't seen him yet today."

"Really? Did he call in?"

"I don't think so." She turned to the others and said, "Girls, did anyone hear from Dr. Goldstein today?"

No one had heard from him was the response.

"Could he be in a meeting?" he persisted.

"There's none on his schedule."

Cesari waited for more of an explanation, but none was forthcoming. "That's it?" he asked.

"What more do you want?"

"Your boss doesn't show up for work and doesn't call with a reason and you're okay with it?"

"It's only noon, Doctor. Give him a chance."

Cesari thought about that. She sort of made sense. "I will, thanks."

He hadn't come to work today or called in sick. What did that mean? Maybe he wasn't thrilled at what the SEC had to say. Cesari walked away and called Arnie on his cellphone wondering if the older man wasn't feeling well although he appeared fine yesterday. The call went to his voicemail box which was full and not receiving any more messages. He sighed and decided to do what the secretary suggested and give him a chance. Maybe he had some sort of appointment he forgot to tell them about or maybe a plumbing emergency at his apartment. Just about anything was possible, he supposed. There was no point in jumping to conclusions prematurely.

Less than an hour later, as he wolfed down a slice of hospital pizza on his way to his office to see patients, his phone buzzed with an unknown number. He thought there was at least a fifty-fifty chance it might be spam. But he was a physician in a busy hospital and there was at least a fifty-fifty chance it might be another physician who had gotten his number from the switchboard, so he answered it.

It was Sylvia, Arnie's wife, and she sounded stressed. "John... Dr. Cesari, I mean. Have you seen, Arnie?"

Although Arnie and he were friends at work, their relationship pretty much ended at the hospital's main entrance. He had met Sylvia on several occasions, such as hospital picnics, Christmas parties, and the like. He had even had dinner at their apartment a couple of times, but they weren't close and he hadn't seen or spoken with her in months. Hence, the somewhat stilted, semi-formal address. Overall, he liked her and thought she was a nice person, like Arnie.

"John is fine, Sylvia. And no, I haven't seen him today. His secretary told me he didn't come to work this morning."

"John, I'm worried. He didn't come home last night."

Cesari let that sink in for a minute before saying, "He didn't come home?"

"No..."

"When was the last time you talked to him?"

"Around noon yesterday. He was having lunch in his office. He seemed fine. Maybe a little nervous about going to the SEC."

"You knew about that?"

"Yes, he's been very upset. That's all he could talk about lately, but he was sure it was the right thing to do."

"Why was he nervous if he was sure it was the right thing to do?"

"He was worried about the fallout, the potential scandal at the hospital. He knew he was placing himself in the eye of the hurricane and would surely lose the confidence of the board."

Cesari nodded to himself. He had no doubt the coming firestorm would have engulfed Arnie and burned him to a crisp. That's just the way these things went. No good deed ever went unpunished.

"And he seemed perfectly fine to you otherwise, Sylvia? He didn't mention any appointments later in the evening? Or perhaps going to a friend's home?"

Her voice was frail and trembled a little. "He was perfectly fine, and we had dinner reservations last night at 7:00 p.m. at our favorite restaurant in the Village. He wouldn't have missed that for the world. He said it was the only restaurant in Manhattan that made matzah ball soup the way his mother did."

Cesari didn't like the sound of this and felt the hairs go up on the back of his neck. He'd heard Arnie talk about that restaurant many times. Arnie loved it. "What have you done so far, Sylvia?"

"I called him multiple times, but he hasn't answered. I called my children to see if any of them had heard from him, but they hadn't. Needless to say I have them all worried now. I didn't want to press the alarm too soon, but I think something bad may have happened. I called everyone I knew at St. Matt's, but no one has heard anything. His secretary told me you were just up in his office looking for him. She gave me your number. I didn't mean to bother you. This is very unusual for him to just disappear like this."

"You're not bothering me, Sylvia. What about local hospitals? Have you called any of them?"

"I called the police last night, but nobody seemed to think it was a big deal, as if grown men decide to up and leave their wives all the time without warning."

"Unfortunately, they do, Sylvia. All the time. And women leave their husbands without warning all the time too."

"Arnie wouldn't do that."

"No, not Arnie. I agree. I can't believe that either... Look, try not to think the worst. I'll start calling all the hospitals in the area to see if he was admitted anywhere. Who knows? Maybe he was in an accident. Maybe he tripped, fell, and has temporary memory loss. At this point, it could be anything. He could be lying on a stretcher in an emergency room somewhere with a bump on his head."

"I thought about that too. I thought to myself, what if he had a stroke and wandered off and can't remember who he is or what if he was robbed and got hit in the head or shot and dumped in an alley. This is New York. It happens every day."

"Sylvia, please. I know you're worried but don't let your mind dwell on the absolute worst. I'll get cracking on this right away. I have a friend in the police department who might be able to help. I'll give him a call."

"Thank you, John. I just don't know what else I'm supposed to do. Last night was the first time in forty-five years I slept alone. It was unnerving."

He heard her weeping into the phone and said, "Sylvia, is there someone who can keep you company until we sort this out?"

"My son lives in New Mexico with his wife and my daughter teaches at UC Berkeley. Both are tied up with work and kids but said they will break away as soon as they can, but I don't want that. At least not until I'm absolutely sure I need them, so I told them not to come just yet. I'm still hoping he'll walk through the front door with a big smile and a dozen roses. In the meanwhile, my neighbors are good people. I'm sure they'll pop over as soon as I tell them."

"I'll call you immediately if I learn anything, Sylvia. I promise."

"Thank you," she said, greatly relieved to have an ally.

He hung up as he entered the reception area to his office. The place was jammed with people checking in. Amy, the GI office's nurse practitioner and all-around Girl Friday was talking to his other nurse Monica as they readied themselves for the afternoon onslaught. Both women were short, petite, late thirtyish, and very Italian.

He said, "Ladies, I have an emergency. I need to cancel my afternoon."

Monica's eyes went wide. "You have four people sitting in the waiting room since twelve o'clock, and four more registering as we speak, two of whom you canceled last week when you had to see someone in the emergency room."

"It can't be helped. It's something I can't ignore or put off. Amy, maybe you can see one or two of my patients? I'm afraid the rest will have to be rescheduled. I really can't stay. Dr. Goldstein's wife just called me. He didn't come home last night or show up for work today. No one knows where he is. She's worried sick. It's probably nothing, but he's almost seventy so who knows?"

"Sure, I can see your patients," Amy replied sarcastically. "I'll just squeeze them in between the twenty-five patients I'm already scheduled to see. I like Dr. Goldstein. I really do, and I don't mean to seem unsympathetic, Cesari, but when did you become head of the missing person's department? Why doesn't she just call the police?"

"No need for acrimony, Amy. She sought me out as a friend, and she already did call the police. They blew her off."

Monica interjected, "I am not walking out there and telling a room full of patients who have been waiting over an hour for you that they need to reschedule their appointments. No way, Jose."

Cesari smiled and said, "Okay, it's like this. If you guys play ball, I'll make it worthwhile for the both of you. I'll do anything it takes to make it right." Then he leaned in close, winked impishly, and whispered, "Anything it takes… If you know what I mean."

Amy rolled her eyes. "Give me a break, Cesari. You got nothing I want."

Mona laughed. "Now hold on a minute. I'm interested in hearing more. You said anything?"

He stepped closer and with a husky voice, repeated, "You heard me right, girlfriend… anything."

"Okay, then promise me right now you'll come by and clean my house tonight and we've got a deal."

Amy and Monica thought that was hysterical and started laughing out loud, but now in a better mood, agreed to run interference for him. As he left the office, he overheard a heated exchange between one of his patients and Monica at the front window.

Monica said, "I'm sorry, but Dr. Cesari got called away on an emergency."

The patient said, "This is bullshit. I should call a lawyer."

Chapter 17

The first thing Cesari did was return to Arnie's office to speak with the secretaries again. The women were still busy at their jobs but stopped what they were doing when he arrived. He told them of his conversation with Mrs. Goldstein and their demeanor changed as they looked at each other.

"I'd like to ask you a couple of more questions about Dr. Goldstein."

They bobbed their heads in unison and he continued, "It's very important. I need to know when the last time was anyone of you spoke to or heard from Dr. Goldstein."

They were now appropriately concerned. Arnie was a fan favorite around the hospital. One said, "Yesterday around 1:30 p.m. He left for an appointment somewhere and said he wouldn't be back and to call him for any problems."

"He didn't mention where he was going or how he would get there?"

She said, "He didn't say where he was going but he did mention that it looked like a nice day for a walk downtown."

"And he didn't call later in the afternoon for any reason? Think hard."

"No, he didn't," they all agreed.

Cesari sighed, "Okay, thank you for your time. If you don't mind, I'm going to use Arnie's office for a minute."

Thoroughly apprehensive now, they nodded. There was a growing sense of trepidation on their faces. He let himself into

Arnie's office and closed the door to look around. It was a modest ten by fifteen rectangle, but it did have a private bathroom slightly larger than a closet but still... His desk was a collage of papers, folders, unopened and opened mail, sticky notes, family pictures, and hastily jotted down messages and phone numbers on a yellow pad. He sat in Arnie's swivel back chair and searched all the drawers, which revealed more of the same, a variety of work-related folders and papers. The bottom drawer on the right held a bottle of cheap bourbon and two glasses. Cesari smiled. Sometimes he would visit Arnie after hours and have a toot. He closed the drawer and studied the room, trying to place himself in Arnie's mindset.

He had known Arnie ten years and considered him one of the most vanilla guys he had ever met. His favorite meal was meatloaf and mashed potatoes. That said it all and then some. He never heard him say a cross word about Sylvia or their relationship. He had an army of grandchildren he loved and doted on as much as he could. The view from his window overlooked Third Avenue and all its hustle and bustle.

It had been less than twenty-four hours since anyone last saw Arnie. In the absence of some sort of witnessed violence, most people wouldn't even consider him a missing person yet. But it was so out of character for him not to be in a place he ought to be or to call his office or his wife that clearly something was wrong. Maybe it was minor or maybe not. Sylvia was right about New York being a dangerous place. Arnie could have been the victim of random street crime, but there was another possibility, and he dreaded this thought as much as the previous one. Maybe they didn't know Arnie as well as they thought they did. The news cycles were rife with men who had secret lives. Could Arnie have a girlfriend somewhere? Despite his concern, this brought a smile to Cesari's face. Old man Arnie with a woman half his age. The idea was ludicrous, but not impossible. Even more preposterous was the image that Cesari suddenly had of Arnie lying unconscious in an alley with a needle sticking out of his arm or a crack pipe in his lap. He suddenly wondered if opium dens were a thing anymore.

Arnie had a generic computer terminal on his desk. Cesari turned it on and entered his own username and password. Then he did a search of all the hospitals and urgent care centers within a one-mile radius of St. Matt's. It made no sense that if he was suddenly sick, he would have gone somewhere other than his own emergency room, but it needed to be checked out. So using the desk phone, he called each medical center and placed a query about Arnie. It took close to an hour and a half. There were three hospitals and five urgent care centers. There was no record of an Arnold Goldstein M.D. having been treated or admitted to any of them. There were two John Doe's at Bellevue last night but neither of them fit Arnie's description. Both of them were in their early thirties. One was the victim of gang violence and the other a drug O.D.

Cesari hung up after the last call and glanced up at the wall clock. It was 2:35 p.m. He looked up the number to the SEC and dialed it. He told the operator what his call was in reference to, and she transferred him to another line which was answered by a guy called Albert Dunmore. He told Albert that Dr. Arnold Goldstein had an appoint there yesterday and that no one had seen him since he left work to make that appointment. People were concerned and he would like to speak to the person or persons who interviewed him to try to get a bearing on what might have happened and that it was a matter of some urgency.

He was advised that this was a highly irregular request and the nature of the discussion between Dr. Goldstein and the SEC representative was a private matter and could not be revealed to him.

"I understand completely. I'm just trying to figure out if Dr. Goldstein wasn't feeling well at the time of the appointment or if he might have looked ill or complained of anything like chest pain or feeling dizzy."

Albert Dunmore clicked a few keys on a computer before he said, "Dr. Goldstein had a 3:00 p.m. appointment yesterday with our representative, Harold Zimmerman, but failed to make the appointment. He didn't call to reschedule either."

"Are you sure about that?" Cesari asked.

A few seconds later. "Perfectly sure. Can I help you with anything else?"

"No. Thank you for your time."

He hung up and thought about that for a while. He hadn't made his appointment, so something had happened between the time he left the hospital at 1:30 p.m. and 3:00 p.m., the time he was supposed to be at the SEC. Only mildly concerned a minute ago, Cesari was now up to DEFCON 3 and rising. Something really had happened. He thought about Arnie. The last thing he said to his secretaries was that it was a nice day for a walk.

It was about half an hour to forty-five minutes by foot from St. Matt's to the SEC depending on how aggressive a pace you took. Arnie was a big walker and it was perfect weather yesterday afternoon. He had left an hour and a half in advance. The walk would have settled his nerves a bit, and given him plenty of time to find his way around the building and get oriented. On the computer, Cesari pulled up an area map and tracked out the most logical path to the SEC from St. Matt's.

There were several parallel routes he might have taken but the most direct and Arnie-like would have been to go straight down Broadway past City Hall. He glanced at his watch. Then he glanced at a framed picture of Arnie and Sylvia on the desk. It was taken from last year's holiday party at the hospital. It was a good picture. They were both dressed up and happy. Cesari took the photo out from the frame and stood up. There was no time like the present. He planned to walk to the SEC down Broadway and show as many people as he could the picture of Arnie. It would be a laborious process but needed to be done.

A knock on the door distracted him and he looked up. The three secretaries crowded in the doorway. He could tell from their expressions they had made a full about face from a few hours ago when they had more or less given him the brush-off. They were now extremely worried.

One of them said, "Any news?"

"Nothing good, but not necessarily bad. He hasn't been admitted to any hospital and hasn't been treated in any outpatient urgent care in the last twenty-four hours, but I also found out that he never made it to his appointment yesterday."

The secretary closest to him put her hand over her mouth and her lips quivered in fear for Arnie. She whispered, "Oh no. That can't be good."

Cesari let out a deep breath. "Maybe... I knew where he was going so I'm going to try to retrace his steps using this photo." He held up the picture. "With any luck, somebody will recognize him. I hope he didn't have some sort of sudden, inexplicable mental breakdown and is wandering the streets with amnesia."

The three of them gasped simultaneously, and he added quickly, "I apologize. I didn't mean to frighten you. I was just thinking out loud."

The closest one nodded. "Did you call the police?"

"Mrs. Goldstein did yesterday and I'm going to again today."

"We'll be praying for Dr. Goldstein."

"That's not a bad idea."

"Is there anything we can do? We feel so helpless."

"Let's all try to be positive. The prayer thing's a good start."

After they left, he folded the photo and tucked it into his pocket. He looked around one last time not sure if he should let the board of the hospital know. Arnie was acting CEO and he was missing. They may need to start thinking about governance issues. Word was going to percolate organically as the secretaries spread the news by mouth, but they really deserved to hear it from him. He eventually decided to wait until morning. One more night wouldn't change anything.

He walked out of the hospital, passing through the emergency room which was busy as always. All twenty beds and six trauma rooms were filled to capacity with patients, their families, beeping machines, the occasional cop or security guard, and nurses everywhere. The waiting room was overflowing with patients and the ambulances were bringing more in every minute. And this was just an ordinary day.

There were four doctors and four nurse practitioners running around like chickens without their heads evaluating and treating the sick. Cesari was pleased when he saw a friend of his, Rhonda Harrison, sitting on a stool, stitching up some guy's forearm. From the look of the guy, he took a spill off his motorcycle. He was fat with an unkempt beard, and long hair, wearing a leather jacket, jeans, and a dirty t-shirt. Rhonda was black, forty, looked like she was thirty, very attractive, and in charge of the ER. She had great eyes. Big green things that you could really get lost in, like tractor beams in an old sci-fi movie. Once they locked on you, you were helpless to get away as they inexorably pulled you toward the mothership. Cesari really liked eyes. The bigger the better. He never understood that about himself.

He came up to her side and nodded at the fat guy who nodded back. He gave Cesari a sly grin. Apparently, he noticed Rhonda's eyes as well or maybe her breasts. They were nice too. When he got close, she looked up.

"Cesari, what brings you to my neck of the woods? I don't remember calling GI."

"You didn't nor did anyone else. I just needed to ask you something."

"Is it personal because I have to tell you, Cesari. You're a nice guy, but I'm already seeing someone. Don't be offended but why would I go out for hamburger when I have steak at home. Know what I mean?"

The fat guy laughed. "I already tried, buddy. I should have warned you."

Cesari grinned. "No, nothing like that, Rhonda. It's something a little bit more serious."

His tone said it all and she replied, "Okay, give me a minute. I'm just about done here with Mr. Hell's Angel."

The fat guy looked at his forearm and said, "Great job, Doc. Thanks."

She put in one more stitch, cleaned the area, and gave instructions to the nurse assisting her. Then she rose off her stool, and they walked a short distance away for privacy.

She said, "What's up?"

"It's Arnie."

"Goldstein?"

"Yes, he's been missing since 1:30 p.m. yesterday afternoon."

She instinctively glanced at a wall clock and did a quick calculation in her head of how long he'd been missing. "You're kidding?"

"No, I'm not. He hasn't been seen or heard from by anyone since that time. I can't be sure what happened, but head trauma or mental confusion are high on the list right now. You know, perhaps a neurologic event that prevented him from identifying himself. Maybe he lost his wallet and had no ID on him. Is there any chance, he came to this ER and wasn't recognized?"

She looked at him like he was crazy. "Are you kidding?"

He shook his head. "I wish I was."

She said, "Oh my goodness... Well, everyone knows Arnie. I don't think there's even a slight chance he could have walked in here without being recognized...What do you think?"

"Not sure. He left the hospital at 1:30 p.m. yesterday and no one has seen him since. I called every medical center in Manhattan this side of the Empire State building, but I realized I should have checked here first."

She walked over to a computer terminal and pulled up a roster of all the patients seen in the ER from the last twenty-four hours including all DOAs and John Does. She glanced up and down the screen and then sorted the patients by age and gender.

Eventually she shook her head and said, "There were no unidentified males treated here in the last twenty-four hours. Sorry, but I'll put the word out with the other docs just in case."

"Thanks, Rhonda."

He turned to leave, and she said, "I was just kidding about calling you a hamburger, Cesari. You're a steak in my book."

He smiled, "Thanks."

Chapter 18

Cesari hoofed it from the entrance of St. Matt's all the way down Broadway to City Hall, showing as many people as would stop long enough to hear his story the picture of Arnie and his wife. The process was dizzying as the streets and sidewalks were packed with people, cars, vans, trucks and storefronts. But Cesari was highly motivated. He started at just after three and wound up at the SEC on Vesey Street at just after five. No luck. It had been a long shot and although he was disappointed, he hadn't been overly optimistic to begin with. It was something that had to be done.

He was thankful that it was a nice afternoon, warm but not hot, with a gentle breeze and no sign of rain. The temperature had reached a high of eighty degrees at one o'clock but was cooling off. Cesari was hungry, tired, frustrated, and now officially worried for his friend's safety. Something bad had definitely happened. He could feel it in his bones. He walked back to Broadway and hailed a passing yellow cab to his apartment.

In the back seat, he dialed Detective Tierney. "Cesari, I was just thinking of you."

"And why is that?"

"Because the medical examiner just called me. He finished the autopsy on Mrs. Loomis. He found traces of propofol in her body and identified a puncture wound in her femoral vein from what had to have been a hypodermic needle. He has definitively concluded that although she had cancer and a shitload of narcotics in her system, it was the propofol that pushed her over the edge."

"Why the femoral vein and not one in the arm?"

"Not sure. Maybe whoever did it thought it would be less likely to be noticed and he would have been right if it hadn't been for the discovery of the needle cap. But it does suggest a detailed knowledge of anatomy like a doctor might have. You better tell Goldstein he has a public relations nightmare on his hands. The daughter is going to want blood."

Cesari sighed. The day was going from bad to worse. "I wish I could tell him, but Arnie's missing. He's the reason I called you."

"What do you mean, missing?"

Cesari reviewed the events for him. It didn't take long. After a while, Tierney said, "You sure he didn't take off somewhere like to Tahiti to be with his other wife?"

"You never know but I'm pretty sure."

"He could be in an alley somewhere or a dumpster."

"I get it, Detective. There's the river, any number of land-fills, a car crusher, and so on, but why? Arnie never hurt a fly."

"Why has nothing to do with it, Cesari. You should know that. He could have just been in the wrong place at the wrong time. On the other hand, he might walk through the front door tomorrow morning suffering from the worst hangover of his life."

"That's what I'm hoping."

"Let's keep our fingers crossed. I do kind of like the guy. He's feisty. I'll ask around, but you already did the kind of leg work I would have done. If an old guy doesn't come home and there's no evidence of violence or bodily harm, you check the hospitals first, retrace his steps, and keep your fingers crossed. Nobody had it in for him?"

"Not that I know. He was a pretty well-liked guy. Is there anything else we can do?"

"If he doesn't show up by morning, I'll open a file on him and go talk to his wife. We'll start there."

"Thanks… Have you started interviewing the pain guys?"

"Yes, I spoke to Xi and Jaskaran. Nice guys and very cooperative. It'll take time to process their DNA. It's unfortunate that Jaskaran doesn't have an alibi, but we'd need more than that to move forward. I was supposed to talk to Macallan tonight, but he begged off. Said he wasn't feeling well so we rescheduled for tomorrow night."

Cesari smiled at the thought of Jeremy nursing a massive headache from the night before. He said, "What about Parikh?"

"The big guy? I was saving him for last."

"You don't really think one of them went to her apartment to finish her off?"

"Anything's possible, Cesari. And if they thought they were doing her a favor? Sure why not? In their minds, it would make them the good guys. But to be honest, I'm no more suspicious of them than the other nine million people living in this city. All I care about at the moment is evidence and motive, and so far the evidence is weak unless DNA, fingerprints, or an eyewitness places them at the scene. I will need to review policies and procedures for the handling of propofol in your hospital. If you don't mind, I'd like to take a tour of the OR and its pharmacy with you."

"I don't mind, but I'm not sure what authority I have. Arnie was the acting CEO. I'm just the chief medical officer, a mostly honorary position. Which reminds me. Tomorrow, I'll need to tell the board he's missing if they haven't figured it out already. They'll probably have to designate a new acting CEO. Right now, we're a rudderless ship."

"In the short term, that's good for me. If there's no one there to approve my visit to the OR, then there's no one there to deny it either. I'll meet you at eight in the lobby. Then there'll be no need for warrants and hard feelings."

"I guess it will be fine. Arnie's intention was to fully cooperate with the investigation. I can vouch for that. Eight it is then. Should I bring the lattes?"

Silence.

Then, "Lattes? Do you think I'm light in the loafers, Cesari? I'm a marine and a cop."

"Ex-marine, and would you like whipped cream and a drizzle of caramel."

"Once a marine, always a marine, Cesari," he growled. "Don't forget it and don't forget a healthy amount of freshly ground nutmeg as well."

Cesari hung up just as the cab pulled to the curb in front of his building. He ducked into the Polish deli and ordered a pastrami sandwich to go for dinner. He glanced at his watch. It was almost six and he was supposed to pick Vito up at seven to drive out to Morristown. While he waited for his meal, he called Sylvia to let her know where he was at in the hunt for Arnie and alerted her to Detective Tierney's visit tomorrow. She was relieved that steps were being taken in the right direction.

When his order came, he went to his apartment, ate quickly, and changed into more casual clothes for the ride to Jersey. As he left to get his car parked two blocks away, he texted Vito that he was on the way. At seven sharp he pulled into the garage on Mott Street, drove three levels up, and found his friend waiting by the stairwell. There he was in his imported silk suit, Italian shoes, white shirt and tie, diamond cuff links, and Rolex with his hair perfectly coiffed. Cesari tried picturing him popping out of the trunk of a Rolls Royce.

He simply couldn't imagine it.

Vito took his suit jacket off and tucked himself into the passenger side of the Honda reclining the seat as far back and as low as possible. When he was nearly horizontal and his head was below the level of where the window began, he threw his suit coat over his face and shoulders and said, "Drive. I'll give you directions once we're out of the city."

Cesari found his antics amusing and smiled. "Hello to you too."

"This is no joke, Cesari. These guys are making my life a living hell."

"I'm pretty sure that's the whole idea. Squeeze you until you squeak is the expression, I believe."

"Well screw them. I can take it a lot longer than they can dish it. Eventually they'll run out of funding, or a new director will come along and redirect their energy."

Cesari laughed as he put the car in drive and stepped on the accelerator. "That's your long-term strategy? Wait until the FBI runs out of money or there's a new director? I'm sorry for laughing but I would consider other options if I were you."

"Such as, smart guy?"

Cesari mulled that over as they exited the garage onto Mott Street and headed for the Holland Tunnel to New Jersey. He said, "Give me some time to think about it, but I have no doubt there's a better way than what you're doing."

"You're all talk, Cesari... Let me know when the sign for the Holland Tunnel's in view. That should be safe enough."

Ten minutes later, they were in the tunnel and Vito propped his seat back to a normal position, folding his suit jacket in his lap. He looked around as if for the first time and remarked, "I can't believe with all your doctor money you drive a piece of junk like this, Cesari."

"And I can't believe with all your gangster money you have to rely on this piece of junk to get around. A word of advice, my friend. I wouldn't pick on my car again if I were you. She's sensitive and sometimes has a mind of her own when it comes to who she lets ride in her. If she decides she doesn't like you she might take control of the steering and drive you to the nearest FBI field office."

Vito snickered at that and reached into suit jacket pocket. He came out with a pack of Camels, shook one out, rolled down the window and lit it. He said, "Tell your car to relax. She's as uptight as you are."

Changing the subject, Cesari asked, "Do you have directions?"

"Take I-78 W to NJ-24 W all the way into Morristown. We'll wing it from there. I have the directions written down in my pocket. It should be easy. It's not that big a town."

Traffic was light and Cesari kept to within five miles of the speed limit as he brought Vito up to speed on Arnies's disappearance. Vito was of the Arnie was probably off somewhere getting laid school of thought.

Cesari said, "That's not very helpful and extremely unlikely."

"What do you want from me? I make people disappear. I don't usually find them."

After an hour, they pulled into Morristown. Vito reached into his pocket and retrieved a piece of paper with the directions. "Find the village green. Then take South Street for half a mile until you reach George Washington Lane. That leads into a cul-de-sac. His house is number fifteen George Washington Lane. Gerry said it's an enormous two-story white colonial with blue shutters and a gigantic American flag on a pole in the center of his front lawn."

"Gerry did his work, didn't he?"

"Yeah, I have to admit. He's pretty good at this stuff."

"Are you starting to like him?"

Vito blew a puff out the window and said, "Almost as much as I like the flu, Cesari."

Chapter 19

Cesari made the turn into the cul-de-sac and slowed the car to a stop about a hundred feet before the entrance to the home's driveway. It was 8:30 p.m. and the last glimmer of the summer sun had ducked below the horizon leaving only the serenity of the night sky. The two-story house with two brick chimneys was in a very upscale neighborhood with lots of trees and manicured lawns. It was set on a two-acre lot with a large front lawn leading up to a wraparound porch with a glider and Adirondack type chairs. There was a three-car attached garage and a brand-new silver Mercedes sedan parked just outside one of the bays. Cesari judged the house to be about five or six thousand square feet. The white flagpole in front of the house was thirty feet tall, and an eight by twelve-foot flag swayed gently in the breeze lit up by flood lights at the base which switched on by timers as they watched.

Vito commented, "Nice house."

"Yeah, the guy must be doing pretty well."

Vito got out and Cesari followed him. Vito said, "I thought you were going to wait in the car?"

"I changed my mind."

"What's the matter? You don't trust me to be civilized?" Vito grinned.

"No, I don't, and I have a soft spot for guys who fly Old Glory on their front lawns."

"Give me a break."

They walked up to the front door and Cesari pressed the doorbell. Less than a minute later, the overhead porch lantern turned on, and a well-groomed fifty-year-old man opened the door. He was an inch shy of six feet, clean shaven, in reasonably good shape with a full head of graying hair. He wore a green short-sleeved polo shirt, khakis and loafers. In the background, they could hear piano music.

The man sized them up with curiosity and asked, "May I help you, gentlemen?"

Vito said, "I think so. Are you Alan Chamberlain?"

"Yes, I am."

"And you manage the Mercedes dealership on Madison Avenue?"

"I don't manage it. I own it and who may I ask are you?"

Vito took a step closer, lowered his voice and said, "Alan, trust me. You don't want to know my name. My associate and I represent a certain individual who doesn't like it when his expensive Rolls Royce just disappears. This individual can, at times, be unpleasant. So I hope you'll cooperate."

Alan grew a little pale as he suddenly seemed to appreciate Vito's great size and intimidating appearance. He gulped and unconsciously glanced back into his living room.

"Alan, can we sit down…out here on the porch?" asked Cesari politely in a not unfriendly tone. "We'd rather not disturb your family."

The man hesitated but then nodded. He called into the house to tell his wife that he would be chatting with friends for a while and then stepped outside. They took seats on the Adirondack chairs.

Alan said, "I already told Hugo I don't know what happened. When my guys went to collect the car, there was nothing in the container."

Vito and Cesari shot each other looks and Cesari took the lead. "Tell us about Hugo. Who is he?"

Alan looked surprised. "You don't know Hugo?"

Vito said, "Alan, I'm only going to say this once. We ask the questions, and you answer them."

"Sure, I get it. Hugo is the guy. You know…. The guy. A few years ago, I ran into financial difficulties from bad investments… I lost everything. I couldn't make my mortgage payments on the house. I was about to lose the dealership. I was sitting in my office contemplating how best to commit suicide when in walks Hugo with two million dollars in cash in a bulging suitcase and tells me there's more where that came from."

"What is he…a banker or something?" asked Vito.

Alan shook his head. "I never heard of a banker doing something like that and I don't know how he heard about my problem. He seemed more like Robin Hood at the time. Anyway he was working for someone else who I never met. There was no paperwork involved and all he wanted in return was for me to pick up things for him from the Port of Newark from time to time."

Cesari said, "You didn't think that was a strange request?"

"Maybe you didn't hear me right the first time. When I met Hugo, I was sitting in my office wondering if the light fixture would support my weight if I hung myself. I didn't want to wake up in some nursing home with brain damage. Of course it was a strange request, but I didn't care. My job was to send a crew down to the port with an eighteen-wheeler, pick up a container and bring it to Morristown. In exchange I got my life back. Are you guys cops…or reporters?"

Vito grabbed his arm and shook it. "What did I tell you about questions?"

"Okay, take it easy. I'm sorry."

"Did you ever look in the containers, Alan?" asked Cesari.

"Once or twice, maybe more. I was told never to do that, but you know how it is. I was curious. There were always luxury items such as high-end cars, like Ferraris or speedboats. Once there was a 1932 Bugatti Royale. Twenty-one feet long. Unbelievable. It looked like it had never been driven. Every time I did peek inside, however, I was surprised because the item inside never matched up with the invoice. I assumed that Hugo's boss was trying to avoid paying taxes and customs duties on his toys. List a car on the invoice that was of much lesser value than the actual item for the customs people was the idea. Better to pay taxes and duties on a fifty or sixty thousand car than a ten million dollar one. I had no problem with that. As far as I was concerned, the guy was a hero. The government already takes too much of our money." Alan looked down. "That's how I felt until recently, that is."

"What happened to change your mind?"

"Look, I don't mind tax dodging. I really don't. That's as American as apple pie, but I had always assumed the items inside the containers were legitimately purchased. Something happened not too long ago that made me start to wonder if I needed to end my relationship with Hugo."

Vito and Cesari exchanged glances. This tale wasn't what they had expected when they had driven out to Morristown. It was also obvious that Alan was exhausted from stress and needed to get it off his chest, so they let him talk.

Alan continued, "Six months ago a container came in. The invoice said it was a World War I British fighter plane, the kind with two wings. I think it was a Sopwith Camel. Supposedly, it was part of a private collection of World War I memorabilia bought at auction and in reasonable condition. Naturally, I was interested to see it. I opened the container and found a trunk bolted down securely like it was the Ark of the Covenant. Now I was really curious, so I opened the chest and found an oil painting." He paused a minute to catch his breath and actually seemed relieved to tell someone his story. "It was Vincent van Gogh's *Starry Night*."

Cesari's jaw dropped. "You can't be serious? Maybe it was a reproduction?"

"Maybe," Alan said, "But why go through all the trouble? I researched it and couldn't find anything about the original being stolen from the Museum of Modern Art, but I'm not sure that means anything. If it was stolen, they wouldn't announce it to the world. It would be too embarrassing, assuming they even knew it was missing. It could have been replaced by a high-quality forgery. At any rate, the arrival of the container coincided mysteriously with the *Starry Night* making its way through the art museums of Europe on loan from the MoMA. It arrived in the container no less than two weeks after the painting finished the final leg of its grand tour in the Louvre. We're talking a hundred million dollars here…minimum."

Vito whistled and Cesari said, "Wow… Hugo and his boss have balls. That's for sure. I think you were right a few minutes ago when you said it was time to end your relationship with them."

"Thanks, but Hugo made it clear that isn't going to happen. I brought it up with him a few months after I gave the Van Gogh thing time to settle down. I offered to pay him back the money he loaned me plus interest."

"What did he say?"

"He pulled up to my office one day in his limousine with a bunch of goons and asked me to take a ride with him. I didn't really think I had a choice, so I got in the car, and he put a blindfold on me. I don't know where we went but when he took the blindfold off, I was standing in a room that had human heads mounted on the walls. He said that if I ever tried to back out of our relationship, my head would be next on the wall along with my wife and kid's."

"Jesus," said Vito. "This Hugo guy is a maniac."

"Can you guys help me?"

"Help you?" asked Cesari. "You think we came here to help you?"

"You obviously didn't come here to hurt me despite the tough guy routine." He turned to Vito and added, "You need to take some acting lessons. That was the worst gangster act I ever saw. I mean you got the right look and everything but, man, you're not even close. In fact, you're both pretty bad actors. Don't you watch TV? My kids could do a better good cop, bad cop performance. I think you're FBI and you're looking for the *Starry Night* and trying not to make too much noise about it. I'm not stupid. I've been expecting a knock on my door from you guys for months, ever since I saw it. Look, I just don't want my family to get hurt. Hugo is a psychopath."

Cesari smiled. "Alan, this might be a good time to take your family on a long and well-deserved vacation. Maybe Disney World. I wouldn't tell anyone at work where you're going, and I wouldn't book anything through your personal computers. Just get in your car and drive. Pay cash for everything along the way. Credit cards are too easy to track."

"Just like that? Pack a bag, Alan, and go to Disney?"

"Would you prefer to be handcuffed and thrown into a cell?"

"No, but I find it hard to believe you're just going to let me off the hook and send me on my way? I feel like I'm being set up."

"Alan, you're small potatoes and you've been very cooperative. If we need you, we'll find you. But a couple of more things. How do you reach Hugo, and did he ever mention his boss's name?"

"I can give you Hugo's cellphone number, and as far as his boss is concerned, he never mentioned him by name. But the other night he was pissed about the empty container and said the Sommelier wasn't going to be happy."

"The Sommelier?"

"Yeah, that's what he said."

Chapter 20

It was day two of his captivity and Arnie paced like an animal in a zoo. He had banged on the door until his knuckles were raw and had yelled for help until his voice was hoarse. There was zero communication between him and his captors. He had no idea where he was or why he was there. He was unhurt, well fed, and the coffee was good. No one had come in to change the linen or clean the bathroom so apparently this wasn't a full-service hotel, he quipped to himself sarcastically. His sense of humor was returning, and he was starting to feel like he might get out of this alive.

The question that nagged at him incessantly was what did they want? Because he had nothing to give. This couldn't possibly be about money. He didn't have enough for anyone to waste their time on him. And his prison suggested that whoever it was already had way more wealth than he did anyway. There had to be some reason that eluded him.

He went to the bathroom to splash water on his face and while he was drying his hands, he heard a slight tapping sound. Faint and distant. Tap, tap, tap… He looked around for the source but found none. The sound stopped and he froze at attention. A minute later, it started up again, and his heart leapt in excitement as he scanned around the room for the cause. He laughed silently as it occurred to him that his new found hope might simply be an insect or a mouse crawling along a pipe or some duct work in the walls.

Duct work?

There was a metal grate on the ceiling, about a foot square that he presumed contained an exhaust fan for the room. There was another similar sized metal grate along the lower border of the far wall that may have been for heat or air conditioning. He listened carefully, expectantly.

Soon, the tapping began again. It was coming from the wall grate. He suddenly became paranoid and walked over to the bathroom door and closed it. Returning to the grate, he lowered himself to the floor, and lying on his stomach, put his ear next to it. The sound was definitely coming from the duct work. Somewhere distant. Was it a worker, a plumber maybe, fixing something? It could be nothing, a misaligned fan possibly. His thought went back to the possibility of a rodent.

The grate was held in place by four small flat head screws. He took out his keys and using the smallest one was able to remove the screws without too much difficulty. He placed his hand inside the duct and began tapping the side wall with one of his keys as loudly as he could.

The tapping on the other side stopped and Arnie's excitement nearly caused his heart to burst. He kept on tapping for a few more seconds and then stopped and waited. The tapping on the other side started up again and then stopped. He waited some more and was rewarded with the distant echoey sound of a human voice. A high-pitched voice, a woman's voice, a desperate voice. She was too far away for him to hear clearly but it sounded like she was saying help me.

Arnie became frantic to communicate with her effectively. Could it be possible that he wasn't the only prisoner in this place? Maybe there were many others here in similar circumstances. He tapped on the wall of the duct work again and this brought silence to the other end.

He called out, "Who are you?"

She called back repeatedly, over and over, but he couldn't make out her words until the last desperate try.

"My name is Martine."

****

Hugo said, "I have the propofol, Michel. A pharmacist at Morristown Memorial Hospital was very helpful. He says it will be weeks before it will be noticed missing, and even then, will barely raise an eyebrow in a busy medical center like that. Apparently, the working environment there is most accurately described as anarchy."

"How much propofol did you obtain?"

"A box of ten one thousand milligram bottles with a supply of syringes. He told me three hundred milligrams would be enough to kill most people without adequate medical support. We have enough to look like someone was about to open their own OR. Certainly enough to keep Dr. Goldstein occupied. Anything he says about you after this will be seen as a feeble attempt to deflect attention from himself."

"Excellent, although killing him would be so much easier and more conclusive," the Sommelier said ruefully.

"If he dies people will want to know what happened and why. Better this way, Michel, and we will have the added entertainment value of watching him squirm. With any luck, it will be front page news."

"Still, I think we need to gild the lily a bit."

"How so?"

"Is there any way of finding out who else may be dying of cancer at St. Matt's?"

Hugo nodded slowly as he absorbed the meaning of the other's words, "That would take time. Certainly days, if not weeks. I would have to infiltrate their cancer center."

"Bribe a receptionist or a nurse?"

Hugo snapped his fingers. "I could pretend to be a pharmaceutical rep. My understanding is that they are as ubiquitous as flies and just as annoying."

"There you go. Try to find an old patient who lives alone so the scene triggers immediate recognition with the authorities, raising the suspicion of a pattern. You have the address to Goldstein's apartment?"

"I do. It was among his personal effects. He lives in an apartment on the upper West Side with his wife. I will have no problem accessing it. They have two grown children on the west coast. It is unknown whether they plan to visit any time soon. I have no doubt she has made them aware of their father's absence. They will probably be monitoring the situation closely."

"We must act quickly then. We should return him soon before they press the panic button. I would like to deposit him back from whence he came sometime this evening after he misses his appointment with the attorney general. This will give you the better part of a whole day to work your magic with some unsuspecting secretary or nurse."

Hugo smiled and looked at his watch. "It's almost sunrise. I'd better shave and splash on cologne then. I should try to get to their cancer center when it opens, but I will need at least an hour to fabricate a fake Pfizer ID. Once through the door, I'll mingle in the waiting room with the patients until noon, and then I'll have a feast brought in for the staff."

"What about the medical lingo?"

"I'll tell them I'm new at Pfizer, and that I've just begun training. You know, learning the ropes, wet behind the ears, and was hoping for them to give me a few pointers on how an outpatient clinic and infusion center works. It's part of a new program at Pfizer to help the reps better understand our patients and their needs. I'll look up some commonly used oncology drugs they produce. I have a nearly eidetic memory and that will help. The fact that I'm new will allay some of the more obvious missteps I may make. I'll target the non-medical people the hardest. They will be the least suspicious and most susceptible. The secretaries will be ideal. I may be unable to avoid the nursing staff and will wing it as best I can. I will only engage the providers if forced to."

"Don't forget to get Dr. Goldstein's fingerprints on the propofol bottles."

"I won't. I'll do it after he's sedated."

"You are worth your weight in gold, Hugo... How goes it with the search for the Rolls Royce?"

"Not good. The Morristown dealer knows nothing. I am convinced he had nothing to do with it. Our man inside Rolls Royce in London is equally adamant that everything went smoothly on his end. He babysat the car as it was loaded into its container and then on to the ship. He says there is not a chance anyone could have stolen it after that."

"And you believe them both?"

"I believe that both of them know all too well the consequences of disloyalty. But yes, I believe them both. Mainly because of the most recent wrinkle in the story. I went down to the Port of Newark and reviewed the security tapes for that night and there was a thirty-three-minute gap in the recording from 2:00 a.m. to 2:33 a.m. at one of the gates."

"A thirty-three-minute gap?"

"The security official is calling it a glitch in the system. For some unknown reason, the system went down and then back on again. He says that although it is unusual it does happen from time to time."

"What do you think?"

"The gate in question just happens to be nearest where the container was located and the container with the Rolls Royce just happened to be on ground level. If the cameras went down, then it would have been a straightforward matter to get the Rolls out of the container. And if the guard at the gate was duplicitous whoever the thief was could have simply driven the car out into the night."

The Sommelier nodded. "I see your meaning, Hugo. There had to have been a conspiracy, but how could anyone have known the true value of what was inside that container? The Port of Newark is one of the busiest in the country."

"I'm not sure, but it's entirely possible they didn't know, and this was just an ordinary heist and they got lucky. Theft of this nature down on the docks happens all the time. It's so common it's factored into the retail costs of almost everything we purchase."

The Sommelier paused a beat to digest that and then said, "I agree with everything but the they-got-lucky-part. They don't know it yet, but they are the unluckiest people on the planet right now. In the history of unlucky, they will go down as the unluckiest ever, but first we must catch them... So what's the next logical step on our part?"

"We question the security guard manning the gate in question and the one manning the security cameras on that particular night. They would necessarily had to have been in on it together. I'll get working on that as soon as I finish with Goldstein."

"You have enough to do, Hugo. I'll see to the guards personally. I'm feeling very much like I want to roll my sleeves up on this one. It's almost unbelievable that people who pay union dues could have pulled this off. Do you have their contact information? I will send men to collect them."

"I will send their personal data to you shortly. Is there anything else?"

"No, you should go now. Time is of the essence."

Chapter 21

At 8:00 a.m. Friday morning, just as the St. Matt's cancer center was opening its doors and an hour before the first secretary walked through the main entrance to the office of the New York State Attorney General's office on Liberty Street in lower Manhattan, Cesari walked through the lobby of St. Matt's with a twenty-ounce freshly brewed mocha latte topped with whipped cream, drizzled with caramel and sprinkled with a generous amount of freshly ground nutmeg.

Detective Tierney grinned, accepted the gift, sniffed it and then took a sip. He made a contented sound before saying, "Thanks, Cesari. There's nothing like starting off the day right."

Tierney was wearing the same brown three-piece tweed suit, bowtie and bowler derby hat as the other day. Without the hat, he was about an inch taller than Cesari, twenty pounds heavier and solidly built. Like many men with military backgrounds, a disdain for facial hair had been beaten into him. He shaved twice daily and went to an old-fashioned barber weekly for a trim. Cesari knew Tierney could be an asshole, but at least he was a well-groomed asshole.

Cesari said, "I'm glad you approve. Would you like to enjoy your coffee first or get right to it?"

"Lead the way, Cesari. There's no time like the present."

They went to the operating room and Cesari explained, "I'm going to show you how the endoscopy suites handle their meds. To go into the general OR would require you to change into scrubs and wear a mask and hair covering. It's a lot more convenient this way, and it's the same process and the same doctors."

"That's fine. I'm just trying to get a feel for things."

In the first endo room they went to, the nurses were in the process of hooking up a male patient to his monitors and blood pressure machine. The case hadn't started yet. Xi was in an adjacent, closet-sized room preparing his meds for the procedure. He stood in front of small gray metal cabinet with a built-in keyboard, multiple drawers, and a computer screen on top. It looked a little like an ATM machine.

Xi saw them coming, flinched just a little in surprise, and said, "Good morning, Detective Tierney... Cesari."

Tierney said, "Good morning, Doctor."

Cesari nodded. "Detective Tierney was curious to see how you guys handle medications. It looks like we arrived at a good time. I hope you don't mind?"

"So this is just random. It's not me in particular you're observing?"

Tierney grinned. "Just random, Doctor. You can relax now. This was the first room we walked into. We had no idea you were in here."

"You can at least try not to act guilty, Xi," added Cesari.

Xi took a deep breath and turned to Tierney. "Okay, I feel better. I thought maybe I said something to you last night that made you suspicious."

Tierney shook his head. "No, you spoke well for yourself, and you had a great alibi. It's hard to argue with four nurses and another doctor who say they were with you all night. I just thought it would be good to familiarize myself with the process."

"Well then you picked a good time. I was just about to draw up meds for the next case." He turned, pointed at the machine and continued, "This is called a PYXIS machine and they're strategically located all over the hospital where nurses and doctors need to give medications to patients. It's a way of securing medications that need to be obtained and distributed in a decentralized manner. For a nurse or a doctor to access the machine, they need a username and a secure password. The machine records all entries and medication withdrawals in a central server. The drawers are filled and refilled daily, depending on need, by pharmacy personnel who perform manual counts every day."

Tierney asked, "So there's one of these little machines all over the hospital loaded with propofol?"

"No," Xi replied. "It's a medication commonly used here in the OR and nowhere else. So these machines up here in the OR have propofol but not the ones on the general wards or in the ER."

"Can anyone access these machines? Like Cesari or a nurse?"

"No, only anesthesia providers can access the PYXIS machines in the OR, but that does include our nurse anesthetists and there are five here in St. Matt's. On the general wards, the nurses have access to their own PYXIS machines to dispense their patient's daily meds. And as I said, every entry is recorded and digitally stored somewhere in the hospital. The meds are counted every day in every machine and then reconciled by pharmacy."

"Reconciled?"

"Think of your checkbook, Detective. You write checks and at the end of the month you compare the checks you wrote to that of the bank statement. If there's a discrepancy, you search for where the error is and try to reconcile it. The pharmacist places the meds in the machines and does a count. At the end of the day there is a record of which meds and how much of them were withdrawn. He or she then compares that to what's left in the machine."

"So there are errors in the counts?"

"All the time, but usually just small ones. Try to imagine hundreds of busy nurses and doctors accessing the various machines throughout the hospital all day long. The pharmacist then comes along and says there's an aspirin missing or there's one too many. They narrow it down to which machine and which nurse or provider handled aspirin that day and for which patient. It's usually something simple like the pill fell on the floor and had to be thrown away and another was taken out of the PYXIS but the nurse forgot to record the incident."

"What about one too many?"

"That's even worse. The implication at first glance is that a nurse accidentally didn't dispense a medication she was supposed to. So if a patient is supposed to receive a blood pressure pill three times per day and at the end of the day there's still one pill left it suggests the patient didn't receive all of his medications. But it's also possible the pharmacist put one too many in the machine by accident."

"Wouldn't the nurse notice an extra pill?" Tierney asked genuinely curious.

"Of course, but a busy nurse might have been distracted and not said anything."

Tierney nodded. It was a lot to take in and clearly despite everyone's best effort, was still a flawed system. "Okay, walk me through the propofol process. I believe you were just about to begin, and thank you for your time, Doctor. I know you have a patient waiting. We'll leave after that."

"It's no problem at all. The GI guy is running late anyway. He won't be here for another ten minutes… So the first thing is I type in my username and eight-digit secure password, which changes every six to eight weeks. Then I punch in the patient's name, date of birth, and unique medical record number. Then I withdraw the medication I need, which I estimate based on experience and patient history because everyone's a little different. A one hundred pound, ninety-year-old woman isn't going to need as much propofol as a twenty-year-old, three-hundred-pound football player."

He took out a small bottle of a milky white liquid and showed it to Tierney. Tierney studied it without touching as if it were radioactive or inherently dangerous.

Xi continued, "This is a standard-sized bottle which I'll draw up into a syringe when we're ready to start. Now, I'll close the drawer and log out."

Tierney thought about that and said, "Now that you've removed the bottle legitimately from the machine what would happen if the case were suddenly canceled?"

Xi raised his eyebrows and said, "That's a great question. I'm impressed. If the bottle hasn't been accessed, I'll return it to the PYXIS. If it's been accessed, the procedure is to waste it all into a trash can and record the wastage."

"You waste it? Why can't you save it to use on another patient?"

"State regulations for one thing, but between me and you, if the next case were to start right away then I might do just that. If there were a long delay in between cases, then I would have to waste it because it's not good to walk around the hospital with open bottles and syringes full of propofol."

"It's not good but nobody would stop you, right?"

"No, probably not."

"Next question… Do you ever need to grab a second bottle in the middle of a case?"

"Yes, all the time, and it's the same process repeated."

Tierney was zeroing in on something. "Let's pretend you're a bad guy for a minute."

Xi coughed uncomfortably, "I'd prefer not to, if you don't mind."

"Okay, let's pretend Cesari is a bad guy and wants a bottle of propofol for nonmedicinal purposes. He could be in the middle of a case, excuse himself for what, thirty seconds, grab a second bottle of propofol, shove it into his lab coat and no one would be the wiser. Hell, he could even pull two bottles out at the start and put one in his pocket. True or false?"

Xi hesitated and then said, "That's possible, but the anesthesia record would reflect that he only used one bottle during the case."

"Who fills out the anesthesia record?"

"The anesthesiologist."

"By himself or is someone looking over his shoulder to verify what he's writing down?"

Xi shook his head. "No one checks. Everybody's doing their own thing."

"So it's an honor system. Just like replacing the bottle for a canceled case. I mean who would really know if it went back into the machine or not?"

Everyone was silent for a minute. Tierney had just made stealing propofol from a secure system look easier than taking candy from a baby.

Xi concluded, "I guess it's possible but if anyone suspected..."

"Why would anyone suspect anything? Nothing's really missing. The PYXIS was accessed properly for the right reasons and the medications withdrawn properly. As far as the machine is concerned everything was done on the up and up, and when the pharmacist swings by at the end of the day all the counts match up just like a check book, only in this case the anesthesiologist wrote the check out to himself in a manner of speaking. The only way to catch the theft would be if the person was dumb enough to not cover his ass in the anesthesia record, but I assume you guys aren't that dumb. I mean I checked your resumes, Harvard, Yale, Columbia, Princeton..."

Xi looked like he was going to be sick, and his left eye started to twitch.

Tierney was on fire. "I didn't even ask what happens in a case if you draw up a syringe full of the stuff and only use a little bit. I assume it's the same procedure. You tell a nurse you're wasting it. You fill out the record that you wasted it and then you dispose of the syringe, but what if that's not what you do? Like you said, no one really watches. What if the syringe finds its way into your lab coat or your briefcase after you say you wasted it? Would anyone question it or even know it? But you have nothing to worry about. Unlike your buddy, Jaskaran, you have an alibi. There are four nurses you were on call with that night saving lives who will swear they were with you, and that you couldn't possibly have murdered anyone. On the other hand, you're doctors and nurses, right? Everybody knows how tight you guys are. You all know each other, work together, trust each other, respect each other. It's you guys against the world or something like that. Am I right?"

Xi was speechless.

Cesari said, "Time to go, Detective."

Chapter 22

They left the OR and boarded an elevator to the main floor. Cesari was upset. "What was that all about?"

Tierney grinned. "You think I was out of line?"

"I think you're an asshole and what you just did was completely uncalled for. He was cooperating as best he could, and you went out of your way to give him an anxiety attack. You practically accused him of murder. Now he's going to spend the rest of the day looking over his shoulder instead of concentrating on the patient in front of him."

"He's a professional. He'll get over it."

"Still, it wasn't nice. He didn't do anything wrong, and he has the best alibi of all of them."

Tierney sipped his mocha latte which he had neglected during his recent tirade. He said, "Cesari, maybe I came on a little strong, but you need to understand a few things. This is no longer just a casual question and answer session with my good friends at St. Matt's. This is a murder investigation. We're not just speculating anymore. Somebody shot that woman up with propofol, and I just found out that the people highest on my suspect list can literally walk away with as much of the stuff as they want, any time they want. That wasn't what I expected to hear this morning."

"That's nonsense, and you know it."

"Is it? Look at it from my point of view, I'm not even half as smart as the district attorney. If I could blow holes in your security procedures the size of basketballs, try to imagine what he'll do. What I just did in there is nothing to what a prosecuting attorney will do if it ever comes to it, so he better prepare himself and get used to harsh questions. And you guys need to tighten things up around here."

"We follow standard protocol set by the state of New York in accordance with national guidelines and Joint Commission recommendations. Our system is not only a good one but better than most of the other forty-nine states."

"Then the other forty-nine states are in deep shit. You have to admit. The policy and procedure for the handling of such a potentially lethal drug seemed kind of weak."

The elevator doors opened, and they stepped out. Cesari didn't have an answer for that, and before he could come up with a response, Tierney continued, "Look, tell your friend to relax. I didn't mean to imply that he was guilty of anything. It's just the way cops are, okay? We like to shake the tree a little and see what falls out."

"Is that an apology?"

"You can think of it any way you want."

"Perhaps it would be best if I asked you to leave and come back with a warrant, and then I'll warn my guys to not speak to anyone without a lawyer."

Tierney laughed. "And thus ended the golden age of cooperation… You can do whatever you want, Cesari, but so can I. Keep that in mind. After I get that warrant, I could stop at the New York Times and spend a few minutes with the editor there on my way back. It's a great story. When you read about it, they'll refer to me as a reliable source inside the NYPD. There's something else you should consider before drawing any lines in the sand. That nine-foot-tall Pakistani doctor I'm meeting with tonight? I can't remember his name?"

"He's only seven feet tall and he's Indian, not Pakistani, and his name is Parikh."

"That's right, Parikh. I haven't met him yet, but you should consider the following before declaring war on me. I did a little background check on him and guess what?"

"What?"

"Here's the thing. He's here illegally."

"Like in the country illegally? You're nuts."

"That's a little true too. I admit that, but I'm also right. It seems your pal's green card expired a year ago and he never applied to re-up so his ass is mine any time I want."

"He didn't reapply?"

"No, he didn't. You can check for yourself. It's not that hard."

Cesari let out an audible groan. "What's that mean? He's been in the U.S. almost fifteen years. He has a wife, kids, a house, timeshare at Disney. He pays taxes. He has season tickets to the Yankees for Christ's sake. You're not going to find anyone more American than that guy."

"Immigration laws are tricky, Cesari. Maybe if he reapplied in a hurry, they might be sympathetic and rush him through or maybe not. They could make him start all over from scratch. You know what pinheads bureaucrats can be. Then there's the real problem that only you can help him with."

"And what is that?"

"He never applied for citizenship and then he lets the card run dry. Maybe he's just been busy or maybe he's had a change of heart about his adopted country. Maybe an extremist muslim relative from back in Islamabad got to him. Maybe he decided that rather than go back he'd stick around and slaughter Americans one propofol injection at a time."

Cesari got red in the face. "This is outrageous bullshit even for you and you know it. And I already told you he's Indian not Pakistani. Islamabad is the capital of Pakistan, and another thing, he's Hindu not Muslim. If you knew anything about world history, you would know Hindus are not very fond of

Muslims and don't share their more fanatical elements' desire to destroy democracy."

"Thanks for the social studies lesson. The question you have to ask yourself is what do you think would be the result if somebody made a phone call to the department of Homeland Defense and ICE with the news that your buddy is a suspect in the homicide of an American citizen and then planted the idea in their heads that he may have been radicalized? At a minimum it would derail his chances of having his green card application renewed, and possibly, no, probably worse. You know how those guys are when they find out someone's a nutcase from the Middle East."

"He's not from the Middle East. He's from India."

"You think they know the difference?"

Cesari was growing frustrated. "You would do that to one of my guys?"

"Your guys?" Tierney whistled. "You're chief medical officer for one and a half days and they're already your guys?"

"Look, you're harassing the wrong person. Parikh is a nice guy."

Tierney wasn't finished. "Did you say, Parikh? Because what I heard was, Achmed the destroyer."

"You're not even close to being funny. Now what do you want from me, Detective?"

"Nothing really. I just want us to be friends and continue doing as we have been. I like it when my chief suspects are cooperative, and I want you to keep them that way unless you'd like to see immigration agents swarming over this place."

"That's not going to happen, and you know it."

Tierney grinned. "You want to take the chance? Now back up a few paces. We both want the same thing, which is justice for the old lady. We're on the same side, right? So no more talk about warrants. We're pals and pals don't make their pals get warrants."

Cesari bit his lip and said, "Can you at least take it down a notch with my boys? They're not used to your kind of rough foreplay."

Tierney rolled his eyes. "Fine, I'll try, but I'm doing you a favor. You and everyone else here need to start seeing things the way a grand jury or a prosecutor would. You live and work in a cocoon called a hospital. You get a pass on things that no one else would because you're doctors and nurses and take care of grandma and grandpa. But people out there in the real world have expectations for their healthcare heroes. They're not going to want to hear about sloppy, lax, and totally inadequate procedures for the safeguarding of dangerous drugs such as what I heard this morning. They're going to think you have a shitshow going on here. It behooves you to have me on your side, Cesari. I can paint this thing any way I want with the D.A. so how about we play ball together and not let Xi's ruffled feathers get in the way of doing what's right for the hospital."

Cesari was silent for a moment as they approached the lobby and neared the exit onto Third Avenue. Eventually he said, "I can't stop them from getting lawyers, especially Xi. You didn't do yourself any favors in that regard this morning."

"No, it's their right, but you can smooth things over and reassure them that I'm only after the truth. I have no interest in locking up innocent taxpayers."

"Can we talk about Arnie now?"

"Goldstein? Sure. Any news?"

"Nothing. Not a word."

"I'll take a ride over to his wife's apartment later today. You want to come with me? It will put her at ease if I'm with somebody she knows. She's probably a basket case by now."

"I can do that. What time?"

"I'll give you a call. When are you free?"

"Usually by five."

"Nothing earlier in the day like noon or one?"

"I have patients scheduled, and lots of them. Lots of angry ones. I had to cancel people yesterday." He glanced at his watch. "Which reminds me, I need to get going."

Tierney thought it over and said, "Your guys are coming tonight to give their statements. The big guy with the green card issues and Macallan. One's at six and the other's at seven. I really won't be free until at least eight at the earliest… By the time we get there it will be nine or possibly ten o'clock? Is that too late for the old lady or should we just put it off until tomorrow?"

"That is kind of late, and if we take an hour or two of her time, we could really stress her out. Let me call her and tell her the police are now involved. That will greatly relieve her. Tomorrow is Saturday and I'm free all day and can go see her with you anytime if that works?"

"That works fine. Tell her 9:00 a.m. I'll pick you up in front of your apartment at eight sharp. You still live at the north corner of Washington Square Park over that Polish deli?"

"Yes, I do."

"I'll see you then. Okay, I got to roll. By the way, have you seen your boyfriend, Gianelli, recently?"

Cesari shook his head. "No," he lied. "Why?"

"A guy was shot while having coffee in his neck of the woods. I was wondering if he knew anything about it."

"I'll ask him the next time I see him, but I don't see why he would. You know as well as I that he's a legitimate businessman."

"Yeah, right, and there's no such thing as the mafia."

"Anti-Italian slander."

Chapter 23

Cesari watched Tierney leave the building before returning to the elevator bank. He glanced at his watch. If he hustled, he could make it to his office on time for his first patient. The medical office building was attached to the hospital through a walkway on the fourth floor and Cesari went directly there at double pace speed. He was going to work as hard and fast as he could today. He didn't want any delays or old people yelling at him for being late.

Which is why he became suddenly demoralized as he swung the door open to his office and found three board members sitting there along with Steve Brennan, the CFO, and a mousy looking woman he didn't recognize. Two board members were sitting in his consultation chairs, another was studying the diplomas hanging from his walls, Brennan leaned against the edge of his desk and the unknown woman was standing at attention. She was slender, mid-thirties, with wavy, brown, shoulder-length hair, and stylish glasses wearing a business suit and carrying a briefcase. Her makeup was subdued and professional. She was attractive in a mousy sort of way and Cesari thought she might cry if he raised his voice. The room was small enough to begin with, and now reeked with claustrophobic energy.

All the board members were well-off businessmen and women in and around lower Manhattan and had a vested interest in the financial well-being of the hospital and the community. One of the sitting board members was a woman named Marjorie Sunderheim. Marjorie was in her mid-sixties, well preserved and well kept. For years, she had run a major retail clothing chain with divisions up and down the east coast. She was Valentina's aunt by way of marriage and had a vested interest in Valentina's well-being.

Cesari took a deep breath, unconsciously peeked at the wall clock, and sat in the leather chair behind his desk.

He said, "Hello everyone."

Leo Trautman was the chairman of the board and in his late seventies. He sat next to Marjorie Sunderheim in one of the two consultation chairs. He was bald with long white sideburns and gold-rimmed spectacles. He was a throwback to the days when cranky old men ruled the world. He had been the president of a bank for thirty years and only recently retired when his son had been promised his pop's position. His connections with that bank and throughout Manhattan's money circles was the hospital's pipeline to credit and much needed cash during times of difficulty. They were all well-dressed.

Leo cleared his throat and started, "Good morning, Dr. Cesari. I don't suppose you would care to tell us where Dr. Goldstein is?"

"I most certainly would if I knew, but I don't. You obviously know he's missing."

The old guy nodded. "Were you going to inform us yourself or simply rely on the rumors sweeping through the hospital along with Mrs. Goldstein's frantic calls?"

Cesari looked down, chastised. "It's been less than forty-eight hours since he was last seen. I didn't want to press the panic button too soon. I've been hoping he'll walk through the front door."

"I see. Have the police been notified?"

"Yes, by myself and Mrs. Goldstein. They plan on interviewing her tomorrow morning."

"Tomorrow? Isn't that being a little cavalier?"

"A missing person without evidence for a crime is complicated, Mr. Trautman. Statistically, ninety-nine percent of those people simply don't want to be found."

"You can't be serious? The man is just a few years younger than me. He may have had a stroke or been hit by a car. What kind of a friend are you?"

"I've talked to Mrs. Goldstein. I've called every hospital in lower Manhattan, and I've retraced his last known steps as best I could. Yesterday, I must have shown his picture to a thousand people from here down to city hall. He has simply vanished. I don't know what more I can do at this point except hope for the best."

Marjorie Sunderheim interjected sympathetically, "I told Leo you were taking this seriously, John, and that you didn't want to alarm anyone unnecessarily."

"Thank you, Marge," said Cesari.

Leo looked frustrated. "Is it okay to be alarmed now, Dr. Cesari, or should we wait until happy hour?"

Cesari said nothing and Leo continued, "Do you think this had anything to do with his appointment at the SEC?"

Cesari sighed. He wasn't sure who knew about that. "I called the SEC and he never made it to his appointment. Something must have happened on the way."

"Something like what?"

"I really don't know, and I hate to speculate about all the bad things that can befall a person in this city. There are medical things and non-medical things. You can use your imagination about that, but without proof or witnesses, we'd be banging our heads against a brick wall. My suggestion is we give him some more time and let the police do their thing. We're very fortunate in that I was able to get one of New York's best detectives to take a personal interest in the situation. That will help a lot."

"Well, that's something at least," muttered Trautman. "But I'm not sure how much time we can give Arnie. He was the acting CEO and was in line for the full-time position. We can't allow the ship to be without a captain. Decisions have to be made. Arnie was a good man, but sadly, the show must go on."

"I understand but I disagree that Arnie was a good man. My working assumption is that he still is a good man."

Marjorie Sunderheim smiled approvingly. "Well-spoken, John. Like a true friend."

Trautman made a grunting sound and said, "I know you are aware of this, Doctor. Arnie was very upset about losing the hospital's money and placing us in a disadvantageous situation financially."

"I'm well aware of it."

"Is it possible that he was so distraught, he may have committed suicide? Perhaps he jumped off the Brooklyn bridge?"

The room collectively gasped. Marjorie placed a hand over her mouth in horror at the suggestion. Cesari hadn't even considered something like that and replied, "Anything's possible, I suppose, but I really don't think so. And just for the record, I doubt a jumper off the Brooklyn bridge at two in the afternoon would have gone unnoticed. Furthermore, describing Arnie as being distraught over the lost funds isn't quite accurate."

"How would you have described him?"

"Angry... He was angry. He was convinced that we were being scammed by the financial company he used for the investments."

"I know. He told me that."

Brennan spoke up for the first time since the meeting began. "He told me that too."

Leo turned to Brennan. "And are we?"

Brennan shook his head. "There's no evidence to support that. I've gone over the financial sheets multiple times. The initial investments were rock solid and fairly cautious. We weren't trying to get rich quick with risky stocks and fly by night startup companies. Everything was blue chip and conservative. The portfolio was diverse and risk averse. We were in it for the long term."

"Then what happened?"

"Like I explained to Arnie, the Middle East happened, at least that was part of it. Terrorists blew a hole in an oil tanker coming through the Suez Canal six months ago, and coincidentally, our government shut down the pipeline from Alaska due to environmentalist pressure. The net effect was to cause the price of crude to shoot through the roof. This, in turn, caused a sudden spike in inflation and investor unrest. It didn't help that the economy had already been staggering along the edge of recession and the last jobs report was abysmal, showing higher than expected unemployment rates. The market tumbled, we took a hit...a big hit, but lately things have been turning around. I tried to explain this to Arnie, but he wasn't buying it."

Trautman nodded. "No, he definitely wasn't buying it. I can vouch for that. When you say lately things have been turning around, what do you mean?"

"I mean the situation in the Middle East has calmed down and tanker traffic is back to normal levels. Whatever animal they thought was becoming extinct because of the pipeline has been found thriving and the courts have ordered the pipeline open for business again. Inflation has stabilized and investor confidence has returned. I examined our portfolio and we've already recouped ten of the one hundred million that was lost. At the rate the market is trending upward, I think we'll have it all back and then some in about six months."

"Did Arnie know this?"

He nodded and said, "I reviewed the financial data coming in from the markets the night before he disappeared. I told him I was very optimistic for a full recovery."

"Well, that's good news anyway. At least there's a silver lining to this cloud," said Trautman. "Okay, everyone, here's the game plan. I'm appointing Brennan interim CEO pending Arnie's return, God-willing. The board will vote on it tonight, but I have every confidence they will support that decision. We need to have someone in charge. Brennan will consult with Dr. Cesari concerning medical issues. We can't have an accountant trying to run a hospital by himself. Now, for the second order of business...."

Cesari looked at him.

Trautman went on, "Before he disappeared, Arnie mentioned that an old woman with cancer being treated in our pain clinic may have been murdered and that one or more our doctors may be involved."

Cesari shook his head. "Not may have been murdered. She was definitely murdered. I just found that out myself. The autopsy report has returned, and the results are not in dispute, but there is no evidence that any of our doctors are involved."

"Not even the tiniest bit?"

"Only by inference. The cap of a syringe containing a controlled substance that is used in OR's everywhere was found at the scene, but there is no evidence that any of our physicians put it there."

He nodded. "And they all have rock-solid alibis, I presume."

"All but one, Jaskaran Singh. He was alone the night she died."

Trautman's eyes went wide. "So he may have done it?"

"Sure, and I may have done it or anybody in this room for that matter. Anybody that could figure out how to use a syringe could have done it."

"This is not a joking matter, Doctor."

"And neither is accusing someone of murder without evidence. He's a good man and deserves the benefit of the doubt, and there's plenty of doubt."

"Should we terminate him or at least remove him from patient care pending the outcome of the investigation?"

"Only if you want to send the signal out to the public that we think he may be guilty or that we're so spineless we'll throw anyone and everyone under the bus to protect our own asses, the truth be damned."

There was an uneasy silence after that which was eventually broken when Marjorie cleared her throat. She said, "This may be a good time to introduce you to the hospital's legal counsel, John." She turned to the mousy woman standing quietly off to the side. "John, this is Michele Kislovsky. She's an attorney at Goldblum, Finebaum, Meyer and Keith. The hospital has retained her firm to represent us in case the inquiry winds up with charges being filed."

The woman stepped forward to offer him her business card. He rose, took it, and shook her hand. She said, "I'm looking forward to working with you, Doctor. For the record, I agree with Mr. Trautman. I would cut this guy loose like driftwood. End of the PR problem for the hospital should it go in that direction."

Not mousy at all, thought Cesari but said nothing.

Trautman added, "In the coming days, we'll consider our options, okay? We need to stay ahead of this, Doctor. I'm sure you understand. Michele will also act as the spokesperson for St. Matt's with the press. Please defer to her at all times and let her do all the talking."

"I'll be sure to do that."

Michele Kislovsky added, "I would like to be kept in the loop on all matters concerning Dr. Goldstein's whereabouts and the case for or against the pain management doctors. I think we should meet or conference by phone at least twice daily to stay on the same page. In order to stay abreast of all the issues my firm has relieved me of my other responsibilities until the St. Matt's crisis has stabilized. In view of that, I will be setting up shop temporarily in an office here in the hospital on the third floor."

Cesari didn't react and simply said, "How nice."

"I knew you would see the wisdom of that. Coffee or tea?"

"What?"

"Do you prefer coffee or tea for our morning briefing?"

Cesari looked around the room for help and said, "Coffee, black and sweet."

"See you at 7:30 a.m. tomorrow morning. I'll expect a call from you today no later than 5:00 p.m. for my update. If anything comes up, call me sooner. You have my number. It's on my business card and I already got yours from Mr. Trautman."

Almost on cue, the meeting ended, and they filed out of the room. Marjorie Sunderheim lingered at the entrance after the others had left. She had something on her mind and closed the door once they were alone. She sat back down and signaled him to do the same.

She smiled and said, "That could have gone a little better, I suppose."

"You think? That made shock and awe seem tame by comparison."

"Leo's a cranky old man. You know that. Don't take him so seriously."

"I learned a long time ago not to take threats lightly, Marjorie, whether those threats are directed towards me or my friends."

She nodded. "He wasn't entirely wrong. From a public relations point of view we have a nightmare on our hands. The CEO of the hospital is missing. A hundred million dollars of hospital money has been lost and four of our physicians are being investigated for the murder of one of our patients. If any of this gets out our credit rating would tank. If all of it gets out, we'll sink like the Titanic. Leo is just trying to mitigate the damage."

"Well, you should make him aware that, while I'm sympathetic to his concerns, I'm not on board with sacrificing a fellow physician to protect St. Matt's image. So relay to him this personal message from me. If he terminates, suspends, or in any way impugns the reputation of one my physicians before the police conclude a meticulous and thorough investigation, I will quit. Then I will go right from this office to NBC studios news division and really make some noise."

Marjorie laughed. Apparently, she found him amusing. "Take a deep breath and don't be so hotheaded. I'll caution Leo to not overreact until we have all the facts. But that's not what I remained behind to talk to you about."

He took a deep breath and let it out. "And what about this lawyer you just sicced on me? I hope she doesn't think we're going to be best friends."

"I don't think she thinks that at all. She's here to help. She and her firm handle things like this all the time. Just give her a chance."

"Give her a chance? Does she really think I'm going to conference with her twice every day?"

"You'll work it out with her, I'm sure. Now, may I speak?"

He grinned. "I'm sorry, Marge. What did you want to talk about?"

"You're not a spring chicken, John. Forty is knocking on the front door whether you like to think about it or not."

"What's that supposed to mean?"

"How many chances at love do you think you're going to get in this life?"

"I see. We're talking about Valentina."

"Of course that's who we're talking about. She loves you, John. I have never seen anything like this in my entire life."

"I don't know about that. She's seems pretty happy with that hand surgeon she's dating. He's got a Lamborghini and six-pack abs. She told me so herself. He told me so too."

Marge laughed. "Joe Fusco? Please… She's just trying to make you jealous. It's you she wants. You're going to have to trust me on that one."

"Marge, we already tried it. It didn't work. She's really sweet and beautiful and I honestly do like her. But dating her is like dating…"

As he searched for the right word, Marge said, "Like dating crazy glue?"

Cesari concurred, "You took the words right out of my mouth. She's a very intense person."

"She's not like that with everyone, John. There's something about you that drives her wild. She is firmly convinced that you are her soul mate, and that you two are meant to be together."

"She scares me, Marge. On our first date, we went out to dinner. She had me walking down the aisle and picking out baby names before our entrees even arrived. That's pretty damn intense."

Marge smiled. "I agree. That is pretty intense. She can't seem to help herself when she's around you. I can tell you this. She doesn't feel that way about Fusco. I don't care what she's told you. They're just friends."

"I want to be nice to Valentina, but she's overpowering... and smothering...very smothering. You ever read that book, *Misery*?"

"The one where she breaks the guy's ankles so he can't leave her?"

"That's the one. When we were dating, I used to think about it all the time."

Marge laughed. "Oh, John, stop. You're exaggerating."

He smiled, "Only a little."

"Well, I'll leave you now. I know you have a lot of work and I've held you up too much already, but please think about it. You two are so damn cute together. All Fusco ever wants to do is look in the mirror. I swear. I've never met such a narcissist."

A few seconds after she left, his nurse Monica stuck her head in the doorway. She was frowning and said, "Are you going to see patients today or do you want to start another riot? They're starting to go wild again."

"I'll be right there."

Chapter 24

The last patient walked out the door at 5:30 p.m. and Cesari breathed a sigh of relief. He had been so far behind when he started that he was forced to skip lunch and see appointments right through. The trouble was that if he had to skip lunch then everyone else had to as well. Amy missed a nail appointment and Monica put off a trip to the supermarket as well as her cigarette break. To partially compensate them for the inconvenience, he ordered in pizza and soda. Monica wanted beer but that was against hospital policy.

He finished his paperwork and called Mrs. Goldstein. "Hi, Sylvia. How are you holding up?"

"Not very well, John," her voice quivered. "Have you heard from Arnie?"

"No, I haven't, but in some ways that's not necessarily a bad thing."

"You mean that he hasn't been found run over or shot?"

"Something like that. Sometimes no news is good news."

"I choose to be optimistic but it's very hard right now. My daughter is flying in tomorrow night and my son, the day after."

"That's good. You should have company."

"I'm staying at a neighbor's apartment tonight. I can't bear to be in our bed alone."

"That's understandable. On a positive note, I talked to a friend in the police department. He's a detective named Tierney.

He's opened a file on Arnie and will begin an investigation. He'd like to come over to your apartment tomorrow morning and interview you, if it's okay?"

Her spirits lifted at once as he introduced this ray of hope. "It's more than okay and I'm glad they're finally taking this seriously. But why the change of heart? I thought you said the police aren't usually interested in cases like this?"

"They aren't, but once I explained the details to him, he agreed that this isn't your run of the mill situation. Would you mind if we dropped by around 9:00 a.m.?"

"You're coming too?"

"Yes, if that's all right?"

"Of course it is. I can't thank you enough. Should I make breakfast?"

Cesari smiled. "That won't be necessary, but thank you."

"No, thank you," she replied emphatically.

He hung up, closed his laptop, and walked out of his office. He was all alone. No one moved faster than hospital employees at the end of the day. He glanced at his watch. It was 6:00 p.m. and he had agreed to pick Vito up at 8:00 p.m. using his Honda and the suitcoat over the head trick again. He dialed him to make sure they were still on, but the call went to voicemail. As he left the hospital, it crossed his mind that Jeremy and Parikh were just now sitting in some interrogation room being photographed, fingerprinted, and surrendering DNA samples.

Two days ago, he wouldn't have been concerned but two days ago Arnie wasn't missing, and it wasn't clear that anyone had actually been murdered. And two days ago, Parikh was just another big friendly guy, not a potential target for immigration law enforcement. Xi was mostly safe as was Jeremy, but Jaskaran was truly on the hot seat if there was any hint he was in that apartment complex that night or any other night for that matter. All it would take would be for one person in that building to look at his picture, scratch his head and say maybe.

Trautman would have a heart attack and want Jaskaran's head on a platter.

Cesari decided to go to the precinct to assess the situation and support his friends. He arrived there by taxi fifteen minutes later and told the woman officer behind the bullet proof glass he was a friend of Detective Tierney's. She checked and two minutes later, he was buzzed through into the main chamber. He walked through a metal detector and was guided to the interview room which was still in progress. He took a seat in a hard-plastic chair and waited while under observation of an officer and a variety of security cameras.

A few minutes later, the door opened and Jeremy came out looking none the worse for the experience. He smiled when he saw Cesari.

"How'd it go?" Cesari asked, shaking his hand.

"I thought it went well."

Tierney came up behind Jay and added, "He did fine. What are you doing here, Cesari? You're not his mother."

"I came down to make sure you weren't giving any of my staff the rubber hose treatment."

Tierney and Jay grinned. Tierney said, "Rubber hose? My God, Cesari. You watch too many old movies. We don't hit suspects with rubber hoses anymore. There are too many cameras around this place. The best way to convince someone to cooperate is to put him in lock-up for a night with fifteen other guys, one open-air metal toilet and no bed to sleep on. After an hour or two, they usually start to see things my way."

Cesari said, "You really are a sweet guy."

"I've been trying to tell you that... Okay, Dr. Macallan. Thank you for your time. If I need anything else, I know where to find you."

"Sure, no problem," replied Jay and then turned to Cesari. "I hope you didn't come all the way down here just for me?"

"You were part of the reason, and Parikh too, but I also needed to speak with the detective."

"Well, I wish I could stick around and chat, but I really have to run. My girlfriend's waiting for me, and given what happened the other night, I better not keep her waiting."

Cesari laughed. "I understand perfectly, Jay. That's why I never settled down. Too many rules and expectations, but it's okay. You have a great weekend."

"You too."

He walked away and Tierney said, "What happened the other night?"

"Me and him had one too many glasses of wine. Mostly him. I had to practically carry him into his girlfriend's apartment. She was not very pleased."

Tierney shook his head. "You're a bad influence, Cesari... Where's Parikh? He's late."

Cesari glanced at his watch. "Give him a chance. You have any coffee around here?"

"Nothing that qualifies as a latte, but I'm sure I can find you something. Come with me..."

As they walked to find a coffee machine, Cesari asked, "No problem with Macallan?"

"Should there be?"

"None whatsoever. Just making small talk."

"So to what do I owe the honor of this visit, Cesari?"

They stopped in front of a counter with an industrial strength coffee maker and a half-filled glass pot sitting on a burner. "First off, I set up the appointment with Mrs. Goldstein tomorrow morning at nine. She was greatly relieved to hear that the NYPD was taking an interest in her husband's disappearance."

"Just doing my job, Cesari."

"Not really. You're doing me a favor so thank you for that."

Tierney looked at him for a minute and then said, "You're not going to start crying with joy or try to hug me, are you? Because I'll tell you right now, if you do anything that even vaguely smacks of homoerotica, I will, and have no doubt about it, throw you in the holding tank for the night with ten or twelve of the biggest and horniest MS-13 members I can round up."

Cesari laughed. "Have no fear on that score and I would expect no less."

Tierney poured them bad coffee into small foam cups, and they sat at a small metal table. Tierney said, "All right, Cesari, what's on your mind? You could have called me about the appointment with Mrs. Goldstein tomorrow. You didn't have to come down here."

Cesari said, "I know that. Something came up at the hospital today and I just thought it would be easier to discuss it in person."

"I'm all ears, Doctor."

"Well, the possibility that Arnie might have committed suicide was raised by one of the board members this morning. I hadn't considered that and was curious to see what your view on the subject might be."

Tierney sipped his coffee and winced at its bitterness. He mulled over the question for a bit and said, "Suicide's always a possibility but vanishing into thin air in the middle of the afternoon doesn't quite fit with that. And you never mentioned anything about a suicide note. They almost always leave one especially for their loved ones. They want to explain themselves and their actions. They want everyone to understand."

Cesari nodded. "As far as I know there isn't any note unless it's on his computer waiting to be found."

"Or coming by snail mail," countered Tierney. "It happens once in a while, but that's very unusual. For a guy like Arnie it would have been in a tender, loving card, handwritten and filled with emotion."

Cesari nodded again. "You're right about that. Still, we should take a look at his computer. I used the one in his office the other day but only to do an internet search. We should check it more thoroughly."

"Can't hurt, but that's probably just a work computer, right? He probably has one for personal use at home. Are you going to ask his wife if you can search their personal computer for a suicide note? That might be kind of harsh. We don't even know that he's dead."

Cesari thought it over and said, "That's a very good point. She's already stressed out enough. But I could just say we're looking for clues. There's no need to embellish it, and we really are doing just that."

"That sounds a lot nicer for sure, but I doubt we'll come up with anything either on his home PC or his office workstation. Let's be realistic, Cesari. Arnie made an appointment at the SEC. According to you, he was all hot under the collar to blow in that financial guy. He had lunch and a pleasant phone chat with his wife just prior to leaving the hospital to go to that appointment. It seems highly improbable that on the way he would suddenly decide to end his life."

They batted it around like that until Parikh walked into the station house almost an hour late for his interview. Tierney nudged Cesari and under his breath said, "Holy shit. He really is nine feet tall."

Cesari whispered back, "Knock it off. He's sensitive about his height. Everybody's always ribbing him about it."

Parikh saw Tierney, walked over, and bowed apologetically. "I am sorry for my lack of punctuality, sir. Good evening, Dr. Cesari."

"Take it easy with the bowing, Doctor," Tierney said. "We don't bow and scrape to anyone in this country."

"Except maybe to our wives," laughed Cesari. Never having been wed made him somewhat less than an expert in the area of marital harmony but it was always fun to bash the institution.

Parikh smiled, "It's funny what you say, sir, because that is the reason for my tardiness. My wife insisted I vacuum the living room before my appointment with the detective. I tried to explain to her the importance of this visit, but she would not yield."

Tierney stared at him in astonishment and then looked at Cesari, and said, "Is this guy for real?"

Cesari grinned, "He's for real, all right."

Parikh looked confused. "Of course I am for real, sir. What else could I be, a robot?"

Cesari shot Tierney a private look and mimed the words, "I told you."

Tierney nodded, stared at Parikh some more and finally said, "Come with me, Doctor. I have a feeling this won't take too long. I'll see you tomorrow, Cesari."

Chapter 25

About a half mile from Vito's apartment, Cesari said, "You can come out now."

Vito took his suit jacket off his head and shoulders and propped his seat up. He said, "This is starting to get irritating."

"Just starting?" Cesari laughed. "You've got a lot more patience than I would have guessed. Do you do something like this every single time you leave your apartment or just on special occasions?"

"Not every time. If we were just going out to eat, I wouldn't care too much."

Cesari drove the car over to the West Side, navigating through some side streets as the neighborhoods got increasingly run down and sparsely populated. He eventually reached a section of abandoned factories and warehouses.

Vito said, "Over there… The building with the garage door open."

He pointed toward the middle of the block where two of his men were standing guard outside. Cesari drove the Honda into the warehouse and the door closed behind them. He pulled the car to a stop just a few feet from another car covered with a protective cloth. Vito's men hustled to his side of the car and opened the door for him. He stepped out, put his suit jacket on and brushed his hair back.

"Any problems?" he asked.

The two guys were big. One was just fat and round, the other was muscular and large like a linebacker. They were well-dressed and groomed. Vito would not tolerate anything less.

The linebacker shook his head and said, "Nothing doing, Vito. All quiet on the Western Front."

"Good. Take the tarp off the car and let's see what we have."

The two men ran to the front of the car, grabbed an end on either side and pulled the cover off, letting it fall to the floor at the rear of the Rolls.

Vito whistled. "Man, this is some car."

Cesari was in absolute awe. It was the kind of car that was fit for nobility or the Great Gatsby. It was a nineteen feet long, four seat, two-door convertible, white-walled tires, royal blue in color with wood veneer panels on the twin trunk doors that opened from the sides inward dividing the trunk into two compartments. The doors swung open from the front to the back in an old-fashioned style. The designer was trying to achieve the feel of a vintage yacht or cigarette boat from the 1920's. Cesari felt small and unworthy as he walked around it eventually lingering in the front to study the classic grill and *Spirit of Ecstasy* traditional Rolls Royce hood ornament.

"I did some additional research last night, Cesari. I lied when I said it was worth twenty-five million dollars. It's closer to forty million."

"And it was stolen before Gerry stole it. That does raise some interesting possibilities."

"I'll say. It raises the ransom price by quite a bit. I was originally thinking one or two million but now I wouldn't accept a penny less than five."

"What if he screams foul?"

"He won't. We have too much ammunition. We know about what's been going on down at the port. Besides, he probably has a buyer already lined up and hot to drive his new car around. He's not going to want to disappoint the guy."

"What kind of security do you have keeping an eye on it?"

"Aside from the fact that we're in a deserted warehouse in a skanky part of town with padlocked doors, I have three teams of two guys rotating at eight-hour intervals standing guard."

Cesari nodded. "That's a lot of man hours you're devoting to this project."

"I can't imagine it will take more than a few days to negotiate a deal. When it's all said and done, I'll have Gerry drop the car off so me and my guys can stay clear."

"What about the money? Five million is a lot in cash. Too dangerous. A lot could happen."

Vito nodded. "Yeah, I agree. It's too much. I'll have it wired to an offshore account in the Caymans. Once the transaction is confirmed, I'll give him the car."

"And you trust Gerry?"

Vito laughed. "Of course not. We'll be following him. Personally, he's too small time to think outside the box. For the record, this is a nice payday for him. In addition to his finder's fee, I plan on waving the ten grand I gave him to pick up the first Rolls Royce, and as an added bonus, I'm willing to overlook his incompetence in that fiasco."

"That's very generous of you, but as long as we're speaking of Gerry…"

"Just a few more days, Cesari. I can't have him stay with me. He's too disruptive, and I can't have him running around a hotel in Manhattan shooting his mouth off."

Cesari sighed and said wryly, "Great."

Vito took out his cellphone, turned on the camera, and began snapping photos of the Rolls from multiple angles. When he was done, he said, "Okay, let's see if Hugo wants to play ball."

"Won't he be able to trace your phone potentially?"

"He can try. I picked this one up at Walgreens this morning. I'll get a new one tomorrow and so on. One step ahead of you as always, Cesari."

He messaged the images of the Rolls to Hugo using the number that Alan Chamberlain, the Mercedes dealer, had provided.

They waited as the pixels on the phone were converted to electronic particles, sucked up invisibly through cyber space, and delivered to the recipient on the other end of the line.

Five minutes later, a text message from Hugo buzzed on the phone. It read, "Who is this?"

Vito replied via text, "Hey Hugo, do you want your car back?"

"Of course."

"Five million dollars. Run it by your boss. Then stay tuned for instructions. Don't call this number. I don't need to hear your voice and you don't need to hear mine. I'll give you till morning to make up your mind or I call Rolls Royce and ask them if they're missing one of their cars."

Vito added a smiley face to the end of his last text and then turned the phone off. Cesari said, "I like the way you kept control of the conversation."

"He's just a soldier and I wanted him to know that I know that."

"What now?"

"Now we wait."

****

Hugo sat in the back of the limousine pondering the text messages he had just received. The tone was confident, knowledgeable and quite serious. Whoever it was knew the Rolls was already stolen. How could he have known that? He also knew his name and cellphone number and that he worked for someone higher up the food chain. Also a puzzle. He was dealing with a well-informed, very confident adventurer.

He called the Sommelier, "Michel, I have found your car."

"Tell me, Hugo."

Hugo forwarded him the text messages from Vito and after a few minutes to digest their contents, the Sommelier spoke, "Tell him yes to the five million. It is a small price to pay. Besides, it's not like he is going to live long enough to enjoy the fruit of his labor. The security guards from the port are being brought to me as we speak and then we will know the identity of this thief in the night."

"How did he know all those things?"

"Clearly, we have a leak somewhere. The fact that the Rolls was already stolen might have been an educated guess based on the misleading packaging invoice and the fact that it is unusual to ship cars overseas in containers like that. But knowing your name and cellphone number and that you are employed by someone else is another matter. Intimate details like that could only have come from within our ranks. Someone is trying to cash in on such knowledge. I will think about it. In the meanwhile, play along with him."

They hung up and Hugo glanced at his timepiece. He waited two more hours and exited from the back of the limo. He was dressed all in black and wore surgical gloves as he entered the building and found the apartment he was looking for. He glanced furtively in all directions. It was late but not that late. He retrieved the tools from his pocket and crouched as he picked the lock. He was on the third floor of an old apartment building on East 11th Street just off First Avenue. Other than the recent, unsettling text messages, the day had gone much more smoothly than he had anticipated. He had been welcomed by the staff at the oncology center like a breath of fresh air. They had taken him under their wing and merrily walked him through the process of patient care. Several of the nurses had told him that it was about time the pharmaceutical companies started thinking of the patients and their families as people and not just statistics. Those in the waiting room eagerly told him their stories, their problems, their concerns, their fears. He was a good listener. Help was on the way he told them.

That was where he met Murray. Murray was the only patient there without family because he had none. What he had was prostate cancer that had spread to his bones that, so far, was only causing him moderate discomfort but not necessarily extreme pain. Still, it was enough that he required analgesics and the occasional epidural injection. He'd undergone total prostatectomy several years earlier, but the cancer had returned and metastasized. Eventually he had been referred to the pain clinic where they treated him well. He was divorced and his wife was but a distant memory, having left him for another man thirty years earlier. He had no children and his only sibling, a sister, had died two years earlier. He was living out his days in a low rent apartment on the East Side, going for palliation and pain management once every week.

He didn't mind really. The treatments did help, and he got to meet other patients who had cancer. It was a great way of socializing and he actually looked forward to the appointments. He had made it to seventy-five years of age. That was more than his father who had died of a heart attack at sixty. Poor guy. He had worked hard his whole life to support their family, and just on the cusp of retirement, went down like a rock buying a cup of coffee and a bagel.

Today was a good day for Murray. Better than most. The monotony of the visit to the cancer center had been broken by the presence of the young man from Pfizer. Such a nice young man. Well-dressed and clean shaven. Respectful and polite. You hardly ever saw that anymore. He was interested in Murray's story from start to finish and not just the side effects of the treatments or out of pocket costs for his care. He wanted to know every detail of his life. What he ate for breakfast, who he ate with, what he did in his spare time, who he did it with. What time did he go to bed? Things of that nature. He was so damn nice that Murray had given him his address. The nice young man had promised to pick him up for breakfast in the morning and maybe play a game of chess with him in Washington Square Park to get to know him even better. You didn't get nicer than that.

It was almost midnight, the door slid open without a sound, and Hugo stepped inside. The old man was undoubtedly asleep in his bed, but he had brought chloroform anyway. He couldn't have him struggling at just the wrong moment. He wanted everything to appear just as it had with the first patient, down to the wayward syringe cap with propofol. Only this syringe cap would have Dr. Goldstein's fingerprints on it. Once he was done here, he would go to Goldstein's office and add the finishing touch. The piece-de-resistance as they say. If he had time, he might even drive uptown to Goldstein's own apartment to gild the lily. But only if he had time. It was getting late, and he still had much to do.

Then he would release Dr. Goldstein back into the wild like on some nature show. But first things first. He scanned around the dimly lit apartment. The old man had several night lights on to prevent him from tripping in the dark. Once acclimated, Hugo had no trouble navigating the small room. The bedroom door was ajar and he slipped inside. There was the small figure of a man lying face up under the covers, breathing quietly. Hugo went around to the right side of the bed and took the bottle of chloroform and rag out from the bag he had with him.

Showtime.

Chapter 26

A t 2:00 a.m., the limo cut its lights and pulled into an alley in a seedy part of town. They were only six blocks east of St. Matt's but in lower Manhattan the landscape changed drastically every quarter of a mile. They might as well have been on the moon, the difference between the two neighborhoods was that extreme. This area was dominated by denizens of the night; the homeless and the hopeless; drug addicts and hookers. The East Side of Manhattan adjacent to the FDR drive at night was the live version of the dark web. It was where people went to be swallowed up by corruption and to wallow in their own sins.

The alley was dark and deserted. Refuse, rats and dumpsters. Hugo got out and went to the rear of the vehicle. Still wearing the surgical gloves, he glanced in both directions and popped the trunk. Arnie lay curled up, snoring in nothing but his underwear. Hugo reached into his pockets and came out with a bottle of propofol and a syringe. He wrapped Arnie's hands around both items and then drew up most of the liquid into the syringe and stuck the needle into one of the veins of the sleeping man's right arm. He injected just enough to ensure he remained comatose but not enough to kill him, although from what he had learned, that last part could be a bit of a crap shoot. It all depended on the person's cardiopulmonary system and whether or not it was compromised by underlying disease or poor conditioning. He then tossed the needle and the bottle to the ground, picked Arnie up and dropped him unceremoniously next to the drug paraphernalia. He looked down admiringly at his handiwork. Hugo considered himself an artist in his own way.

"Hey man, what are you doing?"

Hugo spun around quickly. A crack addict who had been sleeping behind a dumpster stood three feet away. Long disheveled hair, unkempt and emaciated, the man could not have weighed more than a hundred and thirty pounds, less than half Hugo's weight. He reeked worse than raw sewage. Hugo's mind raced at the new development. The crackhead's brain was addled but he had seen Hugo's face and the license plate. There was no telling what if anything he would or could remember.

Like a provoked tiger, Hugo reacted instantly and without hesitation. He stepped forward and with his left hand grabbed the man by the throat and squeezed hard. The man struggled weakly and futilely, his eyes bulging, his hands flailing. Hugo was a large and powerful man and had no trouble immobilizing the malnourished wreck of a human being in his grasp. With his right-hand Hugo fished out a four-inch stiletto from his pocket, flicked it open, and stabbed the man in the forehead with great force. The knife pierced skin, bone and gray matter up to its hilt, and the man went limp. The tragic scene was over in seconds.

Hugo removed his knife and cleaned it on the man's shirt before tucking it back away. It was a quiet death and a quick one. There are much worse ways to go, Hugo mused as he lifted the corpse and dumped it into the trunk of the limo. He briefly considered leaving it right there next to Arnie but felt that would complicate things too much. If he was discovered, no one would believe that Arnie would have stabbed a man in the forehead. That would go against the angel of mercy theme they were trying to promote, and what about the weapon? He couldn't leave it there. It had been custom made for him. The engravings on the handle were unique and possibly traceable. No, much too complicated. He would have to get rid of the body.

No rest for the weary, he thought as he settled on a course of action. He stared at the lifeless body and felt no remorse.

The man had wasted his life. No one's fault but his own. He would bring the body to the meadowlands in New Jersey. At least there, he will do some good. He will decompose, providing nourishment for plant life. Those plants will produce oxygen and nutrition for other living things. The environment will benefit greatly from his death. He might even run into Jimmy Hoffa.

Hugo slammed the trunk closed and smiled.

****

Cesari rang the buzzer and waited. It was 9:00 a.m. Saturday morning and he and Detective Tierney held coffee cups with plastic lids on them. Cesari said, "Can I ask where Parikh stands on your suspect list now that you've met him?"

Tierney shook his head and chuckled. "You were right. That guy couldn't hurt a fly. Not only was he late for his interview because his wife made him vacuum the living room, she told him that he'd better not waste too much time with me because when he got home she had more chores for him. He mentioned something about emptying the dishwasher and folding the laundry. Personally, I think he needs domestic abuse counseling."

Cesari whistled. "It's even worse there than I thought."

"You're telling me? My assessment of him is that if he was going to kill anybody, he'd start with his wife. On a scale of one to ten, where ten is Charles Manson and one is Dolly Parton, I rate him a minus two in the potential killer department."

"That's good to know, and his immigration status?"

"I told him to get working on his renewal application for his green card and gave him a number to call. I doubt it will be a problem. I'm telling you, Cesari. By the time we were done I was feeling so sorry for the guy, I almost offered him to come stay with me for a few days to decompress."

Cesari let out a sigh of relief at the change in attitude, and as he reached to press the buzzer again, the door swung open and Sylvia stood there. She didn't smile and appeared haggard and tired from stress. She wore a bathrobe and slippers, and had made no attempt to put herself together. She was thin, frail and pale, and Cesari wondered if she had slept or eaten at all in the last few days.

Cesari said, "Good morning, Sylvia. This is Detective Tierney."

She nodded and said quietly, "Good morning to you both. Please come in."

They entered a nice upper West Side apartment with a great view. Easily the size of Cesari's unfinished, no-frills loft, but closer to five or six times the rent money. But it was a thousand times more pleasing to the eye with a large well-furnished living room, kitchen and formal dining room. The balcony was spacious enough for a small table and a couple of chairs. Sylvia had exquisite taste which was reflected in the furniture, wall coverings, and years of fine tuning the decorations and other smaller accent features.

They sat at the kitchen table and Tierney said, "I'm sorry we have to meet under these circumstances, Mrs. Goldstein. I also have to apologize in advance for some of the questions I need to ask."

"Thank you and I understand. I doubt that you could say anything worse than what half of my neighbors and even some of my own family have suggested. Between television and the internet, everyone's imagination has been working overtime."

Tierney smiled politely and Cesari sipped his coffee as he glanced around. Tierney took a small notebook from the inside pocket of his jacket and placed it on the table along with a pen he had brought with him.

"Mrs. Goldstein…"

"Sylvia, Detective. Please…"

"Sylvia, Dr. Cesari has filled me in on the basics. I know your husband has been missing now for over forty-eight hours and the last time you spoke to him was around noon on the day he disappeared. Is that correct?"

"Yes, it is. More like twelve-thirty, if it matters."

"How did he seem to you?"

"He was fine, a little jittery perhaps, like butterflies in his stomach, over his afternoon appointment at the SEC. I could tell from his voice."

"And that appointment was concerning his feeling that the investment company he gave the hospital's money to was possibly swindling him?"

"Yes, it was, although swindling is too strong a word."

"What word would you use?"

"Arnie was leaning toward incompetence more than criminal theft. You know, mishandling of the money...plain old stupidity."

"I see. Did he have any evidence to support that claim?"

She shook her head. "No, not really, but Arnie was never good with numbers. I pay all the bills and balance our check book. It was just a feeling he had that something wasn't right. It seemed like too large a sum to just disappear into the void in too quick of a time period. Plus, it bothered him that the financial company didn't seem in the least bit concerned. They had sort of an easy come, easy go attitude which irked Arnie to no end. He felt they should have been upset. At least that was Arnie's take on it. It was their laissez-faire attitude that made him feel something was wrong more than anything else."

Tierney jotted down a few notes. "So he was a little jittery on that day, but how was he in the days leading up to that appointment?"

"He was uncertain if he was doing the right thing. He was concerned it might cause a scandal for the hospital and perhaps tarnish his reputation."

"Was he depressed?"

She nodded. "I think so... A little. Who wouldn't be? He spent his whole career at St. Matt's. It bothered him a great deal that his final act was to lead them into economic ruination."

"Is it possible that he might have felt so responsible for the loss of the hospital's money that he might have…despaired?"

"You're trying to be kind. Thank you. But if you mean do I think Arnie was suicidal, then the answer is definitely not. When he wasn't fuming about that man, Beaujolais, he was looking forward to retirement and maybe moving to the West Coast to be with our grandchildren."

"Who's Beaujolais?"

Cesari said, "He's the financial guy I told you about. Arnie used him to invest the hospital's money. His company is called Fidelity Financial Services and is headquartered in New Jersey."

Tierney sipped his coffee and wrote that down. He said, "Sylvia, was your husband happy? I mean in general terms."

She thought about it. "I think so. When you've been married for as long as we have you don't always think of things in black and white terms like that."

"Let me put it another way then. Was Arnie ever unfaithful to you?"

She lowered her eyes, and it took her a minute to respond to that. Eventually, she shook her head and said, "No, never. I would swear to it."

"There's no chance in the world that he purposely chose to not return home?"

She shook her head again even more vigorously. "I don't believe that for a minute."

"And no enemies?"

"There have been minor disagreements on occasion with other tenants, the sporadic family squabbles, and the endless hospital politics but all of those combined wouldn't amount to a hill of beans."

"What about places he liked to go such as night clubs, theatres, bars?"

"We went everywhere together, and after a lifetime, the number of places would be too numerous to rattle off. Certainly he liked museums, Broadway shows, the opera, and he loved to eat out. I don't know that I can be more specific other than we didn't go to many bars unless they had a nice dining room attached."

"Any friends, male or female?"

"Just people from work. He liked John here more than most, probably more than anyone else in the hospital. He spoke of you often, John."

Cesari nodded and Tierney continued, "Has anything unusual happened recently or odd that maybe caused you to be concerned?"

She shook her head. "Not really. My door was unlocked this morning if that counts. I slept at a friend's last night to not be alone, and when I returned, the door was open. At first, I was excited because I thought Arnie had come home, but he wasn't here. Under normal circumstances, that would have rattled me because I never forget to lock the door, but I've been under so much stress and so distracted the last few days that I chalked it up to that."

"Was anything disturbed when you entered the apartment?" asked Tierney.

"No, nothing that I could tell, and nothing was missing. I guess it was just a mental lapse on my part."

Tierney let out a deep breath before saying, "Sylvia, a moment ago I asked you if Arnie had ever been unfaithful to you and you hesitated before replying. Why is that?"

Sylvia stared at him and then turned her gaze to Cesari. Her eyes welled up and she sniffled. "Arnie was never unfaithful... but I was. Once, a long time ago. Arnie forgave me."

Tearful, she started weeping uncontrollably. Cesari and Tierney waited patiently. After a minute, Cesari said, "Sylvia, we're sorry for bringing up painful memories."

She nodded and whispered, "I understand it has to be done. You're just trying to figure out what happened and need to know all the dirty laundry, but that was it. The last thirty years have been unblemished as far as I know. If he was harboring ill will toward me, he never let it show and never brought it up ever as a reproach."

Tierney said, "Did Arnie have a private room or study? I'd like to see it."

"He did. Arnie converted one of the bedrooms into an office to work from home. It's cluttered as badly as his office in the hospital. I'll show it to you."

They followed her across the living room to a twelve by fifteen-foot room with a desk, a swivel chair, several filing cabinets, bookcases, and its own closet and bathroom. The desk was a jumble of paperwork, manila folders, medical books, pens, pencils, notepads and a laptop. Arnie was a perpetually busy guy. On the floor were boxes of papers and more folders, maybe a dozen or so.

"Do you mind if we poke around?" asked Tierney.

"Not at all."

Cesari said, "May I peek at his laptop, Sylvia? He may have had an appointment no one knew anything about or some type of correspondence that could hint at his whereabouts."

She nodded enthusiastically. "Anything that will help. His username is Goldstein, and his password is *I love my wife!* with a capital I and an exclamation point at the end. I'll write it down for you."

She went to the desk, found a piece of paper and a pen and jotted it down. As she handed it to Cesari, she added, "His laptop is networked into the hospital's system. He uses the same username and password there as well. Arnie likes to keep things simple."

"It might take a while to examine it thoroughly. Would you mind if I borrowed it so I could take my time?"

"You can take anything you want. Just bring my husband back to me."

Cesari nodded. "Thank you, Sylvia. We'll try not to disturb the room too much."

"I'm going to put on some tea while you do that. Let me know if you find anything."

Tierney sat at the desk and started sifting through the myriad of papers and then the desk drawers looking for clues. Cesari packed up the laptop in its case to review later. He then began scanning the bookshelves and the contents of the boxes hoping to find anything that might shed some light on the situation.

After a few minutes Tierney said, "You better look at this, Cesari."

Cesari came over to the desk where Tierney had pulled out the lower drawer and moved aside a bunch of papers, revealing four small bottles containing milky white liquid and an assortment of hypodermic needles.

Tierney said, "Is that what I think it is?"

Cesari knelt down to get a better look. He nodded and said, "It's propofol."

Chapter 27

Sylvia was cooperative, albeit confused, as Tierney presented her with a warrant for the propofol and syringes. He had gone down to his car and phoned a judged who gave him verbal approval and faxed his signature. Tierney bagged up the items with gloved hands and tried his best to reassure Sylvia that everything he was doing was routine. The problem was that no matter how you cut it Arnie wasn't just a missing person anymore. He was possibly a fugitive from justice.

On the way back downtown to search Arnie's office, Tierney said, "Didn't expect that, did you, Cesari?"

"No, I didn't. There has to be some logical explanation."

"When you find one, please tell me. Just the other day, your friend Arnie told me that no one other than anesthesia personnel should be handling that stuff, and they should be doing so only in a hospital setting. Yet, he has it in his home along with syringes."

"Arnie didn't kill anyone, Detective."

"And I want to believe you, but look at what we found. You better face it, Cesari. There's a distinct possibility that Arnie is missing because he's on the run."

"I just can't believe that."

They arrived at St. Matt's, and as Tierney jockeyed for a spot in the hospital's parking lot, Cesari's phone buzzed. He picked it up and said, "Hello."

"Dr. Cesari, this is Michele Kislovsky, St. Matt's attorney. Remember me?"

"Hi Michele, of course I remember you. What can I do for you?"

"You didn't call me last night and you missed our briefing this morning in my office."

He was silent for a minute. Apparently, she had been very serious about all the updating and conferencing. He said, "I'm sorry… Today is Saturday. I thought you meant beginning on Monday during the regular work week."

"I see. No, I meant effective immediately. So what have you got for me?"

Cesari didn't feel comfortable with telling her about the propofol in Arnie's apartment. He barely knew her and from what he had seen, he guessed she would throw Arnie overboard at the first sign of trouble.

He said, "Nothing at all. There have been no changes since I saw you yesterday morning in my office."

"Anybody from the press try to contact you?"

"No, they haven't or at least I'm unaware of it. They can be pretty stealthy."

"Don't I know it, and that's my reason for wanting you to stay in close contact with me. These guys don't play fair and we can't afford to let our guard down. What about Arnie and the investigation of our anesthesiologists?"

"Status quo," he lied again. "If I hear anything, you'll be the first to know."

"Okay, Doctor, I'll let you go and I forgive you for missing our meeting this morning. In retrospect I can see the misunderstanding. I pride myself on being clear but perhaps in this instance I wasn't."

"Forget about it. I don't hold grudges."

"I'm glad to hear that. My door is always open. I'll be here all weekend."

"Here?" he asked. "Where?"

"In my office in St. Matt's. I brought a cot to sleep on."

"Is that necessary?"

"We're at war, Dr. Cesari. You may not realize this, but there are those out there who love to take pot shots at hospitals and providers. They look for any reason to take down the healthcare system no matter how unjustified that reason may be. My goal is to nip that in the bud any way I can. To do that I have to be on the forefront of any and all that happens here at St. Matt's. I would love to discuss counter-attack measures with you some time. I have a few ideas how we can silence critics if it comes to it."

Not mousy at all, thought Cesari. He said, "Does it involve blood?"

She laughed. "Now we're talking."

"Well, I'd love to hear your thoughts on the subject."

"Okay, we'll talk later. Say fiveish?"

He thought about that. Valentina had invited him and Georgina out on a double date. He had said Georgina was away for the weekend, but there was no Georgina, and therefore no real reason he couldn't take someone else. It might help convince Valentina that he was doing quite well in the romance department. In fact, if he brought someone else, she might think he was a real player. His main girl was unavailable, so he effortlessly substituted a replacement, a lawyer no less, the hospital's attorney and mouthpiece for the press. Technically, she was way up the food chain. That should keep Valentina in check for a while. Cesari laughed to himself. He loved this idea, but he needed to do some prep work with the lawyer.

He said, "Do you like to eat?"

"Are you kidding? When I'm in battle-mode like this I burn calories like an Olympic athlete."

"Maybe we could have dinner sometime, my treat?"

She hesitated for a minute and then said, "It's not a date, right? That would be a conflict of interest. I'm not saying it's on my agenda right now, but there may come a time when I have to recommend to the board that you be terminated for the good of the hospital."

"I appreciate your frankness, and no, it's not a date. Heaven forbid. We need to conference on a regular basis. We might as well do it while we're eating. The way you're burning calories you could become malnourished."

"Okay, then. We'll call it a business expense and I'll pay."

"Even better."

"I'm sorry for being so blunt, but I believe in laying all my cards on the table so there can be no misunderstandings, and…"

"And what?"

"Well I saw the way you looked at me in your office yesterday morning, and I hate to burst your bubble, but you don't do anything for me. I'm not into that Italian Stallion stuff. I know that schtick works with some women, but not me. I have an older sister who's really into the macho types. Play your cards right and I might consider introducing you. Serves her right. We never really got along. Did I mention she was valedictorian? Anyway, no hard feelings, all right?"

"None at all, and trust me, it will be purely professional."

"Fine, when and where?"

"I'll get back to you. Obviously, everything is very fluid right now."

"No problem."

He hung up and joined Tierney who was already standing outside the car waiting for him. He said, "I'm sorry for holding you up, Detective. It was an urgent call."

"No worries, Cesari. And I'm sorry if you didn't understand the sudden urgency that has just overtaken this investigation. You see, that tends to happen when one of our prime suspects suddenly disappears. Other than that, feel free to take your time."

"Trust me, Detective. If Arnie is your prime suspect, then you need to reevaluate your investigatory skills."

"Let's go to his office and see what's on his laptop, Cesari. Maybe we'll find a confession that he forgot to print out and mail to the police."

They entered the hospital, took the elevators to the tenth floor and found Arnie's office. The door was still unlocked, and they let themselves in. Cesari sat in Arnie's chair and powered up both the laptop and his work terminal. They waited patiently as the machines went through their pre-startup up rituals of loading software and checking connections, memory, and system integrity.

Cesari logged onto both devices with Tierney staring over his shoulder. The first thing he did was pull up Arnie's various email accounts and browse through them going back a week. His work email was mostly ordinary stuff relating to the management of the hospital. There were several exchanges with various department heads concerning run of the mill issues such as staffing, a multitude of emails concerning an upcoming state inspection, and several communiques with maintenance over air conditioning problems in the recovery room. His personal email was even less exciting. It was tedious and mundane work, but had to be done. Certainly there was nothing suspicious, like a threat from a disgruntled employee or a love letter from a girlfriend or a request from a sick patient to come to her apartment and put her out of her misery.

After reviewing the emails, he opened the web browsers and going back and forth between the two screens, studied Arnie's internet history. He was relieved when he didn't find any recent porn surfing activity. It did look like he may have been considering a vacation to Hawaii with Sylvia the following year, perhaps for their anniversary.

Tierney said, "That's interesting."

"What is?"

"Arnie was looking into vacation getaways."

"What's your point?"

"Who was he interested in getting away with?"

"Give me a break. There was nothing in his emails that suggested he even pursued this beyond a casual search in his spare time. He didn't receive any emails confirming he booked a flight or a hotel or anything, not even additional information."

"Relax, Cesari. I'd rather we find out he flew the coop with a nineteen-year-old girl than murdered anyone. Let me take a look. I think you're too biased."

Cesari stood up and allowed Tierney to sit in front of the computers. For the next forty-five minutes they poured over every folder and file they could find. They went through directories and subdirectories. There were a lot of directories and a lot of subdirectories. Tierney eventually sat back in the chair and let out a deep breath.

"Is it noon yet? I could use a drink."

Cesari grinned. "He keeps a bottle of bourbon and two glasses in the bottom right drawer."

Tierney opened the drawer and looked inside. He reached down and came out with the bottle of bourbon but when he went to retrieve the glasses, he stopped short, seemed surprised, and said, "Oh shit…"

Cesari came close and looked. There were five bottles of propofol and a couple of syringes set deep in the drawer behind where the bourbon had been. Echoing the sentiment, he agreed, "Oh shit…"

"Your boy has a lot of explaining to do and now I have to get another warrant."

"This doesn't make any sense. I looked in that drawer less than two days ago. There wasn't any propofol in there."

"Did you move the bottle of bourbon like I did? It wasn't readily visible at first."

Cesari hesitated and then said, "No, I didn't."

"I'm sorry, Cesari, but Arnie's missing for a reason, and I think I know what that is."

Cesari's phone buzzed, and he looked down at the screen. It was Rhonda in the ER. He answered it, "Hi, Rhonda. What's up?"

"It's Arnie. He's here in the ER."

Chapter 28

The ER was in an uproar as word sifted around that Arnie had finally made an appearance. Cesari found Rhonda first to see what was going on. She was on the phone at the nursing station and waved when she spotted him. She hung up just as he and Tierney arrived.

Cesari said, "Rhonda, this is Detective Tierney of the NYPD. He was looking into what happened to Arnie."

She smiled and shook hands with Tierney. "Nice to meet you."

Tierney replied, "Likewise."

Cesari said, "So what happened?"

She said, "Your guess is as good as mine. He walked in off the street, disheveled, naked, and babbling. He was very confused and dirty like he had been lying in filth."

"Jesus," Cesari said. "Naked?"

"Mostly, he had on a pair of boxers."

"That's close enough. Any injuries?"

She shook her head. "No, and so far, no signs of anything medically wrong. No fever... His vital signs are stable and we're waiting for his bloodwork. He was dehydrated so I hooked him up to an IV for fluids. I'm also giving him a couple of doses of broad-spectrum antibiotics too just in case he has an occult infection somewhere. His EKG and portable chest x-ray were negative and he's not complaining of anything in particular. He doesn't know where he's been for the last forty-eight hours or how he got there, but he's been telling some whoppers about his experience wherever he was. If I didn't know better, I'd say he was tripping on LSD. He wants to speak to the FBI and the police. We cleaned him up as best we could, and I was just on the phone with radiology. They're going to bring him over for a head CT to rule out a stroke or a bleed or even a tumor. Then we'll need to get neurology and psychiatry to see him."

"Did you call his wife?"

"Yes, she's on the way down as we speak. Why don't you go in and say hello? He's been asking for you. When he's not ranting about his recent experiences, he's pretty lucid. He's in room 7. He'll be happy to see you too, Detective. I'll be over in a few minutes."

Outside room 7 was a gaggle of nurses and doctors humming and speculating about Arnie. It wasn't everyday a doctor and CEO showed up naked exhibiting signs of delirium. He could forgive their nervous energy. The door to Arnie's room was closed and the curtains drawn. Cesari and Tierney pushed their way through the crowd and entered without knocking. Arnie's nurse looked up. Her name was Susan.

Arnie saw them, got all excited and agitated, and tried to sit up. Susan gently pushed him back down. She was taking his blood pressure and his movement had unsettled the machine. Cesari walked quickly to the bedside to reassure Arnie. He sat on the edge of the bed and clasped Arnie's hand. Arnie laid back down and let Susan finish.

Cesari said soothingly, "Hey Arnie. Long time, no see."

Tierney came up behind Cesari. "Hello Dr. Goldstein. Remember me? Detective Tierney?"

Arnie was restless and his eyes gleamed. He gripped Cesari's hand tightly and tried to rise again. "Of course I remember. I haven't lost my mind, Cesari. I know what I saw and what I heard."

Cesari put a gentle hand on his shoulder and said, "You're a little ahead of us, Arnie. Why don't you tell us what you saw and what you heard? Susan, do you think we could have a moment with Dr. Goldstein? Detective, why don't you grab a chair?"

Susan left them alone and Tierney sat down on a metal folding chair. Cesari said, "Tell us what you know about the last couple of days, Arnie."

"You don't understand, Cesari. We don't have time for this. There's a woman being held prisoner. She needs our help."

He tried to rise for a third time and Cesari felt it might be smarter not to fight with him, so he helped him sit up in the bed and propped pillows behind him for support.

"Arnie, I'm gathering you've been through a lot, but you have to help us understand. Who's being held prisoner and where?"

"It's Beaujolais' wife, Martine. That bastard has her prisoner."

Cesari glanced at Tierney who sat forward and said, "Beaujolais? The financial guy?"

"Yeah, his wife. We were both held captive somewhere. It looked like a fancy hotel or a mansion."

Tierney said, "Can you roll it back a bit, Dr. Goldstein. Two days ago you were on your way to the SEC. That's the last anyone saw or heard from you until this morning. What happened on the way?"

Arnie furrowed his brow in thought and said, "I don't know. I can't remember. I was walking down Broadway. I remember somebody called out my name but that's it. I woke up in an amazing five-star bedroom with a chandelier and oil paintings. The bathroom had a porcelain tub and gold-plated fixtures. I had plenty of food and water. They even had ice cream, but the doors were locked, and I couldn't leave."

"Did you meet your captors? Did they give you instructions or any explanation?"

He shook his head. "No, not a word from anyone. I woke up in an alley on the East Side near the FDR. I'd been drugged. I think. It felt that way."

Tierney was perplexed. "You were kidnapped but your kidnappers didn't want anything, and they gave you ice cream? That's a bit unusual."

Cesari said to Tierney, "I think we should give him some time to recuperate. He's been through a lot."

"Stop talking about me like I'm not here. I know what I know, and we need to help that woman."

"I apologize, Arnie," Cesari said contritely.

"Me too, Dr. Goldstein. Tell us about the woman. If no one spoke to you, how do you know she's a prisoner?"

Arnie spent the next few minutes describing how he and the woman communicated through the duct work in their respective bathrooms.

Tierney was skeptical and said, "Beaujolais' wife, Martine, is being held prisoner in another part of the house and managed to convey this to you through the duct work?"

"Yes, that's what I'm trying to tell you. It's like a house of horrors wherever it was."

"Or a hotel of horrors. What's the last thing you remember, Doctor?"

"I went to sleep and woke up in the alley. I stumbled my way over here."

There was a knock on the door and Rhonda poked her head in. "Hi guys. Transport is here to bring my patient to radiology. Are you ready, Dr. Goldstein?"

Arnie nodded. "As ready as I'll ever be. Don't go far, Cesari. We need to do something to help that woman. Beaujolais is a monster. I told you so."

Several nurses entered the room and assisted Arnie into a wheelchair. Cesari and Tierney left the ER and stood outside the hospital taking in the late morning air. They leaned against a cement wall in the receiving area where the ambulances pulled up to deliver their patients. Neither one spoke for a long time. Thirty feet away and out of earshot, a weathered nurse was taking a cigarette break and speaking on her cellphone.

Cesari finally said, "What do you think?"

"First impression?"

"Is there any other kind?"

"I think your friend has gone over the deep end, Cesari."

Cesari said nothing.

Tierney then laid out his case for Arnie's insanity. "In broad daylight, in the middle of the afternoon with hundreds and perhaps thousands of witnesses, he simply vanishes off the street with no recollection of what happened. He wakes up in a five-star hotel with a bathroom the size of a two-car garage that has a chandelier and gold-plated fixtures. He's provided with food, wine, great coffee, ice cream, the works. No one hurts him, explains anything to him or demands anything, and then just as suddenly, he's lying naked, in an alley by the FDR drive. And all he can tell us is he heard voices through the wall. You're the doctor, Cesari. What does that sound like to you?"

"You think he's had a psychotic break? But what about the woman? What if she's real?"

Tierney shook his head. "All part of his delusion. I'm no psychiatrist but it's pretty clear he hates this guy Beaujolais, so his subconscious came up with this fantastical story about how he's mistreating his wife. It's a metaphor for the way he feels Beaujolais has been mistreating him."

Cesari grinned. "Are you sure you're not a psychiatrist?"

"Just doing my job, Cesari. Do you have an alternative explanation for what we just heard in there?"

"I'm still thinking about it. And the lying naked in the alley part?"

"He ripped off his clothes and ran around the city until he got exhausted and passed out. Not that unreasonable if he was psychotic. Don't quote me, but I'm pretty sure it happens not infrequently like that with some forms of untreated mental illness."

Cesari nodded. "Possibly, but where's he been for the last two days? Don't you think if he was acting that crazy somebody would have noticed and called it in?"

"I don't have an answer for that."

Cesari paused a beat and asked, "Shouldn't we at least go out to Jersey and talk to Beaujolais? I've been to his house in Bernardsville. It really is a mansion although I never saw the bedrooms."

"Did you meet his wife and was her name Martine?"

Cesari shook his head. "No, I didn't meet his wife. I didn't even know he was married."

"And I'm still not sure he is. Arnie could be delusional. What were you doing at Beaujolais' house?"

"He invited me and another doctor to tour his wine cellar. We were there from noon until ten that night."

"That's quite a tour."

"It's quite a wine cellar."

"When was this?"

"The day Arnie disappeared."

"You mean the day Arnie thinks he was kidnapped by Beaujolais?"

"He didn't say that exactly."

"No, but he inferred it."

"Yes, he did. I agree."

"That's quite an alibi Beaujolais has. He was with you the whole day... That's kind of funny when you think about it."

"What is?"

"Arnie was on his way to the SEC to file a complaint about Beaujolais while you were hanging out with the guy in his wine cellar."

"Hysterical," Cesari said wryly. "You didn't answer my question. Would it be worth it to talk to Beaujolais?"

"New Jersey is out of my jurisdiction, Cesari. Not to mention kidnapping is an FBI matter. And besides, what are you going to say to Beaujolais? Did you kidnap my friend for two whole days for no reason?"

"I could ask him if he has a wife named Martine?"

"And what if he does? Arnie could have found that out on the internet or simply by asking Beaujolais' secretary. I think I would chill out about Beaujolais until Arnie has had a complete psychiatric evaluation."

As they hashed it out, Tierney's phone rang and he answered it, "Tierney here."

He listened for a minute and said, "I'm two blocks away. Tell them not to touch anything and get the forensics people up there as soon as possible. I'm on my way. Also, send a guy over to the East Side by the FDR drive, say between Houston and East 14th Street. Have him check out the alleys, door stoops and dumpsters. A guy showed up in the St. Matt's ER, naked and delirious. He says he woke up in an alley over there. It's a long shot, but he may have left his clothes and wallet there. If they find anything have them call me. It's a pretty big area, you may want to send two guys."

He hung up and turned to Cesari. "Things just got a little bit more interesting."

"How so?"

"An old guy with cancer was just found dead in his bed a couple of blocks from here. They found a syringe cap with a milky substance in it on top of his bedsheets."

Cesari said nothing, but felt a growing knot in his stomach. Way too many coincidences for his taste.

Tierney added, "Want to come check it out? You can be my medical advisor."

Cesari took in a breath and exhaled. "Sure, why not?"

"First I need to get a warrant to collect the propofol from Arnie's office. We both agree that it has no business being up there, right?"

Cesari nodded and said glumly, "I agree."

Chapter 29

They entered the apartment building on East 11th Street where Murray had lived and died. It was an old building only ten stories high, built at a time when ten stories seemed huge, but was now dwarfed by skyscrapers everywhere. There were no doormen and security was a door that led to the street with a lock that had broken many years ago. The paint was peeling in the foyer and the wood steps groaned under their weight. There was a musty odor that permeated the building from the lack of adequate ventilation. The third-floor apartment door was open and a uniformed officer greeted them. They put on plastic gloves and booties and stepped inside.

The apartment was shabby but clean. The small living room was dominated by a worn-out sofa and chair. The linoleum was faded and cracked in places. The kitchen was miniscule and ancient. In the bedroom, there was an officer snapping photos and another bagging evidence.

Tierney nodded at the guy with the evidence bag containing the syringe cap and asked, "What do we know so far?"

"The guy's name was Murray Templeton, age seventy-five, lived alone and no family. The neighbor who found him says he was a nice guy who lived a quiet life. He had metastatic prostate cancer and was a patient at the St. Matt's cancer center for pain management. The last time the neighbor saw him was at 5:00 p.m. yesterday afternoon. Murray had just returned from a grocery store carrying a paper bag and the neighbor presumed he was getting ready to make dinner. This morning, the same neighbor noticed the door was ajar and called out for the guy. When he didn't answer, the neighbor went in to investigate and found him."

"What do we know about the neighbor?" Tierney said.

"Arthur Borowitz, seventy-eight years old, retired mailman, lives with his wife one or two doors down. Apparently, the neighborhood isn't that great and they look after each other."

Tierney said, "Anything else besides the syringe cap?"

"A drop of blood and a tiny puncture wound in the right groin, but no evidence of a struggle. The apartment's all in order. The guy's wallet was on the night table with forty bucks in cash and a credit card. There wasn't a whole lot here to begin with, but it doesn't appear that anything was taken."

Tierney and Cesari approached the pale body on the bed, frail, cold and stiff from rigor mortis. Tierney said, "Not looking good, Cesari. It's the same MO as the other one."

"So the finding of a syringe cap wasn't an accident the first time?"

"It couldn't be. I can't believe the guy would make the same mistake twice. It could be his calling card. Like he's taunting us. Daring us to figure it out."

"And it has to be the same guy?"

Tierney looked at him sideways. "Give me a break, Cesari. A propofol injection to the groin in a cancer patient? Yeah, it's the same guy. Besides, it wasn't common knowledge that we found a syringe cap in the other case. No one outside a small group of people knew that."

"And the same set of suspects?"

"Well, the list just got a little longer now that we found propofol in Arnie's home and in his office, but that's still a little circumstantial."

Cesari said, "If it's the same killer then that would suggest organizational skills and would require a certain amount of planning, a certain amount of mental coherency. Would it not?"

"I agree but what are you getting at?"

"Judging from the condition Arnie's in do you think he would be capable of such lucid thinking?"

"Spare me the psycho-babble, all right? Just because he's a little unhinged at the moment doesn't mean he was unhinged when he did this."

"You mean, if he did this."

"Fine, if he did this... You asked me earlier where Arnie might have been for the last two days. Maybe he was right here babysitting this guy?"

"The neighbor said he saw the victim last night at five carrying a grocery bag. He didn't say there was anyone with him."

"Maybe Arnie was already in the apartment?"

"A lot of maybes, Detective."

"I know... Well, let's move outside and let these guys remove the body and sweep the apartment for prints."

They left the apartment and walked outside onto the sidewalk. The air was thick with humidity. It was almost one and a lot had happened since Tierney had picked him up that morning to interview Arnie's wife, Sylvia. They were both hungry and grabbed hot dogs and waters from a street cart. Cesari was worried. He was worried that the thing hadn't quite hit bottom yet.

And he was right. As they munched on their dogs, Tierney received a call from one of the officers assigned to search the alleys on the East Side. He had found a used bottle of propofol and a syringe. He did not find Arnie's clothes or wallet. Tierney told him to bag it up and bring it back to forensics.

He turned to Cesari. "So far, it looks like propofol is the least guarded secret in Manhattan."

"Where'd he find it?"

"Four blocks east and two blocks south of here. Within walking distance."

"Not good."

"Not at all. I'm going to have to send someone over to Arnie's room and fingerprint him. We'll need to match his prints to any we find on the bottles or the syringe cap."

"Best case scenario?"

"Either there won't be any prints at all or whatever prints we find aren't Arnie's. I'm also going to leave a patrolman outside his room for now."

"Is that necessary? It will upset his wife."

"It will upset me even more if he decides to disappear again. We found propofol at his apartment, at his office, and now in an alley where he claims he just came from. And after what's just happened, I have to consider Arnie a bit of a flight risk."

Cesari saw his point and was having trouble finding an argument to defend Arnie. He said, "I understand. Look, Arnie's probably back from his CT scan. I'm going back to see how he's doing. Sylvia's probably there too. I should say hello."

"I'll catch up with you later, and don't let anybody into Arnie's office including yourself. I'm sending people over there to collect the propofol and search for anything else that might be germane."

****

The two security guards from the Port of Newark had died nearly two hours earlier. They sat mutely in their respective chairs. Their deaths were unnecessary and unnecessarily gruesome. The one on the right had lost an eye to a kitchen knife and a hand to a machete, amongst the many highlights of his ordeal. The other had watched his friend scream and spit and beg for his life before his turn came. His face was swollen to twice its original size and his eyes were closed tight and purple. His jaw was broken as well as most of his ribs, his femurs and his tibias. A bloody machete and a baseball bat sat on the table as the Sommelier sat catching his breath. His fury was unparalleled at the moment. He didn't like it when people stole from him, especially when it was people he felt were inferior in social rank.

They had freely given up the name of the individual who had paid them off. In fact, they had given up the name almost before he had begun. The sight of the machete alone made one of them piss in his pants. The rest of the beating had to take place if only to placate the Sommelier about the loss of his property. The idea that a work of art such as the Rolls Royce Boat Tail was in the hands of someone so trivial, so unworthy, actually made him physically ill. Gerry Acquilano… Who was he? He was nothing more than a speck of sand in the Sahara. A petty and soon to be dead thief.

The Sommelier stood, picked up the baseball bat, and began whacking the corpses some more. Hard and fast and furious until he was panting and covered in sweat and flecks of their blood and flesh. It was a pretty good work-out, he thought. When he was finished, both men were unrecognizable, bloody, pulpy messes. Hugo stood at the ready with plastic body bags. Both men were destined for a landfill in Bayonne. After that, plans would be made for how to deal with Gerry Acquilano. But first they had to find out who he was and what his pressure points were. The guards had only known him through their illicit relationship and not on a truly personal level. The phone number they had given him for Gerry was no longer functional and they didn't know where he lived.

Gerry had suborned his way into their world with promises of easy money for little or no risk if they simply followed the plan. It was only the fifth time they had worked with him. The first four times went as smooth as silk. No one asked any questions. There had been no investigations. Gerry had slinked in and slinked out completely unnoticed and they were both thousands of dollars richer each time. Ten thousand dollars each time to be exact. For a thirty-minute glitch in the cameras, it wasn't a bad payday. It wasn't like they actually stole the merchandise themselves. They had plausible deniability on their side and insurance usually covered the loss. There were frequent malfunctions in the cameras and the IT guys were always playing catch up. The guards made sure the cameras had problems all the time so there would be no easy pattern to pursue should it come to it. And they had used different gates each time for the same reason.

The way the American justice system worked, it could never be definitively proven that they did anything criminal. They were quite comfortable that as long as they didn't turn on each other they would be safe. What they didn't count on was the swift trial by machete action of the Sommelier. Large, clean cut, well-groomed men in trench coats, suits, ties, and holstered 9mm Glocks had met them as they left work and politely piled them into the back of a stretch limousine. The men were well-mannered, respectful but very insistent. Saying no didn't even seem like a remote possibility. It was hard to believe that a bad outcome could possibly arise in that situation. It all seemed too civil, too upscale, too courteous. It was like the secret service had collected them for a meeting at the White House. That thought had even crossed their minds. No one spoke but no one threatened either. It had been a quiet ride. There was a dichotomy of what was happening and who was doing it that their brains couldn't reconcile.

It had ended very badly for both men.

Chapter 30

Cesari called ahead to Rhonda in the ER to see what Arnie's status was. She sounded harried and answered with, "It's becoming a circus down here. His CT scan was negative, his labs are okay, and except for his persistent agitation about being held prisoner in a palace with some woman, he's fine. Right now he's with neurology, and psychiatry is in the wings. The decision's already been made to keep him overnight for observation. Now for the bad part. The entire board is down here along with Mrs. Goldstein, and the CFO, Brennan. They're all hovering outside his room. There are cops everywhere and half the staff have wandered through at various times to catch a glimpse, but I haven't reached the bad part yet."

"You haven't?"

"There's a mob of reporters with their camera crews trying to stampede through the ER doors. The hospital's attorney is outside giving them a statement."

"Michele Kislovsky?"

"Looks kind of mousy?"

"Don't let that fool you."

"Well, I don't know what she's telling them because she never spoke to me."

"I wouldn't worry about it. She can handle herself... All right. Thanks for the head's up. I should probably steer clear then."

"I whole-heartedly recommend it. You can't do anything anyway and it's going to be hours before we're finished with him. Besides, I don't think you'll want to deal with the board right now."

"Got it. How's Mrs. Goldstein?"

"Are you kidding? I've never seen anyone so happy."

Cesari smiled, "Thanks, Rhonda, and keep me posted, all right?"

"Roger that, Cesari."

Cesari hung up and cabbed it over to Mulberry Street where he took a seat in a small café and ordered an espresso. He had a lot on his mind. Arnie was in trouble. Deep trouble. He could feel it in his bones. The evidence was starting to pile up, but it didn't make any sense. Unless you threw in mental instability, which was starting to seem very likely. His story was preposterous. Kidnapped and held in a gilded cage, well treated with food, wine and ice cream. No ransom demands. No extortion. No physical threats. A damsel in distress. The story was completely absurd. Almost like a fairy tale.

His coffee came and he called Vito. "Vito, where are you?"

"I'm doing a little book-keeping. What's up?"

"I'm having an espresso at the Café Vivaldi. I'm sure you know it. It's down the block from your apartment. Why don't you join me?"

"Not a bad idea. We can review the car situation. I have an update."

"And I have an update for you about Arnie."

"I'll be right there."

Ten minutes later, Vito walked through the door, spotted Cesari, pulled up a chair at the small wood table and signaled the waiter for a double espresso.

"You first, Cesari. What's going on with Goldstein?"

It took less than ten minutes to fully explain the situation with all of its underlying legal and psychological implications.

When he was done, Vito said, "Damn, no matter how you cut it, your buddy's in hot water. He's either certifiable and going to an asylum or he's just an ordinary homicidal maniac and going to prison."

Cesari let out a deep breath. "We're waiting for the fingerprint analysis on the syringe cap and the propofol bottles but I'm getting a sense of impending doom in that regard... I just can't believe Arnie would do anything like that."

"You're too close, Cesari. You have to step back and be objective. He had access to the medication. He knows how to administer it and how it works. He has access to all the clinic records of the cancer patients. And he may be psychotic. You said yourself he's been under a lot of stress because of the money. Maybe he just snapped."

"Maybe..."

"I'll bet those pain management guys are jumping for joy. They're off the hook."

"I'm not sure if they heard the news yet. Sure, they'll be relieved but not in a good way. They're too nice to take any pleasure in Arnie's downfall. Anyway, what's new with the Rolls? Did Hugo get back to you?"

"Yes, he did and is totally agreeable to the five million in exchange for the Boat Tail. We're working on the details right now, but I'm thinking of using the Mercedes dealership in Morristown as the drop off point."

"Is Alan still in town?"

"The Mercedes guy? I don't know, but it doesn't matter for my purpose. I just need a public place where people won't notice another high-end car."

"How will you get it there? You're not going to let Gerry drive it on the highway?"

"No, of course not. I can't risk something happening, like a stone kicking up and cracking the windshield. I'm going to rent or borrow an eighteen-wheeler and pack the Rolls in there for transport to the dealership. Gerry's going to handle the car on either end, loading and offloading. He's a pain in the neck, but I trust him with cars. He's got a lot of respect for a quality vehicle like that and will know how to take care of it."

"Like the way he took care of your other Rolls at the biker bar?"

"I can hardly blame him for what happened that night. From what you told me it was the bikers who started it. They were out of control but don't worry. I'm planning on teaching them some manners."

"All right. It's your car. So what happens next after you bring the Rolls to Morristown?"

"I'll let Hugo know where the car is after he transfers the money to my account in the Cayman's."

"Won't he want to see it and possibly inspect it before he coughs up five million?"

"Like I said, I'm still working on the details. Enough about the Rolls. What about you?"

"What about me?"

Vito snorted. "C'mon Cesari. I know you too long to believe you're just going to roll over about this Arnie thing."

"Do I have a choice?"

"Why don't you at least go out to Jersey and ask this Beaujolais character if he's married?"

"Give me a break. I could check online for that. Even if he is, it wouldn't mean anything."

"Unless she really is being held captive."

"Which I doubt he would tell me."

"Probably not."

"And if he's not married, then Arnie's story truly is the product of an overactive imagination."

"You got a smart phone. Google it up. A successful financial company will probably have his bio online. It's good PR in this day and age."

Cesari took his phone out from his pocket, found the search bar, and typed in Beaujolais' name. Nearly instantaneously he was inundated with hits about his company and his reputation as a Wall Street wizard, but nothing about his marital status. Then he typed in the name of the company, Fidelity Financial Services Inc. Numerous results popped up including Fidelity's website which Cesari clicked on. The website listed the company's services, specialties, and many accolades from customers and other financial institutions, as well as tributes from the *Wall Street Journal* and *Forbes*.

The brokers were listed in order of seniority and rank. Beaujolais was on top of that list with his name in large letters next to a small picture of Mike B. himself. There was a blue hyperlink and Cesari followed it to Mike B.'s personal biography. Cesari read through it and at the very end it revealed that Mike B. was indeed married and lived in Bernardsville with his wife and young son. Her name was Martine.

Cesari looked up at Vito. "He is married and his wife's name really is Martine, but Arnie could have googled it up just the way I did."

"Still, if you want to give him the benefit of the doubt then you should look into it."

"How? Just call up the mansion and say I'd like to speak to Mrs. Beaujolais?"

"It couldn't hurt to try but you won't know if she's under duress that way. He could have a gun to her head every time she picks up the phone."

"This is ridiculous. Did you hear what you just said?"

"Arnie's your friend, Cesari, not mine. Suppose she is being held captive. Then Arnie would have been telling the truth about being kidnapped."

"Why would anyone kidnap Arnie?"

"Not anybody. Why would Beaujolais kidnap Arnie is the question?"

"Feel free to tell me the answer."

"You tell me. Arnie suspected him of robbing the hospital's money and was going to file a complaint with the SEC, right? Maybe Beaujolais didn't want that."

"True, true and totally ridiculous. Of course, Beaujolais wouldn't want that. Who would? But consider this. One; Beaujolais couldn't have known Arnie was on his way to the SEC, and two; what's the point of kidnapping a guy, treating him well, and then letting him go unharmed. You would think that if the idea was to stop Arnie from filing a complaint, they would at least have roughed him up and told him why. Anyway, it's just a complaint. Every company on Wall Street must get hundreds of them every year. Ninety-nine percent of them go nowhere. Most are just sour grapes."

"Maybe there was something different about Arnie's complaint? Have you discussed it with your money guy at the hospital?"

"The CFO? No, not the specifics. I didn't think it was necessary. His name is Steve Brennan by the way, and he's now the acting CEO. According to pre-kidnap Arnie, Brennan wasn't very concerned about the hospital's losses and he thought Arnie was overreacting. Just a day ago Brennan told me and the board the markets are reversing themselves and heading back up again. He says we've already started to recoup our losses and is very optimistic we'll have recovered it all in due time."

"And Brennan knows his stuff?"

"I assume so. He was Arnie's hire a year ago. I wasn't involved with it. He's got the usual degrees and background and seems to know what he's talking about. Not to be overly cynical, but most of high finance is voodoo if you ask me. Warren Buffett passes gas after lunch, and everybody loses their shirts kind of stuff."

Vito scratched his head and said, "Then I don't understand."

"Neither do I. That's the problem."

"Is Arnie still hell bent on filing the complaint?" Vito asked.

"I think Arnie's way past the complaint phase. He wants Beaujolais in handcuffs in front of a firing squad."

Vito laughed. "I kind of like the guy's spirit. What's going to happen in regard to the complaint?"

"Nothing. The complaint thing is ancient history. Arnie doesn't know it yet, but his whole world is hanging by a thread. If he keeps sounding delusional, he may lose his job and his credibility. He may even wind up in inpatient therapy on antipsychotics. And I don't even want to think what's going to happen if they match his fingerprints on that syringe cap they found this morning."

"So you're not going to see if Beaujolais' wife is okay?"

"Wrong, I'm definitely going to see if she's okay because it's the only thing I can do."

Vito made a snarky grin. "I knew it. You can't help yourself."

"No, I can't."

"But you can't just walk up to the front door and ask. What if he really is a bad guy?"

Cesari thought about that for a minute and said, "You're right. I'll have to be a bit more circumspect. I'll think of something."

"I'm sure you will."

Chapter 31

Later that afternoon, Cesari called a meeting with the pain killers. It was Saturday but they were all bursting at the seams to find out what was going on and agreed to meet him in the anesthesia breakroom in the OR. Cesari went directly there, avoiding the emergency room as if it were ground zero for some new kind of plague. When he found the guys, they were huddled around a small television watching a clip of Michele Kislovsky talking to reporters earlier in the day. They were all in a state of shock as was most of the hospital. Cesari hadn't directly addressed Arnie's absence with them, and they were now hearing soundbites and rumors from other doctors and emergency room nurses.

They looked up at him wide-eyed and speechless. Cesari closed the door behind him and said, "I see you've heard about Arnie."

Xi turned off the television. "Was he really kidnapped?"

"It's what he says or implies, but there are a lot of ifs. He doesn't quite recall key elements of the last few days, and says he never met his kidnappers."

"What did they want?" Jaskaran asked.

Cesari shook his head. "Nothing apparently. There were no ransom demands or ultimatums for some type of action on Arnie's part."

Jeremy said, "That doesn't make any sense."

"No, it doesn't. And it's even more complicated in that Arnie wandered into the emergency room nearly naked, disheveled and somewhat incoherent."

"Wow," they all whispered simultaneously.

"Wow is right," added Cesari. "And there's more so brace yourselves. This part hasn't hit the airways yet and I need it to stay right here. I don't want what I'm about to tell you to leave this room. Are we all agreed?"

They all nodded their heads and waited.

"Obviously, there is a suggestion here that Arnie may have suffered some type of nervous breakdown which we're trying to sort out. He's being evaluated from head to toe by neurology and psychiatry, but there's something else that's happened that may alter the outcome of recent events and I think you should know because of recent speculation about your involvement in the death of Mrs. Loomis last week."

Cesari paused to take a breath before continuing, "Just this morning another one of St. Matt's cancer patients was found dead in his bed with a syringe cap lying on the sheets. The cap had a milky substance in it and I have no doubt that it will turn out to be propofol."

Their jaws dropped and Parikh said, "Dr. Cesari, sir, may I ask you the name of the patient?"

"For the ten thousandth time, it's just Cesari, Parikh. Hardly any of my patients even call me Doctor, and absolutely no one calls me sir. The patient's name was Murray Templeton."

Shocked glances at each other went around the room. Parikh said, "We all knew him. He was a very nice gentlemen."

Jeremy added, "He had metastatic prostate cancer. I saw him yesterday morning. This is so sad."

Cesari nodded, "Very sad and it gets worse... The police have found bottles of propofol with syringes in Arnies's apartment, his office, and in the general vicinity of where he says he woke up this morning. We're waiting for fingerprint analysis on the bottles and the syringe cap."

The silence in the room was deafening. You could have heard a pin drop. Everyone, including Cesari, was at a loss for words. The enormity of the implication was not lost on anyone. They all knew they were innocent but to be freed from the shackles of suspicion like this was a bittersweet victory. They all liked Arnie. He was their boss, but he was also one of them. This was not how they wanted this to end. It was like they were staring down at the grave of a fallen comrade.

Xi said quietly, "What do you think, Cesari?"

"I don't know what to think. Things are happening so fast, it feels like a blur. On the one hand, my mind and my heart cannot accept that Arnie is capable of any wrongdoing, let alone murder or euthanasia or mercy killing or whatever you want to call it. You guys don't know Arnie the way I do. If you're on Third Avenue and you stand still too long, he'll shove a ten-dollar bill in your hand because he'd think you might be homeless and could use a cup of hot coffee. That's just the way he is. But facts are stubborn things, and these facts look really bad for him."

Jaskaran said, "Is there anything we can do? I mean he's innocent until proven guilty, right?"

"You're right and I'm working on that. I'm not going to let Arnie get railroaded for a crime he didn't commit just because it's convenient, but I need help. So far, we've recovered a total of ten bottles of propofol; four in his apartment; five in his office and one in an alley on the East Side. I need you guys to fan out and ask around. That's a lot of propofol. Too much to go missing and no one notice. So start by talking to the pharmacists here. Ask them if their invoices have come up ten bottles short recently. Say, going back eight or ten weeks. Start there. Ask them how it could happen. What would be the procedure if it did? I doubt that much propofol could have gone missing from a PYXIS machine. That would certainly have raised an alarm."

"And Arnie doesn't have access to the PYXIS machines," commented Jeremy.

"So the propofol would have had to come from downstairs in the pharmacy before it made its way up to the OR."

"Exactly."

Cesari said, "I want everybody to start thinking real hard how you could steal ten whole bottles of propofol and not cause a general alarm. You'll have to be as discreet as possible in your inquiries. Are you guys with me on this? It's a voluntary mission and I would understand if you wanted no part of it."

Parikh raised his hand, "I am with you, sir. We will be superheroes."

"I don't know about that, but I appreciate your enthusiasm. What about the rest of you? I won't hold it against you if you don't want to get involved."

They all raised their hands and one by one said they wanted to help. Cesari thanked them as his phone rang. He looked at the screen. It was Tierney.

He put the device to his ear and Tierney barked, "Big problem, Cesari. Actually, two big problems and I wanted you to be the first to know about them. Where are you?"

"I'm in the OR, why?"

"Come up to Arnie's office. You need to see something."

Tierney clicked off without waiting to hear Cesari's reply. Cesari looked at the pain guys and said, "I've got to go. Jeremy, would you mind coming with me? I want to talk to you about something."

Jeremy nodded and stood. They left the OR and found an elevator to the tenth floor. Cesari said, "I didn't mention it in there but there's another wrinkle to consider. In addition to Arnie claiming he was kidnapped, he also claims he made contact with a woman who was also being held in captivity."

Jeremy's eyes widened. "Seriously?"

"I'm very serious. He claims that he spoke to the woman through the duct work of the bathroom where he was being held prisoner."

Jeremy shook his head despondently but didn't say anything. It was clear, that like everyone else, he thought Arnie was missing a few marbles.

Cesari couldn't blame him and went on, "I know. It sounds crazy but Arnie is insistent. He says the woman told him her name was Martine Beaujolais, the wife of Mike B."

"Jesus, Cesari, Arnie's clearly lost it. I feel bad for him, but talking to a woman through the duct work? That's over the top."

"I know it looks bad, but before we put him in a straitjacket, I was thinking I ought to check his story out. I mean, what if everything he said is true?"

"C'mon Cesari. You can't believe that. We were just there. In fact, we spent the whole day there. Do you really think that if Mike B. was holding people prisoner in his house, he would have invited total strangers to a party there?"

"I understand and I agree. It would be nuts to do something like that, but as you said, we were there all day and what didn't we see?"

"What?"

"Martine Beaujolais. Would it make sense to spend an entire day at someone's home and not meet his wife?"

Jeremy was quiet as he contemplated that. Eventually he said, "I guess not, but that doesn't mean she was locked up somewhere. That place was huge. She could have been anywhere we weren't, watching TV or reading a book or anything. She might have been out with a friend or visiting a relative."

They exited the elevator thinking about it and made their way to Arnie's office where they found Tierney and two uniformed policemen opening drawers, checking closets and taking pictures. The propofol and syringes from Arnie's drawer were in plastic bags inside a small evidence box.

Tierney said, "Good afternoon, Doctors."

Cesari and Jeremy greeted him. Cesari said, "I hope it's okay that Jeremy joins us, Detective."

"As long as you're okay with it, I'm okay. He and the others are no longer suspects."

"That's good news."

"Not for Dr. Goldstein, it isn't. The lab just called me. His prints were already on file, and they matched the ones on the bottles of propofol in his home office and the one in the alley as well as the syringes they found in both places. The syringe in the alley was missing its cap. They think they have a partial print on the cap they found in the old guy's bed and are trying to match it as we speak. Not a good day for Arnie at all."

"Why were Arnie's prints on file?" Cesari asked.

"About a million years ago, right out of high school, your boy served two years as a Marine Security Guard at the U.S. embassy in Stuttgart. It was routine to fingerprint all embassy staff."

Arnie hadn't told him about his brief stint in the military. "Arnie was a jarhead?"

"For two whole years and two more in the reserves. You didn't know that?"

"It never came up and I never would have guessed it. He doesn't seem to have the temperament."

"Maybe he was trying to find himself and needed direction. A lot of kids that age sign up for that reason."

"Depending on how you look at it, he got lucky. Stuttgart is a great gig. I was there for a while. Embassy work is pretty cushy too. The food is good and the girls are pretty. He never saw any combat, but I still have to respect the guy."

Cesari said, "I agree. Does this mean you're going to let him off the hook?"

"Just the opposite. I'm going to hold him to a higher standard, and I don't care how old he is. I won't tolerate any Marine dishonoring the Corps."

"I was afraid you would say that."

Tierney asked, "Are you a betting man, Cesari?"

Cesari shook his head no.

"What about you, Dr. Macallan?"

He also shook his head no.

"Why?" asked Cesari.

"I'm thinking that it's almost a sure bet that the print on the syringe cap is going to match Arnie's. Anybody want to take me up on it? I'm offering a million to one odds."

No one said anything.

Tierney said, "But that's not why I asked you to come up here."

He reached into the evidence box and retrieved a small plastic bag. In the bag was a square, black object about half the size of a modern cellphone and just as thin. It had a short wire dangling off one end and several operational buttons. He showed it to them.

Cesari asked, "What is it?"

"That, my friend, may be the only thing that stands between Arnie and multiple life sentences. It's a listening device."

"Somebody bugged Arnie's office?"

"It appears that way. I found it taped to the undersurface of his desk. I was just groping around, seeing what I could find. Routine grunt work in the detective business. My arms are much longer than Arnie's. He never would have reached it by casual feel."

"How does this help Arnie?" asked Cesari, optimism surging through him.

"Somebody wanted to know what he was saying and to who he was saying it. Right there you have the beginnings of a conspiracy. Whether it has anything to do with his alleged kidnapping or the deaths of the two patients or simply a rival hospital trying to get an angle on how well the competition is doing is anybody's guess right now."

"Is it on right now?"

"No, I turned it off and I'll have people sweep the room for other devices."

"So this doesn't really help Arnie?"

"Don't be negative, Cesari. Where there's smoke, there's fire. We need to find out who was keeping an eye on Arnie and why. He's still suspect number one, two, and three mind you, but at least there's a glimmer of hope that there's more going on here than meets the eye."

Chapter 32

Cesari glanced at his watch. It was close to 3:00 p.m. and he was already exhausted by the day's events, news, twists and turns. He stood on the sidewalk on Third Avenue outside the hospital's main entrance with Jeremy. Teeming throngs of pedestrians passed by in both directions. Traffic was heavy and noisy. Cesari signaled Jay to follow him across the busy thoroughfare to a waiting bench on the other side. There they sat for a long moment lost in thought.

Jay finally said, "What do you make of the listening device in Arnie's office?"

"I don't know what to make of it. This whole thing is insane. Up until the last few days, Arnie was a candidate for the most boring person on Earth title. A conversation with him could cure insomnia. I can't even begin to imagine who would want to listen in on him. That bit about a rival hospital trying to gain an advantage is ludicrous on the face of it. We're not Tesla or Microsoft that we have some secret or cutting-edge technology that's worth stealing."

"Then what?"

"I don't know, but I can't help feeling that it has something to do with his disappearance for the last few days. Somebody heard something they didn't like and pulled Arnie off the street because of it."

"Maybe he really was kidnapped?"

Cesari nodded his head. "Maybe he was, but that brings us back to Beaujolais. Suppose he was the one listening in on Arnie. Suppose he heard Arnie talking about going to the SEC and the attorney general's office. Would he have felt that was such a threat that he needed to stop him? And if he did snatch Arnie off the street, why didn't he do more than just entertain him for a few days? Arnie could just run right back to the SEC the minute he gets out of the hospital."

Jay said, "Yeah, but who would listen to anything Arnie has to say now?"

Cesari rubbed his chin in thought and then snapped his fingers. "Maybe that was the point? Maybe the object here wasn't to hurt Arnie physically or threaten him into submission, but to use the time he was gone to destroy his credibility, which they have very effectively done so far." Cesari then sighed deeply and forlornly as he added, "But Arnie going on a two or three day bender where he doesn't really know happened doesn't explain why he has propofol and syringes in his office and his apartment."

Jeremy agreed, "No, it doesn't and the idea that he was kidnapped just to stop a complaint from being filed seems a bit extreme to me."

"Me too. I think we may be grasping at straws with that theory." Cesari was quiet for a minute as he processed the information. He suddenly remembered something and said, "When we spent the day in Beaujolais' wine cellar, do you remember what he said?"

"Like what?"

"He said he was a hosting a fund raiser for the governor Saturday. That's tonight."

Jeremy thought it over and nodded, "Yes, he did say that. I remember. So?"

"I'm trying not to be overly paranoid, but if you were rich and powerful enough to hold a fund raiser for the wealthiest and most prominent people in New Jersey, would you want a complaint filed against you with the SEC and the attorney general's office on the eve of that event?"

"Probably not."

"I agree. If it made the papers, then it would be like throwing a bucket of cold water on the whole affair. There's nothing more illusory than relationships based on money and influence. His guests would turn on him the way a pack of sharks would turn on a wounded, bleeding brother. Maybe faster."

"It certainly would explain why Arnie was unhurt and never met or heard from his captors. They couldn't afford to implicate themselves in any way."

"And also why they made no demands. They didn't need to. Just make him look like a nut job."

"Except for one thing, Cesari. He may really be a nut job. Don't forget about the propofol."

"I'm not forgetting about it. It's just another thing that doesn't make sense to me... Okay, let's review the situation. Any defense of Arnie is predicated on whether it can be proven that he actually was kidnapped, but authorities aren't going to take him seriously right now because he seems like a raving lunatic. Lurking in the shadows is the possibility that he is trying to distract attention from himself because of the propofol and its implications. Do I have that right so far?"

Jeremy nodded.

Cesari looked down at his jeans and loafers and for the first time noticed Jay was wearing a sport coat, dress pants and a tie. He was even wearing cufflinks. He asked, "Do you always dress so formally on Saturdays, Jeremy?"

Jay glanced at his outfit and replied, "This is formal to you?"

Cesari said, "Forget I said anything... How committed are you, Jay?"

"To what, fashion?"

"To finding out what's going on?"

"I'm in all the way. Just don't get me killed."

Cesari liked his attitude. "As I said a minute ago, the only thread of hope we have is to prove Arnie was really kidnapped. But we have no clues other than Arnie saying that some woman who identified herself as Beaujolais' wife called out to him via duct work in a bathroom and claimed she also was being held captive. Are you with me so far?"

"I am. Continue…"

"We need to find Beaujolais' wife and ask her directly. If she says it never happened, then it's game over for Arnie."

"And how do you propose we do that?"

"We need to go to the mansion in Bernardsville."

"Just like that?"

"Why not?"

"When?"

"Tonight?

"You're crazy. You want to crash the governor's fundraiser looking for Beaujolais' wife to ask her if she's a prisoner?"

"If I recall correctly, he said we were welcome there anytime."

Jay grinned. "He did say that. I heard it too."

"Then you're in?"

"What does that mean exactly?"

"I need you to come with me. The two of us together can maneuver more easily and will be more disarming to Beaujolais. He seemed to like you. He'll think we're coming for round two in the wine cellar because we had such a good time. We'll pretend we forgot all about the fundraiser he talked about. The crowds may work to our advantage. He won't want a scene with all the hot shots there. Not with two doctors he called friends and fawned over just a few days earlier. With any luck, we might get a free meal and an introduction to the governor of New Jersey. Remember, if he's innocent and Arnie is crazy, he won't suspect anything. He'll think we're simply being crass, but harmless. I don't have a problem with that. I get accused of being crass all the time, but I can understand how that might offend your sensibilities."

"I'm already offended, but it's for a good cause so I'll suck it up. What happens if he's not innocent and really is a bad man?"

"Whenever two guys are in a situation like this, the black guy always gets killed first. I'm hoping that will give me enough time to get away."

Jeremy laughed and then said, "I don't know why I'm laughing because it's true."

"Relax, nobody's going to get killed. Even if he wanted to, the place is going to be packed with politicians and society's elites, possibly the media as well. To be honest, it couldn't be safer from that point of view. If we can get in, that is, which is a big if. If I recall correctly, there was armed security at the gate?"

"Yes, there was."

"Not good."

"No, definitely not good, and I drive a beat-up car that screams riff raff at the top of its lungs. They'll shoot us on sight if we pull up in that thing at a fundraiser. What about you?"

Jay shook his head. "I don't have a car. I'm a city boy. I live and play right here in Manhattan. If my girlfriend and I want to get away for a weekend, we use planes, trains and rented automobiles."

"That makes sense. I only keep and maintain one myself because of the personal freedom it provides, however imaginary, because I don't really drive it that much. It's just nice to know I have it there if I want to. Like tonight for instance, but for tonight, my little Honda is inadequate. As much as I love that car, I would be embarrassed to drive to Beaujolais' palace in it."

"We could rent a car," Jay suggested.

"It would have to be a really nice one."

"Like a Corvette or a Porsche?"

"Something that would impress even the most impossible to impress people. A car that will make security guards gape in awe and unabashed jealousy and hopefully put the safeties back on their submachine guns."

"Such as?"

"A brand-new Rolls Royce Boat Tail convertible."

Jay said, "Good luck with that."

"Luck's got nothing to do with it, Jay. It's all about who you know, not what you know."

"Well I know they're not going to have one of those at Hertz or Avis."

"I'll take care of it. Do you have a tuxedo? It will be a black-tie affair for sure."

Jay nodded. "Of course."

"Let's synchronize then. The fundraiser will probably begin between six and seven, cocktails, hors d'oeuvres, handshaking, the whole bit, but I'm guessing dinner won't start until 8:00 p.m. when people sit down in the wine cellar. If we get there at seven, we'll be in great shape. Does that sound about right to you?"

"It does. There's going to be over a hundred people there at a minimum I would guess. It'll take time to get them moving from one room to the other. They'll probably hang upstairs in the art gallery and bar for cocktails. That seems the most logical place for that while the waitstaff get everything organized downstairs. Somebody will probably be playing the piano."

"I agree... Okay, we better get moving if we want to get there in time for happy hour. I'll pick you up in an hour at your apartment. Be waiting outside."

Jeremy glanced at his watch as they both sprang for the same passing yellow cab.

Chapter 33

Cesari was looking in the mirror, making the knot in his bowtie and adjusting his cummerbund, while he talked to Vito on speakerphone. He owned a classic black tuxedo with matching patent leather shoes he had bought a few years ago for a friend's wedding. He had thought about renting one at the time but figured that owning one outright might encourage him to pursue more sophisticated activities such as the opera and the philharmonic. Of course he had been to neither one yet, but hope springs eternal. After all, look at him now.

He said, "I need to borrow the Rolls."

"Well that's not going to happen," Vito snapped in response.

"Earlier today, you thought it was a good idea that I check out Beaujolais' wife. That's what I'm trying to do."

"I didn't say you could use my Rolls Royce. You aren't worthy."

"You don't understand. I'm going to a fundraiser for the governor of New Jersey that Beaujolais is hosting out in Bernardsville. All the richest and most powerful people in Jersey are going to be there and I'm wearing a tuxedo. I can't pull up in a banged-up, old Honda. They won't even talk to me."

"Even if I wanted to lend it to you, which I don't, I can't. I already packed it up in a transport truck and moved it to a location in Morristown."

"Morristown? At Alan's dealership?"

"Close to it. It's in a parking lot waiting for the signal to bring it to the dealership as soon as I can pin this Hugo character down. He said he needed until Monday to decide on how he wants to proceed with the exchange. In the meanwhile, I have Gerry and a couple of my guys out there watching it."

"Where is Alan?"

"I don't know. I called the dealership. He left the vice president and operations manager in charge. All he told them was he was going to be out of town with his family for a while and that he would settle up with them when he returned."

"So the place is still open?"

"It would seem so."

"Okay look, you'd be doing me and Arnie a huge favor by letting me take the car to the event. It's in no danger of being stolen. The place is guarded better than Fort Knox, and I just googled it up while we've been talking. Beaujolais' mansion in Bernardsville is only five miles on country roads from Morristown. How much trouble could I get in going five miles? I promise to do the speed limit. C'mon, Arnie's life is on the line. He's married and got kids and grandkids."

Vito was silent for a minute and Cesari smiled into the mirror as he put the final adjustment on his bowtie. Vito didn't actually know Arnie, but over the years had heard much about him through Cesari, and at heart, his friend was a big softie. Okay, maybe that was an exaggeration.

Vito said, "Five miles?"

"To and from the mansion and that's it. No joyriding. Strictly business. I need to get in the doorway, and to do that I need to impress them that I mean business. There are some heavyweights attending this thing so it may not be the only Rolls there."

"But it will certainly be the most expensive… I don't like this idea, Cesari," Vito said, his voice softening. "Anything could happen; a deer could jump out of the woods, a drunk at your party could back up into it. Then what? Then Hugo's going to charge me. That's what. He's expecting a brand new, in perfect condition, car."

"I promise you nothing's going to happen. I'll park miles away from any other car and I won't go above thirty miles an hour regardless of the speed limit."

More silence as he decided. Finally, he said, "Fine, I'll let my boys know you're coming."

"Thanks, where is it?"

"There's an outdoor parking lot on Bishop Nazery Way just off of Spring Street in Morristown. Someone will be waiting for you. Let Gerry maneuver the car out of the truck, all right? It requires some finesse. You better not damage that car, Cesari. Five miles there and five miles back. That's it, and don't drink."

"Tell them I'll be there at six."

Vito hung up without saying goodbye. Cesari threw on his tuxedo jacket and left his apartment. He walked over to the garage where he parked his Honda, got in, fired it up, checked to see that he had plenty of gas, and drove over to Chelsea. Jay was standing on the sidewalk all spiffed up in his black tuxedo with white cummerbund and bowtie, a step up from Cesari's black on black standard ensemble. Jay wore his best designer Bono eyeglasses, a diamond and onyx pinky ring and gold cufflinks. Cesari felt a little like Cinderella must have on that fateful night of the ball. He wore no personal jewelry and used whatever inexpensive cufflinks and shirt fasteners that came with the tux. And now he was picking Jay up in an ancient, dented Honda Accord. At least there were no tears in the leather upholstery.

Cesari pulled to the curb, rolled down the window and said, "Your chariot arrives, Dr. Macallan."

Jay looked up and down at the car, didn't make any comments, and got in. He didn't need to say anything. In Latin the expression was, *res ipsa loquitur,* the thing speaks for itself. As Jay buckled up, Cesari pulled out and head toward the Holland Tunnel to New Jersey. His plan was to take I-78 W to NJ 24 W into Morristown, a forty-five-minute drive under good traffic conditions. And they were very good right now. Saturday evening in and around the environs of Manhattan, people were already where they wanted to be.

They chit-chatted nonchalantly most of the time, but half-way into the drive, Jay couldn't contain himself anymore and said, "You can't be serious with this car, Cesari?"

Cesari laughed. "I was hoping you wouldn't be like all the others, Jay. It's a perfectly good car."

"I'm sure it is, but I think we're going to get a little flak trying to get into the party with this thing."

"That's why we're not going to try. I should have mentioned that the car we're going to drive to the fundraiser is waiting for us in Morristown. A friend of mine owns a dealership for high end cars out there. He owes me a favor and he's going to lend me one for the night, but first we have to get there. I should also commend you for holding back for a full twenty minutes before saying something negative about my ride. I think that's the longest anyone has ever gone."

Jeremy chuckled. "I'm sorry about that. It's just that it doesn't seem like you, and you mentioned a Rolls Royce earlier at the hospital."

"And that's exactly what's waiting for us, a brand-new Rolls Royce convertible."

Cesari's phone rang. It was Tierney. "Good evening, Detective."

"Are you with Arnie right now, Cesari?"

"No, why?"

"Because I have bad news. The partial print on the syringe cap matched Arnie's."

Cesari didn't say anything.

"I'm sorry, Cesari."

"So what happens now?"

"I'm going to have to arrest him. There's no way around it. I called you because I know how personal this is, but there's no way around the science."

Cesari felt the wind get knocked out of him. Jeremy's eyes went wide as he listened in over the car's speaker system. Cesari said, "Where is he now?"

"Last I heard, he's still in the emergency room with the shrink but the plan is to admit him for observation. I'm going to have to cuff him to his bed."

"You can't be serious? He's not going anywhere."

"Sorry, Cesari."

"But what if he really was kidnapped?"

"That seems very unlikely but wouldn't change anything anyway. Two separate issues. I'm a cop, not a judge. Just for the record, I ran it by a friend in the bureau, he says there's nothing to go on in terms of a kidnapping case and they wouldn't touch it with a ten-foot pole, especially now that we have hard evidence linking him to two separate crime scenes."

"No offense intended, Detective, but has anyone tried to contact Beaujolais' wife to see if she's okay? I mean, I know it's a long shot, but isn't it worth a try?"

"No offense intended? Kiss my ass, Cesari. How about we wait until the psychiatrist finishes his evaluation? If he declares Arnie to be delusional and hearing voices, then it's case closed as far as I'm concerned. I'm not going to waste time tracking down the ravings of a maniac."

"What if the shrink says he's not psychotic?"

"Then he's in the crosshairs for one, possibly two murders. And in case you didn't hear me the first time, kidnapping is a federal offense, and the FBI are taking a pass."

"But it's just a phone call."

"Yes, and as a concerned citizen, you can feel free to make it."

"Me?"

"Look, Cesari, I like Arnie too, but this whole kidnapping story smells fishy like he concocted the whole thing. There's no hard evidence to support it at all, and stumbling around the city naked, rambling about damsels in distress doesn't exactly smack of veracity. Does it to you? You're being sentimental. Once again, I'm sorry. I got to go now. Stay tuned."

"I will."

Cesari clicked off and glanced at Jay who said, "Shit…"

"You said that right. I felt it coming but I can't believe it. This is nuts."

"Is there any point in still going to Beaujolais' mansion?" asked Jeremy. "The detective had a point about Arnie's story. It is kind of weak for a kidnapping."

Cesari mulled that over for moment and said, "And kind of strong for premeditated murder, but you know what? I need closure. If Arnie is psychotic, it might help me accept that he could be a murderer, but if he's not, then I need to know the truth."

"You weren't listening to Tierney, Cesari. Arnie may not be psychotic, but he could have made the whole thing up to throw people off the trail or maybe to lay the groundwork for an insanity plea."

"You're a ray of sunshine, aren't you? Whose side are you on anyway, Tierney's?"

"Just playing devil's advocate."

Cesari nodded in glum acceptance. "Well, I need to know for sure, but you're right. This could be a desperate ploy on Arnie's part, but that would imply an active imagination. Something I know for a fact Arnie doesn't possess. Do you have any idea how dull he is on a personal level? I love the guy, but I would never accuse him of being creative. Did you know he once very seriously asked me if I thought it was appropriate for him to wear aftershave to work because he was concerned it might send the wrong message to the female secretarial staff about his availability?"

Jeremy laughed and shook his head. "You never told me that."

"Well, he did. Does a guy who worries about the aphrodisiac properties of Old Spice seem like someone who would run around Manhattan shooting people up with propofol, and then create an elaborate ruse to misdirect the authorities?"

"I know what you're saying, Cesari, but you're not factoring in that he may have snapped mentally."

"I know I'm defending him hard. I can't help myself..." Cesari glanced in the rear-view mirror and then in the side mirror, signaled a lane change and then moved over one, watching his mirrors carefully.

He said, "We have company, Jay."

Chapter 34

Cesari had noticed the minivan back in Manhattan, shortly after he had picked up Jay. It was two cars back in the Holland Tunnel. Then he saw it again on I-78 in his mirrors but hadn't paid much attention. It wasn't until, he turned onto NJ 24, that he began to take it seriously and made a series of lane changes to see what would happen. It had changed lanes with him every time. It was a new model, red, Chrysler Voyager, a family car with the vanity plate 007. It sat seven people comfortably and all the rear seats could fold flat for added cargo space if necessary. It wasn't a very exciting vehicle but for a growing family, it was perfect.

He made an unexpected detour into the parking lot of the Frelinghuysen Arboretum on Whippany Road, a short distance from his true destination. The arboretum had closed for the day and the lot was empty. He was angry as he got out of his car and waited for the approaching minivan. It pulled up next to his Honda and Cesari marched up to the driver's side door. Jay followed him.

Cesari banged on the window and the driver rolled it down. Parikh was behind the wheel, Jaskaran was in the passenger seat, and Xi sat in one of the backseats. The other back seat lay flat as was the rear bench seat. A bipodded, scoped AR15 lay on the floor with multiple mags of ammo. The boys were all wearing tuxedoes. Jaskaran wore an emerald green turban with the ornately carved handle of a traditional Sikh ceremonial knife, called a Kirpan, jutting out from his cummerbund. Overall, they looked pretty good.

Cesari scanned around the cabin before saying angrily, "What the hell do you guys think you're doing?"

Parikh said, "We are your back up, sir. We are loaded for tiger."

Jaskaran corrected him, "The expression is loaded for bear, Parikh."

"Bear or tiger, what is the difference?" asked Parikh.

"Stop it," ordered Cesari and then glared at Xi. "You brought your AR15? Really, Xi?"

Xi said, "Jeremy said there could be trouble. We wanted to help. It's got night vision capability."

"Splendid," Cesari said, his voice dripping with sarcasm. "So you think shooting an AR15 at a dinner party where the governor of New Jersey is raising money for his re-election is going to be helpful? I used to think you guys were smart." He turned to Jeremy. "Have you lost your mind? What were you thinking bringing these guys in on it?"

Jeremy had confessed the minute Cesari had positively identified Parikh in his rear-view mirror. He shrugged contritely. "You said it might be dangerous. I mean, what if Beaujolais really did kidnap Arnie and we find that his wife is being held captive? He might not take it too well."

"He is correct in his thinking, Dr. Cesari," added Parikh.

Cesari turned back to Parikh. "He might not take it too well? So you're just going to shoot him? May I remind you gentlemen that you are doctors. You save lives, not destroy them. If Tierney heard about this, he might be inclined to put you all right back on the suspect list."

"Don't you think you're overreacting, Cesari?" asked Xi. "Think of the AR15 as more of a deterrent than an offensive weapon just in case the shit hits the fan. You know what they say. It's better to be judged by twelve than to be carried by six."

Jeremy nodded his approval at that and said, "Beaujolais has a lot of armed security. It may not be so easy to get out of there if he doesn't want us to."

"So what's the plan? Xi lies down in the back of the minivan with the AR15 on its bipod. Parikh opens the rear door, and boom, instant sniper? And what's your role Jaskaran? Are you his spotter?"

In response, he lifted a pair of high-powered binoculars he had between his legs. Cesari was beside himself and continued, "I can't believe you guys, and what's with the tuxedoes?"

Jaskaran answered, "They're for freedom of movement. In case we need to infiltrate the grounds, we'll look like all the other guests."

They were making Cesari's head spin. Clearly, they had watched too many action flicks. He said, "Guys, I want you to turn the car around and go back to New York. You're just going to get yourselves in trouble. Now I really must insist. I appreciate your wanting to help but what you're doing is misguided and extremely dangerous."

They were all quiet for a while and Parikh was the first to speak. "But Dr. Cesari..."

Cesari interrupted him, "But nothing. Turn the car around and return to New York. Do you see what's in the back of your car next to the AR15?"

Parikh turned around and saw his kid's car seat. He turned back and nodded. "I understand."

"I'm glad, and what's with your license plate, 007? What's that supposed to mean?"

"007, sir, license to kill."

Cesari shook his head in disbelief. "You all need to go home. Am I clear? Thank you for your concern but your presence is only going to make things worse for everyone."

Jeremy said, "He's right. Go home guys."

They looked deflated but nodded in agreement. Cesari and Jeremy walked back to the Honda and got in. Cesari waited for the minivan to leave first and when it reached the exit out of the arboretum, it turned left back to NJ 24 and he turned right toward the parking lot with the Rolls Royce. Cesari didn't waste time with rebuke and carried on as if nothing had happened. In his mind, they were adults trying to do the right thing. They get a gold star for that not detention.

They followed Whippany Road, turned right onto Morris Street and then right onto Bishop Nazery Way. One and half miles from the arboretum, they found the parking lot. Gerry was standing outside the back of the truck with one of Vito's men. Cesari pulled into the lot and parked several spaces away. Gerry and the guy wasted no time and opened the back of the truck as Cesari, and Jeremy walked over. Jeremy was confused watching the activity.

Cesari explained, "They keep this particular car in the show room and don't usually let people test drive it. To protect it, they transported here in the truck."

Jeremy was amazed, "How expensive is this car?"

"Too expensive for us. That's for sure, but if you work real hard, one day you'll be able to afford a Honda like me."

Jeremy grinned as they watched Gerry inch the Boat Tail down the ramp onto the pavement of the lot. It had stolen plates on it. Nice touch, thought Cesari. Gerry left the car running and came around to Cesari as Vito's guy packed up the truck.

Jeremy walked around the car in awe. It was big for a convertible and the wood veneer trunk really did make it resemble an old-time cigarette boat. The deep blue paint job was lacquered to a high shine, and you could see your reflection in it. There was no doubt that this car represented luxury of an unparalleled sort.

Gerry said, "I can't believe Vito's letting you take this car out for a spin."

"Neither can I, but it's for a good cause."

"You look sharp. Where are you going?"

"That's for me to know and you not to."

"Just be careful. I can take care of minor stuff and I'll clean it up when you return, but please no accidents. I don't think I'll be able to bear all the screaming and moaning."

Cesari grinned. "I'm with you on that one. I'll be cautious."

He got in the driver's seat and Jay got in on the other side. The leather was high quality and the padding plush. The interior was lined with Wilton wool and trimmed with English walnut. The engine hummed in quiet elegance. Cesari suddenly felt under-dressed in his tuxedo.

They drove out of the parking lot and Cesari could see Gerry waving in the mirror. He said, "Are you happy now, Dr. Macallan?"

Jeremy nodded and smiled. "Oh yeah. This is freaking awesome. Look at this interior... Do you need me to plug the address into Google maps or the car's navigation?"

Jeremy took out his phone, turned it on and played with it for a second. Cesari thought he was turning on his map feature and said, "Nah, it's pretty easy from here. It's a straight run down Rte. 202 into the center of town and a couple of miles out into the country on Claremont Road. I looked it up this afternoon before I picked you up."

Jeremy snapped a few photos of the interior of the car and said, "Do you remember the exact address or are you just doing it by feel and memory?"

"It's number 170 Post Kunhardt Road. I remember seeing the address on the mailbox at the edge of the property when we came to tour the wine cellar."

"170 Post Kunhardt Road," Jeremy repeated. "I remember the mailbox now. You have a much better memory than I do."

"Better than most people," Cesari added, but there was something about the way Jeremy had repeated the address that sounded odd. Cesari let it go.

"What a sweet ride," Jeremy commented. "I wouldn't mind spending a little extra time in it."

Cesari quipped, "When we're done, I'll take you for an ice cream cone. You can get sprinkles on it."

Jay laughed. "You think you're joking but I want to live in this car."

"Jay, call Rhonda in the ER. I'd like to talk to her about Arnie before she goes home. Do you have her number?"

Jay nodded, lifted his phone and dialed. He put the phone on speaker and raised the volume as high as he could holding the device between him and Cesari. They listened to it ring multiple times before Rhonda answered.

"Hey, Rhonda, this is Cesari."

"Cesari? Why are you calling from Macallan's phone?"

Jay said, "Hi, Rhonda. Cesari's driving and wanted to speak to you."

"I'm just calling to see what's the latest news on Arnie, Rhonda," Cesari explained. "I hear the police may be coming for him."

"They've already arrived and handcuffed him to the bed. He got upset and agitated and we were afraid he was going to hurt himself, so I had to sedate him."

"Jesus…"

"His wife, Sylvia, got upset and agitated and started having chest pains. She's in the bed next to him now waiting for cardiology."

Cesari groaned, "Please tell me this isn't happening, Rhonda."

"Oh it's happening all right. In living color, right before my eyes. They read him his rights in the middle of the ER with half the hospital watching. It was pretty bad."

"What did the psychiatrist have to say?"

"He was in the middle of his evaluation when the police came and all hell broke loose. He said because of what happened, he couldn't possibly draw any conclusions and now that Arnie is sedated, he will have to reconsult in the morning. They're moving him to a floor bed as we speak, cops, cuffs, and the whole nine yards. I feel like I just filmed a scene for *General Hospital*."

"Thanks for the update, Rhonda."

There was silence on the other end of the line for a moment before Rhonda said, "This is where you're supposed to tell me this is all bullshit and Arnie's being framed, Rhonda."

"This is all bullshit and Arnie's being framed, Rhonda."

"Thank you. Now at least I have something to tell people."

Chapter 35

A s they approached the street entrance to the mansion, they observed a mass of expensive cars and chauffeur driven limousines lined up trying to get past the guard gate where names were being cross referenced with the guest list while security teams checked out each car. The next step, once you passed through the gate was to drive up and around the circular driveway to allow passenger drop-off and valet assistance. Cesari checked his watch. It was 6:30 p.m. They were earlier than he'd expected, but at the rate the line of cars was moving, he thought his estimate of how the evening would progress was easily off by an hour, possibly two hours. Cocktail hour would clearly have to be extended. He pulled the Boat Tail to the end of the queue, rolled the top down and waited patiently. There was a cool easterly breeze passing through.

They eventually reached the security gate with at least fifteen more vehicles behind them. A muscular guard with a holstered pistol on his hip and a clipboard in his hands approached them. A video camera from the guardhouse whirred as it focused in on him, Jay, and the car. Another guard holding a submachine gun stood directly in front of the grill, relaxed but alert. The tip of his weapon pointed downward at the engine block. The gun he held was a Heckler & Koch MP5 which used 9mm parabellum ammunition. It was a very successful weapon, used widely all over the world and lauded for its accuracy and reliability. He probably had it loaded with a thirty-round clip. Cesari was a good judge of character and could tell from the man's expression he would not have any significant moral objection to emptying the weapon's entire magazine into the Rolls' windshield.

The guard with the clipboard sized up the car and said, "Nice wheels."

Cesari said, "Thanks."

"May I have both your names please?"

"Dr. John Cesari and Dr. Jeremy Macallan but our names aren't going to be on the guest list. We're friends of Mr. Beaujolais and he told us we could drop by anytime for a glass of wine. We had no idea there was a party going on."

The guard in front of the car didn't change his expression but Cesari thought he sensed him tense up a little. Cesari felt Jeremy's blood pressure rise and his heart start to pound. But outwardly, he remained calm, which was impressive. It wasn't every day you tried to pull the wool over two guys who looked like ex-special forces types, armed and ready to rumble. The guard looked at Cesari and Jay, taking their measure, judging their appearance, their tuxedoes, their attitude. Then he looked at the car, back and forth. Clearly, they fit in. Cesari saw it in his eyes. He didn't want to turn them away. They belonged here.

Cesari said, "Maybe you can call Michel and ask him if he would make an exception for us. We just had lunch with him here earlier in the week when he made the offer."

Cesari deliberately did the first name drop. It had a subliminal effect of adding intimacy to the visit as if they weren't just casual acquaintances but very close friends.

The guard said, "Let me call the head of security. He'll know what to do."

He stepped into the guard house and picked up a phone. The guard in front of the car was frozen like a statue, staring straight at them. The nose of the gun had inched upward slightly, from the front grill to Cesari's face. Cesari guessed that in the time it would take him to put the car in drive and slam on the accelerator, he and Jay would already be dead. He watched as the guard spoke into the phone. Jeremy slowed his breathing to a controlled easy in and easy out yoga type rhythm to settle his nerves.

Cesari heard the surveillance camera whizz as it zoomed in to maximum magnification. The lens moved up and down the length of the car, settled on Cesari and stayed there. The guard hung up and returned, waving at his pal in front of the car to allow them to pass. The guard relaxed, lowered his gun, and withdrew to the side as the gate opened.

The guard who had just spoken on the phone said, "Have a great night, Doctors."

Cesari thanked him, put the car in gear, and moved forward. Jay exhaled loudly in relief. Cesari said, "You're big time now, Macallan."

Jeremy was too stressed to laugh, but he did manage a grin as he nodded. Cesari drove forward slowly, intending to park the Boat Tail as far from the other vehicles as possible, but realized that to prevent mass chaos and a possible accident, all the cars were funneled around the circular drive to the front entrance where they were greeted by valet attendants.

Cesari said, "I don't like this. They don't want people parking their own vehicles."

"I can understand why," Jay surmised. "Look at all these expensive cars and limos. Try to imagine the confusion when everybody's soused at the end of the night."

"I can see that, but I hate the idea of giving the keys to anyone. Vito will kill me if something happens to his car."

"Who's Vito?"

Cesari realized he shouldn't have mentioned Vito's name but recovered quickly. "He's the owner of the dealership where the car came from."

Jay nodded. "I can understand his concern. Well, drive around to the front and ask the valet if you can park your own car. He may say yes and give you directions to where you should go."

"It's worth a try."

Cesari pulled up to the front of the house where doormen, and a team of valets stood waiting. The limo in front of them had just let out an older well-dressed couple. The man was portly with a white mustache. He wore tails, white gloves, a top hat, and used a walking stick. He looked a little bit like the guy on the monopoly board, Rich Uncle Pennybags. The woman was slender, wearing an evening gown and a diamond necklace with matching earrings that dazzled brilliantly in the light. She walked hesitantly as if struggling with arthritis in her large joints. Her face was much younger than he would have thought and Cesari suspected plastic surgery and many, many trips to the spa. Nonetheless, she was attractive.

A valet came around to his side of the car and opened the door for him. He was in his early twenties. Not a kid. Not yet a man. The valet said, "Cool car."

Cesari said, "I know. Is there any way I can park the car myself? It's not that I don't trust you but as you can see it's rather special."

"I can understand that. It's a fine machine. You don't see many of these around, but we were told to not let the guests park their own cars for safety reasons. The boss was very clear on that. The parking lot is quite a distance from here and there's too much traffic. It might not seem too bad right now but at one in the morning it's going to be a madhouse. I'll park her far away from any other cars. I promise."

Cesari thought it over, got out of the car, and said, "I guess I can live with that. What's your name?"

"Taylor."

Cesari took a hundred-dollar bill out from his wallet and handed it to him. "Take good care of my car, Taylor."

Taylor thanked him and handed him a numbered ticket to retrieve the car. "I promise to keep an eye on her. Nothing will happen. Ask for me when you're ready."

Cesari and Jay watched the Boat Tail pull away, adjusted their tuxedoes, and approached the front door of the mansion.

They passed through a portico where another team of security guards were processing everyone through a metal detector.

Cesari said, "I'm not happy."

"The car?"

"Yeah, the car. I have a sinking feeling about it."

"Relax, Cesari. You were going to have to park it and get out at some point. The kid seemed reliable. At least you know there's not going to be some random theft or smash and grab in this place."

"That's some reassurance, but I just gave some kid with pimples the keys to the most expensive car in the world."

"That's true but at least you don't actually own it, which is more than I can say for all these Bentleys and Maseratis I see."

They came out on the other side of the metal detector and entered the grand hallway of the mansion. Jay said, "Security's pretty tight tonight."

"You'd think the governor was coming or something," Cesari joked.

The sound of piano music filled the air and a multitude of well-dressed people circulated about studying the art on the walls as they sipped cocktails and champagne. Waitstaff cruised the room with caviar, oysters and foie gras. Cesari had been wrong. Before arriving, he had guessed between one hundred and one hundred and fifty guests. There were at least twice that many. The more the merrier, he thought. They grabbed champagne flutes from a passing waiter and toasted each other. They had made it through the front door.

"What now, Cesari?"

"Good question. My plan kind of ended at this point. To be honest, I didn't even think we'd get this far."

Jay laughed.

"So tell me, Macallan," Cesari said with a slight edge in his voice. "Where are the boys, right now?"

"What boys?"

"Parikh and company? The geek squad, remember them?"

"I would think they're well on the way back to Manhattan."

"Your left pupil dilates when you lie, Jay. Did you know that? You'd never make it as a spy. You had them on the line when we were driving here. That's why you asked me to tell you the exact address of the mansion and then you repeated it out loud, very slowly and very deliberately, because they were listening. It took me a while to understand why it seemed strange, but I figured it out. So where are they right now?"

Jay looked contrite and said, "About a hundred yards from the main entrance, parked on the side of the road, out of sight under a huge tree. Xi just texted me."

Cesari shook his head. "If they shoot me by accident, I am going to kill you."

Jay didn't say anything.

Something on one of the walls caught Cesari's eye, and he signaled Jay to follow him. They walked over to see it better and were now ten feet behind the grand piano where a beautiful Chinese woman in a lavender evening dress was hammering out Mozart's Piano Concerto No.21. She was as attractive as she was talented and owned the keyboard as if it was simply an extension of her body. As if when she came out of the womb, instead of crying for her first meal, she demanded to see the piano.

Cesari looked at a painting on the wall and said, "What do you think of the artwork in here, Jeremy? When we were here earlier in the week everything was so overwhelming, we didn't really talk about it."

"I don't know a whole lot about art except for a class I took in college and a semester I spent abroad in Europe. I went to a lot of museums then."

"Well, that's better than me. I know nothing about art. Take this one for instance." He pointed at the wall. "I couldn't tell if it's real or fake. All I know is it looks pretty good."

"I agree, but it's just a high-quality reproduction."

"Are you sure about that?"

Jeremy looked as if he didn't hear the question right. He said, "It would have to be."

"I guess you're right. I mean you couldn't just walk into the Museum of Modern Art and say, 'Excuse me, ma'am, I'd like that Van Gogh over there and I'm in a bit of a rush. Be a dear and pack it up for me. Do you accept Visa?'"

Jeremy chuckled at that. "Absolutely not. You couldn't even begin to put a price on a Van Gogh anyway, especially this one."

They both paused a beat and looked up at the *Starry Night*.

Chapter 36

Hugo patiently stood several feet away waiting as the Sommelier chatted up a group of local businessmen in support of their favorite governor who had yet to make his traditional and fashionably late appearance. In due time, he turned his attention to his head of security. They stepped into the Sommelier's office for privacy.

"I am sorry to bother you, Michel," Hugo began. "Something urgent has come up."

"What is it, Hugo? As you can see, I am inundated with my guests' needs. God forbid someone's martini glass should run dry before I can refill it."

"It's your car, the Boat Tail. It has just been delivered to us."

The Sommelier quietly digested that and said, "I don't understand."

"Your Dr. Cesari and his friend, Dr. Macallan just drove through the front gate with it. He said he didn't know there was a party going on and that he was just coming to visit you as per your open-ended invitation the other day. He was driving your car."

The Sommelier sat back in his chair and propped his hands together, fingers splayed wide. "My car? Are you sure it was the Boat Tail and not some gaudy low-end roadster?"

"I am quite sure. I was sitting in front of the security cameras downstairs and studied it from end to end. Of course I will check the vehicle identification number, but I have no doubt."

"What did you do?"

"I had security let him in. One of the valet's parked the car and I now have the keys. I will move it into the garage for inspection and safe-keeping, and will store the keys with the others in your vault. I felt you should know about this miraculous turn of events as soon as possible."

The Sommelier smiled. "I don't know what to say, Hugo. I never anticipated this."

"Good things happen to good people, Michel. Although, I suppose there is always a chance the Boat Tail actually does belong to Dr. Cesari. I will need clarity on what to do in that situation."

"Hogwash, Hugo. A mere physician in New York could never afford a car like that. It's royal blue, right?"

"Yes, I saw it clearly."

"Steering column on the left?"

Hugo nodded.

"Then it's my car. What are the odds of two brand new royal blue Boat Tails made for American roads running around my back yard at the same time?"

"Astronomical…"

"Exactly… The real question is how did he come across my car, although he obviously doesn't know it's my car."

"Do you think he purchased it from Gerry Acquilano?"

"Why would Gerry do that? I readily agreed to his five-million-dollar ransom demand. The logical choice if he wanted more money would have been to renegotiate the sale price or at least try to before abandoning me for another buyer. Besides, even five million would have been too steep for Cesari. I've accessed his bank records and IRS filings for the last five years. There is simply no way. He's more of a Boxster type. No, there's something going on here, Hugo. Something that is not readily apparent. Something that is suspiciously clandestine."

"Do you think this is somehow related to recent events with Dr. Goldstein?"

The Sommelier shook his head. "I don't see how. Do you? Dr. Goldstein's stay here was quite uneventful. He was fully unconscious when he arrived and equally so when he left. He spoke with no one and saw nothing but the inside of his room. According to the news, our plan went over even better than expected. Dr. Goldstein is now handcuffed to his hospital bed."

Hugo nodded. "I would feel better if our contact inside St. Matt's hadn't suddenly gone radio silent on us."

"Under the circumstances, his skittishness is forgivable. He had no idea we were behind Dr. Goldstein's kidnapping, but has probably figured it out by now. And being a clever man, he's suddenly realized that he's now waist high in multiple felonies and probably has concluded he should put as much distance between himself and us as possible. I can understand his logic. He just needs some time. I've known him forever, and I know he'll come around. He always has… At any rate, you have done well, Hugo. I am indebted to you once again and will express my gratitude appropriately."

"Thank you, Michel, but there is no need. Tell me, what are you going to do with Cesari and Macallan?"

"I'm going to have the waitstaff add two more place settings for dinner. This has the potential to be most amusing. Where are they now?"

"I believe they are in the gallery sipping champagne and listening to piano music. No doubt they think they have won the lottery showing up here tonight."

The Sommelier thought about it for a minute and said, "Who was the valet that parked the Boat Tail?"

"Taylor… He's worked for us on several previous occasions. He's a fine young man, a local boy."

"Pay him for the night. In fact, overpay him. Double what he would have made including tips, but send him home immediately. Thank him and tell him we've accidentally overstaffed and that we will keep him in mind for future events."

"What are you thinking, Michel?"

"Hugo, I think I want you to make a trip into Morristown to find me a car."

"A car? But you own at least three dozen cars?"

"Yes, but they are all too good for Dr. Cesari. I'd like you to find him one befitting his true status. When you find the right car, preferably something boring like an old, rusted station wagon, bring it here and park it in the lot with the others. Put the keys on the valet board attached to the numbered ticket that previously belonged to the Boat Tail. Then, at the end of the night, we'll sit back and have ourselves a giggle."

"Oh my, you are clever, Michel. You get your car back and a good laugh in the bargain, but if you want the keys too, then I'll have to jack a car not just steal one."

"I have every confidence in your abilities, Hugo. Off with you now and let me know when you return. In the meantime, I'll keep the Bobbsey twins occupied."

"Poor Dr. Cesari. He arrives in a golden chariot and leaves in a…"

"Bucket of bolts..."

"You took the words right out of my mouth, Michel."

"Serves him right for having the audacity to touch my Boat Tail."

"Wouldn't it be just as amusing to detain both doctors for interrogation?"

"The thought crossed my mind, and to be honest, the verdict is still out on that option. I'm concerned that there are too many witnesses, and there's always the chance of a commotion. We wouldn't want to do anything to harm the governor's re-election bid. I don't know what's going on, but for now, it will suffice to send the good doctor on his way with his tail between his legs unless some new information comes my way. Instruct the staff that for the time being he is to be treated like a VIP, every bit as much as our fat governor."

Suddenly reminded of his guest of honor, the Sommelier glanced at his watch and added, "Which reminds me, if he doesn't get here within the next five minutes, I'm going to deny him access to the bedrooms."

"I don't mean to question your judgement, Michel, but is it wise to let the governor upstairs during this sensitive time?"

"If you're referring to Martine, then fret not. She is heavily sedated and will sleep through the night. Her door is locked, and her room is on the other end of the hall from where the governor will be spanking his trollop. Simone will act as his chaperone and make sure he does not wander."

Hugo nodded. "Then I will take your leave and go find Dr. Cesari a fitting ride home."

After he left, the Sommelier sighed deeply, strummed his fingers on his desk thinking about Cesari and Macallan and the Boat Tail. Did they really come just to drop by? How did they come by the car? He simply could not connect the dots no matter how hard he tried. The Sommelier was an intelligent human being with a naturally inquisitive mind. He had graduated summa cum laude, phi beta kappa from Columbia University. He had been a member of Mensa since the age of ten when he had scored one hundred and fifty-five on his IQ test. His father had told him he would have scored higher, but he had a bad head cold on the day of his examination. That memory of his father always brought a smile to his face.

He took his cellphone out and dialed Simone. She answered on the first ring as always. "Yes, Michel."

"All is well with Martine and Jean-Claude?"

"Yes, Michel. They are both sleeping comfortably. I doubt they will wake before morning."

"Good. Come down to my office. I'd like to discuss a new problem with you."

"I'll be there presently."

The Sommelier hung up and opened the top drawer of his desk. He pushed aside some papers, reached inside, and came out with a small plain metal box. He opened it and examined the snow-white powder. He tapped a small amount onto his desk surface and then using a razor blade he kept in the drawer for this purpose, proceeded to map out several thin lines. He reached into his back pocket and took out his wallet, found a hundred-dollar bill and rolled it up.

By the time he had inhaled his second line of coke, Simone entered the room. She was wearing a short, tight black dress, black stockings and matching heels. She observed Michel and then closed and locked the door behind her. She slinked and swayed over to him shaking her head like a lioness. Without hesitation, she sat in his lap as she had done many times before, took the hundred-dollar bill and snorted a line of the nose candy as she ground herself into his crotch.

They both sighed contentedly, and she asked, "So what is this new problem, Michel?"

"Problem is too strong a word, Simone," he replied as he stared at her cleavage. "There is someone I would like you to meet. I need information."

She cupped his face in her hands and kissed him. "Someone you would like me to meet or someone you would like me to seduce?"

"I need information, Simone. I would never question your methods. You know that."

"What kind of information and how much time do I have?"

"The individual had the temerity to drive my Boat Tail to the affair tonight."

"Your missing Boat Tail?" she asked with incredulity in her voice.

"Exactly, and I want to know where he obtained it and what his role was in its theft. Plus, there are others involved in the conspiracy and I want to know where I can find them."

"Certainly this person doesn't know it's your car or he would never have brought it here."

"I'm inclined to believe that as well although it doesn't absolve him of culpability."

"I see, and you don't want to question him yourself because it might cause a scene in front of three hundred and fifty of New Jersey's wealthiest and most important people and their entourages."

He smiled. "You see my dilemma? I don't have the necessary guile you possess."

"And naturally, you would like to have all this information before the night is over so you can plan an appropriate disposition for this fellow."

"You understand me so well, Simone, which is why I couldn't survive without you. It would be so much easier to deal with him if he enters his cage voluntarily."

"You're not giving me very much time. What if he is reluctant to answer the mating call?"

"Nonsense, you are severely underestimating your charms. This particular man will be easy pickings in my opinion. Take him somewhere quiet on the second or third floors. He'll be putty in your hands, but here, take these just in case."

He reached past her into his desk drawer and handed her a small nickel plated .22 Colt semi-automatic pistol and a vial containing several pills.

He said, "The pills are chloral hydrate, your basic date rape drug. If you feel it is necessary, just drop them into whatever glass or beverage he's drinking from, and he'll be out for hours."

"And the gun?"

"You'll be alone with a man whose temperament and appetites are unknown. Who knows what base instincts you may arouse in him? If he gets out of control, you may not have time to rely on the chloral hydrate."

Simone grinned. "He sounds so primitive. Who is this unfortunate individual?"

"His name is Cesari. Come, I'll take you to him."

Chapter 37

Cesari and Jeremy mingled with the other guests, gradually making their way around the room, trying to come up with a strategy. The wine cellar was two stories down and the bedrooms were upstairs, but upstairs in a four-story building as large as this covered a lot of territory. Then there was the issue of just how many bedrooms were there? Cesari had no idea. He needed some sort of floor plan or a personal guide.

As they meandered about, they saw Mike B. closing in on them from across the room. Hanging on to his arm was a tall, stunningly beautiful woman, with long dark hair, wearing a revealing dress, a long dangling pearl necklace, diamond stud earrings, and multiple gold bracelets. In her free hand, she held a designer evening bag. Maybe in her early thirties, she looked like she belonged on a catwalk surrounded by adoring photographers. Her measured, steady gait, calculated to maximize the undulation of her hips, reinforced Cesari's image of her slinking down a runway.

Multiple guests tried to get Mike B.'s attention but he was focused on his destination and waved them off politely. It was obvious by the time he and his companion were ten feet away that his destination was Cesari and Jeremy.

Cesari whispered out of the side of his mouth, "Here we go, Jay. Put your game face on."

"I'm already there, Cesari."

When they were close, Mike B. smiled and extended his hand. Cesari and Jeremy clasped it warmly in turn. Cesari said,

"Mike, before we begin, I want apologize for crashing your party. When we had lunch with you the other day you had mentioned tonight's affair, but we drank so much that afternoon we completely forgot."

"Nonsense, Dr. Cesari. I said you and Dr. Macallan were welcome here any time and I meant any time. Tonight is as good as any."

Cesari winked, "It's just plain old, Cesari, remember?"

Jeremy said, "Jay here."

"Yes, of course… That was a great afternoon, wasn't it?"

Jeremy said, "Epic, to say the least."

"Totally," added Cesari.

Mike B. said, "Yes, my chef was certainly on top of his game that day, wasn't he?"

"As was your sommelier," Cesari pointed out. "The wine selection was brilliant."

"Thank you, Cesari. I'm genuinely flattered. I am the sommelier for the estate, and I take a compliment like that from a connoisseur such as yourself as high praise indeed. But the memory of our historic gathering the other day has caused me to misplace my manners." He turned to the woman by his side and presented her to them, saying, "Gentlemen, allow me to introduce to you, Simone. Simone is my chief of staff and runs my household for me. My wife and I would be lost without her."

"You are too kind, Michel," she said.

"I speak only the truth, Simone."

Up close, she wasn't just beautiful she was out of the park gorgeous. Her eyes were large and brown with long lashes, her cheekbones were high, and her lips were full and sensual. She smiled demurely and extended her left hand, held high, palm down, to Cesari and Jeremy. Cesari wasn't sure what he should do; shake it or kiss it. He decided the safer thing to do was to touch it lightly and make a slight bow. Jeremy followed suit and did the same.

The awkwardness of the moment passed and Cesari said, "Nice to meet you, Simone."

"Likewise," concurred Jay.

The Sommelier said, "I see you wore tuxedoes even though you were unaware of tonight's function."

"Yes," explained Cesari. "The other day, we realized we were painfully underdressed and a little embarrassed by it. We hoped to make up for it tonight."

The Sommelier smiled. "You have both done well, and as you can see just by looking around, you are a perfect fit."

Cesari changed the subject. "I look forward to meeting Mrs. Beaujolais."

Mike B. looked sad. "Unfortunately, she is out of the country at the moment. She is on an extended tour of Africa and Asia. Something she has always dreamed of doing. I was to go with her, but at the last minute, business and politics delayed me. I will catch up with her in a few weeks."

Jeremy said, "That's too bad. Won't she be lonely?"

The Sommelier smiled. "The better question, Jeremy, is will I even be missed? She is traveling with five of her closest friends and their families."

Simone said, "Of course she will miss you, Michel. You are the light of her life."

"I can only hope, Simone. The hardest part about her absence right now is that she is in a part of the world that has only spotty, at best, cell phone coverage. She sends an email here and there when she can, but she is largely incommunicado."

Cesari glanced briefly at Jay and said, "I can understand how emotionally difficult that must be. Well, thank you for allowing us to have a glass of champagne and enjoy the atmosphere. We don't want to keep you from your guests. We'll be on our way when the dinner bell rings."

"Nonsense," protested the Sommelier. "You and Jay must dine with me. I've already had my staff set a place for you both in the wine cellar. Jay, I understand you play the piano?"

Jay looked confused and said, "Yes, I do, but how…?"

The Sommelier grinned, "I make it a point of knowing as much as I can about my dinner guests, my clients, and my friends. And after our Homeric adventure the other day, I can honestly say that I now think of you as my friends."

"That's very flattering, Mike. Thank you, and I assure you it's mutual," Cesari said. "So what did you learn about me?"

The Sommelier turned to him and said, "That you are a physician in excellent standing, well liked and respected by your peers and patients alike. If and when I ever need a colonoscopy, you will be my gastroenterologist of choice."

"I appreciate the vote of confidence," replied Cesari. He then turned to Jay and grinned. "See, Macallan, if Mike will let me do his colonoscopy, you should let me do yours. I've been trying to convince him, Mike, but he's stubborn."

"But I'm only thirty-two years old," argued Jay.

"Yeah, but you're uptight. They're the ones who need it the most. A colonoscopy will loosen you right up."

The Sommelier laughed at the friendly banter. "Gentlemen, gentlemen, I order you to lay down your weapons. But seriously, Jay. My research tells me you are classically trained in both piano and violin. You studied a year at Julliard before deciding to pursue a career in medicine and enrolled in Yale for your undergraduate studies eventually winding up in Harvard medical school. Something tells me that type-A personalities such as yourself don't just surrender their skills, so I suspect you have quietly kept up your quest for musical perfection."

Jay said, "I'm impressed, and yes, I have continued to take lessons and practice both instruments as often as I can."

Cesari was astonished, "How come I didn't know anything about this?"

Jay shrugged modestly and the Sommelier said, "When I heard you were here, I took the liberty of speaking to our pianist, Yuja Wang, and she has graciously agreed to perform a duet with you. As you may know she is accomplished in many instruments, and we have a violin, viola, and cello available."

Jay's eyes went wide. "That's Yuja Wang playing the piano? She's world famous. I can't believe I didn't recognize her."

"A friend of yours, Jay?" asked Cesari.

"More like an idol. I can't possibly perform a duet with her. I'm not up to her level."

"You're being humble, Jay," added the Sommelier. "Do something uncomplicated like Eine Klein Nachtmusik. You on violin and Yuja on cello. It's written for a four-piece ensemble, but it will be fine with two. I have every confidence in you. Consider it the price you must pay for you and Cesari's ten course dinner."

Cesari encouraged him, "C'mon Jay. It'll be great, and on a selfish note, I've never had a ten-course dinner."

Jay was quiet as his mind raced. After a minute, his face broke into a big grin and he said, "Sure, why not? I'd be crazy to pass up on an opportunity like this."

"Excellent," said the Sommelier. "Then come with me and I'll introduce you to Yuja. There is a private room where you two can warm up and get used to each other. Simone, please entertain Dr. Cesari, but keep the governor away from him at all costs." He turned to Cesari. "Trust me, you can't afford that kind of an encounter. The man would cajole his own mother into mortgaging her ancestral home in order to make him a campaign contribution."

Cesari said, "Thanks for the warning."

Jeremy and the Sommelier walked away to find Yuja, and Simone stepped close to Cesari, slipping an arm through his. With heels she was almost as tall as he was, putting her at five-feet-seven or eight in her bare feet. Her hips touched his and he could smell her perfume. There were different rules for the rich and famous, he thought. In any other situation, you couldn't have paid him enough to get this close to a woman he had just met five minutes earlier. This was the modern age, and he was sure he was already guilty of something just by not pushing her away. But the idea of pushing her away gave him brain freeze. She was, to say the least, mesmerizing, so he went with the flow.

She whispered, "Fundraisers are so tedious. I find politics such a bore."

"I'm inclined to agree with you. You can't believe a word anyone of them says anyway."

"Isn't that the truth…I know you've been to the wine cellar, but have you seen the rest of the house?"

"No, we saw the bar and the cellar and of course where we're standing right now."

"You haven't been upstairs?"

"No, what's upstairs?"

"The mansion has four floors not counting the cellar. On the fourth floor are the bedrooms, but the fun part of the house are the two floors in between. Did Michel tell you about the planetarium?"

"The planetarium? There's a planetarium somewhere in here?"

"It's on the third floor. It's only five thousand square feet, but with computer graphics and 3D imaging you will feel as though you are lost in space." She glanced at her watch. "We have time. Let's go there. I never tire of it."

She grabbed his hand and led him to a small elevator. A waiter was walking by with a bottle of 1975 Dom Pérignon and a tray of empty glasses. She deftly grabbed the bottle with two flutes, and then pressed four numbers into an electronic receptacle outside the elevator. She made no effort to hide her code and Cesari memorized it. The car arrived and they boarded it upward to the third floor.

They walked down a corridor past several rooms, some of whose doors were partially open. One of the rooms was a billiard parlor and yet another bar. Cesari stopped to peer inside. There were ten professional pool tables each with its own

Tiffany lamp overhead, leather sofas and chairs everywhere and a massive humidor along the back wall.

"Amazing," he murmured to no one.

"You haven't seen anything," she laughed.

Two doors down from the pool hall, they arrived at the planetarium, a circular room, fifty feet in diameter with a twenty-foot-high domed ceiling. The walls and ceiling appeared to be made of the same material, a reflective glass of some type. There was nothing on them and he couldn't discern any seams, but there was a strangely comfortable familiarity with the appearance of the room. In the center, was a round couch which faced outward at the wall. It had armrests every five feet or so separating it into six love seats. When occupied, each couple would be facing a different part of the room. The sofa was very soft and made of the highest quality leather and each seat reclined back. He sat down next to one of the arm rests and realized each seat also had a car-like safety belt. He was so busy studying his surroundings that he didn't notice at first how near to him she sat, setting her bag down on her other side. After settling in, she pressed a button and a tray slowly rose from alongside her armrest. She placed the champagne bottle on it and filled the glasses, handing him one. They toasted each other and she snuggled uncomfortably close.

"I'm supposed to advise you to buckle your seatbelt as per the people who set up the room," she said.

"I think I'll be fine."

"I think you will too," she smiled and sipped champagne. "Besides, if a man doesn't wish to use protection what can a girl really do?"

He raised his eyebrows at that but didn't say anything. She was flirting as fast and furious as any woman he'd ever met. As if her life depended on it. As if humanity itself depended on it. As if he were the last man on Earth and she was the last woman. He liked it but was also curious as to why.

"The room is going to start moving," she warned him. "Don't be alarmed."

"Won't the champagne tip over?"

"If you're worried, I can hold it between my legs."

He blinked and said, "That won't be necessary."

"Are you ready?" she asked.

"Somehow, I don't think so."

The lights went out.

Chapter 38

It was dark. Pitch black dark. Cesari held his hand inches from his face and couldn't see it. She was close, very close and getting closer. He could feel her breath, hot and moist. She crossed her leg and swung it over hers and his in a clear and indisputable violation of his air space. He had every right to shoot her down. She was making all sorts of presumptions about his availability and his moral compass. She had some nerve making an assumption that this was somehow okay. If his mother was alive, she would have said, she's a bold one. He should just push her away. But he didn't. He couldn't. The man who could do that hadn't been born yet. A million years of evolution had programmed the human male to pursue not to evade the human female. When the tables were turned, the male had no adequate defense.

But what about, Valentina? He'd been running from her for months. That was different, he reasoned. Valentina wasn't after sex. She was trying to imprison Cesari for life in a world she had already constructed in her mind; the two-story house in the burbs with blue shutters, the white picket fence, the inground pool, the vegetable garden, the two-point-five rugrats riding their tricycles... He involuntarily shuddered at the thought.

Then the room started to rotate slowly in a clockwise direction as the sofa reclined and tilted backward like they were in a spaceship. The entire room suddenly lit up with bright white light. There was a sense of forward motion as air blew in their faces, and they felt like they were being propelled through space and time to the outer limits of the universe. Millions, perhaps billions of computer-generated stars flew by them in the blink of an eye and just as suddenly everything stopped, leaving them in a virtual reality extravaganza that rivaled any experience anywhere in the world. He realized why the walls and ceiling seemed familiar. They were one massive computer screen from the floor to the peak of the ceiling, and they were now playing tricks on his senses as they bent and distorted reality.

Cesari held his breath as they circled first the sun and then the planets and then the Milky Way itself before they shot off in another direction to another galaxy in another solar system to see other suns and other planets. They followed asteroids and rode the tails of comets. They watched stars implode and die, and they traveled through wormholes. They rode the crest of the fabric of the universe, bouncing along the space time continuum. It was a magnificent experience.

Twenty minutes later when the lights came back on, Simone was more in his lap than not. He looked at her leg resting on top of his and said, "You make friends pretty fast, don't you?"

"Not with everyone. Just handsome doctors in tuxedoes."

He glanced around the room. "Let me know when one arrives."

"Don't sell yourself short. You're remarkably good looking… Don't you want to be friends?"

"I always want to be friendly."

"Don't be shy, Dr. Cesari. I saw the way you looked at me earlier."

"Women have been saying that to me a lot lately. I think I need to work on that."

"You don't find me attractive?"

"I didn't say that, but I'm Mike's guest. There are rules of etiquette. It's kind of rude for me to…you know? With his chief of staff. What are we doing anyway?"

She laughed at that. "Nothing yet."

"I just don't think it's a good idea," he said.

"Well I think it's the best idea I've had in weeks," she countered. "You have no idea how boring it is working here."

"But we've only just met."

"Am I moving too fast?"

"You think?"

She thought it over and conceded, "You're right. Maybe we should get to know each other first."

"Shouldn't we go to dinner?"

She got all excited. "Are you asking me out on a date?"

"I meant downstairs with everyone else."

She giggled and glanced at her watch, saying, "We're good. Dinner's not for another thirty minutes."

"Dinner's at 8:00 p.m.?"

"If it starts on time and that's usually a big if. If you haven't figured it out yet, it's going to be a long night. We'll have plenty of time to catch up with the crowd."

He nodded. She wanted to be alone with him and had it all figured out, but why? He liked women and they liked him, but he wasn't stupid. This didn't add up. He said, "Don't you have a boyfriend or something? You're too beautiful to be unattached."

She smiled and poured them both more champagne. "Thank you, but no. I am unattached and have been for some time."

He asked, "How did the champagne bottle stay upright during all of that?"

"The tray is designed to stay level no matter the position of the sofa or its movement. I don't know the science behind it exactly. Some sort of gyroscopic mechanism, I presume."

"Interesting… So you're a bit deprived in the romance department?"

"Maddeningly so…"

"What about you and Michel? You seem…close.

She laughed out loud, "Heaven's no. I am nothing to him but another warm body with a function to perform. In any event, he is hopelessly devoted to his wife, who he dotes on. He loves her in the extreme."

"And yet she's in Africa on a safari and he's here with hundreds of his best friends."

"Lifestyles of the fabulously wealthy can be difficult for the rest of us to understand I'm afraid."

"So you're just another cog in the machine around here?"

"Unfortunately, yes, and I pay a heavy price for it in that I lead a very lonely existence. Managing the house and its staff is like two jobs in one. I frequently work sixty or seventy hours a week and every weekend. Michel pays me well, but he is a slave driver, and there are no men here other than gardeners and plumbers, and it wouldn't be smart to get involved with one of the staff anyway. It could undermine my authority. I am truly sorry if I misjudged you. I thought I saw something in your eyes, but I guess I was mistaken."

"There's no need to be sorry. I think what you saw in my eyes was true admiration for your beauty. I thought you were a model when I first saw you downstairs."

She seemed to like that. "Tell me about yourself now that we're putting the horse back in front of the cart."

"What would you like to know?"

"I know you're a doctor. A gastroenterologist, Michel said. He didn't say if you're married or have a girlfriend?"

"Neither," he laughed.

"Why do you laugh?"

"I can't help it. It's kind of funny that you asked me that as an afterthought."

"You're making fun of me."

"Absolutely not. Please don't take offense. I meant no harm."

"What about hobbies or interests? You obviously spend a lot of time in a gym." She squeezed his bicep through his tuxedo jacket and then ran her hand over his chest in admiration before continuing, "Do you read books or travel? Maybe you like cars the way many men do?"

"I read for entertainment sure, when I have the time. The same thing for travelling, and cars? I guess I like them."

"Fast cars?" she asked, her eyes lighting up. "I like fast cars."

He shook his head. "Truthfully, cars are just tools I use to get from one place to another. As long as they're comfortable and reliable, I'm fine."

"What kind of car do you own?"

"A Honda Accord. It's ten year's old and not much to look at. It's got a few lumps and bumps here and there, but it gets the job done."

She seemed surprised at that and nearly gasped, "You drove an old Honda here wearing a tuxedo? And they let you in?"

"No, I didn't drive the Honda here. A friend of mine owns a Mercedes dealership in Morristown. He also sells other high-end cars. He owed me a favor and let me borrow one of his nicer models for the night. I didn't look out of place."

She said, "That's too funny. So what kind of car did he lend you?"

"A Rolls Royce convertible."

"Seriously, a Boat Tail? I've never ridden in one."

"Neither has ninety-nine percent of the world's population."

"You must take me for a ride."

"After tonight, I have to return it. It's a very expensive car."

"Then tonight, after dinner… please."

He thought it over and said, "Sure, why not? A short ride, okay?"

"I'm liking you more with each passing minute, Dr. Cesari."

"Once you scratch past the crusty exterior, I'm a barrel of laughs, and it's just plain, Cesari, like I told Mike."

She smiled. "I concur about you being a barrel of laughs, but honestly you don't seem that crusty."

"Don't let the tux fool you. Somebody once told me I'm like the difference between Paris and New York... Have you been to Paris?"

She clearly found him amusing. "Yes, many times. So please expand on that thought."

"Well, when people travel to Paris for the first time, they immediately fall in love with it because of its grandeur, its artwork, its cuisine, its sophistication, but the longer you stay, the more the luster wears off revealing all of its flaws, the class divisions, the hubris of its citizenry, the shallowness of its soul. In time, you can't wait to leave. Whereas when people first arrive in New York, they are overwhelmed by its great size, its industrial nature, the pace of its life, and the rudeness of its citizens. But as time goes on New York becomes a treasure trove of tiny nooks and crannies, bars and cafes. The quirkiness of its people become the marvel of life and the city itself begins to feel like an old comfortable sweater that fits you and only you. In time, you don't ever want to leave."

When he finished, she looked at him and was quiet for a long moment. Finally, she said, "That was the most intriguing self-description I've ever heard."

"Was it?"

"Yes, it was... And now I want to kiss you more than ever."

They held each other's gaze. She was still half on top of him, her face inches away. He whispered, "I suppose one kiss wouldn't violate any host-guest rules of etiquette."

"Not at all," she purred. "We could pretend it's my birthday."

"Or mine..."

"Exactly, there's nothing wrong with a birthday kiss, is there?"

"Nothing at all, but just a little one, all right?"

"I totally agree."

She said that and completed her turn onto him hiking her dress up a little to allow for greater freedom of movement. Then she wrapped her arms around his neck, and let her hair fall over his face before pressing her lips against his, lightly at first and then with more pressure and more passion. Her tongue slithered into his mouth and played with his. He stopped breathing and felt blood rushing in all directions. For a moment, he considered trashing all the rules about host-guest etiquette, but he calmed himself down, remembered his mission, took a breath, and gently pushed her back. Her eyes were wild with lust and her hair was now tousled. She was breathing hard.

Cesari said, "Happy birthday."

Chapter 39

"Happy birthday?" she giggled and tried to kiss him again, but he held her firm.

"One kiss, remember?"

She looked at him. "You can't be serious?"

Before she could add to that sentiment, her cellphone buzzed. She reached over to where she had placed her evening bag and retrieved it. It was the Sommelier.

She listened for a minute and said, "Yes, Michel, I will come now."

After she hung up, Cesari asked, "Work?"

"Always," she replied. "The governor requires urgent attention."

"Is he all right?"

She laughed. "Yes, he would like to tour one of the bedrooms with his young female staffer."

At first Cesari didn't quite get it, but his eyes grew wide as her meaning sunk in. He said, "You're kidding?"

"I wish I were. His carnal appetite is legendary, but he's not the only one. The bedrooms upstairs will see robust usage with quite a few of our guests tonight. It is but one of the reasons Michel's parties are renowned."

"Doesn't it get a bit confusing up there with all that traffic?"

"Believe it or not, it's all quite organized. We have do not disturb signs on the doors when they're occupied. If the door is unlocked and there is no sign on it, you can assume the room is available. The maids are constantly running around changing linens."

"Jesus… How do you keep track of it all?"

She grinned. "Now you understand. It's my job to make it all run smoothly, and believe me, it's not easy. But this is early. The governor likes to get a head start. None of the rooms are in use yet. Usually, things don't start picking up until after the third course. Look, I have to go, but I'll be right back. I want you to stay here. We have a lot to talk about, starting with this happy birthday stuff. I will be gone no more than fifteen minutes. I promise."

She raised the seat back to its starting position, climbed off him and adjusted her hemline and hair. She took out a small compact mirror from her bag and tweaked herself back to perfection. She pressed a button on the side of her arm rest and soft music filtered into the room. She smiled, blew him a kiss, and then left the room.

Cesari jumped to his feet, ran after her, counted to ten and opened the door a crack. He saw her enter the elevator down the hall and glanced at his watch. Fifteen minutes. He might never get a better opportunity. He sprinted down the corridor looked right and left and spotted a staircase with wide steps and luxurious carpeting. He bounded up two at a time, reaching the fourth floor in seconds. Probably before Simone even made it to the ground level, he thought.

The big problem was that he was now confronted with a very, very long hallway with multiple doors on either side. The plush floor rug would keep the noise from his footsteps down to a minimum, and there were large potted plants positioned at regular intervals which would provide casual cover. As he got his bearings, he noticed the corridor branched off to one side leading to even more bedrooms. He had a lot of ground to cover and needed to move quickly.

He decided to start with the bedroom furthest down the hallway from the elevator just in case Simone and the governor arrived prematurely. There was always the chance they might come up the stairs, but he deemed that very unlikely. Important people didn't walk when they could ride. The decision made, he dashed to the room, and was surprised to find that it already had a do not disturb sign on it. That was odd. He scanned around. It was the only one with a sign on it. But Simone had said the liaisons hadn't started yet and that the governor was getting a head start on everyone else. Maybe somebody was up here that she didn't know about? Would that make sense if she was in charge of keeping track of things? He gently tested the knob. It was locked. Pressing his ear up against the door, he listened carefully for any sounds.

At first, he heard nothing, but he slowed his breathing down and listened more carefully. He wasn't sure. He furrowed his brow in frustration and determination. Could he have been this lucky on the first try?

Wait!

What was that? He pressed his ear against the door. He thought he heard a small child crying or whimpering. It was faint and distant, and he was unconvinced. It could have been the wind whistling through a partially open window or a radio someone forgot to turn off.

He went to the adjacent room and turned the knob. The door opened and he entered. It was the largest, most lavish bedroom, he had ever been in. He studied the room carefully; fireplace, four-poster, canopied king bed, chandelier, desk, chairs, Persian rugs, paintings on the walls. His heart raced and the hair on the nape of his neck jumped to attention. It was just as Arnie had described. He'd really been here or in one of the other rooms assuming they were all similar.

A quick check of two more bedrooms confirmed that theory. Different paintings, different color schemes, but all were enormous and fit for kings. As he left one of the rooms, he heard the elevator door open at the other end of the hall and ducked back inside. They were quite a distance away, but he heard a deep male voice laughing and a feminine voice giggling. Then he heard Simone wishing them a good night. He looked at his watch. Damn, it had only taken her ten minutes to get the governor settled in, not fifteen. He heard a bedroom door open and then close. He peeked out into the hallway and saw Simone walking toward the elevator with her back to him. He quietly closed the door behind him and raced over the carpeted floor to the staircase and leapt downward three and four steps at a time soaring to the third floor, beating her by seconds at the most. He hustled to the planetarium and plopped down on the love seat just a moment before she entered the room with a big smile on her face. He stood up to greet her.

She said, "You're still here? I wasn't sure if you would be."

"I thought about going downstairs to listen to Jay play the violin. You know, to give him some moral support, but then I thought about how charming you are and how well we were getting along. So I said to myself, self, you can go listen to another doctor play stupid Mozart or you can... Well, let's just say that you won that coin toss."

She smiled and laughed. "Well, well, well, that certainly was fifteen minutes well spent, but why do you seem breathless?"

He stepped close to her and gazed longingly into her eyes. "Now if you have to ask a question like that, then you really don't understand men at all."

She didn't say anything but stepped into him, pressing her body against his.

"Is the governor all settled in?" he asked.

"You never know what's going to happen with him, but for the moment, yes."

He wrapped his arms around her, and she reciprocated. He said, "Refresh my memory. Where did we leave off?"

"You were very rudely limiting me to one kiss, I believe."

"I did that?" he smiled. "That doesn't sound like me."

"You did and now you need to make up for it."

"And how shall I do that?"

"Kiss me now, like you mean it."

He leaned into her and kissed her for a long time. His hands traced down her back to her bottom where they lingered, teasing her of what was to come. She looked into his eyes to make sure this wasn't another false start. It wasn't and she pulled him into her tightly.

She whispered, "Let me turn out the lights."

"No," he said. "Not here. This feels cheap. Let's go to one of the bedrooms and do this in style. You said they're not in use right now except for the one the governor is in."

She smiled again. "You're adorable, did you know that? I think that's a marvelous idea."

"Do you have keys to the bedrooms in case they're locked?"

"They're generally not locked at this time, but yes, I have a master key that opens all the rooms in case of an emergency."

"What kind of emergency?"

"You're sort of naïve, aren't you?"

"How so?"

"Think of it; a bunch of liquored up, coked up, filthy rich, political animals romping around behind locked doors with their harlot du jour. Seems like it has the potential for trouble, don't you think?"

"When you put it that way…"

"Is there any other way to put it."

"I guess not, but what would you do if there was trouble?"

"I'm a first responder. I call security and then barge into the room and politely yell fire hoping that will settle everyone down."

"What if it doesn't?"

"I'm a first-degree black belt in taekwondo and Brazilian jiu jitsu. It usually doesn't take much to bring someone back down to Earth however large he might be. Besides, the idea is to just slow them down a little until the big boys arrive."

"I'm impressed, and maybe a little bit frightened."

Smiling she said, "You should consider yourself lucky. When you pushed me away earlier, I was tempted to put you in a headlock."

He laughed. "Thank you for being so patient with me."

She grabbed his hand. "C'mon let's go find us our own little paradise."

"I hope Jay doesn't miss me."

"I doubt it. I called downstairs and had them move your seats. You'll be sitting next to me now and he's sitting with Yuja. By the way, they were playing when I went down to collect the governor. He was holding his own with her very well."

"I hope I never have to hold my own."

"Then I suggest you never get married."

"That would be reason number five hundred and fifteen."

They both laughed at that as they approached the door. Cesari paused, looked back, and said, "Should I bring the champagne with us. It looked expensive."

She shook her head. "I wouldn't bother. There's champagne, wine, scotch, and snack food in every room. If we wind up spending more time than we planned, I'll send for something more substantial, like lobster or filet mignon."

"I like a girl who can snap her fingers and have a steak appear."

"I have many more talents than that. As soon as we find a bedroom, I'll demonstrate a few of them to you."

He gave the room one last look and they left.

Chapter 40

They exited the elevator and strode down the corridor arm in arm passing the bedroom where the governor was exercising his right of eminent domain. They heard no sounds coming from within.

Cesari commented, "I presume the rooms are all very well insulated for sound."

"Yes, of course. It wouldn't do to have the entire fourth floor filled with the howls of old men and their whores wailing in sexual frenzy."

He laughed. "You do know how to turn a phrase."

"Forgive my cynicism."

"I can understand it," he said and added, "If the rooms are sound proofed how do you know when there's trouble?"

"That is an excellent question. There are listening devices in the rooms that trigger on when the decibel level reaches a certain threshold. Ordinary conversation won't activate them but a girl screaming in pain or terror will."

"Fascinating... All the rooms?"

"All but Michel's master bedroom, but fear not. There is an electronic keypad in every room to control the device. I will turn ours off when we arrive. No one will hear you cry out in climactic ecstasy."

"Thank you," he laughed, and looking in all directions noted, "This is probably the largest personal residence I've ever been in."

"Me too, unless you count Buckingham Palace or Versailles."

"Does Mike have any children? This place is practically begging to have kids running up and down doing their best to mess it up."

She grinned at that. "Yes, they have one child, Jean-Claude. He is three years old and is with his mother in Africa at the moment. He is an extremely well-behaved child although he does suffer from night terrors occasionally, but many children his age do."

Cesari contemplated that and thought about the sound he heard coming from the room at the far end of the hall. Was it a child crying out in his sleep? He said, "I feel bad for Mike. His wife and kid being away and all. That has to be hard."

"It is very difficult, so he throws himself into his work to take his mind off their absence."

They walked halfway down the hallway when Simone stopped, and said, "This one will do."

The door opened quietly, and they entered a dark room. He closed the door behind them and when he turned back, she was waiting, flung her arms around him and pushed him back against the door. She kissed him ardently and took his breath away.

Eventually she let go and reached for a dimmer switch that controlled several low voltage electric candles on the walls. She said, "I will turn off the listening device and turn on the fireplace. Go get us a bottle of wine or scotch if you prefer. There is a refrigerator over there by the desk with ice. Glasses are on a silver tray."

As he walked over to the desk, he sketched out in his mind how things should proceed. Glancing around the room, he saw two large floor to ceiling windows with expensive, maroon colored velvet curtains and got an idea. He found some ice and dropped a few cubes in rocks glasses and poured them two-fingers of thirty-year-old Oban. Not a bad way to kick off the night. When he returned, he found her sitting on the edge of the massive bed with her legs crossed. The shimmering hue of the fireplace cast a romantic glow over the room. She patted the space next to her for him to come and sit.

He handed her a glass of scotch as he sat down, and they clinked their glasses. She said, "This is very exciting."

"The first time always is."

"Talk to me. I feel like I'm floating on air right now and need to calm myself."

"What do you want me to say?"

"Tell me about the Boat Tail. Is it expensive?"

She said it again. But why did that bother him?

He said, "I assume, but I didn't ask the guy the exact price. I asked him if I could borrow a nice car for the night to impress some people. I didn't say who I was trying to impress. I didn't feel it was any of his business. I thought he'd give me a Mercedes or its equivalent, but I guess he felt he owed me big time, so he said to take the Rolls. He told me it was the most expensive car on his lot. He didn't say how much exactly but I figure we're talking about one or two hundred thousand, probably."

She laughed at that. Almost spit up her scotch to be more accurate. "Are you all right?" he asked.

"Yes, I'm fine. I just enjoy listening to you. This person who owed you big time. Was his name Alan Chamberlain by any chance?"

"Yes, do you know him?"

"Not on a personal level, but he showed me a Mercedes last year. Ultimately, I went with a BMW."

"Both very good cars."

Cesari was spinning a good story and was pleased with himself, but there was something about her reactions and her questions. He felt like he was being interrogated. She seemed to be trying to understand the bigger picture about something.

"If he's a Mercedes dealer, why would he have a car like that?" she asked.

"I have no idea. I didn't ask. Why would I? He's a car dealer. And when I said he was a friend, I kind of stretched the definition of friend a little. I took care of a relative of his in Manhattan and he was very grateful. He made one of those offers people do when they're feeling good. He probably never expected me to take him up on it."

"And now you're driving a brand-new Rolls Royce Boat Tail."

She said it again, and then it came to him. All the pieces started to fall into place. His mind raced connecting the dots. He just needed one more thing to be sure. He said, "Well, good things happen to good people... May I you a question, Simone?"

"Of course."

"There was a guy outside the house when I drove up. The cars were all waiting in line to pass through the security checkpoint, and he was giving orders to the security guards like he was in charge. I was just wondering who he was. He had a different kind of name. The kind you don't hear very often at least not here in the States. I heard the guard say it..."

"Was it Hugo? He's the head of security here. That was probably him."

"That was it...Hugo."

"What about him?"

"Nothing. I was just curious. He seemed important, but I think we've broken the ice enough," he said smiling devilishly. "Now let's talk about you."

She grinned seductively. "What about me?"

"I'm not going to lie, Simone. You're driving me wild. If you're okay with this, then I'm more than okay with it too."

She stood, took their scotch glasses, and placed them on a nearby credenza next to her bag. When she returned, she stood in front of him and then turned away, saying, "Help me undo my dress."

He rose off the bed, placed his arms around her, and kissed her on the neck, first on one side and then on the other. She moaned in appreciation and anticipation as he unzipped the back of her dress. She swung around to face him and let it slide to the floor. Standing there in her undergarments and pearl necklace in the flickering light of the fireplace, she was a sight to behold, and his heart skipped a beat. Studying her, Cesari suddenly understood how the Trojan War started. Helen of Troy was a woman whose beauty was so great, it caused men to throw their reason and common sense out the window. It would be an easy thing for him to do at the moment.

He pulled her close. His voice was hoarse. "May I make a suggestion?"

She kissed him and whispered, "I'm pretty sure you can do anything you want right now."

"Do you trust me?"

"We wouldn't be here if I didn't."

He leaned close and whispered into her ear. She smiled as he spoke, thought about it, nodded, and said playfully, "You are bad, aren't you? What an interesting night this is turning into. Shall I lie face up or face down?"

"Face up. Make yourself comfortable."

She laid down in the center of the bed and watched him with great interest. He walked over to the curtains and pulled off their gold, braided tiebacks with their tasseled edges and returned to the side of the bed. He then tied one of her wrists to the bed post, firmly but gently.

"It's not too tight?" he asked. "I don't want to hurt you."

She tugged on it. "Not at all."

"Good. The idea is to have fun and enhance our pleasure, not to cause discomfort."

He walked to the other side of the bed and repeated the procedure. When he was finished, and both her wrists were firmly bound, he looked at her from head to toe. She was still wearing her high heels. The temptation to finish what they had started was almost overwhelming. The desire in her eyes was at a fever pitch as her chest heaved up and down with primal need. Instead of putting out the fire, he went over to the credenza, picked up her bag, brought it back to the bed and emptied its contents.

She looked confused. "What are you doing?"

He picked up the Colt .22 the Sommelier had given her and examined it, saying, "I hope this wasn't for me?"

"Of course not. I am always armed. You never know what's going to happen with this many important people in one place."

He nodded, put the gun down and picked up her key ring. "I guess that makes sense. Are any of these the master key to the bedrooms?"

Bewilderment spread over her face. "Yes, the silver one with a purple mark on it, but I don't understand."

"Simone, we need to have a frank conversation. I'm going to give you ten minutes of my time and then I have to go."

"What are you talking about?"

"Simone, you've been lying to me from the first second you saw me, and I want to know why."

"Lied to you about what?"

"Let's start with this. I'm old enough to have been to a few rodeos before and beautiful women who live in mansions do not come charging across art galleries to throw themselves at me. As much as I would love that to happen, it just doesn't. So I had to ask myself a difficult question. What do you really want from me? Certainly it wasn't the sausage in my trousers, so what was it?"

Sudden realization that the game was over swept across her face. She pulled on her restraints, and said angrily, "Let me go. You have no idea what you are doing."

"Maybe not the full picture, not yet, but I have a pretty good outline. I was a little too focused on the lies I had been telling to pick up on the ones you were telling. Plus," he smiled, "I was a little bit smitten too."

From the corner of his eye, he saw her begin a slight hip rotation as she planned a kick to his head with her high heeled foot. A well-placed kick from a blackbelt might easily render him unconscious if not worse. Before she could gain any momentum, however, he lunged himself across her thighs and stomach eliciting a grunt as the wind rushed out of her. She struggled, but he was much too heavy, and all she could do was curse under her breath.

"Now, now… I haven't hurt you, Simone, so let's not break the truce, all right?" he said in a chiding manner.

"Once again, I'm warning you. Let me go now and I'll forget about this. We can go downstairs as if nothing happened."

"But I haven't finished my story. You see I came here to determine whether a woman named Martine Beaujolais is being held against her will and now I'm convinced she is. You see, that was the lie I told. I didn't come here to have a drink with Mike. I came to find her. Had I told the truth, I'm certain I would not have been let in the house."

She was quiet, confirming in his mind that she knew all about it. He added, "No comment? You're the chief of staff, aren't you? You have the master key to all the bedrooms, don't you? Would it be possible for someone to be a prisoner here and you be unaware? I don't think so. And you all but confessed it to me out in the hallway."

"And how did I do that?" she hissed through clenched teeth, seething with rage.

"I asked you if Mike had any children and you told me he had a toddler who was in Africa with his mother, but Mike never mentioned once how much he missed his child. That was kind of odd. When you were tending to the governor, I was down the corridor. I found a room with a do not disturb sign on it at the end of the hallway and I heard a child crying inside. Maybe he was having a night terror."

She now pulled violently on the tiebacks in a futile effort to escape. Cesari watched her struggle helplessly. He knew his knots well and was confident they would hold. They'd better, he thought. He wasn't looking forward to a tussle with an expert in any kind of martial arts. But they held.

"One last time, Simone. Are Martine Beaujolais and her child being held against their will in the room down the hall?"

Red-faced and apoplectic, she spit at him, saying with contempt, "Michel will kill you. You bastard."

Cesari wiped his face. "I'll take that as a yes. Perhaps, I should enlist the aid of the governor. After all, if Michel told everyone his wife and child were in Africa, then won't he be surprised to see them right here? And won't Michel be surprised to see you all tied up and naked? He'll probably be very disappointed in you. Does he take disappointment well?"

She didn't say anything, but from the look in her eyes, Cesari realized he'd hit a nerve.

He went on, "But I'm curious about something else. You didn't come on to me like gangbusters to protect his little secret about his wife or else we never would have left the main floor. Bringing me up to the bedrooms would have been incredibly stupid, and you don't seem stupid. Therefore, you must have had something else on your mind."

She said nothing as her eyes darted in every direction looking for a way out of her predicament.

"It was about the car, wasn't it? You asked me one too many questions about cars tonight. When I told you I drove here in a Rolls Royce convertible, you immediately called it a Boat Tail. No hesitation at all. The first time you said it, it went over my head, but the second time I knew something wasn't right. There are many different models of Rolls Royce convertibles, and you went right to the rarest, most exotic, most expensive one of all like a homing pigeon. And moments ago, when you asked me the price, I threw out one or two hundred thousand dollars and you gagged on your scotch because you knew it was worth tens of millions. But the clincher was Hugo. I heard from a very reliable source that a nasty guy named Hugo was looking for his boss's Boat Tail and was none too pleased that he couldn't find it. I wonder how many Hugos there could be in Bernardsville that fit that description? All things considered, I was forced to conclude that you were sent by your employer to find out what the hell I was doing with his property. Except it's not his property. He stole it. Probably, like he stole everything else in this place, like Van Gogh's *Starry Night* on the wall downstairs. Yeah, I know about that too. A word to the wise, princess. There are lots of things you can steal in this world and get away with it, but national treasures aren't one of them. You're on the losing side, Simone. Federal agents are going to be swarming this place soon enough, so I suggest you take a deep breath and hear me out with an open mind."

She was defeated, but her wheels were spinning fast and furious. He recognized the look. She was gradually becoming pragmatic. That's what smart people did. You accepted your losses and moved on.

"What do you want?" she asked reasonably, the hostility gone from her voice.

"I'm going to need help getting out of here and I'm taking Martine and Jean-Claude with me. It occurred to me that if Mike knows I brought his Boat Tail here and sicced you on me, he's probably not going to let me just drive away in it."

She laughed derisively, "No, not at all. He already has the car secured in his garage with his fleet of other expensive automobiles. He has substituted another vehicle for you to leave in. Last I heard it was a canary yellow mini cooper with gaudy white stripes down the hood. That is, if he decides to let you leave at all. He was waiting to hear from me to make that decision."

"A canary yellow mini cooper with white stripes? Seriously? He must have a very low opinion of me."

"Very low indeed."

"So what was he waiting to hear about?"

"Whether you were involved in the conspiracy to steal the car or not. You had more or less convinced me that you were very possibly an innocent bystander, although your explanation of Alan Chamberlain lending you the Boat Tail for the night didn't quite ring true. I know Alan very well. He has worked for us for years. If he had stolen the car, he never would have let it out of his sight. Why anyone would have lent you a car like that is beyond my comprehension. Thieves are clever but sometimes not very smart was my analysis. If it means anything, I was planning on advocating for your release."

"Thanks for that, and what would happen if he didn't let me go?"

"You don't want to know."

"But I do want to know, because the other reason I came here is he did a great disservice to a friend of mine. He held him captive here for two days, and now everyone thinks he's nuts and possibly a murderer. But he's the one who tipped me off about Martine. He managed to talk to her through the duct work in their bathrooms, and now I need to clear the air. So I want to know just how bad this guy is."

"Ah, Dr. Goldstein. Now I see. That is interesting. So you are just a do-gooder helping a friend? Great job," she said dryly. "You have gotten us both killed tonight, Dr. Do-Gooder."

Ignoring her sarcasm, he asked, "Did your pal, Michel, frame Dr. Goldstein for murder?"

"Of course. Isn't it obvious? It was Hugo who did it on Michel's behest. They heard that the anesthesiologists at your hospital were under suspicion for murder using an anesthetic, so they thought to seize upon the opportunity to discredit him before he sang to the SEC."

"They heard? They're the ones who placed the listening device in his office?"

She nodded and said, "Yes, but you are concerning yourself with the wrong things at the moment, Dr. Cesari. It's true. Michel sent me to find out about the car, and he might have given you a pass over that if he believed you had nothing to do with its theft. But when he discovers your true purpose was to rescue Martine and avenge your friend, his wrath will be volcanic. You have sealed your fate and mine I'm afraid. You were right in that when I am found like this, he will know that I have failed him.

His disappointment in me will have catastrophic consequences. As for how bad he is… Let's just say that we will probably both wind up on the wall."

"What's that supposed to mean?"

Chapter 41

Simone told Cesari about the trophy room in the wine cellar and why Martine was being confined to quarters. He listened in stark disbelief at her description of the macabre chamber. He had seen and heard a lot of things in his life but this one trumped them all.

After a time he said, "And you can prove this?"

"Martine will confirm it, but if you need visual confirmation, I know where he keeps the key to that room."

He glanced down at the bed and noticed the little bottle of pills. "What are those?" he asked.

"Roofies. If I decided you needed to remain here for Michel to interrogate, I was to knock you out and lock you in. The rooms have one-way deadbolts."

Apparently, Simone had decided that full disclosure was better than being left tied to the bed. Nonetheless, her sudden frankness irked him. "You were going to have sex with me and then turn me over to your boss to cut my head off? What do I look like, a male praying mantis?"

"I don't know what he was going to do with you, but I've already told you. I was going to advise him to allow you to leave."

"That doesn't mean he would have taken your advice, and what about Martine? He can't keep her locked up forever."

"I don't think even he knows what he has planned for her. He does care for her, but right now, he feels betrayed."

"And you're okay with this?"

"No, I'm not okay with this, but I'm powerless, and I can't just leave. He would come after me. He would send Hugo, and he wouldn't just kill me." She shuddered. "It would be slow and painful."

"Cry me a river, Simone. We all have to make choices, and you made some pretty bad ones." He glanced at his watch. "Time's up. Will you help me or not?"

"And what happens to me if I do?"

"What's going to happen to you if you don't?"

"He will kill me no doubt, but it may be quick if he thinks you simply overpowered me. If I betray him, then I will find out what hell is like before I die."

"I'm not the police, Simone. I just want to get out of here safely with Martine, her child, and my friend downstairs. If you help me, then I don't care if you disappear into the woodwork. I'll even help you. The only people I want brought to justice are Mike and Hugo."

"You truly mean that?"

He nodded. "Yes, I do, but we need to move fast. We've already spent too much time up here. Mike will be wondering where we are."

"I will help you, but you will need to trust me."

He hesitated and then said, "How so?"

"Let me call Michel to buy us more time and to reassure him all is going well."

It took him a minute to make up his mind before he said, "Make the call."

"Untie me."

"No, I'll hold the phone to your ear."

He opened her phone and she directed him to her contact list where the Sommelier's phone number was. He pressed the dial key and held the phone to her right ear. He flipped the safety off the Colt .22 and pressed it against her forehead.

He said, "Talk."

When the Sommelier answered she began to speak, quietly as if she was afraid of being overheard, "Michel, we are upstairs in one of the bedrooms. I am delayed. He is in the bathroom so I must hurry. I am sure he knows more than he is letting on, but I am confident he will tell me all. Unfortunately, he is obsessed with sex, and I will have to submit. The thought disgusts me but I will find out what you want. I must go now. Give me an hour."

She waited a second, looked at Cesari, and signaled the end to the call. He clicked the phone off and tucked it into one pocket and the gun into the other. He said, "Not bad, but you didn't have to add the, he disgusts me, part. You were just trying to bug me."

She grinned. "We are lucky. Dinner was delayed waiting for the governor to arrive and they are just serving the first course now. You can untie me. I just signed my death warrant with that call. I am no longer a threat to you."

"I'll untie you and you can get dressed. I'm tired of seeing you in your lingerie. It disgusts me."

She snorted. "Touché, we are even."

He untied her wrists and she slid off the bed and put her dress back on. He zipped her up and said, "We need a plan before we leave here, and I still don't trust you."

"As far as a plan is concerned, I suggest we get Martine and Jean-Claude and take the elevator down to the underground garage. From there, we can commandeer one of the cars. He keeps all his keys in a safe in his bedroom."

"And then what? Just drive through the front gate?"

"More or less. All the security guards know me. I doubt they will give it a second thought. Their job is to keep unwanted people out, not in. It is Martine that will be a problem. She is heavily sedated right now as is the child. If a guard sees them like that, he may call in to Hugo or Michel."

"Are there any Rolls Royces in the garage besides the Boat Tail?"

"Of course. At least six, why?"

"All their trunks are enormous and lined with luxurious wool. If we take a few pillows with us, they won't know whether they're in their own beds or not."

"That would work."

"Okay, let's go get the keys."

"Michel's bedroom is down the fork in the corridor. It is the last bedroom and has a fingerprint scanner protecting it."

"Naturally, your fingerprint can get us in?"

"Naturally, and I also know the combination to the safe. He sends me to retrieve things for him or to put things away for safekeeping."

"He's pretty trusting."

"No one in their right mind would willingly betray Michel. I already dread the thought of what will happen to me if I'm caught. Beheading will be the least of my worries."

"If you're looking for sympathy, you got the wrong guy. I doubt Mike will treat me any better, but before we go anywhere, I need an insurance policy."

"What kind of an insurance policy?"

Picking up one of the tiebacks he had restrained her wrists with, he wrapped it around her waist and tied a knot. Then he looped the other end around his hand several times until there was one foot of gold cord separating them.

"Now we're ready," he said.

Her eyes went wide. "Seriously, a leash?"

"You're complaining? Be glad I didn't tie it around your neck."

"There's no need for incivility, Doctor."

Cesari yanked on the leash and gave her a stern look. "No need for incivility? I strongly disagree with that. I think there's plenty of need for incivility after what you just told me. I should have warned you. I have a tendency to be impolite to people who want to mount my head on their wall like a twelve-point buck."

"Fine, but I'm on your side now."

"I'm glad to hear it, and the closer you are to my side, the less likely it will be that you'll try to kick me in the head... Let's go."

They opened the door an inch, determined the corridor was safe and scurried to the master bedroom. She pressed her thumb into a fingerprint reader and there was an audible click as the mechanism unlocked. Inside they found a room that was easily twice the size of the others. There was a ten-foot-wide working fireplace with piles of neatly stacked wood nearby. This room had a fully stocked bar with two leather chairs. The bed was a king and half in size and needed a step ladder to climb onto it. The room reeked with ostentatiousness.

She led him to a massive walk-in closet the size of a two-car garage. Cesari glanced around and estimated there were at least five hundred suits on hangars with row upon row of shirts, ties, belts, and shoes. She pushed aside a section of clothes and revealed a large combination safe built into the wall. It was three feet wide by three feet high. She turned the dial to the right, to the left, and back to the right. As she lifted the latch to open the door, he grabbed her wrist.

She looked at him and he shook his head. "I'll look in first. Lots of people keep handguns in safes."

"Go ahead. He has another safe for his guns. It is much larger than this one."

She stepped to the side, and he opened the door. There were no handguns, but there was plenty of other fun stuff including stacks of cash in their bank wrappers, in multiple currencies from around the world, bags full of diamonds, stocks, and passports with various aliases. There was a box with many sets of car keys organized by manufacturer. Cesari grabbed all the Rolls Royce keys and stuffed them into his pockets.

He said, "So far, so good, but where's the trophy room key?"

She looked inside the box, then the safe, and reached in with her arm, pushed things around and eventually came out with a large key which she handed to him. She closed the safe and they left the bedroom in all its majesty and headed toward the room with Martine and Jean-Claude. When they reached the door, Cesari took her personal set of keys from his pocket and handed them to her. She unlocked the door, and they went in. On the bed and under the covers was Martine Beaujolais and next to her lay Jean-Claude.

They were breathing comfortably and in no distress. Cesari shook Martine gently but elicited no response. He called out her name and shook her more vigorously to no avail. She groaned a little and made unintelligible sounds, but that was all.

Cesari let go of the tieback and said, "We're going to have to carry them. You get Jean-Claude, but I have to make a call first."

Simone nodded and walked to the other side of the bed as he dialed Jeremy. Jeremy answered, "Cesari, where have you been? Dinner started."

There was a lot of noise in the background, music and people conversing. "I've been busy. I found Mrs. Beaujolais. She really is being held against her will. She's with her son, and I'm going to try to get them both out of here. I'm not going to sugar coat it, Jeremy, you're in a lot of danger. We're all in a lot of danger. Don't react, all right? Beaujolais might be watching you. Just pretend it's a friendly call and you're having a great time. Smile a lot. Got it?"

"Got it. What should I do?"

"You're sitting next to Yuja, right?"

"Yes…"

When there's a break in between courses. Tell her you'd like to play the piano or violin with her a little more to pass the time. It will seem natural after your duet. That will at least get you back upstairs."

"And then what?"

"I haven't gotten that far, but whatever you do, if Mike or one his guys say they want to show you something at the far end of the cellar where there aren't crowds of people, don't agree to go."

"Oh shit…"

"Keep smiling Jay. It's going to be all right. Just hang onto Yuja. They won't touch her. That would precipitate an international crisis. It would be like starting a war with Red China itself."

He could hear Jeremy take in a deep breath and let it out.

Chapter 42

Cesari picked up Martine and Simone picked up Jean-Claude. Martine was light and he would have no difficulty carrying her for an extended period if he had to. They each held a pillow in one hand and left the room. His hands were occupied so he decided to trust Simone and didn't bother taking hold of the tieback again. It dragged along the floor behind her as they walked down the corridor to the elevator. Simone punched in the code, and they waited a minute for the car to arrive. Cesari's brain raced, thinking about the next step.

The elevator door opened, and a large man stepped out. They all froze in place. He was as surprised to see them as they were to see him. He was thick all over, six feet tall, and extra-large in the chest and shoulders. He wore a suit and was well-groomed. They all stared at each other for a moment in awkward silence. Eventually, the man registered recognition when he saw Simone. He was very confused at the sight.

He said, "Simone, Mr. Beaujolais asked me to make sure you were all right."

She knew him too. "Thank you, Lawrence. I'm fine, but I can't say the same for Mrs. Beaujolais and Jean-Claude. They were coughing terribly when I went to check on them. I fear that something is wrong with the ventilation system on this floor. I thought to take them downstairs to the planetarium. Dr. Cesari was good enough to assist me. Please help me carry Jean-Claude. He is quite heavy for his age. Too heavy for me. In fact, I must put him down now. She knelt and lay the child on the floor, fluffing the pillow beneath his head.

Lawrence just stood there, bewildered by the unusual scene. Cesari nodded at him and barked, "You going to help us or not? These people are ill."

Cesari wasn't sure what Simone had in mind but buying time couldn't hurt. Lawrence bristled at Cesari. He was a newcomer, friend of Simone's or not, but Simone was the chief of staff, the boss's right-hand woman as it were. He stepped out of the elevator to see how he could help and knelt down beside Jean-Claude. Simone quickly and deftly rose and stepped over to Cesari, slipping her hand into his pocket.

As she did, Lawrence noticed her golden leash. A puzzled expression came over his face, but before he could say anything, she fired the .22 into the back of his head. Cesari blinked and Martine twitched in his arms at the report. Lawrence slumped forward to the floor, blood oozing from the wound. He was dead instantly. There was no exit wound and Cesari guessed the bullet might still be rattling around his cerebral cortex. Simone put the gun back in Cesari's pocket, and he could feel the warmth of its barrel against his thigh.

She said, "Put Martine down and let's drag him into a bedroom or a maid might find him."

He nodded and said, "Or an amorous guest."

He lay Martine on the carpet and grabbed Lawrence by the ankles. She walked ahead and opened one of the bedroom doors and he dragged the body inside. As he did, he spotted a shoulder holster with a Glock 17. He relieved Lawrence of his weapon and placed it in his waistband at the small of his back. They went back out, and she placed the do not disturb sign on the doorknob before locking the door.

They gathered up Martine and Jean-Claude and entered the elevator, a little out of breath and considerably wound up from the experience. They didn't speak until they reached their destination. The door opened and they stepped out into the garage.

He said, "I guess you've earned the right to have the leash removed."

She smiled wryly. "We're in it now for sure."

"I hesitate to argue with success, but did you have to shoot him?"

"Would you have preferred I slip him a roofie?"

"No, but couldn't you have karate chopped him or something?"

She grinned. "Martial arts aren't magic, Doctor. The man weighed more than a hundred pounds more than I do. Even more importantly, he is equally trained in martial arts, and I've sparred with him often. Trust me when I say it would have been a miracle for me to have subdued him physically. Not to mention, he was armed, and either Martine or Jean-Claude could have been hurt in the process. It was a hasty decision, but I feel it was the right one."

"Enough said. Where are the Rolls Royces?"

"Follow me."

The garage was well-lit and they found a row of seven Rolls Royces. The Boat Tail was now officially part of the collection and took its place among them. But the Boat Tail was not optimal for their purpose. The trunk was poorly designed for storage and the trunk doors opened awkwardly for placement of large or bulky objects like a human body. Additionally, it stood out like a sore thumb because of its unique design.

They walked down the row until they came to the largest of the cars. It was a Rolls Royce Phantom, jet black and brand new, polished to a mirror reflection.

He said, "This one."

They lay Martine and Jean-Claude down gently on the cement floor with their heads propped on the pillows, and Cesari fished the keys out from his pockets. They were all slightly different but weren't labeled, so he pressed the trunk release on them one at a time until he finally got the result he was looking for. The trunk popped open, and a light came on inside. The beige fleece interior was thick and soft. The trunk was spacious and would easily fit both Martine and her son and possibly a third person.

Simone said, "It looks like there's plenty of room."

He nodded, picked up Martine and carefully placed her in the trunk. Simone assisted him by positioning Martine's pillow under her head. They repeated the procedure with Jean-Claude, and when they were done, stood back, and looked at the mother with her child snuggled in her arms.

He said, "It's sad that it's come to this. I bet it didn't start out this way."

"It never does," Simone replied. "Come, we should leave."

"I have to make a call first."

He closed the trunk and handed Simone the keys to the Phantom. She sat in the driver's seat and started the engine. Then he retrieved his phone from his pocket, walked a little distance away for privacy and dialed Parikh.

"Yes, sir," Parikh answered the phone brightly.

"Are you guys still nearby?" There was hesitancy and Cesari added, "I know you didn't go back to New York, Parikh. Jay told me."

"Not exactly close, sir, but not too far away. Maybe a quarter of a mile. We have been waiting patiently for our mission orders."

"Am I on speaker phone?"

"Yes, sir."

"Xi, Jaskaran, can you hear me?"

There was a chorus of affirmation from the others, and he continued, "Okay, Parikh, I want you to bring your minivan as close to the main entrance as possible with the headlights off. Without being seen, try to angle it to get a clear view of the guard house and front door. It should be pretty dark now but there will be lights on the front porch and by the guard house. Are you with me so far?"

Parikh said, "Yes, sir."

"Good, when you're as close as you can get, turn your van around so the rear end is facing the mansion. Xi and Jaskaran, this is where you come in. Parikh, you open the rear door, and Xi, you line up your AR15 on its bipod in the back. Watch the guardhouse and front door and be ready. Jaskaran, I want you to exit the minivan and creep closer to the mansion with those high-powered binoculars. Keep an eye out for trouble, but don't come too close, all right? You don't want to trigger a general alarm. Stay behind trees, keep your phone on, and most importantly, stay out of Xi's line of fire."

"You going to tell us what's going on?" asked Xi.

"In a minute or two, there's going to be a black Rolls Royce coming out to the guard house. The driver is a woman named Simone. Inside the trunk of the car is another woman and her three-year-old son. They're names are Martine Beaujolais and Jean-Claude. They were both being held prisoner here. They've been drugged and will need medical attention. I don't know if they've been abused in any other way. Take them to Morristown Memorial Medical Center for care and call the police. Simone may or may not take a powder on you. Don't be alarmed by that. It doesn't matter."

Parikh said, "That doesn't sound too difficult. What about you and Macallan. Will you be coming out too?"

"This is the tricky part. Jeremy and I are separated. Right now he's entertaining a beautiful Chinese pianist." There was a roar of approval from the three in the minivan at that. He continued, "Not so fast. These people here are cold-blooded killers. I can't emphasize that enough, but the priority is to get the mother and the kid to safety. When Simone reaches the gate, the guards may or may not play ball. That's where you come in, Xi. If you see them point weapons at her, you're going to have to shoot. It doesn't necessarily have to be a head shot. I know you're good with that gun, but it would be nice if you didn't have to kill anyone tonight. Anyway, if you fire, Simone will just bury the gas pedal and plow through the gate."

Xi said, "I could try to shoot him in the arm or the leg, but at this range with an AR15, he may bleed to death."

Cesari let out a deep breath. "Do your best, and make sure there are no vehicles in pursuit of her either. If there are, feel free to fire at will into their engine blocks."

"What about you and Jeremy? You didn't say."

"He's next. I'm hanging back to make sure he's okay and then we'll figure something out."

Jaskaran said, "We're supposed to just leave you both here?"

"That's right," I want you to take care of Mrs. Beaujolais and her son. They've been traumatized, and in all likelihood will wake up in the emergency room confused and frightened. They won't have a clue as to what just happened and will need advocates. I don't think we can count on the woman driving the car. She's got her own problems."

He hung up and turned around. Simone was standing right next to him. He hadn't expected that and said, "You heard?"

She nodded. "Every word."

"I'm sorry…"

She interrupted him. "Don't be. You didn't say anything unkind or untrue. These friends of yours are waiting out by the road?"

"They will be in about five minutes. They're doctors and will take care of Martine and Jean-Claude. I would just leave them in the trunk for now. The hospital is only five or six miles from here. Once you reach Morristown, you're going to have to figure out another means of transportation. My guys won't hinder you, but I assume you won't want to use Beaujolais' car to make your getaway."

"No, of course not. I'll figure something out. I can always Uber it somewhere. There's the train too, but what about you? You're going back in there? That will be suicide."

"I have unfinished business with your boss. I need to kick some Beaujolais ass."

Despite the dire situation, she laughed softly. "Michel told me you were sort of…"

"Primitive?"

"Yes…"

"Well, he was right."

She took a step closer and looked him in the eyes.

"What is it?" he asked.

"I'm trying to understand you. Your best chance to get out of here alive is to get in the car with me, and yet, you choose to remain behind."

"Just because I'm primitive doesn't mean I'm smart."

She smiled and seemed genuinely sad. "I'm sorry."

"For…?"

"For everything, but mostly because I wish we could have met under less obscene circumstances."

He said, "Take care Simone and good luck."

Chapter 43

Simone waited for Cesari to give the signal, which arrived in the form of a text message from Xi that they were all in position, before she left the garage. Ten minutes later he received another text that she had passed through the security gate without incident and was now approaching their position. Cesari breathed a sigh of relief and returned to the elevator. He pressed in Simone's four-digit code he had memorized and rode it to the main hall where he got off and found Jay and Yuja sitting at the grand piano all by themselves in the massive reception room. She was tickling the keys as Jay watched admiringly. Jay stood up as he arrived and Cesari saw stress lines etched into his features. He was trying hard but was out of his element.

Jay asked, "How'd it go?"

"Good, but now we have to get you out which may be a bit more complicated. You and I may be on a no-fly list at the security checkpoint." He looked past Jay and saw that Yuja was smiling at him.

He said, "Hi, I'm John Cesari."

She nodded and said in stilted English, "Hello, I am Yuja."

"Nice to meet you."

She kept smiling and nodding. Cesari said, "You are an amazing pianist."

She said again, "Hello, I am Yuja."

Cesari glanced at Jay. "She doesn't speak English, does she?"

"We left the interpreter downstairs at the banquet, but she can say thank you too."

"Great."

"So what's going on and why did we go to DEFCON 1 all of a sudden?"

"It's a long story which boils down to our host Beaujolais is psychotic. He imprisoned his wife, kidnapped Arnie, stole the *Starry Night* on the wall behind you, murdered multiple people he didn't like, and is now mad at us for stealing his car."

"Jesus," murmured Jay. "When did we steal his car?"

"That convertible we drove here tonight was his."

Jay shook his head in disbelief. "Seriously? I thought you borrowed it from a friend?"

"I did, but my friend stole it from Beaujolais. Look, it's complicated and we don't have time to go into it all."

"Don't have time? You made a black guy drive around the wealthiest town in America in a stolen Rolls Royce? Are you insane? Do you have any idea what they'll do to me?"

"Relax, it wasn't his car. He stole it from someone else."

"Oh, that's sweet. What the hell did I let you talk me into?"

"Time to go, Jay. We'll hash out the recriminations when we're far from here," Cesari said, as he reached into his pocket and handed Jay the rest of the Rolls Royce keys. "Take Yuja down to the garage. The Rolls are all in a row toward the right side as you get off the elevator. I don't know which key belongs to which car. Just test them out. Some of the trunks are open. You may want to close them before driving away. Personally, I'd pick the Boat Tail. It's the nicest car there, and you might as well leave here in style. Get in but hang tight until you hear from me."

"Where are you going?"

"To create a diversion. If you see people running for their cars, then it's safe to go. Let's roll."

Jay waved to Yuja to come with them. She stood, looked a little lost but came anyway. In just a short period of time, she had come to like and trust Jay. Cesari brought them to the elevator, punched in the code and they all got on.

When they arrived at the garage level, he stepped out first and scanned around for trouble, saw none, and said, "All good."

Jay said, "See you later. Be careful."

"Always..."

Yuja smiled and said, "Thank you."

Cesari smiled back but didn't say anything as they made a bee line for the Rolls Royce section. He then pressed the button for the wine cellar and arrived a moment later. The doors opened and he adjusted his cummerbund and tweaked his bowtie as he entered the hallway. The main entrance to the cellar was fifty feet away. There was a small table at the entrance attended to by an attractive young woman with a guest book. Next to her stood a large, decidedly unattractive man in case your name wasn't in the book. The stairs leading down from the main floor were directly in front of them, ten feet away. Cesari was approaching from their side which seemed to catch them by surprise. That made sense, he thought. If everyone had valet parked, then the majority of guests would have come down the stairs unless they had some disability. He hadn't noticed a whole lot of elderly or wheelchairs, but he hadn't been looking either.

The big guy stood next to a set of closed, oak doors, and Cesari could hear music and voices coming from within as he neared the table. They were heavily invested in merriment inside. What Cesari was relieved not to see was a metal detector. He had passed through one entering the mansion earlier, and he guessed Beaujolais thought that was good enough, except now he had a .22 in his pocket and a Glock 17 in the small of his back.

The young woman smiled affably and said, "Name please."

"Cesari, John Cesari."

She opened her book as Cesari studied the big guy who was relaxed but attentive, casually observing Cesari and assessing his threat level. This guy's hair was moussed back into one of those little man-buns and he sported a neatly trimmed, close cropped beard. He was in his mid-thirties, and probably lived inside a gym in his spare time, Cesari surmised.

Cesari said to the guy, "You must get numb standing here all night?"

The guy grinned. "I can think of worse jobs."

Cesari nodded. "You got that right."

The guy must have been bored to death. They both must have been or one of them would have asked the obvious question of why he had arrived by way of the elevator and how did he rate an access code? But they didn't. Maybe they felt that was above their pay grade to ask questions like that to guys in tuxedos. Maybe the fact that he did arrive like that had automatically raised his status in their eyes even though they had never seen him before?

Interesting, he thought, and just a little tragic. The girl looked up from her book and said, "Here you are...Dr. John Cesari. You're at table ten, place setting number eight. Enjoy your evening, Doctor."

The big guy opened the door for him, and Cesari was enveloped in a cacophony of sounds and a dizzying array of sights indicative of a party in full throttle. Cesari revised his estimate of how many people were in attendance yet again as he scanned the room. There were at least five hundred of New Jersey's elite in all their splendor, packed like sardines in a tin can. The massive central table had multiple leaves placed, extending it to twice its original length, and it now seated well over a hundred and fifty people. There were dozens of smaller round tables surrounding it, seating anywhere from ten to twenty guests each. A five-piece band was banging out swing music and professional dancers dressed as 1920's flappers were twirling for the crowd's entertainment on a makeshift hardwood dance floor.

They must have been in between courses because most of the crowd were standing and talking to one another as an army of waitstaff changed plates and silverware and refilled glasses.

Cigar smoke filled the air and bottles of champagne and expensive wines dotted every table. Cesari guessed that they probably just finished the third or fourth course. He couldn't be sure. Three or four of ten. He glanced at his watch. It was almost 10:00 p.m. It really was going to be a long night. Well, maybe longer for some and shorter for others, he mused to himself.

He spotted Beaujolais in the distance encircled by a throng of sycophants lapping up whatever pearls he threw at them. Beaujolais saw him, looked past and then all around, probably wondering where Simone was. Beaujolais waved to him and Cesari went over, nudging his way through the tangled mass of humanity.

"Cesari, so glad you finally made it to dinner. You must have hit it off with Simone which is quite an accomplishment. She can be rather aloof at times."

"Really? I never would have guessed. She was very warm to me. In fact, she struck me like the All-American girl next door type."

Beaujolais smiled. "Interesting. I don't think I've ever heard her described that way before... Is she here now? I've been trying to reach her."

Cesari was nonchalant and completely unconcerned as he said, "I don't know. We were playing a game of pool upstairs with another guest when she excused herself. She said there was something or someone she had to check on and that if she didn't return to keep playing and head down to dinner without her. That was about thirty minutes ago. She never returned so here I am."

The Sommelier seemed baffled by that and said slowly, "I see..."

"This is some party. I never would have guessed you could throw a bash like this down here. I'd like to make a donation to the governor's campaign. I don't have much but every little bit counts, right?"

"You don't have to trouble yourself but if you insist, I'll let you know who to write your check out to."

"Can you point out the governor? I'd like to meet him."

Beaujolais chuckled. "You can't miss him. He's nearly four hundred pounds of hot air, but at the moment, he's sitting at the main table smoking a cigar, talking to the lieutenant governor on his left and the attorney general on his right."

As they chatted, a swarthy, sinister looking man about five feet, ten inches tall with a wiry, powerful build came up behind Beaujolais. Built like a fireplug, he was a full head shorter than Mike, but his neck was twice as thick, and he was easily six inches wider at the shoulders. His appearance was three times as dangerous as anyone else in the room and made the hairs on Cesari's neck stand at attention. He was one of those guys Cesari had learned a long time ago never to turn his back on. They simply couldn't hide who they were on the inside. No amount of window-dressing could mask their evil natures. He whispered something into the Sommelier's ear.

Beaujolais nodded and said to him, "Are you sure, Hugo? The Phantom? That doesn't make any sense. Where is she going?"

Hugo shrugged.

Lost in thought, Beaujolais momentarily forgot Cesari's presence. Finally, he looked at him and said, "You'll have to excuse me Dr. Cesari I have some urgent business to tend to. Please make yourself at home."

They walked away and Cesari allowed himself a quiet moment of satisfaction at Simone's daring escape. He tempered his exuberance with the knowledge that he didn't have long before they pieced together what had happened and focused their attention back to him. With this in mind, he turned toward the main table where the governor was enthusiastically engaged in conversation with his subordinates, and strolled over.

Governor Bernard von Steuben claimed to be tenth generation German American and a direct descendant of Baron Friedrich Wilhelm von Steuben, a Prussian military officer who volunteered and served first as Inspector General and then as a Major General under Washington during the American Revolution. It phased the governor not one iota that the original Baron von Steuben never married, had no known children, and was widely considered by historians to have been homosexual. The governor was finishing up a moderately successful, albeit scandal plagued, first term and had every intention of making it through a second.

The man was rotund, grotesquely so, with jowl upon jowl upon jowl. His wispy gray hair was matted with sweat, and his ruddy cheeks shook like jelly as he laughed at some witty comment. He puffed on the fattest cigar Cesari had ever seen and sat with his legs splayed wide to accommodate his overhanging belly. Cesari couldn't even imagine the size of his tuxedo jacket. Did they even come larger than a size one hundred? Cesari reminded himself that he shouldn't pick on the guy too much. He had gotten laid tonight and Cesari hadn't.

He tapped the governor's shoulder, and everyone looked up at him. Cesari bent low to his ear and in a very hushed voice said, "I need to talk to you privately, Governor."

The governor glanced up at him and then at his companions and then back at Cesari, "And may I ask who you are?"

"I'm the guy who's going to save your re-election campaign, but I need you and your friends here to take a walk with me while we talk."

The governor turned to give him a more serious once-over and then back at his friends. "But I'm in a very important meeting," he laughed and took a long swallow of scotch.

The lieutenant governor and attorney general both sniggered with him. Cesari expected something like that and hissed through his teeth loud enough for all to hear, "You can laugh all you want fat man, but you're going be kissing my ass when you hear what I have to say."

Chapter 44

They all stared at him in quiet disbelief. Finally, the governor said, "You have balls…"

"The size of coconuts, but that has nothing to do with it. I'm trying to save your hide."

"Fine, I'll give you five minutes you little pissant, and then I'm going to have Beaujolais' security throw you out onto the front lawn. With any luck, you'll land in a rose bush."

"Thanks for the well-wish, but this is show and tell, and I want your two friends to come with us. We're all going to want witnesses."

"Where are we going?"

"Not far, just to a different part of the cellar, a less well-traveled part."

The governor mulled it over, saw how serious Cesari was and relented. "Come lads. Let's watch this upstart commit political suicide. This could be entertaining."

They stood up and the governor said to the attorney general, "Don't forget the scotch, Franklin."

The attorney general picked up the bottle and a couple of glasses and they all followed Cesari through the mob of people. It took a few minutes as every two steps somebody stopped the governor to say hello and congratulate him in advance of his upcoming election. Eventually, the crowd thinned, and they wormed their way to the periphery.

Once they were alone and had put some distance between them and the party, the noise died down to a dull background hum. Bernard von Steuben said, "Are you going to tell us your name or is this some super-secret spy game you're playing?"

"My name is John Cesari and I'm a physician from New York."

"New York? Do you practice in New York and live in New Jersey?"

"No, I live in Manhattan and practice there."

"Are you trying to tell me that you can't even vote for me?"

"Not only can't I vote for you, but I don't think I would if I could. From what I've seen and heard tonight, I'm decidedly underwhelmed. Personally, I'd make you enter some sort of food, alcohol, and sexual rehabilitation center and not come out until you sobered up, lost two-hundred pounds, and agreed to stay away from teenagers. Right now, all you're good for is a pie-eating contest... Don't look so shocked. It's good for a politician to hear the truth once in a while. Besides, despite my personal disenchantment, what I'm about to do for you is far more important than pulling a lever in a voting booth. I'm going to prevent millions of people from voting against you."

The attorney general and the lieutenant governor looked uneasy but said nothing. The governor snorted indignantly, "Damn, you're an impudent whelp, aren't you?"

"You started it. You shouldn't have called me a pissant."

The governor cleared his throat and decided to move on. He said, "Well I'm all ears, Dr. Cesari. Pray tell, how will you prevent millions of people from voting against me?"

"A picture is worth a thousand words, governor. Please be patient. I was only here once before so forgive me if I'm a little slow finding my way around."

They made multiple turns as Cesari struggled with his memory to find the right aisle. At one point the attorney general coughed uncomfortably and said, "Governor, I'm not sure this is wise. Perhaps, I should call security."

Cesari turned to him and said, "You're not going to call anybody until I show the governor what he needs to see."

"Do you have any idea who you're talking to?" said the attorney general with hubris.

"Apparently not, Franklin," chortled the governor. "But after the way he just spoke to me a moment ago, I'm not sure he cares."

"I know exactly who he is," retorted Cesari. "He's the attorney general for New Jersey, and you're right, Governor. I don't care, but he and you should know that I'm a bit of a clairvoyant and I also know where he's going to be if he tries to make a call."

"And where's that?" attorney general asked.

"Somewhere in the middle of next week in an ICU bed asking your nurse for more pain medication. That is, if you wake up."

"Please gentlemen," the governor interceded. "No more rancor, Franklin, until after this fool falls on his face. Then we can descend on him like sharks. You have just five more minutes and counting, Dr. Cesari. I feel I have been generous so far, but I have no intention of missing the next course. Death slowly hunts the living, and despite your taunts and childish attempts at body-shaming, I will never allow myself to fall victim to malnutrition."

With one minute to spare, Cesari fortuitously turned down the right aisle. They were now completely out of sight and hearing from the party. They couldn't even catch the pulse of any music drifting in their direction.

Cesari said, "Here it is."

It was the right aisle but there was no steel door at the end of it. Someone had placed a large wood riddling rack for making champagne up against the steel door to hide it from view and inquiry. The rack was nearly flush against the door and was filled with champagne bottles pointing downward at thirty-five-degree angles. Cesari got close to one side of the rack and inspected it. It wasn't fastened into the wall or doorframe, but was held firmly in place by the weight of the bottles.

"Now what, Dr. Cesari?" asked the governor sarcastically. "Do we open a bottle of champagne and toast each other's health? I'm game for that."

"Now, you move out of the way. C'mon, everybody step to the side. This is going to be messy."

Once they were safely away from him, Cesari grabbed the side of the riddling rack and with a mighty heave using his back, legs and shoulders, and mustering all the force he could, inched the rack upright and then forward and then with a little nudge, the weight of the champagne bottles did the rest of the work as they all went crashing forward onto the floor. Glass shattered and the sweet, aromatic scent of some of world's best champagne filled the air.

The governor shook his head. "What a waste. Beaujolais is going to be pissed for sure, but what do we have here?"

Cesari pushed the riddling rack out of the way, and they all gathered around the odd-looking steel door. The governor added, "Okay, lad, you have my attention now."

Retrieving the key from his pocket, Cesari said, "Good… Just for the record, I've never been in here, but a former employee of his has, and she informed me that what we're about to see is evidence that your host tonight, the sponsor of your fundraiser, Governor, is a depraved psychopath. Are you ready?"

He inserted the key into its slot and turned it. There was an audible clank as the bolt turned, and then, triggered by a motion sensor, overhead lights flickered on as he pushed the door forward. They entered the chamber and collectively gasped in horror. Speechless, they moved slowly, gazing all around. Cesari too was unnerved, but he had more reason to be. He might have been one of those heads. There were animal heads from trophy hunts alternating with preserved human heads, three dozen in all, and all men. On the metal table in the center of the room were two more heads, waiting to join the collection. Their wood plaques and tools for mounting were lying at the ready on the table nearby. They were the Newark port security guards, and they had been beaten so badly they were almost unrecognizable as human beings. The lieutenant governor suddenly lurched to his knees and vomited on the floor. He gagged and wretched continuously for five full minutes as they helplessly watched.

The governor went close to one particular head and shrunk back in dismay. "Franklin, is this…?"

The attorney general came to his side. "Oh my God. It's Joel Abramson."

"Who's Joel Abramson?" asked Cesari.

"The New Jersey Comptroller. He went missing two years ago," explained the attorney general. "There was an extensive manhunt, but his remains were never found."

"I appointed the man," whispered the governor softly. "It was widely assumed that one of his many audits of the misuse of public funds had triggered a nerve somewhere."

"I guess it did," Cesari said.

The governor's mood was subdued. "I presume there's a story behind this, Doctor."

"You presume right, Governor," Cesari said and turned to the attorney general. "You can call the police any time you want, and I would take plenty of pictures."

The attorney general took his phone out from his pocket, but the governor suddenly came back to life and said, "Wait, Franklin… I need to think."

"Think about what?" demanded Cesari.

"Son, I appreciate your bringing this to my attention, but you may not understand the finer points of political hegemony the way I do."

The guy's wheels were spinning fast. Cesari said, "The finer points of what…?"

"Dr. Cesari, a man waits his whole life and suddenly, when opportunity knocks, he has to know enough to answer with enthusiasm. Look around you. This room is shear gold. This is Tutankhamen's burial chamber. Beaujolais will pay a king's ransom to keep this quiet."

Cesari couldn't believe his ears. "Are you insane? Beaujolais will cut your head off and put it up on that wall if he thinks you're a threat."

"He is a beast, a wild tiger. I totally concur. We will have to deal with him carefully."

"You're nuts, Governor, and if you won't call the police I will."

"Wait, Doctor, let's talk about this. I agree that you have a right to an opinion here. You discovered this treasure trove, and I am indebted to you. Name your price. With a finding like this we own Beaujolais. Do you have any idea how much he's worth? Close to a trillion dollars..."

The fat man's eyes gleamed as he spoke. He was scheming so hard how to milk Beaujolais he wasn't seeing straight. "I'm done talking, Governor. I know you have your flaws, but deep down, I thought you were an honest man, and you too, Mr. Attorney General. I can't believe you would even consider letting this happen under your watch."

The attorney general looked down in shame and then slowly raised his gaze up to his boss and benefactor. His was an appointed position not an elected one. He gently shook his head, "Bernard, we can't. There are three dozen human heads here. If it ever got out... There's no way we would survive. We're talking jail time for you, me... everyone involved."

Cesari breathed a sigh of relief. "I take back any evil thoughts I may have had about you, Franklin. Now, if only you can convince the governor to come down to earth and see this for what it is."

The governor looked around and let out a loud sigh. "You're right, of course. I don't know what I was thinking."

"I do," Cesari growled. "You're a ruthless, power-hungry, son-of-a-bitch."

The governor looked contrite and said, "I deserved that... Thank you, Dr. Cesari, you've done the state of New Jersey a great service. Cicero, would you please get off your knees."

He leaned down and helped the lieutenant governor off the floor and then turned to the attorney general. "Franklin, you know what you have to do. Give me a chance to leave first though... If that's okay with you, Dr. Cesari?"

"I can live with that. In fact, I think everybody should leave. We don't know how Beaujolais' going to react, and his men have all the guns."

The governor's eyes went wide. "He wouldn't dare."

"Look at the walls, Governor. I'm okay with you leaving first, but as soon as you're out of sight, I think everyone else should be encouraged to go as well."

"How are you going to do that?"

Cesari reached into the small of his back and came out with the Glock. A big thing, black and menacing. "A couple of shots in the air should do the trick. Now get going. Me and Franklin will wait ten minutes."

Franklin said, "I can't condone firing shots into a crowded room, Doctor, in the air or not. We're supposed to be the adults here. What if you create a panic? A stampede? What if Beaujolais' men fire back? Someone could get hurt."

He was making sense. Cesari returned the gun to the small of his back and said, "Let me think about it."

He had barely finished the sentence when there was a soft clapping sound behind them. They all swung around to look. It was the Sommelier, and he was holding a .44 magnum revolver.

He said, "Bravo! Bravo, gentlemen."

Chapter 45

Beaujolais stepped into the room and closed the door behind him. He drew himself up to full height and said, "I'm impressed, Cesari. I really am. You managed to undo years of work and turn a valued employee against me in one night. That has to be some sort of record for subterfuge."

The revolver he held was very large. It was a Remington .44 magnum with a four-inch barrel and weighed nearly three pounds. From six feet away Cesari could easily see the hollow point bullet chambered in the barrel. At this range, he couldn't miss. An ordinary round would be bad, really bad, but a .44 caliber hollow point would be devastating. There would be an entry wound the size of a dime and an exit hole the size of an orange, maybe even a grapefruit. It would smash through bones, tear apart arteries and plunder your internal organs as it traveled through you. Absolutely no chance of survival. Beaujolais was a big, strong guy and not only did the immense gun look small in his hands, but he waved it around as if it were as light as a feather. Cesari sensed that if for some inexplicable reason he missed with all six rounds, he would just walk around the room and club them to death like baby seals.

Cesari said, "I'm impressed too. That was some quick deduction on your part."

"It wasn't too hard. When one of my security team was found dead with a .22 caliber hole in the back of his head and Simone was seen leaving in my Rolls Royce it became rather obvious. But no worries, the Phantom she stole has a GPS anti-theft tracking device. Hugo will find her soon enough and bring her to justice."

Cesari said nothing as he appraised the new situation. Big guys didn't scare him. They were usually dumb and slow, but he already knew Beaujolais wasn't dumb, and he didn't want to find out if he was slow. At least not while he was holding one of the largest handguns ever made.

"What's the matter, Doctor? Cat has your tongue? Do me a favor and take the pistol from the small of your back and place it on the floor. Please don't deny you have one. I was watching and listening from the side of the door. Do it slowly, please. I would hate to shoot you in here. A gun this big in a room this size will make our ears ring for an hour."

The governor started to speak, "Beaujolais, you can't..."

"Quiet, Bernie, you'll get your turn. First let us disarm the good doctor."

Cesari let out a quick breath, and slowly took the Glock from his back, holding the grip between his thumb and index finger. He crouched and placed it gently on the floor in front of him before standing up again.

Beaujolais said, "Now kick it over here, nice and easy."

With his foot, Cesari pushed the gun across the tiled floor to the Sommelier, who seemed to breathe easier after the surrender of the weapon.

Beaujolais relaxed a bit. "Now what are we to do with this merry group of conspirators? I hope that you found my trophy room entertaining?"

The governor found his courage and said, "Beaujolais, we can work something out. You know I'm a pragmatic man."

The Sommelier grinned. "That I do, Bernie. That I do. I readily concede that you are the ultimate politician."

The governor let out a sigh of relief. "Put the gun down and let's talk."

"I don't think so. Not yet anyway. Unfortunately, I can't think of a solution that doesn't involve killing all of you."

The three politicians paled, and the lieutenant governor fell to his knees again retching and crying at the same time. He pleaded desperately for his life, "Please, Mr. Beaujolais, this isn't necessary. We didn't even want to see this room. That man made us." He pointed at Cesari. "Just let us go home. I have children. We'll never speak of this again. I promise."

The governor kicked him gently. "Get a hold of yourself, Cicero."

The Sommelier sneered in disdain. "I couldn't agree more, Governor. Sniveling and begging only makes me upset, not sympathetic." He then seemed to come to some conclusion and said, "As much as it goes countercurrent to my instincts, I can't kill you all. That would be too problematic, especially since the governor is scheduled to give a short thank you speech after the fifth course in about thirty minutes. And since no one saw any of you leave, questions will be asked. Again, very problematic. So what am I to do?"

The attorney general said, "Beaujolais, Cicero had a point. We didn't seek this room out. No harm, no foul. We move on. It's what we do."

The Sommelier snickered, "Just like that, Franklin. We move on as if nothing happened? What about you Dr. Cesari? Are you in agreement with that sentiment?"

Cesari replied, "No offense, but I'd like to cut your balls off and serve them as the next course. Perhaps, paired with a California cab."

The governor's eyes went wide in fright, but the Sommelier grinned. "Spoken like a true warrior. I would have expected no less. Take note, gentlemen. Dr. Cesari is the last of a dying breed of men, the last knight of the round table, the last samurai. You are Shaka of the Zulu."

"Thanks, but I feel more like Napoleon at Waterloo."

The Sommelier glanced at his watch and Cesari knew he was out of time. Things were about to start happening, so he took a slight step toward the attorney general who was closest to him and to his right. Outwardly, it didn't look like much, almost as if he were simply shifting his weight from one leg to the other.

The Sommelier turned to the governor. "Bernie come over here. I've made my decision. You live tonight."

The governor waddled over as fast as he could.

"Pick up the gun off the floor," the Sommelier instructed him.

The governor knelt down and picked up Cesari's Glock. He said, "What do you want me to do with it?"

"Handle it. Grab the barrel, then the grip, over and over. Get your fingerprints all over it."

"Why?"

The sommelier pointed the .44 at the governor's head. "Because if you want to live, you're going to have to shoot Cicero."

The attorney general gasped, and Cicero cried out, "Please... No... I'm begging you. I'll do anything. Please..."

Cesari slid six inches closer. He was only a foot away from the attorney general now who was frozen in place.

The governor was white as a sheet. "I don't understand, Beaujolais."

"It's easy Bernie," the Sommelier explained. "I need you to live. No one will miss Cicero. Most people don't even know who he is, but I also need assurance that we will never speak of this night again. Therefore, you and I have to be on the same footing. That is, equally guilty of a crime we can never publicly acknowledge. After you kill him, I will keep the pistol with your fingerprints for safe-keeping."

The attorney general found his voice, "This is insanity."

"Maybe, but it's the only way for Bernie to leave this room alive." He pushed his .44 into the back of the governor's head. "Go ahead, Bernie. Don't make me wait too long. I might change my mind."

The governor was drenched in perspiration. He gulped and raised the gun, pointing it at Cicero who was weeping uncontrollably. The governor's hand shook and trembled badly. He said, "I'm sorry, Cicero."

The explosion was deafening. Smoke and cordite filled the room as the bullet ripped off the top of Cicero's skull. His body collapsed backward. He wound up in a nearly sitting position against the wall with his head propped upward as if he was looking at something on the ceiling. Blood continued to gush out of the gaping wound down his face. Cesari took another step and now his right hand was hidden from view behind the attorney general's back.

The governor started crying and the Sommelier took a handkerchief from his pocket and gently grabbed the Glock from him lest he do something unpredictable. As the Sommelier was distracted momentarily doing that, Cesari slowly slid his right hand into his pocket for Simone's .22 Colt. He flicked the safety off and inched it out. The pistol had a ten round magazine and Simone had used one on the guy up in the bedroom. Nine rounds left. He glanced at the attorney general. He was paralyzed by fear. It happened to the best of them, and he wasn't the best. Not even close, but Cesari didn't want him to do anything. Just stay where you are for now.

The Sommelier said, "Excellent work, Bernie. Now we are equals. Your turn Franklin. Do you wish to live?"

The attorney general was barely able to speak and nodded. His voice was hoarse and raspy, "Of course I do."

The Sommelier held the Glock up for the attorney general. "Then come over here, take the gun, and shoot Dr. Cesari. Then we can finish dinner and talk about the future of our great state under the leadership of Governor Bernard von Steuben's second term."

Cesari watched the Sommelier's eyes, which were focused on the attorney general. It was now or never. Franklin made his decision and stepped toward the offered handgun.

His cover gone, Cesari quickly raised the concealed .22 and started firing before Beaujolais could even register surprise on his face. Pop, pop, pop. As the gun moved from left to right, he didn't have time to aim and relied on instinct. The first shot hit Beaujolais in the right shoulder causing his trigger finger to involuntarily twitch. The .44 caliber canon roared, and flames leapt from its mouth. He had been facing the attorney general and the wild shot tore into Franklin's wrist, shattering bone, cartilage, and tendons. The violence of the round nearly severed his hand from his forearm and the man crumpled to the floor screaming in agony, blood spurting out of the stump. They all went deaf from the report and then everything seemed to move in slow motion as Cesari kept pulling the trigger.

The second shot hit the Sommelier in the neck and judging from the color of the blood gushing out, Cesari guessed he got lucky and struck the carotid artery. By that time, he had steadied the gun and the next three shots hit Beaujolais directly in the face. They say the .22 isn't a very powerful weapon with poor stopping power, but it really all depended on where your shots landed. In a man as large and muscular as the Sommelier, body shots might not have done a hell of a lot, but three shots in the face from six feet away was another story. He fell backward and Cesari's next two shots went into the wall behind where his head had just been. Seven shots and five hits. Not bad. The man was already dead, but Cesari walked up to him, pressed the muzzle into his chest over the heart and fired the last two rounds, just because.

The governor had slumped to the floor and was sitting with his back against a wall and his hands buried in his face blubbering unintelligibly. He was useless at the moment, so Cesari put the .22 away and ran to the attorney general who was already in shock. He was lying face up, unconscious, pasty and clammy, his right hand attached only by the thinnest thread of tissue to the rest of him. He was swimming in his own blood which was still pouring out of his arm. It was sticky, slimy, and gooey and all over the place. The stench of it in combination with the burnt gunpowder was nauseating.

Cesari knelt down and flattened him out on the floor, propping his legs up on Cicero's body for elevation. It was the best he could do to help blood flow under the circumstances. Then he took the man's bowtie off him and used it to make a tourniquet on his forearm to slow the bleeding. He also loosened his collar and undid a few of his top shirt buttons for comfort. Whether he would make it or not was too hard to guess at this point. It all depended on how quickly he got to a hospital and the care of a trauma surgeon. His golf game would never be the same, that was for sure.

Cesari looked at his own blood-covered hands and clothes. He was nearly drenched in blood especially his pants because he had been kneeling in it. He went over to the sink and cleaned himself as best as he could. His tuxedo was black and would disguise much of the carnage as long as no one got too close.

When he was done, he looked around. He needed a weapon. The .22's ammo was spent. He eyed the Glock but hesitated to take it. It had just been used to commit a murder and had the governor's fingerprints all over it. Unfortunately, his prints were on it too. Tough decision, but he needed something, so he picked it up and placed it in the small of his back again. He'd make it disappear when it was all over. He hated to bail out the governor like that. The man was just as completely devoid of a moral compass as Beaujolais. But Cesari had no choice. Hugo required urgent attention, and for that, he would need a weapon.

He glanced around the room. This was one forensic nightmare he didn't want to be a part of. He turned to the governor and knelt down beside him. The man took his hands from his face and looked at him. His eyes were red and swollen. He was nearly catatonic.

"I have to leave now, Governor."

He clutched Cesari's hands. "Don't leave me here. Please… I can't be found like this."

"Unfortunately, I just killed a guy worth a trillion dollars, and I don't want to find out how the Bernardsville police will feel about that."

"What am I going to do?"

"I suggest you call 911. You still have time to save Franklin. He's wounded pretty badly, but he might make it."

"And tell them what?"

"That you're a damn hero, that's what. You accidentally stumbled upon this room with your pals and Beaujolais confronted you. There were guns on the table. A struggle ensued, he killed the lieutenant governor and shot the attorney general. You grabbed a gun off the table and killed him in self-defense."

His eyes lit up. "That could work."

Cesari took the .22 out from his pocket, wiped it down quickly with the governor's tuxedo jacket and told him to handle it the way he had handled the Glock earlier.

Cesari watched him and said, "Now grab the trigger and pull."

"Why?"

"If you want to be the hero, then you have to be the one who pulled the trigger. They're going to check the gun for fingerprints."

He did it and asked, "Now what?"

"After you call the police, you call the curator of the Museum of Modern Art and tell him to get his sorry ass out of bed because you recovered Van Gogh's *Starry Night* for him. It's upstairs on the wall behind the piano. You'll be a national sensation for your courageous actions. I smell a landslide re-election in your future."

"The *Starry Night*? I didn't know it was missing."

"Neither does he, I suspect. Insist that he examine theirs for authenticity and then come out here to look at this one. Just remember one thing. I was never here, and you never heard my name before. Because if I get called out on this, I'm going to tell everyone what really happened and who shot who."

"I understand."

"Here comes the part where you're going to have to be a little more proactive in showing your appreciation for me saving your life. I think you know that Beaujolais was negotiating with you out of desperation, just to get through the night, and I also think you're smart enough to know that he would have turned on you in a heartbeat once he felt he could kill you safely."

"I'm not stupid. That much was obvious. What do you want?"

"I'm going to need a favor."

"Anything…"

"I may need a get out of jail free card. Beaujolais' men may not let me pass through the gate, so I'm going to wait for the police, and they might not take kindly to anyone leaving the property if they hear there's been a double homicide involving the governor. I need you to sugarcoat the 911 call. Just be vague and that you need help urgently, but if they stop me, I'd like to be able to call you for help. I have to leave one way or the other. I think Beaujolais' guy, Hugo, is going after my friends."

He nodded. "I'll give you my cellphone number, and don't worry about the 911 call. My whole career is based upon being deliberately vague."

"Thanks."

"Who are you?"

"You already know who I am."

"I mean who are you really?"

"I'm nobody."

Chapter 46

Cesari left the governor and walked hurriedly back through the wine cellar. Dinner had resumed and everyone was busily engaged in polite conversation. If anyone had heard gunfire they weren't letting on. Their host and guest of honor were absent but that didn't seem to perturb the guests as the music played and the wine flowed.

He walked out the same doors he had entered. The same woman and security guard were standing there chatting. He told them he was just getting some air and they nodded. His original intention was to create a disturbance and possibly cause a mass exodus allowing Jeremy to drive out, lost in a mass of other cars, but upon reflection, the attorney general had been right. A panicked flight from the mansion would very possibly result in unnecessary injury to someone, possibly some older person, possibly someone Cesari might have liked had he met them under different circumstances.

The elevator dropped him off in the garage and he headed toward the fleet of Rolls Royces, Maseratis, Ferraris, Aston Martins, and Lamborghinis. He spotted the Boat Tail twenty feet away but didn't see anyone sitting behind the driver or passenger seats. He had asked Jeremy to procure the Boat Tail if possible, mostly to keep Vito quiet. Even though the buyer was gone, Vito still considered the Boat Tail his property. The underworld was like that.

Ten feet away, Cesari started to get concerned. He glanced at the row of Rolls Royces and none of them were occupied.

What did that mean? He stopped, focused, and listened. He heard music, soft and low. He spun around. It was coming from the Boat Tail. He walked over and looked through the driver's side window. The engine wasn't running but the dashboard was lit up and the radio turned on. He pulled on the handle, opened the door, and looked into the back seat where he saw Yuja sitting on Jeremy's lap. They were kissing and seemed to be having a grand time. They both suddenly looked up, embarrassed.

Cesari said, "Seriously, Jay?"

Jay had lipstick smeared on his face and was breathless, "It wasn't my fault. She jumped me."

"She jumped you? And dragged you into the back seat after she turned on romantic music? May I remind you, Dr. Macallan, that she is a card-carrying commie from the People's Republic of China and that you already have a girlfriend who hates me because every time we go out something happens that she doesn't approve of. I'm pretty sure this would fall into that category. Now lose the chick, we have to go. There's trouble on the horizon."

"More? What happened? I thought there was going to be some sort of signal?"

"There will be," Cesari promised. "Give me the keys and say goodbye."

The governor had given him five minutes to get to the garage before calling the police and the media. Cesari estimated that given the distance and mobilization times, the Bernardsville police would arrive first, in ten to fifteen minutes. The troopers after that, the news vans after that. The gates would be wide open at that point, and no one would dare try to stop them even if they were so inclined. Beaujolais was dead and therefore the head had been cut off the beast. Without instructions from the boss, the whole thing would collapse like a house of cards on a windy day. At least that's what he hoped. Hugo, however, was an unknown variable. Cesari suspected that guys like Hugo were too close to the top and had too much invested to go down easily.

Jeremy got out of the Boat Tail with Yuja and walked her over to the elevator whose doors were still open. She was confused but apparently happy. He put her in the car and punched the right floor for her before returning to Cesari, who was sitting in the driver's seat with the engine running. Jay sat in the passenger's seat, looked in one of the mirrors, wiped the lipstick away, and buckled up.

They left the garage but hung back a healthy distance from the guardhouse and waited. Cesari took that time to bring Jeremy up to speed on events in the wine cellar.

Jeremy whistled and said, "Damn...The lieutenant governor and Beaujolais are dead? I didn't see that coming."

"Neither did they, and right now the attorney general is clinging to life by a thread."

Jeremy shook his head. "Unbelievable... What's the latest word on Mrs. Beaujolais?"

"Let's find out," he said, and dialed Parikh. "How goes it?"

"Good, sir. We are in the emergency room with mother and child. I am happy to report they are slowly waking up, vital signs are stable, and they appear in no distress. The police have been notified."

"What about the woman, Simone?"

"She is here with us, sir. She is waiting for the police to tell them what happened."

Cesari was confused. "She's doing what?"

"Waiting for the police. So they know what happened. We really don't know too much. Is better for her to tell story."

Cesari didn't know what to make of that. Apparently, Simone had a change of heart. That was difficult to believe considering the consequences she would be facing, but it was what it was. At least they all got to the hospital before Hugo caught up with them.

He said, "Can you put her on?"

"No, sir. She is at this very moment having a cigarette outside somewhere and as you know this is a very big place."

"Okay, thanks and good job. Everybody happy? You're heroes."

"Everybody but Xi, sir."

"What's wrong with Xi?"

"He very much wanted to shoot a bad guy tonight and is now greatly disappointed."

"Tell him there's always next time."

"That is exactly how I counseled him."

Cesari hung up and told Jeremy that everything was going smoothly. Jeremy said, "What happened to Hugo?"

"Good question. He obviously failed to catch Simone and to prevent Mrs. Beaujolais and her child from being transferred to the emergency room. So what would he have done if he realized he was too late?"

"Probably he would have called for instructions."

"Yes, and since his boss is dead, there would be momentary confusion and inaction."

"But he wouldn't know his boss was dead."

"No, not right away. He would think that he simply couldn't answer the phone for some reason. Tonight was a fundraiser after all. He might be dancing with the governor's wife."

Jeremy thought about that for a minute and said, "Hugo's probably outside the hospital somewhere waiting for a call from Beaujolais for guidance."

"That's what I think, but not just outside the hospital. He was tracking the Rolls Royce Simone had commandeered. He'll be lurking somewhere near it, watching it."

Cesari tried to put himself in Hugo's shoes. He tracks the GPS unit on the Phantom, and it leads him to Morristown Memorial Hospital. That's no surprise since he knew she had Mrs. Beaujolais and her child with her, and they would require medical care. But he arrives too late, and his boss isn't picking up. What would be his mindset as he waited?

Uncertainty, of course. Fear? Unlikely. He hadn't really met Hugo, but anyone that would participate in the atrocities

Cesari had seen probably didn't register fear the way most people did.

He would be angry. Yes, definitely angry at Simone's betrayal. They were all in it together and one breaking rank would destroy the others. She was willingly embarking on an action that would destroy him and Beaujolais. The why of it wouldn't really matter although he could always beat it out of her when the opportunity arose.

But as time passed and the Sommelier didn't call to lend advice, Hugo would eventually have to decide independently on a course of action. To do nothing in itself was a decision. Probably not a great one since when Martine awoke, she would probably tell the authorities everything she knew to protect her child. And if Simone went to this extreme to help Martine, then Hugo might very well come to the conclusion that she was most likely planning on turning herself over to the police in exchange for leniency. The facts bear themselves out or else why would Simone stick around? Hugo had two choices, and he didn't strike Cesari as a cut and run kind of guy.

Cesari looked over at Jay and said, "I've got a bad feeling about Hugo's state of mind."

"You don't think he's waiting in the parking lot of the hospital?"

"I don't think he can afford to be that complacent. We have to get out of here now."

The robust wail of police sirens and ambulances filled the air as a procession of vehicles entered the property at speed, two hundred and fifty yards away. The guard house was a buzz of activity as the security team came out to see what was happening, but rightly assumed that some awful and unexpected tragedy had occurred inside the house. Some fat guy had a heart attack or a stroke, they would presume. They glanced at each other and then at the long procession of police cars aiming right at them and opened the gates without having to be asked. Cesari threw the car in gear and slammed on the accelerator. He flew by the guard house before the first police car reached the entrance and then swung off to the side to allow them unimpeded passage. He drove on the manicured lawn right past the caravan.

Clearly the police weren't happy to see that, honked and blared at him over loudspeakers to pull over. He declined, pressed on the gas, and they decided they had bigger fish to fry. New Jersey's ruling class awaited inside the mansion and the wealthiest man in Bernardsville was rumored to have died. The circumstances were unknown. Their instructions were clear and emphatic; secure the governor's safety at all costs, without delay or distraction. No one knew exactly what had happened other than the governor had requested immediate assistance. Pursuing a half-wit, probably drunk rich guy in his Rolls Royce paled in comparison to the task at hand.

For his part, Cesari wasn't overly worried about being detained. One call to the governor would get him off the hook. It was the possible delay in reaching his friends that bothered him more than anything. Besides, once they reached the front gate, the cops would be busy relieving the security guards of their submachine guns. This whole place was swarming with weapons that needed to be neutralized.

After Cesari and Jay passed the emergency vehicles, they steered back onto the road, and sped off into the night. Jay held on for his life as Cesari took every turn with the tires screeching and the engine straining.

"Call the boys," Cesari barked as he blew past a stop sign at nearly thirty miles over the speed limit. "Tell them to physically surround Mrs. Beaujolais' and her child and to not let either one of them out of their sights. I think they both may be in grave danger right now."

Jay had one hand on the dashboard to stabilize himself and with the other made the call.

Chapter 47

They skidded into a parking spot close to the emergency room entrance and jumped out of the car. It was close to midnight and their hearts pounded with adrenalin.

Cesari said, "Do you think they have metal detectors, Jay?"

"Why?"

"I have a Glock in the back of my pants."

Jay was way past being alarmed by anything he saw or heard anymore. "Most hospitals don't but there's no guarantee."

"Best guess?"

"No, probably not."

"Good enough."

The emergency room was buzzing and the nurse at the reception window wasn't surprised in the least at the sight of two doctors in tuxedoes flushed and out of breath. The EMS and police had alerted them that some type of incident had occurred in Bernardsville and to be on standby for high profile casualties. The arrival of Martine and Jean-Claude had kicked off what was in their minds going to be a remarkable night. It was also a night in which normal rules of operation were going to be bent. After they introduced themselves and stated their purpose, Cesari and Jeremy showed the nurse their New York State physician ID's.

She said, "Good evening, Doctors. Mrs. Beaujolais and her child have already been moved to a private telemetry room for close monitoring and observation. When they left a few moments ago, they were very stable and resting comfortably. The young doctors who brought them here went with them."

"Can we see them? I know it's late."

"I don't see why not. We already let your friends in. You don't look drunk, and I have a feeling tonight's not the night to go to the mat about visiting hour rules. The press has already started calling, and the CEO of the hospital is on his way in. He was down at the shore for the weekend, so I guess this is going to be a really big deal. Elevators are down the hall and to the left. Third floor, red zone, follow the colored lines on the wall. She's in room 3008. I'll call up to let the staff know."

They boarded an elevator and rode to the third floor, walked a short distance, and found the room. It was easy to find because Jaskaran, Parikh, and Xi were sitting on folding chairs outside. They stood and greeted each other.

Cesari asked, "What's the current status?"

Jaskaran answered for the group, "They're both in there now sleeping but easily arousable. There's a nurse in there as well keeping an eye on them. Their lab work is still pending but everything else looks great. They've been snowed is all. What about you?"

Jeremy shook his head solemnly with a don't ask look and Cesari said, "Not here. Suffice it to say that things went sideways. For now, the situation is this; a white male, average height, clean-shaven, built like a tank and wearing a tuxedo is probably looking for Mrs. Beaujolais to harm her. His name is Hugo. Avoid him if you can, but do your best to keep him away from her."

Jaskaran asked, "Harm her as in…?"

"As in permanently silence her, Jaskaran," responded Cesari. "As in scorched earth. His side lost and he may want to mitigate the fallout from any eyewitnesses."

Xi said, "I knew I should have brought the AR15 in here with us."

Parikh said to Cesari, "We had a big argument about that in the car."

Cesari said, "I bet you did, but you can't shoot an AR15 in a hospital, Xi. The walls are too thin and there are too many people. One shot and there could be five or six hundred dead people."

Xi scoffed at the hyperbole. "That's a bit of an exaggeration, wouldn't you say?"

"Maybe, but not by much. Look, if you see this guy or someone you think might be him, keep an eye on him but don't try to engage him. Trust me, he's extremely dangerous. Call me, the police, hospital security, the FBI, or whoever. There's safety in numbers. I'm going to check in on Mrs. Beaujolais now and then we'll come up with a plan... Anybody see Simone?"

They all shook their heads and Jaskaran said, "She went out for the smoke like we told you, and then they moved Mrs. Beaujolais. She could still be outside or down in the ER waiting room."

"We just came in that way and didn't see her, although we weren't looking that hard. Did she give anybody her number?"

They shook their heads again. He didn't have her number either. He didn't think he'd ever see her again. Once he was confident Martine and Jean-Claude were safe, he would search for her. If he was right about Hugo, then she was in grave danger as well. And since she helped Martine make her escape and was considering talking to the police, he owed her that much.

"All right. Let me know if she shows up."

He entered the room while the guys surrounded Jeremy, peppering him with questions about the night's events. He closed the door behind him and saw Martine lying in her bed with Jean-Claude cuddled in her arms. Her eyes were open but mostly blank. She looked at him as he approached. A middle-aged nurse sat next to her, and he introduced himself while Jean-Claude slept.

He said to Martine and the nurse, "My name is Dr. Cesari. I'm with the other doctors outside. How is everyone?"

The nurse replied, "Hello, Dr. Cesari. They called up from the ER about you. They're both doing well. Dr. Malmoud is caring for her tonight and was just in. He thinks she just needs time, and that whatever she was given will wear off."

He looked into Martine's glassy eyes and asked, "Has she been talking?"

"Not a whole lot, but she's definitely more alert than she was when she arrived. She did ask for water ten minutes ago. Other than that, she's rock stable as is her child. He cries out and fidgets from time to time as if in a bad dream."

Cesari nodded and agreed, "A really bad dream."

"Would you like me to call Dr. Malmoud? He'll be here all night."

"That won't be necessary. I can tell she's in good hands. I just wanted to say hello."

He sat on the edge of the bed and studied Martine and Jean-Claude. She was beautiful but looked vacant and exhausted. The kind of exhaustion that comes with extreme and prolonged stress. He had never met her before, but thought she looked gaunt and underweight. It didn't surprise him that she hadn't been eating well. Jean-Claude on the other hand appeared healthy and peaceful. He had no clue how severely his innocence had been disturbed, and Cesari hoped he would never find out.

He held Martine's hand and her gaze drifted toward him at the touch. He smiled comfortingly and said, "You're all right now. You're safe."

She didn't reply but he thought he saw a tear begin to form in the corner of one eye. He stood and said goodnight to Martine and her nurse. In the hallway, he found the pain guys bunched up in deep conversation.

Cesari cleared his throat, "Gentlemen…"

They turned to him. Jeremy said, "How is she?"

"Pretty out of it, but overall, no worse than a typical patient after a colonoscopy."

"That's good. So what now?"

He gave everyone the short version about Hugo and why he might be prowling in the shadows. They were duly impressed and equally committed to seeing their mission through to its concluding chapters.

Cesari said, "It's after midnight. I want you guys to stand guard here in shifts two at a time. There's got to be a patient lounge around here somewhere for the other two to try to get some rest or coffee. Your job is mainly to act as a deterrent until the authorities take over. The local police and state troopers are preoccupied right now with the governor at the mansion in Bernardsville. When they get here, we can try to convince them of the danger we feel Martine is in although without any hard evidence of a threat, it may be difficult to persuade them to allocate resources to protect her... The plan is pretty simple. Keep everyone away from Martine who can't prove his name isn't Hugo. Are we all in accordance?"

They all nodded. Parikh said, "And what will you do, sir?"

"My job is pretty simple too. I'm going to hunt for the hunter."

"And then what?"

"You're in America, Parikh. You don't ask questions like that. The less you know, the less likely it will be that your testimony will put me in the slammer."

He smiled but seemed baffled. "I definitely do not want to put you in the slammer, sir, but please tell me. What is the slammer?"

"Jeremy will tell you. I have to go. Good luck and stay awake."

Leaving them to fend for themselves, he went to find Simone or Hugo or whoever he ran into first. He figured she might still be somewhere in the vicinity of the ER and decided to give that area a more thorough look. Every emergency room in the country had light security in the form of unarmed uniformed guards standing around in highly visible locations to discourage unacceptable behavior. These guys weren't particularly well-trained or even necessarily experienced ex-law enforcement types. Most of them were young or very old and not looking for an argument as long as you showed a modicum of respect and courtesy to them and everyone else. What Cesari found was that on a night when they were expecting the governor and some of the wealthiest people in New Jersey, a tuxedoed doctor pretty much got a free pass to come and go at will. He walked past two security guards with a nod and a serious look of determination. They both nodded back.

She wasn't in the emergency room or the waiting area, so he went outside where the ambulances parked and unloaded. There was a three-foot-high brick retaining wall which was the universal smoking area for every hospital in every part of the country. He sat down on it and stared into the parking lot in the distance where the Boat Tail was parked, thinking about where he might find her. Maybe she was a chain smoker? Maybe she was a chain-smoker who decided to take a walk and blow off steam. Maybe she was just under a lot of stress and needed air? It was a nice night out. Not too cool, not too warm. Working for a homicidal psychopath and then betraying him could cause anyone to abruptly become a chain-smoking alcoholic, he thought. Then again, she may have reversed her decision about talking to the police and had decided to go her own way. He could understand that. He was no expert on the law, but she was facing kidnapping charges, conspiracy to commit premeditated homicide, homicide, money laundering, theft. She was a willing co-conspirator in a laundry list of sundry high crimes and misdemeanors. The Sommelier may be dead, but someone was going to have to go to jail. No prosecutor in the country would completely let her off the hook. He'd look like an idiot, like a weak idiot, like a guy who should be fired.

Then it crossed his mind that possibly Hugo got lucky and caught her while she was smoking. The thought made him upset, and he didn't know why. He didn't want her to get hurt. He didn't want anyone to get hurt, right? No, he didn't want her to get hurt. She almost had him killed, but for some reason he couldn't condemn her for it. At one point in his life, he had worked the wrong side of the tracks too, but not even close to the degree she had. Still, he felt a little compassion for her, especially now that she was close to doing the right thing. It couldn't possibly make up for all the wrongs, but it was a step in the right direction. All his handwringing stopped when he saw the Phantom pull into the parking lot across the street just two cars over from the Boat Tail. The area was well-lit and he could clearly see Simone get out holding a large paper bag in one hand. She studied the Boat Tail and walked across the road to where he was sitting.

Chapter 48

She placed the bag on the wall between them and sat down, saying, "Dr. Cesari, we meet again. I guess all went well in your effort to get Dr. Macallan out of the mansion safely."

He nodded and looked at the bag she was holding. "It all depends on your definition of what went well means... You went out for McDonalds? Seriously?"

She shrugged. "I missed dinner and I thought your friends might be hungry. They've been very busy. I have ten Big Macs and fries. The big guy looks like he could eat three of them easily. You're welcome to one. I'm sure there's plenty. I didn't buy any beverages though. I was counting on using the vending machines inside the emergency room."

"That'll be fine, thank you. I think I will have one. I missed dinner too."

She handed him a burger and fries and took the same for herself. "Are you going to keep me in suspense?" she asked. "Was there any trouble?"

"Hugo is after you," he said quietly. "I guess that qualifies as trouble. He's tracking the GPS in the Phantom. I think he saw you on the security cameras leaving the property. I was with Michel when Hugo informed him. He could be here right now."

She didn't say anything for a while and then spoke with resignation, "That was to be anticipated, I suppose. I didn't expect them to catch on quite so quickly. I guess I got lucky on the fast-food run, didn't I? He might have been following me the whole time, although shooting someone while they're in line at a drive-through is not his usual way. He would want to take me somewhere for a more prolonged, and in his eyes, fitting punishment."

"I hate to agree with such a morbid line of reasoning, but I do. You didn't have that much of a head start on him so he must be around here somewhere biding his time. He knows that you're eventually going to have to find somewhere to sleep. Maybe he's just going to wait it out."

She nodded in agreement. "How angry was Michel when he discovered I betrayed him?"

"Michel doesn't feel anger anymore. In fact, he doesn't feel anything anymore. He's dead."

She stared at him in shocked disbelief for a long moment, and asked, "How?"

In between mouthfuls of his Big Mac, he told her of the night's events in their entirety. She listened with great solemnity thoroughly aware that her whole world had crumbled, no, burned to the ground.

She said in an oddly indifferent tone, "You bested Michel? I can't pretend that doesn't surprise me. Somehow, I always thought he would come out on top no matter what the odds. He was one of those men that everything he touched turned to gold. It's hard to believe he could lose at anything."

"I hope you're not going to cry over him."

"Hardly. He would have killed me in a heartbeat. I'm not going to lie to you about my feelings for Michel though, mixed as they are. I was drawn to him the way women have been drawn to powerful men for a million years. He was handsome, fabulously wealthy, and sculpted like a Greek god, but I could never have true feelings for him. I always understood what he was and what he was capable of. My heart could never cross that line with him in that way. Despite appearances, ours was strictly a business relationship."

He listened but didn't say anything.

"Are the police here yet?" she asked.

"Not yet, but soon. They're probably tied up at the mansion. There's a lot going on there right now… My guys told me you were planning on cooperating with the authorities. That made me kind of happy."

An ambulance siren howled in the distance, approaching rapidly. Cesari guessed it was coming from the Bernardsville chateau. The attorney general would probably be the first one to receive medical attention if he was still alive. They both looked up.

She said, "I thought about running, but honestly, look at me. How long do you think I would last?"

He looked at her high heels, her tight dress, her pearl necklace. She was used to living the good life. The fall from grace was too steep. He said, "I get it, but for the record, if you were to call a taxi right now to take you to a train station or an airport, I wouldn't stop you. In fact, I can't even remember your name already."

"Are you trying to save me, Dr. Cesari?" she asked with a smile, "You're a hopeless romantic, aren't you? How refreshing, but the majority of my funds are inextricably tied up with Michel's accounts, and now I'm essentially cut off. I do have some money that is completely independent, but not nearly enough to live life for long on the down low as they say. Fake identities, phony passports, hotel hopping, and bribes can be quite expensive. And I have no doubt, that by tomorrow morning, the authorities will have put a stop on my credit cards. No, financially I am ruined. I could last a few weeks, maybe months on what I have if I was frugal, but then what? Can you picture me waitressing in some truck stop for tips or whoring myself for the big bucks? Then there's Hugo skulking in the background somewhere. No, attempting to cut a deal with the authorities is my only reasonable option."

She smiled a sad, wry smile, full of anguish and fear of the future. He said, "I could trade you the Boat Tail for the Phantom. It's worth forty million dollars."

"You're adorable. Really you are. Imagine me making my daring escape in the most conspicuous car ever built, and what would I do with it? Park it in the lot of the budget motel I'm hiding in and put a *For Sale* sign on it? *Will not entertain offers under ten million.*"

"I'm sorry."

"Don't be. I'm a grown up and it's time to pay the piper. I was part and parcel to everything that went on in the Chateau. More than a few of those heads you saw in the trophy room, I lured to their demise."

Cesari let out a deep breath. "Like me?"

"Yes, exactly like you with one slight exception."

"What's that?"

"I was truly looking forward to making love to you."

He didn't say anything.

"You'll have to promise me you'll make a conjugal visit from time to time when I'm in prison," she joked.

He laughed softly at the idea. "I've always liked the color orange."

The ambulance siren was deafening as it pulled into the driveway and then backed up into its bay next to the emergency room doors fifty feet away. They watched as a team of nurses and doctors rushed out to meet it, take report, and offload their patient. It was the attorney general and he looked awful. He was unconscious, intubated, and had saline and antibiotics dripping from an IV bag as a medic squeezed lifesaving oxygen into his lungs. The gauze bandage on the stump of his right arm was soaked with blood.

The siren died down and they resumed their conversation. He asked, "Satisfy my curiosity. What are you going to tell the police they won't already know? The mansion is pretty self-explanatory, lots and lots of dead guys, stolen artwork on the walls, the garage probably filled with stolen cars, financial fraud, kidnapping, and that's just scratching the surface."

She smiled. "There's lots more, but I think my best play is to explain that I know where all the other bodies are buried. The ones that weren't worthy of a place on the wall in the trophy room. Then there's the long list of politicians on Michel's payroll…"

Cesari interjected, "I'd be careful with that last one, Simone. They might lock you up just to shut you up. And people in prison have been known to accidentally commit suicide brushing their teeth if you get my drift. I heard of a guy in solitary confinement who had a bad dream and fell off his cot. He somehow got tangled up in his bedsheet and strangled himself on the way down even though he was only twelve inches off the floor to start."

"Your point is well taken. I'll have to be very delicate about any name-dropping, won't I?"

"You better believe it."

"Of course, there is also some good I can do. Your friend, Dr. Goldstein, for instance. I should have mentioned to you that Hugo obtained the propofol to frame him right here from Morristown Memorial. He bribed a pharmacist named Gupta to steal a case from the pharmacy. I'm sure you can match the lot numbers with the bottles that were discovered in Goldstein's office to the ones missing from here. While Dr. Goldstein was unconscious, they wrapped his hands around the bottles to get his fingerprints on them. Gupta will fold like a cheap suit when he hears the propofol he stole was used to murder someone and frame another for the crime. He thought that some guy was using it as a sleep aid."

"A sleep aid?" asked Cesari.

"We all tell ourselves fanciful stories to help us get through the night, John. Hugo paid him fifty thousand dollars for five minutes' worth of work on his part. Naturally, he wouldn't want to consider any negatives about the transaction. Anyway, I was present throughout the planning of that murder. I'd be willing to testify to that."

Cesari nodded, "Thank you. That will be very helpful in clearing Arnie of any wrong-doing."

"You should also be aware that Michel and Hugo have a mole inside St. Matt's who helped them keep tabs on you and your friend. He even planted the listening device for them."

Cesari raised his eyebrows at that. "Who is it?"

"I don't know. They never used his name in front of me and prying is never wise in an environment like that. But I can tell you this, Michel knew this person well. At times, I thought they may have been childhood friends or went to school together."

A second ambulance pulled up and delivered two dead guys in body bags for delivery to the morgue, one very large body and one average sized. Beaujolais and the lieutenant governor, thought Cesari. The faces on this ambulance crew were grimmer than the last. Two police cars followed seconds later. The officers got out and seemed to be securing the area. Within a minute a third ambulance arrived, and the governor came wheeling out the back strapped to a gurney with an IV and an oxygen mask. This got Cesari's attention. The man was fine when he left him, but he was massively overweight, over sixty years of age, and had quite a night of stress, booze, and sex. He could very possibly have had a heart attack. Multiple state troopers and police cars followed, and the place soon teemed uncomfortably with law enforcement and the flashing multicolored lights of their vehicles.

Cesari said, "I think we should move further away, don't you? I'm getting claustrophobic."

"I agree."

The retaining wall stretched another one hundred feet to their left before ending abruptly. As they walked to the end of it, Simone said, "I wonder what happened to the governor? You said he was unharmed when you last saw him."

"He was, but that doesn't mean he didn't have a stroke or a coronary after I left. Physically, he's a disaster waiting to happen... Then there's always the possibility he's faking it for the sympathy vote. I wouldn't put it past him. He's as slippery as they come."

"Is there anybody you trust?"

"You're asking me that after the night I've had?"

She nodded in silent agreement.

"I hate to keep bringing up a sore topic, Simone, but have you heard from Hugo?"

"No, should I have?"

They sat down again and adjusted to their new vantage point of the emergency room entrance and parking lot. They were in nearly complete darkness now. He replied, "Maybe... Wouldn't he try to convince you that you made a mistake and try to talk you into coming back with him?"

She shook her head and wrinkled her nose decisively. "Not a chance on Earth would he ever believe that I would trust him. I know much too well what a sadist he is. If Michel sent him after me, it would be for only one reason, and that reason wouldn't be reconciliation. So therefore, he wouldn't call me and give up the element of surprise. He would love to spring a trap on me and watch me squirm in surprise and terror."

"You don't seem very frightened by the prospect."

"I've learned to hide my emotions well, but what's there to do anyway? Curling up in a ball and crying is not my style in case you haven't noticed."

"I've noticed," Cesari said as he scanned around the hospital grounds. "So he's just lying-in wait out there? He might even be watching us as we speak."

"Very possibly. Do you think he knows Michel is dead?" she asked. "That might temper his actions."

"Or make him thirsty for revenge... I think I should I call him. I'd rather not stay up all night waiting for him to find me."

She looked at him like he was crazy. "What are you going to do? Challenge him to a fight in the parking lot?"

"Why not? I have certain rights here. He was going to cut my head off after all."

"You're serious, aren't you?"

"Very much so. May I use your phone to call him? He'll be sure to answer if it's you."

She shook her head in disbelief but handed him her phone. "Keep it. There's no passcode on it, and I won't be needing it after tonight... We should probably head upstairs. The police may be there by now and I have a lot to clear off my chest."

He took the phone, hesitated, and handed it back to her. "I have an idea, but I can't let you turn yourself in just yet."

Chapter 49

Cesari said, "Hugo's tracking the GPS unit in the Phantom, right?"

She nodded. "Yes…"

"My first thoughts about Hugo were that he would want to silence not just you but Martine as well. But if Michel is dead, and the horrors at the mansion are exposed, then Martine suddenly becomes irrelevant. Everybody will already know what he's been party to, and from what you told me, she's been relatively sheltered from the dark side of her husband's activities."

"That is true, although she must have had her suspicions or else she never would have gone snooping around like she did."

"Yes, but her testimony now is relatively minor in comparison to the overwhelming physical evidence. In fact, you're the only one who can really bury this guy. You know all the details."

"Fair enough, but I don't think I need reminding about how much he would like me dead. What's your point?"

"My point is that Martine is relatively safe now that the cat's out of the bag. And now with cops and troopers swarming all over the hospital it wouldn't make sense for him to try to go after her. The risk benefit analysis doesn't add up. So if you left the hospital, he would probably follow you and give up on Martine."

"And that is what you would like me to do? Draw Hugo away from Martine so he can kill me and no one else gets hurt?"

"No, I want you to draw Hugo away somewhere private where I can kill him so no one else gets hurt."

She stared at him for a minute and then said, "You want to use me as bait?"

"You'll never be safe as long as he's out there. Am I right?"

She nodded and sighed. "Probably... What do you propose?"

"Call him and tell him you know he's out there waiting for you and that you want this to end tonight. Tell him all you care about right now is that Martine and Jean Claude remain safe and that you're willing to surrender yourself if he will guarantee he'll leave them alone."

"But I thought you just reasoned that he will no longer be interested in Martine?"

"Which is why he'll agree to your surrender. If I'm right, it's a no brainer for him. He's getting something for nothing. And even if he thought otherwise, he'd still agree. You'd be the low hanging fruit. Take you first and then come for Martine later."

"I see, and you think this is better than just placing myself in police custody?"

"As I mentioned before, police custody is no guarantee of personal safety, Simone. People die in police custody all the time. And although there's a chance you personally might be safer, there's no guarantee he won't visit Martine at some later date. Who knows, maybe six months from now, he'll decide that Michel's estate owes him for services rendered."

She nodded slowly. "Okay, and where will you be during all of this?"

"That's a good question. If we assume, he's watching the Phantom, I can't just get in the passenger seat with you. The same for the back seat. If he sees something suspicious, he may just start shooting. We have to convince him that keeping you alive will bring him immeasurable albeit delayed gratification... I could follow you in the Boat Tail. That might work."

"I'd prefer to have you in the Phantom with me. In case I haven't impressed it upon you enough, Hugo is not a nice man."

"Hugo's days of not being nice are soon going to be over, but I understand. Let me call my guys. I think they can help."

He took out his phone and dialed Xi. "How's it going with Mrs. Beaujolais?"

"How'd you know I was awake and not sleeping?"

"To be honest, I didn't care. You still want to shoot someone tonight?"

"Are you kidding? It's like having an itch I can't scratch. What's up?"

"I need you and another volunteer to meet me outside the emergency room to plan strategy. Leave two guys with Mrs. Beaujolais. Tell them no one's going to sleep tonight unless I say so."

"That shouldn't be a problem. We're too wound up to sleep. There's a cop up here trying to figure things out, but he doesn't seem particularly concerned. He's pretty uptight about whatever's going on in emergency room. He said the governor's down there with a heart attack."

"Yeah, we saw him get off the ambulance. That's all I know. There's a bag of Big Macs down here for you guys. I'd rather not walk through the ER right now. Tensions are running way too high for my taste, and I can't afford to be frisked."

"You're packing?"

"Always, Xi."

"Okay, I'll find a volunteer and meet you down there."

Cesari hung up and turned to Simone. She grinned. "The calvary is on the way."

"Don't snicker. Xi has an AR15 with a high-powered scope in the van they came in."

"Seriously?"

"And a passionate desire to use it."

"I feel better already."

"You should. Now I'm going to make one more call and then it's your turn."

He punched in the number and waited for Vito to pick up, which he did on the third ring. "Vito, I need some assistance."

"It's one in the morning, Cesari. How'd you know I wasn't sleeping?"

"Honestly, I didn't care."

"What do you want and where's my Boat Tail?" Vito growled.

"Your Boat Tail is safe. I'm in Morristown at the hospital. I'll fill you in on the details later. Right now I want you to call Gerry and the truck driver and tell them I'm coming there with the Boat Tail and a brand-new Rolls Royce Phantom. It's the exact car you wanted. Massive trunk and everything. Five or six hundred thousand dollars new. It's my present to you for being so nice. Have the door to the container open and we'll just drive in and Gerry can secure them."

"You're a lucky son-of-a-bitch, Cesari. I'm in Randolph with my crew. I decided tonight would be a good night to settle up with those bikers from last week. I'm at the New Jersey Bar and Grill waiting to start breaking some heads. I got Gerry with me to identify them, but the Boat Tail takes precedence."

"There's one more thing…"

"There's always one more thing with you."

"There's going to be a guy following us. It's Hugo. That guy Alan Chamberlain from the Mercedes dealership told us about. The one who threatened him and his family. He wants to kill Simone and probably me too."

"Who's Simone?"

"It's complicated, but she's on our side right now."

"I get it. She used to be on Hugo's side and now he's pissed."

"Can't fool you."

"You never could. Okay, you got my attention. Forty million, five hundred thousand dollars' worth of my attention to be exact. I assume you have a plan?"

"Not a great one but here it is. We bring the cars to the parking lot and wait for Hugo. We kill him and put him in the truck with the cars to be disposed of however you see fit, but I presume that shouldn't be that big a deal out here."

"Is Hugo alone?"

"I don't know."

"Pretty big unknown, don't you think?"

"Was there a memo that life was supposed to be easy? Because if there was, I didn't get it."

Vito snorted. "Fine, we get the cars, kill Hugo, come back here and open a can of whup-ass on these bikers."

"I'm going to have to take a pass on the biker rally. If everything goes well, I'm going back to the hospital with Simone and my friends."

"Friends? What friends?"

"You have friends. I have friends, and they're pretty tough too."

"Yeah, right. What time? I need at least twenty minutes to get to Morristown from here and then at least another ten to set up."

"Thirty minutes will work."

After he clicked off, Simone said, "This night just keeps getting more interesting by the minute. So who's this new player, Vito?"

"He's not new. He's the one who now feels he's the rightful owner of the Boat Tail. His friend Gerry Acquilano stole it for him from the Newark port last week."

"Gerry Acquilano? I've heard that name... Hugo and Michel knew he stole it. They were looking for him before everything fell apart tonight."

"They know Gerry?"

"They tortured the two security guards who were complicit with Gerry in the theft. They gave his name up before they died. Michel was going to mount their heads on the wall."

Cesari let out a deep breath. "I saw their heads. They were on the table in the trophy room when I was down there tonight. It looked like someone had used them for batting practice. It was a brutal sight."

She didn't say anything to that, so he continued, "Vito asked me how many guys Hugo had with him. I didn't know. What do you think?"

She chewed on it for a minute and said, "I would think at least one maybe two. One to drive the Phantom back while Hugo drove the vehicle they came in. A third for security just in case something went wrong and they needed back up. A fourth actually would make more sense. Two in each car for balance. Hugo is a very symmetrical person. If he breaks one arm, he will invariably break the other for aesthetics."

"Aesthetics?"

She shrugged.

"And you've watched him in action?"

"It was mandatory. So I could never say I had no idea what was going on."

"Call Hugo and give him your terms. Tell him you'll surrender but it has to be away from the hospital. You understand fully what he has in store for you, and you accept your fate. No, tell him that you deserve whatever he has planned for you but that you'd like to talk first. Maybe you can work something out? You know, maybe you two can move forward and start over without Michel. Tell him you know he's watching and that he should follow the Phantom. You're going to drive around until you find a suitable place for a pow wow. Tell him you need the drive to settle your nerves down, and that you can't be rushed. Your surrender will have to be on your terms, or you'll simply go to the police. This has a ring of authenticity to it. If you give him a direct location, he may become suspicious. I would. There's an outdoor parking lot ten minutes from here. I'll give you directions. At this hour, it will be pretty desolate. There will be an eighteen-wheeler parked there. That's where my friends will be hiding. Eventually, after driving around seemingly aimlessly you'll wind up there. The idea is to make it appear as if by pure chance you wandered into the lot. Call Hugo now and tell him you'll be leaving the hospital in thirty minutes. That will give Vito time to arrive and get out of sight."

"You want me to take Hugo on a joy ride?"

"I want you to make Hugo think you're confused, distraught even. You're O.J. in the white Bronco. You don't know what you're doing, but the one thing you're not doing is setting a trap for him, get it?"

She contemplated that and glanced at her watch. Then she looked at him and asked, "Why are you doing this for me?"

"Hey, we almost had sex. At my age, almost is close enough."

She laughed. "Did anyone ever tell you, you're out of control?"

"All the time."

Chapter 50

In time, a gaggle of news vans and reporters choked off the entrance to the emergency room and had to be forcibly pushed back by the police who set up a strict perimeter beyond which only authorized personnel could pass. From the grimaces on their faces, the media people were not thrilled at what they perceived to be a clear-cut violation of their first amendment rights. They didn't seem to notice or care that their presence created a health hazard to anybody or any ambulance trying to access the emergency room. Cesari watched the circus as Simone negotiated with Hugo on her cellphone. As she was finishing up, Jeremy and Xi arrived and lunged at the bag of Big Macs.

"How goes it upstairs with Parikh and Jaskaran?" he asked them.

"A lot better than an hour ago," offered Xi.

"How so?"

"The nurses switched. A hot, young Indian nurse took over. Jaskaran was falling all over himself when we left, and Parikh wasn't far behind."

Cesari laughed. "You've got to be kidding? Parikh's a player? I don't believe it. He's happily married."

"I'm not saying anymore on the subject," added Xi skeptically.

Simone hung up on her call and gave Cesari an apprehensive thumb's up. She said, "He's out there all right. Waiting and watching. Wherever he is, he doesn't seem to have eyes on us here though. At least he didn't let on that he did, but he knows exactly where the Phantom is. He asked me if I enjoyed my happy meal. Anyway, he's agreeable to the plan and will follow me when I drive out. He sounded very contented to get me away from all police vehicles, although he didn't like the idea of not knowing where we were going."

Cesari nodded and said to Xi and Jeremy, "All right, let's get down to business."

They ate while Cesari laid out the plan for them. When he was done, he handed Jeremy the keys to the Boat Tail.

"Bring it to the parking lot where we picked it up. There'll be guys waiting to tuck it away safely back into the container. I want you to leave now before the action starts. There may not be an opportunity to secure it later."

"And then what?"

"Stay out of sight and try not to get shot. The cab of the trailer ought to be a moderately safe place to hang out. Good luck and stay safe."

"You too," he replied, and walked away.

Cesari watched him for a moment before turning to Xi. "Xi, I want you to follow Simone in Parikh's minivan. You and your AR15 are our back up. There's a car that will be following us so stay back a healthy distance."

"Do you know what kind of car?" asked Xi.

"No, I don't. It may not even be a car. It might be an SUV. Simone will make a few twists and turns. You'll know right away who's following her."

"Where are you going to be?" asked Simone. "You said it wouldn't be smart if they saw you in the Phantom with me."

"I'm going to be in the trunk."

She said, "The trunk? You never said anything about being in the trunk. What if you're trapped in there just when I need you?"

"There's an emergency trunk release on the inside of all new Rolls Royces. Anything made before 1990 and you'd be right. I'd be trapped. The real question is how do I get inside the trunk if Hugo's watching the Phantom? But I think I have a way around that. Xi, do you see the Phantom that Simone drove here?" Cesari asked and pointed out toward the lot. "It's in the second row of cars toward the right side of the lot between the overhead lights."

Xi turned toward the lot just as Jeremy pulled the Boat Tail out of its spot and drove away. Xi nodded. "Yeah, I see it. That grill would make it stand out anywhere."

"That's it. Do you think that if you drove a hundred yards away to a more secluded area, you could hit those overhead lights with your AR15?"

Xi studied the terrain for a bit, and then the lights where the Phantom was parked. Then he looked over at the driveway full of reporters, cops, and state troopers.

He said, "Have you lost your mind, Cesari? I can't fire an AR15 here. Do you have any idea how loud that thing is, even at a hundred yards away? I want to help but spending a year in prison for being stupid isn't going to help anyone."

"He has a point," added Simone. "I don't see how he could possibly shoot two lights out and get away with it. They'd be on him in a heartbeat, and given the level of tension right now, he'd be lucky not to get shot himself."

"Good point. Okay, it was just a thought. It would be nice to have the cover of darkness to sneak into the back of the Phantom, but I might be able to do it as is."

Xi said, "I suppose if I could find a substation or a transformer, I could shoot one of them. It might explode and disguise the gunshot. Then the entire lot would go dark."

Cesari liked that idea but cautioned him. "Shooting the substation could be extremely dangerous. A substation could potentially have several hundred thousand volts of electricity running through it. If it explodes it will feel like an earthquake and if anybody is too close, they'll feel like they've been struck by lightning. It might also shut down part of the hospital and all its life support equipment."

"True, but all hospitals have generator backup. They'd be up and running in minutes, but look, I'll search hard for a transformer and will only target the substation as a last resort."

"Okay, fair enough. When you identify the target, drive the minivan as far away as you can and still get off a safe shot," Cesari said and scanned around for an ideal spot. "What magnification is your scope?"

"It's variable up to ten times, and I routinely practice at two hundred yards. It's not the distance that's the problem. It's the line of sight. Depending on where the transformer is, I may only have a clear shot at fifty yards."

"That's up to you. If it doesn't look good, don't force it. We'll figure something else out. If it looks good, then it's one shot and you pack up and move no matter what happens. We're taking enough risks. If I were you, I'd open the rear door and shoot from inside the back of the minivan like we talked about doing back at the mansion. That will hide the muzzle flash unless someone is looking directly at you. Then wait for Simone and me to come out in the Rolls. If all goes well, and the transformer or substation explodes, no one will even know a shot was fired."

"Okay, I'll drive around the lot looking for one or the other and give you a call with my status."

He left them to find Parikh's minivan and Cesari said to Simone, "Give me the keys to the Phantom and I'll get in position. Once the lights go out, I'll get in the trunk. I may not be able to close it properly from inside. You come over, get the keys from me, and then close the trunk. It'll be very dark by then and I don't think they'll be sure of what you're doing, if they can see you at all."

"And if the lights don't go out?"

"That's a very good question. Probably at that point, you just walk to the Rolls. I'll take the chance and crawl into the trunk as stealthily as possible and hope they're watching you and don't notice me. There will be too much visibility, so it won't be a good idea for them to see you fishing around in the trunk for the keys. It will seem suspicious. In that scenario, I'll just toss them to the ground right where you can find them. Then just lean on the trunk and close it discreetly. It's a bit riskier that way but doable if plan A doesn't work. If they see me get in, they might just fill the trunk with lead when they catch up to you. In that case, it will have been nice meeting you."

She smiled. "You're making me want to kiss you again."

"It didn't end well the last time you said that."

"No, it didn't. But I suppose that as long as I have you trapped in the trunk, I could just drive as far away as possible."

"Interesting idea, and then what? Chain me to your kitchen table waiting for Hugo to show up?" he said and glanced at his watch. "Time to go."

She handed him the keys to the Phantom, and he walked to the parking lot angling away from the Rolls in case he was being observed. He strolled nonchalantly twenty-five yards in the wrong direction, pretended to find the car he was looking for, and jiggled the driver's side door handle of some random vehicle. He then ducked down as if entering the car and began a slow laborious crawl back to the Phantom. When he got to within five cars away, he stopped and sat, leaning back against the rear wheel of a pickup. He was slowly but surely destroying his Tuxedo. The good news was that most of the blood had dried.

Five minutes later, Xi buzzed him. "I found the transformer. It's in the center of the lot, high up on an electrical distribution pole. I'm going to drive off the hospital grounds. Across the main thoroughfare, there are a series of medical office buildings and their parking lots. They're all deserted right now. I'll park in one of them. Line of sight is excellent. The range is little long for me, closer to three hundred yards, but the target is much larger than what I usually shoot at so we should be all right. I may even double-tap it."

"Don't get carried away, Xi."

"I won't. There's plenty of room in the lot to conceal the minivan along the side of one of the buildings. I'll essentially be invisible to the road, and I'll be at an oblique angle to the ER as well. Two quick shots in rapid succession will sound like one and if the transformer explodes then it's a done deal. People won't be able to process what happened. Either way, I'll pack up and move on."

"Okay, be careful."

"I'll let you know when I'm in position. Give me ten minutes."

Xi hung up and Cesari called Simone. "Call Hugo and tell him you'll be leaving the hospital in ten minutes. Then wait for the cue. If you hear shots but no explosion, just proceed to the car anyway and we'll go with plan B."

Cesari put his phone away and crawled to the car adjacent to the Rolls and waited. Ten minutes later his phone buzzed with a text from Xi saying he was ready.

Cesari texted back. *Let her rip.*

A minute later, he heard what he thought was the distant report from the AR15, but almost simultaneously, this was superseded by the exploding transformer in the center of the parking lot fifty feet in the air. It was a large transformer and when it blew, it was like ten or twenty of the most powerful rockets put together in a Fourth of July fireworks display. The noise was deafening, and the sparks flew in every direction showering the lot up to two hundred feet away.

The lights in the entire parking lot went out and Cesari could hear a commotion ensue from the cops and troopers in the ER driveway as he dodged to the back of the Phantom, popped open the trunk, and quickly climbed in. He closed the lid almost completely and held his breath waiting for Simone. She must have been moving fast because he didn't have to wait long. She opened the trunk a few inches, stuck her hand in and wiggled it around.

He handed her the keys and whispered, "Good luck."

Without replying, she grabbed the keys and closed the trunk. He was all alone in the dark and turned on the light from his cellphone to examine his surroundings. Then he took the gun from the small of his back and checked to make sure the safety was off and a round was chambered. Glancing around, he found the trunk's safety release and familiarized himself with it. He heard and felt the engine turn over and was pushed around a little as the car pulled out from its spot. The soft wool lining of the trunk was actually quite comfortable, he thought. Martine and Jean Claude's pillows were still there, so he fluffed one under his head and settled in. All in all, it wasn't that uncomfortable an experience.

Chapter 51

Fifteen minutes into the ride, Cesari called Simone. "Is Hugo behind you?"

"Oh yes. He's quite obvious. He's in a big black Toyota Sequoia maybe five car lengths back. A little hard to miss at two in the morning. Impossible for your friend to miss also."

"A Toyota Sequoia? With a garage full of Bentleys at his disposal? Isn't that kind of slumming it for Hugo?"

"It's a work vehicle. It would appear that he means business tonight... How's the trunk?"

"Very comfortable, and big enough to qualify as a medium-sized studio apartment in Manhattan. All it really needs is a bathroom."

She laughed softly, and he continued, "Okay, just keep driving around for a few more minutes. Vito texted me. He was running a little late, but he's there now with his men and they're ready. Unfortunately, all they have are handguns and baseball bats so this may get personal. I know it's dark, but can you guess how many of them are in the Sequoia?"

"Not really. Their headlights are very blinding. Two for sure. There's Dalton driving and Hugo in the passenger side. I can't see if anyone's in the back."

"Do you know Dalton?"

"Of course. He's security at the mansion. I know them all."

"Would he hurt you if Hugo ordered him to?"

"Is that a serious question?"

"Yes, if push came to shove, is he someone we could negotiate with?"

She let out a deep breath as she considered the question. "I don't know. This kind of situation has never come up before. Blind obedience has generally been the rule with Hugo and Michel, and he must know that I killed one of his friends back at the mansion so I think it's best if we work on the assumption that we can't have a reasonable discussion with any of them."

"Fine, where are we now?"

"We're out in the country somewhere between Bernardsville and Morristown. We're coming up on the Jockey Hollow Preserve."

"You left Morristown?"

"Yes, why?"

He hadn't anticipated that. "I didn't think about it at the time, but I probably wouldn't have left the population center of the city. I presumed you were just going to drive around the downtown area... Hugo's made no attempt to stop you?"

"None whatsoever. I made it clear to him I needed time to think and catch my breath and that I would not be pressured."

"He's being awfully civilized about this."

"What do you mean?"

"I mean if it were me and you just exposed yourself on an isolated country road, I might have considered forcing you to pull over."

"So far, there have been no signs of aggression. He's maintaining his speed and distance. We're only a mile or so outside the city limits, but I'll turn around."

"I think that's a good idea. Can you see Xi?"

"Yes, he's hanging way back, at least ten or twelve car lengths behind the Sequoia. I'm driving very slowly and deliberately so no one loses anyone, but now you've made me nervous."

"I'm sorry. I didn't mean to frighten you, but that's why I'm in the trunk and Xi is back there with his AR15. But there's no point inviting trouble. Turn around at the next opportunity. I'll call Xi…"

There was a massive collision and Cesari was flung like a rag doll to the other side of the trunk. Then the car rolled over and he flopped onto the lid and then it rolled again, and he fell back. He grabbed the pillow and wrapped it around his head for protection as the car rolled twice more, bouncing him up and down and sideways before coming to a jarring stop right side up. He felt like he was in a washing machine or a spin dryer that had just finished its cycle, and he lay there gasping for breath, his heart pounding. Confused and concerned for Simone, he searched quickly for the Glock which he had lost in the free fall.

He found it and his phone although the latter didn't appear to be working at the moment. He put it away and listened for any telltale sounds as to what had happened. He heard nothing, which made him alarmed. Simone was either unconscious or dead. He took a deep breath in and let it out and pulled on the trunk release. Cautiously raising the lid an inch, he was becoming conscious of various pains throughout his body, and as fresh night air rushed in filling his lungs, he heard men approaching. Wherever the Phantom had landed, there were no streetlights. Minimal moonlight was shrouded by the dense foliage of trees. He couldn't see anything, but he could now hear very clearly. Several men, more than two, possibly more than three, and one of them was named Hugo. They were some distance away, but their voices traveled well in the silence of the night.

"I'm sorry, Hugo. In the dark, I didn't realize there was a gully here."

"No worries, Edgar, I didn't know it either, but you really should educate yourself more on physics. This is what happens when a six-thousand-pound vehicle hits another broadside at full throttle. A slightly gentler tap and we may have disabled her without all the havoc, but I think we'll be okay. The damage could have been much worse. The Phantom is no slouch in the weight department and is well-built for personal protection.

You and Karl go retrieve Simone. Dalton and I will move the Sequoias off the road into the woods of the preserve to stay out of view."

"What if Simone requires urgent medical attention?"

"As long as she has a pulse, I want you to bring her to me for her final judgement. You might want to take a crowbar in case the door is jammed, and you have to pry her out. And for heaven's sake put out that cigarette. There could be gas leaking."

The man named Edgar called out, "Karl, get the crowbar from the back of the Sequoia and meet me down there."

Cesari heard Hugo walk away, and as Edgar walked clumsily through brush toward the Phantom, he slowly raised the trunk lid. He hadn't seen any flashlights yet and thought that might have been deliberate so as not to attract attention from anyone passing by. In fact, he realized they had also turned their headlights off. These were serious guys with seriously bad intentions. After a minute, the trunk was fully open, and he lay there trying to figure out a plan as Edgar cursed at some thorny bush that had grabbed him.

There were two Sequoias and four men. Two and two. That's why Hugo was so patient. He had called on ahead to the other Sequoia once he could guess Simone's direction, and had timed the ambush. He didn't believe for one minute that she was going to surrender without a fight. Through the wall of the trunk, he heard Simone moan softly. Airbags were great inventions, but they could be a bitch if you were on the receiving end. At least she was alive.

He heard Edgar pulling on the driver's side door handle and Karl coming down the slope faster than his friend had in order to catch up. Cesari swung one leg over the lip of the trunk and felt an aching sensation run through his body almost from head to toe. He then swung his other leg over the side and crouched to his knees on the ground, the Glock in one hand, just as Karl arrived to assist Edgar. The driver's door opened with a metallic scraping sound as the two men pulled on it forcefully. Cesari listened as the two men tried to drag Simone out of the car. They were having difficulty.

Inching his way around the back of the vehicle toward the front in pain, in the dark was no easy feat, but his eyes were gradually accommodating to the gloom, and he could see now what had happened. The Phantom had passed the entrance to the Jockey Hollow State Park and the second Sequoia had been waiting on a cross street when Hugo had given them the signal to ram them. The Phantom had rolled down a ten-foot ditch which leveled off and had wound up nearly twenty feet from the road in thick brush at the edge of woodland. Cesari couldn't see the Sequoias but knew they were hidden nearby. These guys had their work cut out for them, depending on how far they had to carry her.

He could see two dark, very large figures wrestling with Simone's safety belt, which apparently would not unclasp. It must have been damaged in the impact and they swore under their breaths. Their backs were to him as they sweated, and Cesari decided to act decisively. He rose and grabbed one of the pillows from the trunk and moved quickly forward to the guy nearest him. He pressed the pillow against his back and jammed the tip of the Glock into it firing once into his spine. The sound of the shot was muffled by the pillow, and the guy groaned and lurched forward. Cesari didn't wait to see the other guy's reaction and almost immediately, had the pillow in his back too and placed a 9mm slug somewhere in his right lung.

Both men slid to the ground unconscious. He sensed they were both still breathing but for how long without medical attention would be anybody's guess. The guy with the lung shot was gurgling up blood and wheezing dramatically. Cesari estimated he would die the quicker of the two, but he wasn't too concerned about their fates. The important thing at the moment was that they were no longer a threat, but he needed to move quickly. The two shots were muted but not inaudible and would sound like the clanging of a cymbal depending on where Hugo was.

And he was right.

As he searched the men and threw their weapons into the woods, one of their phones rang. Predictably, it was Hugo. He had heard the sounds and was calling to investigate.

Cesari decided to not answer, though it would have given him a certain amount of grim satisfaction to flaunt his small victory. But he was still outnumbered and out gunned and had an injured woman on his hands. For the moment, he reasoned, it would be better to keep Hugo guessing. So he let the call go to voice mail and pocketed the guy's phone. He still had a minute or two before Dalton or Hugo or both would come to see what was happening. He used that time to evaluate Simone's injuries. She was breathing comfortably but unconscious. As far as he could tell she was mostly intact. Her face was red from the impact of the airbag, and she had a few cuts here and there but was largely unscathed. Her pulse was strong and regular. The seat belt had jammed but he worked on it and gradually pried it loose.

He put his arms under hers and was starting to drag her out when he heard Hugo in the distance calling for Edgar and Karl. He doubled his efforts, freed her from the car and dragged her off into the woods out of sight. He lay her down gently and ran back to the Phantom to grab the pillow and nearly tripped over something. At first, he thought it was Edgar's limp arm but then realized it was the crowbar. He picked it up and quickly retrieved the pillow as Hugo's voice indicated he was closing in. Cesari retraced his steps and fought his way through thorns and vines to where Simone was safely hidden. Kneeling beside her, he propped her head gently on the bullet ravaged pillow. Then, covered in sweat, he breathed a quiet sigh of relief.

Hugo was pissed and howled epithets at the night sky when he discovered his men. Cesari and Simone were a mere forty feet away but in a thicket of brush and woods. Without light, they might as well have been forty miles away.

Dalton said, "How is this possible?"

Cesari could practically feel Hugo shake his head in frustration. "I don't know. Simone's good, but this good? It seems almost impossible that she survived a roll like that without injury let alone still have enough reserve to do this."

Hugo then called out, "Simone...Simone, I know you are there. I am coming for you, Simone. I am impressed by what you have you done here, but you know you cannot escape. I will never stop. Please, I implore you. Make this easier on yourself."

Suddenly, the powerful beams of high intensity LED flashlights flicked on and started scanning the woods. One hundred thousand lumens each, fanning out, one on the right and one on the left, and closing in.

Cesari knew he was in trouble and tried to think of a solution that didn't involve leaving Simone alone. He didn't want her to die like this. She moaned softly again like she did in the Phantom just minutes ago and he lay down next to her, placing the crowbar on the ground and cradling her head in his left arm. In his right hand, he pointed the gun at the closest approaching light.

He whispered comfortingly into her ear, "Shhh... It's all right."

She quieted down, but Cesari's problem grew exponentially as the two lights appeared to be converging on their location and he guessed that their hushed sounds had not gone unnoticed. They were approaching from opposite directions, and he knew, there was no way he'd get them both. And if they had submachine guns, it was game over before it started. They were ten feet away on each side when they stopped. He couldn't see them, but apparently, they could see him.

"Toss the pistol away, Dr. Cesari," ordered Hugo.

He was tempted to shoot directly at the light, but it was like staring into the high beams of a car from just a few feet away. At ten feet, lying on the ground, without a clear target, blinding light, and someone behind him also armed, their chances of survival had just plummeted to below zero. As bad an idea as it seemed, talking his way out of the situation suddenly appeared to be the only reasonable option.

He sat up, flung the gun away in front of him, and rested his hand on the ground inches from the crowbar. Hugo and Dalton saw that and stepped closer, appearing out of the thicket, their lights illuminating each other and everything else. They were holding MP5 submachine guns and heavy flashlights. Hugo had a sneer across his face that Cesari wanted to just rip off. The other guy, Dalton, was huge, broad shouldered and thick necked like a weightlifter. The machine gun looked small in his hands like a toy. His ruddy face was expressionless. Cesari had met guys like this. He was the kind of guy that did what he was told like a good soldier. The morality of it wasn't of consequence to him. Simone was right. There wouldn't be any negotiation with him. If Hugo told him to build a gas chamber or a crematorium, his only question would be how big? Anything to make the boss happy.

They stood over Cesari and Simone, pointing their flashlights directly at them. Hugo was to his right and Dalton to his left. Cesari lowered his gaze to protect his eyes from the glare of lights and could see their legs from the knees down.

Hugo said, "Dr. Cesari… That explains a lot. You were in the trunk, weren't you?"

Cesari said nothing.

"You killed two of my best men… I'm impressed, but there's going to be a price to pay for that and all the other trouble you've caused tonight. You and Simone are going to enjoy my company for quite some time. You see, I have nothing left but my rage."

Cesari said nothing.

Hugo continued, "Dalton, be so kind as to tie Dr. Cesari's hands behind his back and gag him. If you need to whack him a few times to vent your anger, go ahead, but please don't kill him. I want that pleasure, but only after many hours of playtime."

Dalton stepped close and using the barrel of his MP5 back-handed Cesari across the face with it. Cesari fell over Simone, his face on fire with pain, his brain momentarily swimming with confusion. For a few seconds, he was unaware of where or who he was. He shook off the cobwebs, regained his senses and composure, and sat back up. He said nothing.

Dalton and Hugo were smiling.

Hugo snickered, "Dalton, do it again. Dr. Cesari looks like he still has some fight left in him."

He wound the MP5 back for another blow to Cesari's face, but before he could launch it, there was a loud explosion and simultaneously, Dalton's head burst into an expanding plume of pink mist and bone fragments, splattering Cesari, Simone, and Hugo with his disintegrated frontal lobes. His headless torso slipped to the ground.

Everyone flinched and then momentarily froze. Hugo recovered quickly though and swung his MP5 around planning on firing randomly at the source. Before he made it halfway to his intended target area, another shot rang out and passed an inch above his head plowing six inches deep into an oak tree behind him, sending splinters in all directions. That was too close for comfort, and he turned to flee into the deeper woods for cover.

Cesari had other plans and quickly grabbed the straight end of the crowbar and lunged toward Hugo, hooking it around his ankle just as he took his first step. Caught by surprise, he teetered off-balance. With both hands, Cesari pulled back and upended him. Hugo fell flat on his face, dropping his weapon and flashlight. Cesari pounced on his back. Hugo fought furiously to regain some leverage, spitting and cursing. Cesari slammed the back of Hugo's skull with his fists, right then left, right then left, over and over, until Hugo stopped struggling and Cesari's knuckles were covered in his blood. Cesari sat back quietly, regaining his breath, willing his heart rate to come back to earth. His lungs hurt and his body ached from the car crash. Xi came walking into their hiding place holding his AR15 with a flash-light attachment on the end of the barrel.

Cesari said, "Good shooting, Xi. You saved our lives."

Xi said nothing, but as he stared at the headless corpse of Dalton, he fell to his knees and started puking. Cesari watched him retch and heave. There was a first time for everything, he thought. He stood and went over to him.

"You all right?" he asked.

Xi nodded. "I'm fine."

"C'mon, help me get Simone to the hospital. She has a pretty bad concussion."

As they approached Simone, Xi put his arm through the shoulder strap of his rifle and swung the weapon over his back. They were about to lift her when Hugo coughed and sucked in a breath. Xi looked at Cesari.

"Xi, I want to apologize in advance for what I'm about to do."

Xi said nothing but watched intently as Cesari returned to Hugo who had managed to roll over onto his back, gasping for oxygen. Cesari picked up the crowbar and sat down, straddling Hugo's chest. Hugo grunted from Cesari's weight and opened his eyes. He was barely conscious.

Cesari said, "One chance, Hugo. If you want to live, tell me the name of your mole in St. Matt's. I'm going to count to three. One…"

Hugo whispered something almost inaudible, but Cesari heard him clearly and nodded. The news was difficult to digest, but clearly this was a night like no other, and there was apparently no end to the surprises. He stared down at the man who struggled weakly, but there would be no escape tonight. And no mercy. Cesari held the straight side of the crowbar, and with both hands, hoisted it high over his head. He paused at the top to take in a breath, and then swinging the crowbar like an axe, smashed the curved end down hard into the top of Hugo's skull. There was so much force, so much anger and so much primitive ferocity behind the blow that it nearly cleaved Hugo's head into two halves. Like the sword in the stone, it lay embedded deeply in Hugo's head, the flat end angling upward, wedged tightly in place by bone on either side.

Cesari stood and turned to Xi. "Let's go.

Chapter 52

B y the time Cesari had dropped her off in the emergency room, Simone was improving, and he was confident she would make a full recovery. He didn't stick around for long though because his weekend was just beginning, and he had a lot of work to do. The first thing was to call Detective Tierney and bring him into the loop on what had happened at the mansion and tell him there was an eyewitness that would clear Arnie of any wrongdoing. Arnie was already out on bail, but Tierney promised to investigate the pharmacist, Gupta, about the pilfering of the propofol from Morristown and to talk to Simone as soon as possible. If it panned out, then he would notify the district attorney that there was a fly in the ointment of the case against Arnie. He whistled at all the mayhem described and perhaps even caused by Cesari and was glad it was out of his jurisdiction. In a way, he was relieved at Arnie's exoneration. After spending an extended period of time with the man, he was having trouble believing Arnie could have killed anyone.

Then Cesari spent several hours exploring the personnel files at St. Matt's hospital and doing background research on the internet. This led to him waking up multiple hospital administrators in the tri-state area in the middle of the night for questioning. Surprisingly, once they got past their ire at the late hour of the call, most were eager to vent their spleens when they heard the name Beaujolais and hadn't realized there were others in the same boat.

Monday morning came and an exhausted Cesari marched through the halls of St. Matt's with a briefcase and a look of grim determination on his face as he made a beeline toward the boardroom where Leo Trautman had convened an emergency meeting of the board. Cesari had held a conference call the night before with key members of the board, including Leo, to let them all know about Beaujolais' perfidy and unexpected demise at his home in Bernardsville Saturday night. It hadn't quite made the news cycle yet but the question of what to do suddenly took precedence over everything else.

In view of all the negative publicity and accusations swirling around Arnie, and despite his now obvious innocence, Michele Kislovsky recommended cutting all ties with him as if he was a gangrenous limb. She was the mouse that roared. And Arnie was so depressed and beaten down that he had agreed to do whatever was necessary to save St. Matt's.

The next order of business for the board was to decide whether to promote Steve Brennan from acting CEO to permanent CEO. There was a strong sentiment that the hospital needed true and stalwart leadership in this time of crisis, and they wanted Brennan to devote his full efforts to right the good ship St. Matt's. Meaning they wanted him to move heaven and hell to recover St. Matt's money from Beaujolais' financial firm. To do that he would need to have the full backing of the board and whatever resources they could make available. There was only one problem with that.

Cesari glanced at his watch and hoped he wasn't late. He was still pretty banged up from Saturday night's soiree at the Chateau Beaujolais and walked with a slight limp. Last he heard, Martine and child were doing well, but except for the governor's trip to the emergency room for unexplained chest pains, there was an almost complete media blackout on what had taken place. This puzzled Cesari as it should have been the story of the century. But as he mulled it over, most of the action would have taken place after midnight, so it was possible the media was trying to get their facts straight before blasting headlines. Equally possible and more likely in Cesari's opinion was that the governor demanded or begged for some time to get his damage control team organized and on the same page. How long could he suppress a story as big as that? No more than a day or two, Cesari estimated. So that would mean by late afternoon or tonight or first thing in the morning the story would break. And it would break big. It would make national headlines.

In the hallway outside the boardroom stood Valentina, her Aunt Marjorie, and Joe Fusco, the buffed hand surgeon with the Lamborghini. They were sipping coffee from styrofoam cups.

Cesari stopped and greeted them, "Good morning, all."

Valentina and Marjorie said nearly simultaneously, "Hi, John."

Fusco nodded in his direction and grunted, "Cesari."

"Glad you could make it to the board meeting, John. Your presence will definitely help the weighty decisions that face us today," Marjorie said. "And I think Arnie will find comfort in having his friend nearby. Well, I'll meet you inside. Fusco, Valentina, have a nice day."

Cesari waited until she was out of sight before turning to Valentina. He said, "Here's the deal, Valentina. I'm only going to ask once. It's a yes or no question... Will you have dinner with me this Friday night at Les Bernardin in mid-town? I've already made the reservation and ordered a dozen long stem red roses for the table."

Fusco took an aggressive step toward him and bristled, "Now look here, Cesari. You're way out of line."

Valentina stepped in front of Fusco. "What time?"

"I'll pick you up at seven-thirty. Naturally, I'll be wearing a suit and tie."

Fusco's eyes went wide, and a vein suddenly appeared in his left temple as his blood pressure skyrocketed. "Valentina, what are you saying?"

Cesari allowed himself a subtle grin. "I'll see you then, Valentina, but I want to give you fair warning. If you use the M word even once while I'm eating, I will excuse myself to the bathroom and won't return."

She made a big smile and said softly, "I promise I won't."

"Valentina, I'm standing right here," Fusco said indignantly.

Cesari said, "I have to go. I think you and Fusco have a lot to talk about… See you later."

He turned and entered the boardroom. With the door closed behind him, he stood there for a minute assessing the mood of the room. The entire twenty-member board was present including the lawyer. Brennan sat at the head of the table, the mouse to his right and Arnie to his left, then Leo Trautman, then Marjorie, and so on. There was a coffee urn with cups and a tray of pastries in the center of the long table. Arnie had aged in the last week, Cesari noticed. Stress will do that to you. Arnie had trouble wrapping his head around all that had happened. He was an easygoing guy by nature and couldn't conceive of deliberately hurting anyone.

Cesari cleared his throat and said, "Good morning, everyone."

A murmured response greeted him in return. All eyes were on him as he placed his briefcase on the table and opened it. He had done a lot of leg work in the last twenty-four hours and felt he was thoroughly prepared.

He said, "I have told you all about the tragic events over the weekend and the incredible conclusions I have been forced to come to about Michel Beaujolais, but there is one more thing I didn't want to bring up until I had undeniable proof."

Leo Trautman said, "Dr. Cesari, haven't we had enough surprises? What's this all about?"

"Well, Leo, apparently Beaujolais had an accomplice right here at St. Matt's."

"An inside man?" Leo said drolly. "You can't be serious."

"But I am, Leo… Very serious. An inside man keeping tabs on all of us and feeding Beaujolais real time information.

Whispering bad advice into Arnie's ear like the snake in the Garden of Eden. Our very own Machiavelli."

"Thank you for the dramatic introduction, Dr. Cesari. Now please get on with it."

Cesari reached into his briefcase and passed out manila folders to everyone present.

"If you open the folders," he said. "You will see several copies of old photographs. I apologize. I know some of them aren't the best quality. The top photo is the graduation picture from Columbia University of our esteemed CFO and acting CEO, Steve Brennan. Underneath is the graduation photo of Michel Beaujolais also from Columbia, same year, same major."

Brennan held the photos and demanded, "What are you implying, Dr. Cesari? It's no secret that I went to school with Beaujolais."

"Bear with me, Steve… Okay, the picture beneath those is the senior men's crew team at Columbia. I circled two figures, the co-captains, Michel Beaujolais and Steve Brennan. Under that one is a photo of Michel Beaujolais' wedding. I would just like to point out who the best man is standing behind and to the left of the groom. None other than our own Steve Brennan."

Leo Trautman said, "Dr. Cesari, as Steve just mentioned we already knew that he and Beaujolais were classmates and friends, so I really don't understand what you're getting at."

"I want to establish that Brennan and Beaujolais weren't just casual acquaintances at school. They were, in fact, quite close not just back in the day but also recently. The last picture is of both of them relaxing in a ski lodge in Aspen taken two years ago and published in Forbes when they did a very flattering piece on Beaujolais' rising star."

"Okay, you've established they were close. So what?"

"The next page is a chronological outline of where Steve Brennan spent the last decade. It seems that he jumped around every two years or so. First, he was CFO at a hospital in Danbury, Connecticut. Then two years later, he took a gig in Waterbury.

Two years after that, he wound up at the Millard Fillmore Hospital in Buffalo, followed by a two-year stint at Jefferson Hospital in Cherry Hill, New Jersey before winding up here."

Brennan was turning red in the face as everybody was quietly trying to connect the dots. He stood angrily and said, "Are you going to tell us what you're getting at or not, Dr. Cesari?"

"Spare me the false outrage, Brennan. You know exactly what's coming next. Do you want me to spell it out or would you just like to leave now before the police arrive?"

Brennan stammered and began to sweat. Everyone just stared at him waiting for the other shoe to drop. Leo Trautman said, "What is he talking about, Steve?"

Brennan finally collected himself and said, "I have no idea but if someone doesn't call security, I will."

"You'd be saving us all some time if you did, Brennan," Cesari said. "Leo, let me explain what all these hospitals have in common. Our friend here, Steve Brennan, wormed his way into all of them as CFO and shortly thereafter conned them all into investing their cash reserves with a small but hot investment company in New Jersey run by a Wall Street prodigal named Michel Beaujolais. Coincidentally, they all lost their shirts in the process. Each hospital took a progressively bigger hit as Brennan and Beaujolais refined their scam and techniques. St. Matt's was their biggest score to date. I was up half the night talking to the CEOs of those hospitals who told me all the sordid details. They had no proof of any wrong-doing but they're still angry as hell about it."

Arnie looked at Brennan who gulped and protested, "This is absurd and slanderous. Of course none of it's true. I mean, yes, Beaujolais and I knew each other from school and maintained a friendship but that's hardly against the law. Whatever recommendations I made were based on sound analysis of the markets and Beaujolais' track record. I had no idea the man was the scoundrel he apparently was. The notion that I was part and parcel to a con is preposterous."

"Is it?" asked Cesari. "Is the idea that you planted a listening device in Arnie's office at Beaujolais' direct order so he could keep one step ahead of Arnie's plan to file a complaint with the SEC also preposterous? Because if it is, then you'll need to explain why your fingerprints and only your fingerprints were found on the device in Arnie's office."

Brennan turned pale as Cesari reached into his briefcase and came out with a piece of paper, waving it high in the air. "This is the result of the fingerprint analysis by the NYPD on the bug in Arnie's office. It confirms that you were the one who planted the device. You sold Arnie down the river, Brennan. He was kidnapped by Beaujolais and framed for murder in an attempt to discredit him and undermine his complaint to the SEC. You're a son-of-a-bitch, and now you're going to get what's coming to you."

Cesari reached into the briefcase one last time and came out with a big black menacing looking handgun. He pointed it at Brennan whose eyes went wide in fear and horror.

He pleaded, "Wait, no, you can't do this."

The rest of the room collectively gasped and froze in place as Cesari approached closer to the man, and said, "I most certainly can. You're the worst kind of rat, Brennan. You took advantage of Arnie. He was a friend. He's got grandkids and you almost put him in prison for the rest of his life for a crime he didn't commit. You don't deserve to live another day on this planet."

When Cesari got within a few feet of him, Brennan held his head low and started bawling like a baby, "I'm sorry. I really am. Arnie, I didn't mean for any of this to happen. Beaujolais didn't tell me he was going to kidnap you or murder anyone. I swear. I thought the listening device was only to get a sense of just how suspicious you were so that he could return the hospital's money in a timely fashion. You were the first one to ever take it as far as you did. I swear I didn't know they planned on harming you or anyone in any way." He looked at Cesari, his whole-body was trembling. "I admit it was a scam, but it was only supposed to be about money. No one was supposed to get hurt. Please, I don't deserve to die."

Cesari snarled, "You're a dog, Brennan. Now die like one"

Cesari pointed the weapon directly at the terrified man and fired. There was a loud pop, a puff of smoke and a tiny white round plastic pellet weighing a fraction of an ounce struck Brennan in the chest and bounced harmlessly onto the table, rolling directly down the center as everyone held their breath and tracked it with their eyes. Brennan flinched and stared at it in disbelief.

Cesari grinned. "It's an airsoft gun, Brennan. A kid's toy. You can pretty much get them anywhere. Looks real, doesn't it? Anyway, thanks for the confession."

Cesari took a small digital recording device from his sport coat pocket and held it for everyone to see. Then he placed the gun on the table and without warning wound up and slammed Brennan in the jaw with a vicious right cross. Brennan fell backward, stumbled over his chair, and went sprawling onto his ass, dazed and confused. Cesari slid the recorder across the table to Leo Trautman who was slack-jawed and speechless.

Cesari said, "You can do whatever you want with it, Leo... Congratulations, Arnie. I think you're CEO again."

Marjorie grabbed the paper Cesari had said was proof of Brennan's fingerprints on the listening device. She glanced at it and said, "This is the bill for an oil change on your car."

"Is it?" he said and started to leave the room.

The mouse jumped up and cut him off just as he reached the door. She was flushed from the excitement. It took her a second to catch her breath. She said, "Hey, I just want you to know something."

"What's that?"

"What I said about the Italian stallion stuff. I was wrong. That was kind of cool."

"Cool?"

"Yeah…"

"You don't get out much, do you?"

Chapter 53

After the board meeting, Cesari went back to his apartment and crashed for the rest of the day. He didn't wake up until 4:00 p.m. when his phone rang with a call from Jaskaran.

"What's up, Jay?"

"Want to come over and watch the Mumbai Grand Prix with me? Get here at six and we'll have dinner while we watch. I'm making lamb vindaloo and garlic naan."

"Yum, I'm starving. What's the time difference between here and Mumbai?"

"Ten hours, give or take."

Cesari did a quick calculation in his head and asked, "They're running a Grand Prix early on a Monday morning?"

"No, the race was held yesterday afternoon. I was busy, so I recorded it. I meant to ask you earlier in the day, but I got distracted. By the way, I don't know who won so don't google it up."

"I'll be there as soon as I clean up. I've been sleeping in my clothes all afternoon."

"As I said, it's a recording. If you're late it's no big deal, but the food will be ready at six, and I like my vindaloo hot."

"Got it. How are you and the boys? We haven't talked much since Saturday night."

"We're good. We're still reliving the thrill if you know what I mean. That was quite a night."

"Yes, it was. Are they coming?"

"No, Jeremy and Xi had plans and Parikh is on call."

"Can I bring a friend?"

"Sure, why not? Is he into F1?"

"He's into fancy cars. Is that good enough?"

"Sure, the more the merrier. There'll be plenty of food."

"Okay, I'll see you in about an hour. Can I bring anything? Beer, wine, scotch?"

"I got it covered, but if there's something you really want go ahead."

They hung up and Cesari jumped in the shower for the second time that day, then shaved and brushed his teeth again. He combed his hair back with his hands, threw on a pair of jeans and a cotton shirt and called Vito.

"How's the Boat Tail?"

"You owe me a Phantom, Cesari."

"Give me a break. It was a casualty of war. Unavoidable."

"What do you want?"

"I'm going to a friend's apartment to watch an F1 Grand Prix, have a few drinks and hang out like normal people. I need to relax. Want to come?"

Vito thought about it for a moment and then said, "Who's the friend? And it better not be Tierney. I don't socialize with cops."

"It's another doctor, an anesthesiologist."

"One of those pain guys?"

"Yeah…"

"Sure, I wasn't doing anything. Will there be anything to eat?"

"Yeah, he's making lamb vindaloo."

"Lamb vinda-who?"

"It's an Indian dish."

"I don't like curry, Cesari."

"You'll like this. I promise. If you don't, I'll buy you a steak dinner afterward. I'll meet you in front of your apartment in fifteen minutes and then we'll Uber it over to his place in the Flat Iron district."

"Fine…"

After the call, Cesari left his apartment and went down the stairs to the street. There was a shiny black stretch limousine idling outside his apartment with the rear door open and a large guy in a dark navy suit and sunglasses standing next to it. He waved to Cesari who approached cautiously and peeked into the back seat where he saw Governor Bernard von Steuben sitting by himself.

The governor said, "Join me, Dr. Cesari. I'd like to have a chat. I promise not to take up too much of your time."

Cesari hesitated for a moment but then entered the limousine and sat opposite the portly man as the door swung closed. Cesari said bluntly, "I thought you had a heart attack."

The governor smiled, "They now say it was only an angina attack, but I come from very sturdy stock. I'm not worried although my doctors want me to have a cardiac catheterization and go on a diet."

"And how do you feel about that?"

"Me? I don't mind them poking me with needles and making me take a few pills, but you know what I told them when they suggested I lose weight?"

"No, what?"

"Fat chance of that," he chortled, causing his belly to bounce up and down. "Just like that. I said, fat chance of that."

"I'll bet they thought that was hysterical."

"Hardly, but they mean well. You may not know this, but I've always been fascinated by healthcare myself. I've a great admiration for all you doctors do for society."

"Thank you. I'll be sure to pass that along to my colleagues… So what can I do for you, Governor?"

"I've come to say thank you," he replied and reached into a leather satchel by his side and handed Cesari an envelope. "On behalf of the great state of New Jersey, please accept this token of appreciation."

Cesari opened the envelope and looked inside. It was a cashier's check. He raised his eyebrows and said, "That's an awful lot of zeroes, Governor."

The governor said, "The great state of New Jersey owes you an awful lot of gratitude."

"I don't know what to say. Are you sure the great state of New Jersey knows it's missing a million dollars?"

The governor smiled. "That's what I would like to talk to you about."

Cesari sat back in the soft leather seat. Here we go he thought and said, "I'm all ears."

The governor let out a wistful breath of air. "What happened Saturday night was a terrible tragedy. I think we can both agree on that. If I had known what a bad character Beaujolais was, I never would have associated myself with him."

"I can accept that."

"Thank you, but as much as I would like to expose the man for what he was to the world, it would serve only to make matters worse, particularly for poor Martine who could potentially lose everything and possibly even see prison time depending on the zealousness of the new attorney general."

"What happened to the old attorney general?"

"Poor Franklin didn't make it, I'm afraid."

"I see... So the only witnesses to what went on in that room besides you and me are dead."

The governor nodded ruefully. "Would you like a cigar, Dr. Cesari?"

"Sure, why not?"

The governor reached into his suit jacket pocket and took out two six ring, full bodied Nicaraguans and cut them. He handed one to Cesari with a small butane torch and they both lit up, filling the confines of the limo with smoke.

Cesari said, "Thank you... I gather my cover story of you shooting Beaujolais didn't sail with your people?"

"No, it didn't. It was unanimous that it would sink my campaign in a heartbeat if it came out that I was holding a fundraiser just down the hall from a room full of human heads. The issue of judgement, guilt by association… those sorts of things."

Cesari thought it over and said, "I see your point. How do you want it to play out?"

"Have you told anyone yet about what really happened?"

"A few… Some people needed to know but no one knows everything. I tried to compartmentalize it for the most part. I'm not eager to run around telling people I killed the richest man in New Jersey and several of his friends."

"Good, because I'm giving a press conference at 8:00 p.m. tonight, and this is what I'm going to say. Several armed men tried to rob the mansion that night. It was an inside job led by Beaujolais' chief of security, Hugo. They cornered me, the attorney general, the lieutenant governor, and Beaujolais himself in the back of the wine cellar demanding access to his safe. A fight ensued but they were heavily armed. They killed Beaujolais, the lieutenant governor, and the attorney general in the ensuing gun battle. Beaujolais died bravely trying to protect me from gunfire. I collapsed with a heart attack. They left me thinking I was dead or close to it."

"You mean an angina attack."

"Whatever…"

"So far so good. What about Hugo and his gang?"

"They were found dead in the woods in the Jockey Hollow Preserve. Obviously, the villains had a falling out which led to a second gun battle in which they all died."

Cesari sat there for a moment chewing on his cigar. After a while he said, "You didn't really have angina, did you?"

The governor grinned. "That's what it says in my chart so I guess I must have. My cardiologist trained at Harvard. They're pretty smart people up there and rarely wrong."

Cesari laughed softly. "And what do you want from me?"

"Keep your mouth shut. Don't talk about it anymore with anyone. If anyone you told questions my version, just tell them to drop it and move on. You were never there, remember? Because if you were, then you'd have a lot of explaining to do which I presume doesn't interest you in the slightest."

"No, it doesn't... And the trophy room with the heads?"

"What trophy room?"

Cesari nodded. "I get it. For a million dollars, we bury the truth. Hugo was the bad guy and Beaujolais was a hero. He saved your life. No one finds out about the trophy room because you're going to have people sanitize it for the good of the state. The *Starry Night* gets returned to MoMA and they won't talk about it because it's too embarrassing. Martine conveniently develops amnesia about what a scumbag her husband was, and in exchange, she gets to keep her trillion-dollar fortune as long as she promises to continue bankrolling the Von Steuben express. Has a nice fairy-tale feel to it."

The governor blew a smoke ring out the window. "I think so as well. Martine and I had a long and fruitful conversation about what to do. She's a very pragmatic woman who cares deeply about her child's future. I hope you are equally as sensible, Doctor."

"I can be, but there is one thing that needs to be fixed for me to go along with this. You fix it and I'll develop amnesia too. Beaujolais stole a hundred million dollars from St. Matt's Hospital, and I want it back."

"I didn't know, but I'll have it returned double time if it will make you happy."

"It will, and Simone? Where does she fit in?"

"We can't prosecute Simone if there are no crimes to report, now can we? She'll be on a plane out of the country by the end of the week with a hefty severance check from Martine. She has given her word never to return."

"You got it all figured out."

"Can I drop you off somewhere, Dr. Cesari?"

Chapter 54

They sat in the living room of Jaskaran's apartment on East 24th Street just off Lexington Avenue and less than two blocks from Madison Square Park. The sectional sofa was aimed directly at a ninety-eight-inch Samsung flat screen television where the images seemed more real than whatever was going on in the apartment. Although what was going on in the apartment was pretty good too. Three guys drinking and eating and belching and making whatever other sounds that pleased them, watching the Mumbai Grand Prix.

The lamb vindaloo and naan were excellent, and they had finished a six pack of Indian beer called Kingfisher lager. Cesari would have liked more but Jaskaran had brought out a bottle of Rampur Indian whiskey, and they were nearly halfway through that as the Grand Prix itself reached its own halfway mark. Judging from the packed stands and exuberant crowds, Cesari guessed that F1 racing was very popular in India.

Cesari said, "Thanks for the invitation, Jay. This is a lot of fun."

"Yeah, thanks," added Vito. "The food's great."

"Thanks," responded Jaskaran. "Too bad the race is turning into a free for all. I didn't expect so many spin outs this early. They need to settle down."

"Isn't that the fun part?" asked Vito. "Watching guys crash into the walls?"

"Maybe for some people, but not me. I like to see them race. When they get too aggressive it starts to feel like a hockey game," answered Jay. "Plus, it's expensive. An F1 car can cost ten or twelve million dollars."

"No kidding?"

"There's some serious money involved."

"Nice apartment, Jay," Cesari commented glancing around. "You been here long?"

"A year and a half. I'm pretty happy here. The neighborhood's prime. Lots of restaurants and things to do."

Vito stood and asked, "Where's your bathroom, Jay?"

"It's down the hall, second door on the right. Do you want me to pause the race?"

"There's no need to do that. I'll survive if I miss a minute or two."

After Vito left them, Jay said, "That was some amazing stuff that went down over the weekend. Does your friend know?"

"He knows some of it but not all. It's probably best to keep it quiet and let nature take its course."

Jay nodded. "I know what you mean. There are some powerful people involved."

"Exactly... I heard you made a connection with a good-looking nurse Saturday night?"

Jay smiled, "I did. Her name's Nyra and we're going out this weekend."

Cesari grinned, "Good for you."

"Is Martine okay?"

"From what I've heard she's better than okay although the situation is still a little fluid, but I'm pretty sure I don't want to know what's going on in too great a detail."

"You're a little paranoid, aren't you?"

"Not a little...a lot... So who's supposed to win this race?"

"The Indian guy, Karun Chandhok, was favored going in, but he already spun out once. He's trailing pretty badly now, but he's still got time to catch up. It all depends on who makes the most mistakes from this point on or who cheats the most."

"Cheats?"

Jaskaran chuckled softly, "It's India, Cesari."

Vito returned from the bathroom and sat next to Cesari who said, "You good?"

Vito grinned. "Don't I look good?"

"You look like you need to see a urologist."

Jaskaran laughed. "Excuse me, guys. I'm going to get us some more ice. The bottle of whiskey isn't going to drink itself."

Cesari said approvingly, "You said that right."

Jay left to go to the kitchen and Vito whispered, "Cesari, your boy's got a problem."

Cesari was confused. "What are you talking about?"

He leaned in close to Cesari's ear. "I took a wrong turn going to the bathroom."

"You took a wrong turn?"

"Shut up and listen... He said the second right. I took the first right. It's his bedroom. Well, there's a bathroom in there too so that's what I thought he meant."

"Okay, so what?"

"The water was running very loudly in the toilet tank, so I thought the flapper was stuck or something. I lifted the lid to fix it."

"You're a plumber now?"

"Shut up... He's got drugs in there in a plastic bag with needles. It was blocking the flapper. Your friend's a junkie."

Cesari hissed angrily, "You're effin' nuts. Did you know that? Now shut up. He's coming back."

Jay returned with a bucket of ice and placed it on the coffee table. He dropped a few cubes in all their glasses and poured another round of the Rampur.

He said, "Did I miss anything?"

Cesari said, "Yeah, the Indian guy cheated. He threw a handful of rusty nails out of his car and gave the English guy behind him a flat tire and a bad case of tetanus."

Jaskaran laughed. "I'd believe it... Cheers to good times."

They raised their glasses and toasted, but Cesari's mood had darkened, and it was hard for him to sit there. As he stewed, he fidgeted. No one seemed to notice, but a couple of beers and a bottle of whiskey tended to dull the senses. Plus, the race was heating up. With ten laps to go, the Indian guy had actually made his way back into contention. Certainly a top three finish was within his grasp and with a little luck anything could happen. After a while, Cesari couldn't take it anymore.

He stood and said, "I'll be right back. I need to use the bathroom. I know where it is."

Jay didn't even look up. Something was happening on the screen. Vito said nothing and Cesari walked away. Down the hallway and out of sight, he made the first right into Jay's bedroom. He shook his head because he couldn't believe he had let Vito bug him like this, but he had to find out for himself. The bathroom door was still open, and he went directly there and locked it behind him.

He didn't hear any water running and presumed that Vito had fixed the problem. He gently lifted the white porcelain cover to the tank, placed it on the seat and looked inside. His heart sank and the color drained from his face. He was devastated by what he saw. Vito was right and wrong at the same time. Cesari reached in and grabbed the plastic bag. It was twist tied to the flush rod which he easily undid. In the bag was a half-empty bottle of propofol and two syringes. He dried the bag off with tissue paper and put it into his pocket.

Cesari was not a happy camper. He collected himself, and returned to the living room. Walking directly in front of the television, he picked the remote off the coffee table, and with two laps remaining, he turned off the race.

Jay was shocked, "Why'd you do that?"

"Relax. It's taped, remember?" Cesari said, and then turned to Vito. "It's time to go."

"We're leaving now?"

"No, you're leaving now."

Vito looked at him. "What are you talking about? The race is almost over."

"Your office called me while I was in the bathroom. They need you urgently."

"Why would they call you?"

Cesari made a face at him and jerked his head toward the door. After a few seconds, it finally sunk in. Vito stood, and said, "Thanks for your hospitality, Jay, but I have to leave. Apparently, my office needs me urgently."

They shook hands and Vito left with Jay watching him, completely baffled. When Vito was gone, Jay said, "What's going on, Cesari?"

In response, Cesari took the bag with the propofol out from his pocket and tossed it at him. He said, "Want to tell me what this is?"

Jay caught the bag, looked at its contents but didn't say anything.

Cesari said, "Whenever you're ready, Jay."

Jaskaran took a deep breath and let it out slowly before saying, "Mrs. Loomis was in so much pain, Cesari. She had maxed out on what I could give her legally and it wasn't even taking the edge off it. Her primary care physician and oncologist had washed their hands of her and dumped her on me. She begged me to put her out of misery."

Cesari shook his head. "I was afraid you were going to say that. So you admit you did it?"

He nodded quietly.

"Are you insane?" asked Cesari.

Jaskaran replied, "Physician assisted suicide is already legal in several states, Cesari. In fact, it's legal just across the river in New Jersey."

"Don't talk to me about New Jersey, all right? After the weekend I had over there, they just got promoted to asshole of the world. And spare me the bullshit about physician assisted suicide. I know all about it and sneaking into an old lady's apartment in the middle of the night to inject her with a lethal dose of propofol doesn't meet even the loosest definition. In the states where it's legal you're supposed to get a concurring second opinion and then give the patient a prescription so she can overdose on her own at home with her family. This way she can change her mind anytime she wants, and they frequently do. Her poor daughter is a mess right now because of you."

Jay bowed his head and said contritely, "I'm sorry about what her daughter is going through but for obvious reasons I couldn't let anyone know. I was just trying to do the right thing for my patient."

"Look, I'm not completely unsympathetic, but physicians can't play God, Jay. Thinking we have the right to end a life even if we believe it's for their own good is a slippery slope fraught with risks. The road to hell is paved with good intentions. Today, it's an old lady with metastatic cancer, tomorrow it's a demented patient in a nursing home, and the next day it's a kid with a birth defect who's a burden on his family. I took an ethics course in medical school and my instructor used to tell us that physician assisted suicide seems like a reasonable and harmless option, and maybe it is in selected cases, but don't ever forget that it has an evil twin sister called euthanasia. This stuff can get out of hand real fast too. Just ask the nazis. They tried it and it didn't go over well for the rest of humanity."

Jay murmured, "I know that."

Cesari sat down on the sofa next to him and they both stared at the blank television screen. After a while, Jay said, "How'd you find it?"

"I didn't. Vito did. When he went to the bathroom, he got confused and used the one in your bedroom. He heard water running in your toilet tank and decided to be a good Samaritan and fix it for you."

Jay groaned, "Jesus... You've got to be kidding?"

"Jesus is right. How stupid are you anyway? Why didn't you get rid of the bottle?"

He shrugged. "I meant to. When the shit hit the fan, I got kind of paralyzed. You know, deer in the headlights. I didn't want to think about it."

Cesari nodded. "First time?"

"Yes."

"Last time too, right?"

Jay looked horrified. "Of course."

Cesari thought it over for a while and said, "Get rid of the propofol and the syringes later, but for right now pour me another whiskey. You've given me the worst headache of my life, and then turn the race back on. I'm curious to see who won."

"You're not going to turn me in?"

Cesari thought long and hard about that before he said, "I probably should, but I can't bring myself to. She already had one foot in the grave. All she asked for was a little help to end her pain. It was wrong and you shouldn't have done it. Some people would call it murder, but a lot of others wouldn't. Your heart was in the right place even if your brain wasn't. If I turn you in, the system will chew up a good man and a great doctor simply to make an example out of you, and I don't feel you deserve that. No, I won't turn you in, but I'm ticked off. I went to the mat for you with Detective Tierney and the board of the hospital. They wanted your head."

"I'm sorry…"

"This is where you swear to me you'll never do anything like that again."

"I won't. I swear."

"I'm glad to hear it. Now turn on the TV."

"That's it?"

"No, that's not it. From now on, you're my bitch. I want lamb vindaloo and Indian whiskey every week until I decide you're fully rehabilitated."

The End

About the Author

John Avanzato grew up in the Bronx, New York. After receiving a bachelor's degree in biology from Fordham University, he went on to earn his medical degree at the State University of New York at Buffalo, School of Medicine. He is currently a board-certified gastroenterologist practicing in upstate, New York, where he lives with his wife of over thirty years.

Inspired by authors like Tom Clancy, John Grisham, David Baldacci, and Lee Child, Avanzato writes about strong but flawed heroes. His stories are fast-paced thrillers with larger-than-life characters and tongue-in-cheek humor.

His first twelve novels, *Hostile Hospital, Prescription for Disaster, Temperature Rising, Claimed Denied, The Gas Man Cometh, Jailhouse Doc, Sea Sick, Pace Yourself, The Legend of the Night Nurse, Hilton Dead, Bleeding Heart and Under the Weather* have been received well.

Author's Note

Dear Reader,

I hope you enjoyed reading *The Pain Killers* as much as I enjoyed writing it. Please do me a favor and write a review for me on amazon. The reviews are important, and your support is greatly appreciated. I can be reached at johnavanzato59@gmail.com or Facebook for further discussion.

Thank you,

John Avanzato MD

Hostile Hospital

When former mob thug turned doctor, John Cesari, takes a job as a gastroenterologist at a small hospital in upstate New York, he assumes he's outrun his past and started life anew. But trouble has a way of finding the scrappy Bronx native.

Things go awry one night at a bar when he punches out an obnoxious drunk who won't leave his date alone. Unbeknownst to Dr. Cesari, that drunk is his date's stalker ex-boyfriend—and a crooked cop.

Over the course of several action-packed days, Cesari uncovers the dirty little secrets of a small-town hospital. As the bodies pile up, he is forced to confront his own bloody past.

Hostile Hospital is a fast-paced journey that is not only entertaining but maintains an interesting view on the philosophy of healthcare. If you aren't too scared after reading, get the sequel, *Prescription for Disaster*.

Prescription for Disaster

Dr. John Cesari is a gastroenterologist employed at Saint Matt's Hospital in Manhattan. He tries to escape his unsavory past on the Bronx streets by settling into a Greenwich Village apartment with his girlfriend, Kelly. After his adventures in Hostile Hospital, Cesari wants to stay under the radar of his many enemies.

Through no fault of his own, Cesari winds up in the wrong place at the wrong time. A chance encounter with a mugger turns on its head when Cesari watches his assailant get murdered right before his eyes.

After being framed for the crime, he attempts to unravel the mystery, propelling himself deeply into the world of international diamond smuggling. He is surrounded by bad guys at every turn and behind it all are Russian and Italian mobsters determined to ensure Cesari has an untimely and unpleasant demise.

His prescription is to beat them at their own game, but before he can do that he must deal with a corrupt boss and an environment filled with temptation and danger from all sides. Everywhere Cesari goes, someone is watching. The dramatic climax will leave you breathless and wanting more.

Temperature Rising

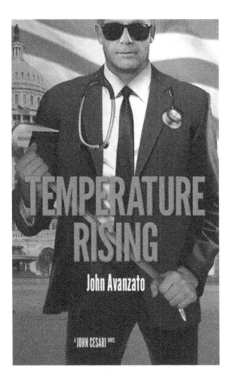

John Cesari is a gangster turned doctor living in Manhattan saving lives one colonoscopy at a time. While on a well-deserved vacation, he stumbles upon a murder scene and becomes embroiled in political intrigue involving the world's oldest profession.

His hot pursuit of the truth leads him to the highest levels of government, where individuals operate above the law. As always, girl trouble hounds him along the way making his already edgy life that much more complex.

The bad guys are ruthless, powerful, and nasty but they are no match for this tough, street-smart doctor from the Bronx who is as comfortable with a crowbar as he is with a stethoscope. Get ready for a wild ride in *Temperature Rising*. The exciting and unexpected conclusion will leave you on the edge of your seat.

Claim Denied

In Manhattan, a cancer ridden patient commits suicide rather than become a financial burden to his family. Accusations of malfeasance are leveled against his caregivers. Rogue gastroenterologist, part-time mobster, John Cesari, is tasked to look into the matter on behalf of St. Matt's hospital.

The chaos and inequities of a healthcare system run amok, driven by corporate greed and endless bureaucratic red tape, become all too apparent to him as his inquiry into this tragedy proceeds. On his way to interview the wife of the dead man,

Cesari is the victim of seemingly random gun violence and finds himself on life support.

Recovering from his wounds, he finds that both he and his world are a very different place. His journey back to normalcy rouses in him a burning desire for justice, placing him in constant danger as evil forces conspire to keep him in the dark.

The Gas Man Cometh

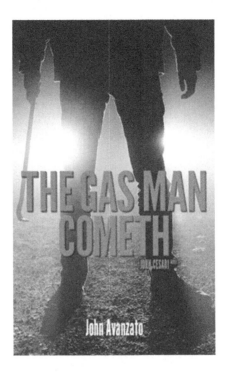

A deranged anesthesiologist with unnatural desires lures innocent women to his brownstone in a swank section of Manhattan. All was going well until John Cesari M.D. came along becoming a thorn in his side.

Known as The Gas Man, his hatred of Cesari reaches the boiling point. He plots to take him down once and for all turning an ordinary medical conference into a Las Vegas bloodbath.

Hungover and disoriented, Cesari awakens next to a mobster's dead girlfriend in a high-end brothel. Wanted dead or alive by more than a few people, Cesari is on the run with gangsters and the police hot on his trail.

There is never a dull moment in this new thriller as Cesari blazes a trail from Sin City to lower Manhattan desperately trying to stay one step ahead of The Gas Man.

Jailhouse Doc

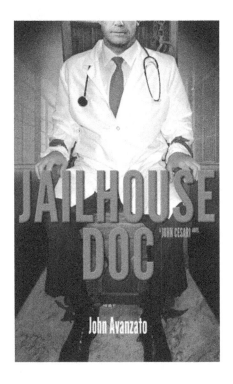

Dr. John Cesari, former mobster turned gastroenterologist, finds himself on the wrong end of the law. A felony conviction lands him in Riker's Island, one of the country's most dangerous correctional facilities, doing community service.

Fighting to survive, he becomes trapped in the web of a vicious criminal gang dealing in drugs and human flesh.

A seemingly unrelated and mysterious death of a college student in Greenwich Village thrusts Cesari into the middle of the action and, forced to take sides, his options are to either cooperate or die. Which will it be?

Sea Sick

Recovering from a broken heart, John Cesari M.D. embarks on a Mediterranean cruise to unwind and clear his head. His goals are to see the sights, eat a lot, and most of all to stay away from women.

A chance encounter in a Venetian Bar with the lusty captain of the Croatian women's national volleyball team just before setting sail turns his plan on its head. When she tells him she is being sold into a forced marriage, he is thrust into the middle of a rollicking, ocean-going adventure to rescue her.

Murder on the high seas wasn't on the itinerary when he purchased his ticket, but in true Cesari fashion, he embraces his fate and dives in.

Pace Yourself

John Cesari's former lover Kelly and her children have gone missing and her husband is found dead in an underground garage. When law enforcement fails to act, Cesari launches his own investigation. He discovers their disappearance is linked to a shady company in Manhattan called EverBeat selling defective pacemakers to hospitals.

EverBeat has ties to both the Chinese military complex in Beijing and to the United States government. Trying to unravel the web of deceit one lie at a time leads to a trail of corpses throughout the city that never sleeps. Hunted by professional killers and thwarted by personal betrayal, his only goal is to save Kelly and her family.

The Legend of the Night Nurse

Our favorite gastroenterologist John Cesari joins a small hospital in rural New York and is beginning to acclimate to the colorful administrators who hired him when Jasmine walks into his life. Single, beautiful and just a little bit odd, he is immediately smitten by her charm. He soon discovers that she is more than just slightly eccentric and is dangerously obsessed with Halloween, witchcraft and devil worship.

Cesari is determined to help her as Halloween night approaches and everyone's excitement reaches a fever pitch. The thrilling conclusion will leave you breathless. The Legend of the Night Nurse proves once again that on Halloween night all things mischievous can and will happen.

Hilton Dead

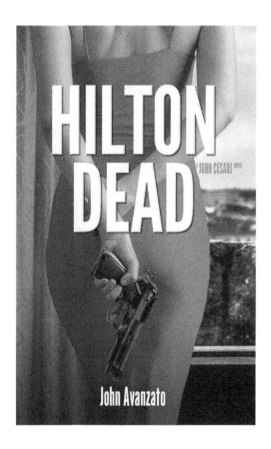

Trapped on a small island off the coast of South Carolina during hurricane season, Cesari finds himself in the company of mysterious yet collegial fellow travelers. The severe weather conditions pose serious challenges for the group, but the odd behavior and quirky dispositions of the hotel staff are even more disconcerting. And then, one by one, the guests start to disappear…

Bleeding Heart

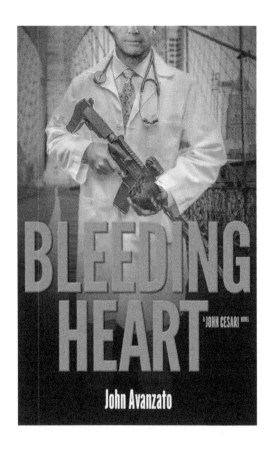

A turf war erupts between rival mobster gangs in lower Manhattan over control of gentlemen's club on Second Avenue. Dr. John Cesari gets dragged into the thick of things as his lifelong friend, Vito Gianelli, the legendary capo of Mulberry Street, fights off encroachment of his territory by Romanian mafiosi from the east side. The action spills over into St. Matt's where Cesari is employed when a new and dirty CEO is commissioned to revitalize the hospital's economic fortunes. In bed with the bad guys, the new CEO makes life a living hell for the employees of St. Matt's but especially for Cesari. The puppet master behind it all is a dangerous, enigmatic character from eastern Europe by the name of Shlomo. At first glance, he seems a kindly, grandfatherly figure with cherubic features and twinkling eyes that belie his black, soulless heart.

Under the Weather

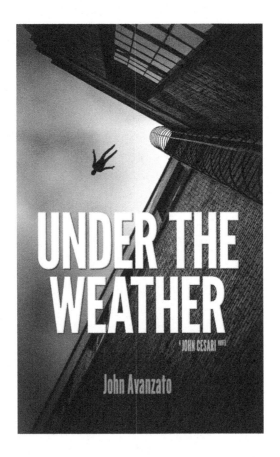

John Avanzato grew up in the Bronx, New York during the turbulent times of the 1960's and 1970's and is now a physician residing upstate with his family. A lifelong dream of writing fiction came to fruition in 2014 with the publication of his first book, *Hostile Hospital*. He has now authored twelve full-length novels and is working on the thirteenth. His stories are loosely inspired by his life experiences as a medical doctor in combination with the rough and tumble memories of an exciting youth. His main character, John Cesari M.D., is a man with one foot in healthcare and the other in the dark underbelly of his past. His two worlds frequently collide with seismic upheaval, and he is forced to make difficult choices. Imbued with a strong sense of justice and not one to hold anything back, Cesari navigates the complex pathway of his life as only he can, and in the process brings hell on earth to those who would hurt others.

KCM Publishing
a division of KCM Digital Media, LLC

Made in United States
Orlando, FL
25 March 2022

16149043R00235